Praise for Joshilyn Jackson

characterizations to be found in contemporary fiction. Don't miss it!'

Bookpage

Also by Joshilyn Jackson

Gods in Alabama
Between, Georgia

About the author

Joshilyn Jackson was born and grew up in the Deep South. A former actress and award-winning teacher, she is now a full-time writer. Joshilyn lives in Atlanta, Georgia with her husband and their two children. You can visit her website at www.joshilynjackson.com.

JOSHILYN JACKSON

The Girl Who Stopped Swimming

HODDER

First published in the United States in 2008 by Grand Central Publishing
A division of Hachette Book Group USA

First published in Great Britain in 2008 by Hodder & Stoughton
An Hachette Livre UK company

3

A CIP catalogue record for this title is available from the British Library

ISBN B format: 978 0 340 92193 7
ISBN A format: 978 0 340 92262 0

Printed and bound in Great Britain by Clays Ltd, Elcograf S.p.A.

Hodder & Stoughton policy is to use papers that are natural, renewable and recyclable products and made from wood grown in sustainable forests. The logging and manufacturing processes are expected to conform to the environmental regulations of the country of origin.

Hodder & Stoughton Ltd
338 Euston Road
London NW1 3BH

www.hodder.co.uk

And for Scott, right now

CHAPTER 1

Until the drowned girl came to Laurel's bedroom, ghosts had never walked in Victorianna. The houses were only twenty years old, with no accumulated history to put creaks in the hardwood floors or rattle at the pipes. The backyards had tall fences, and there were no cracks in the white sidewalks. Victorianna had a heavy wrought-iron gate guarding its entrance. The intricately curled top looked period, but it was new as well. It ran on hydraulics, and it swung wide only for those who knew the code.

Laurel and David had moved into the big house on Chapel Circle thirteen years ago, when Laurel was only nineteen, and since that day she hadn't seen so much as a glimmer of her dead uncle Marty. He was tethered to the three-bedroom brick ranch where her parents still lived, half an hour away in tiny Pace, Florida. As a girl, she had seen him often, mostly on the nights before a storm broke.

She'd be fast asleep on her old Cinderella sheets, faded and soft from a thousand washings, with *Anne of Green Gables* or a

Trixie Belden book lying open-spined on her bedside table. Then he would be there, standing on her side of the room by her bed, mournful and transparent. He didn't belong near the ruffled shade on her reading lamp, and his feet should not have been allowed to rest beside her cotton trainer bra and Thalia's dirty Keds and the abandoned issues of *Tiger Beat* scattered on the floor. The stuffed pony Laurel had loved best was still allowed a place at the end of her bed, but Marty was not reflected in its glass eyes, as if her loyal pony doll refused to acknowledge his presence.

He'd smile at her, one hand tucked easy in the waistband of his faded Levi's, the other reaching out to her, ready to show her secret scenes, her own personal ghost of Christmas never.

A thin finger of moonlight came through the bullet hole left of his center, reaching to touch Laurel's eye and help her lids come shuddering down. She'd leave them closed and roll away. In the morning, the sun would light up dust motes in the place where he'd been standing.

He left a cold spot in the room that she didn't like to walk through, and sometimes she'd see the impression that his blanched cowboy boots had left in the nap of the rug. Once, her sister, Thalia, caught Laurel down on her knees, trying to smooth away those faint footprints.

"Are you feeling up the carpet, Bug?" Thalia asked.

Laurel only shrugged and stilled her hands. Thalia slept light and woke often, but she never saw Marty.

Laurel brought Thalia over to see the house in Victorianna a few days after she and David moved in. They'd been married all of five weeks. Thalia sat in the passenger seat, drawing her upper lip back from her teeth, higher and higher, while Laurel drove her slowly through the winding streets. The lip was practically touching Thalia's nose by the time they'd passed six blocks' worth of the large pastel Victorians with their gingerbread and curling gables and romantic little balconies.

"It looks like Barbie's Dream House threw up in here," Thalia said. "A bunch of times. Like, went full-on bulimic."

"I think it's beautiful," Laurel said. Her tone was mild, but low in her belly, she felt the baby flip, popping sideways like an angry brine shrimp. "Look, this one's ours."

She pulled in to the driveway. Laurel and David's house was the palest blue, trimmed in deep plum and heather. Two gargoyles hidden in the eaves watched over her with fierce eyes. A weathervane on the roof told her the wind's plans for the day.

Thalia glanced from the turret to the sloped roof and then shook her head.

"You say something nice," Laurel said, putting one hand over the swell of her abdomen. She was four months gone, and Shelby was so little, Laurel could only feel her fierce spins from the inside.

"Okay," Thalia said, with the O stretched long, as if to buy her thinking time. Then she lifted her chin, manufacturing a June Cleaver smile. "It looks clean. Like they don't even let dogs pee here."

Laurel laughed. "I think that's in our charter."

She started to get out, but Thalia put one hand on her arm, stopping her. "Seriously? This is what you want? This house, this husband, a baby at nineteen?" Laurel nodded, and Thalia let her go. But Laurel heard her mutter under her breath, "It's like you're living inside a lobotomy."

"Oh, stop it," Laurel said. "That doesn't even make sense."

"Sure it does," Thalia said. "Lots of things live in holes. This place is a hole where your brains used to be."

Thalia never grew to like Victorianna any better, but then she also said Laurel's quilts, with all their jarring elements secreted or undercut, were too pretty to be considered art. Real art, Thalia said, went for the jugular. Laurel would let a bleached bird's skull peek out of the gingham pocket of a country Christmas angel, but she'd never replace the angel's pretty head with it. It wouldn't feel right. Laurel saw her quilts complete in her mind's eye, and she knew every piece—innocent, macabre, or neutral as beige velvet—must be subject to the larger pattern. Likewise, Victorianna's pieces made a whole that Laurel thought was lovely.

Her neighbors might have their own especial favorite sins; they drank or fought, they cheated on their taxes or each other. But they washed and waxed their cars on Saturdays, and they kept their hedges and lamps trimmed. They put up neighborhood-watch signs and kept their curtains open, ever vigilant. Old-fashioned glass lampposts lined the streets, so that even at night, a ghost would be hard put to find a shadowed path to Laurel's door.

Even so, that night the drowned girl came anyway.

A storm was gathering, so Laurel checked that the chain was on their bedroom door before climbing into bed. She was more likely to sleepwalk when the air was humid enough to hold the taste of electricity. She'd rise and undo locks, pull up windows, unpack closets and drawers. Once, she'd left a puffy beaded poppy she was hand-sewing sitting out on her bedside table. She fell asleep thinking that the black beads at the poppy's center were as glossy and round as mouse eyes, and then she rose in the night and picked out every stitch. Her hands liked to open and undo while she was sleeping. The chain was no challenge. Its true job was to rattle against the door frame and wake up David so he could lead her back to bed.

Their bedroom felt like a crisper. David, whose metabolism ran so high his skin always felt slightly fevered, couldn't sleep in summer unless the thermostat was set at 65. Laurel climbed in and got under the blankets, pressing her front against his warm back. She kissed his shoulder, but he didn't stir. He was well and truly out, and his lanky body had solidified into something dense and hard to shift.

David was working fifteen-hour days, adapting simulator code he'd written for the navy into a PC game for a company out in California. He'd probably spoken ten complete sentences to her in the last week. All the pieces of him that she thought of as her husband had moved down to live in his brain stem, while coding took his higher functions.

In another week or two, when the math was done, he'd come up from his office in the basement, rubbing his eyes as if he'd awakened from a long sleep. He'd sit on the floor and lean against her shins, dropping his head back into her lap to look up at her with the same narrow, total focus he'd devoted to his code strings. "What's been happening in the real world?" he'd say, meaning their world.

Laurel would drift her fingers through his hair, holding him rapt with tales of the bride quilt she was working on, her victory at neighborhood bunko, and this new boy at school whom Shelby kept too casually bringing up. David always came back to her, completely, and so she let him be.

She slept soundly until the temperature dropped further, then she shuddered, dreaming that her breath was curling out in smoky plumes like a dragon's breath. She rolled onto her back, rising toward the surface of her sleep. Her eyes opened. She saw the outline of a young girl, twelve or thirteen, standing by the foot of the bed.

"Shelby?" she said, and sat up. But Shelby was built like a blade of grass, her breasts only now budding and the faintest curve to her tum. This girl's puppy fat had shifted into real breasts and small hips, and she was soaked to the skin. She caught the moonlight coming in the window and reflected it, shimmering.

"Honey, aren't you freezing?" Laurel asked her, but the question came out in a strained whisper, as if Laurel had been sleeping so long and heavy that her throat had rusted shut.

The girl didn't answer. Laurel could see her body through the wet fabric, and she realized she could also see the bedroom window. The girl had gone as transparent as her dress. Then Laurel understood what she was, and she checked the corners of the room for Marty; this girl had to be one of his.

He wasn't there. It was unprecedented, but the drowned girl had come alone. Her head was tilted down, and her wet hair was a veil, strands of it clinging like lace to her nose and cheekbones. Her hair was blond or light brown, hard to tell since the water had darkened it.

"You can't be here," Laurel said, swinging her legs out of the bed. David muttered something and rolled over. His long arm moved into the space where she'd been lying.

The drowned girl turned away and walked to the open curtains, as if complying. Dark water dripped from the ends of her hair and the hem of her dress, but the carpet stayed dry. Her bare feet brushed the surface, swaying the thick pile.

"I didn't mean leave," Laurel said, standing up and taking two cautious steps after her. "I meant you can't *be* here."

The girl had reached the bedroom window, and the sound of Laurel's voice did not pause her. She took another two steps forward, melting through the window and arching herself out, spreading her arms and drifting into the darkness without pushing off. Laurel followed, stretching out a cautious hand, but the glass was solid under her fingertips. She watched gravity catch the girl's dress and her long hair, tugging it downward, but her body drifted down easy. She tilted her head up and her feet down as she sank, landing softly on the tiles by the pool.

The yard was dark, but Shelby had forgotten to turn the underwater pool lights off, so the water glowed. The girl glowed, too, as if she had her own light. She swept her right arm down in a smooth and graceful arc, like a game-show hostess modeling the water. Laurel's gaze followed the gesture, and at first she couldn't make sense of what she saw. The drowned girl was resting facedown in the center of the pool, her skirt opening like wings under the water. Her body was slim, with skinny pony legs, her hair curling toward the surface in tendrils like water weeds. Her ghost faded to a moving shadow in Laurel's peripheral vision, blending into the darkness.

Laurel slammed her hands against the glass.

She heard David saying, "Wha—" behind her. He sounded far away.

A long, loud howling split Laurel's sleep in two. It was familiar yet not, and she struggled to place the sound. The effort roused her, and she realized she was hearing her own voice: She was baying in her sleep. Waking further, she found herself standing at the window. She stopped abruptly, disoriented, staring down into the backyard. It didn't make sense. She was awake now. This was her real hand touching her own cool glass. The dreamed girl should be gone, but Laurel still saw her. She was facedown, floating underwater, and the pool lights shone beside her, giving her pale edges and a shadowed back. The water rocked her body as it drifted quietly in the middle of Laurel and David's pool.

Laurel heard David again, closer now, saying, "Baby, what—" But she was already pushing off the window and running to the door, scrabbling to unlatch the chain. She wrenched the door open and ran down the hall toward the stairs. Her head turned toward Shelby's room as she ran past, an involuntary movement.

Shelby wasn't there. Shelby's covers were in a heap at the foot, and Laurel had just seen a small blond body in the pool. Pure adrenaline dumped into her blood, driving her forward. She went down the stairs in three great leaping steps, even as her brain struggled to revise the room her eyes had seen. She fought the instinct to go back and look, to look a hundred times until the bed stopped being empty and her eyes saw Shelby, safe and sleeping where she belonged. Her heart was swelling, taking up too much room in her chest, compressing her lungs so that she couldn't get a breath as she ran. Shelby and Bet Clemmens had been playing Clue in the keeping room when Laurel went to bed, but as she dashed through the room, Laurel saw the board abandoned in the middle of the floor.

Laurel flipped the lock on the sliding glass door and shoved it sideways along its track. The alarm began its pre-howl beeping, an electronic drumbeat of sound, heartless and high, that drove her across the patio. All at once she was too close to the low fence encircling the patio. She'd installed that fence back when Shelby was a toddler whose only goal was to walk straight into the pool and sink like a beautiful, stupid lemming. David, whose gaze turned inward most times, had barked his shin on it so often when it was new that Shelby had grown up thinking a fence was called a "dammit."

Now Laurel stumbled on it and went skidding across the damp lawn. She fell to one knee and then was up again, running to the higher fence encircling the pool. She was praying, a wordless call to God. The gate was unlatched, and Laurel shoved it open and ran across the tiles, straight down the steps into the water.

The cold shocked her legs and shot up through her spine. It was as if she had been wearing a second set of eyelids, sheer as membrane. The cold snapped them open, and she saw that the girl wasn't Shelby. She knew Shelby's every molecule, and the delicate set of the shoulder blades and the contours of the head were not the same.

A wash of red joy bubbled and crashed its way through Laurel's every vein, as if her blood were suddenly carbonated. Her whole body sang with a sick gladness that this was any child but hers. It was as immediate and involuntary as her heartbeat, and in her next breath, shame crept in. Not Shelby, thank God, thank God, but this girl was someone's.

The water forced Laurel into that slow, sodden running she was always doing in her dreams. She waded up past her waist and had to bend, holding her face up out of the water, to reach down and grab the girl's ankle. She pulled the girl up and back, and a reasoning piece of her took note of how lifeless the girl's skin felt, gelid and pliable under her fingers.

Bet Clemmens? Laurel hadn't paused to check the guest room on her way down, but this could not be Bet. Bet was a tall girl, and her hair was a single-toned dark red with an inch of brown at the roots.

The house alarm began blaring. Laurel reached the steps and

tried to roll the girl, to get her face into the air, but her body folded instead of turning. Then it was as if the girl's body pulled itself up, levitating. For one crazy second Laurel clung to her, not understanding, but then she saw David's hands. He was behind her on the pool steps, bare-chested, the water soaking the legs of his pajama bottoms, lifting the girl out.

Laurel grabbed the silver bar and hauled herself up the pool steps. Her heart still felt swollen, taking up all the room in her chest, banging itself against her rib cage. David laid the girl out on the tile. He'd gone to that burny-eyed place he went to in a crisis, his movements precise and spare. He said, "Start CPR. I'm calling 911."

Laurel dropped to her knees, facing the house. She cupped the back of the girl's neck and pulled up, tilting the head back to open an airway, using her other hand to push the heavy strands of hair away. She saw a heart-shaped face, pug nose, and round blue eyes half open under straight blond brows.

Laurel recognized her. More than that. It was Molly, and Laurel knew her, knew her high giggle and the way she walked in quick, small steps with her toes turned in. Just last October, Laurel had snapped at least ten pictures of Molly and Shelby, both of them in red lipstick and the ragged pirate miniskirts she'd made for them. She had wondered if this was the last Halloween they would want costumes and trick-or-treating. They'd refused to ruin their look with jackets; they'd run off with their skinny bare arms linked at the elbow and prickling with gooseflesh in the mild chill. This was Molly's face. It was Molly Dufresne.

Laurel felt like something huge and heavy was rolling fast over her, flattening her and pressing out her breath. There was a film over Molly's pale, familiar eyes. Laurel wanted to stand up and walk inside her house to find a peaceful room where none of this was true. It couldn't be true, and yet her clever hands kept doing necessary things, sending two fingers into Molly's slack mouth to clear it.

She bent to put her mouth on Molly's and pushed air, hard, meeting resistance. All she could see was the cheerful pebbled tile, and beyond that a small part of the lawn and David's bare feet running for the house.

As she sat up, she yelled after him, "David? Where's Shelby? You have to find Shelby."

The alarm cut out as she called the last two words. The siren had shocked the frogs and crickets into silence, and her voice rang out. Her hands were back on Molly's chest, compressing, but Molly's body felt abandoned. Her heart was dense and still.

She looked back toward the house and saw Shelby walking through the glass doors. Her bangs stuck up in tufts, and she was dry and sleepy-eyed and breathing. She was still in her ratty jean shorts and a T-shirt and pink Pumas. She stopped on the patio, her mouth opening in a shocked O. Laurel wanted to run to her, grab her up, but she had to bend and push air for Molly again.

When she sat up, Shelby was taking a hesitant step forward, and Laurel called, "Stay there, baby."

Shelby obeyed.

Bet Clemmens came out of the back door, David right behind her. Bet had the black Hefty bag she'd brought as a suitcase pressed against her chest like a pillow. After her first visit, last year, Laurel had gotten her a wheeled suitcase with a pull-out handle, but she'd come back with a trash bag again this year. "It broke," she'd said in a flat, defensive voice before Laurel had even asked. It had been stupid, sending a nice suitcase like that back to DeLop, expecting Bet would get to keep it.

"Stay," David said to both girls. He stepped over the patio fence and strode fast across the lawn. He was holding the cordless phone from the kitchen by his side.

Laurel could hear the tinny voice of the 911 operator telling him to remain on the line, but as he reached Laurel, he let the handset clatter to the tile and said, "They're coming."

David knelt on the other side of Molly's still form. His stronger hands folded themselves over her chest, and he thrust down, short, hard pushes, demanding a response and not getting one while Laurel breathed uselessly for her.

It went on for a long time like that. By the time Laurel heard the sirens, the pebbled tiles were tiny scissors clipping at her knees each time she shifted.

David heard the sirens, too. He called, "Shelby, go unlock the front door."

The first two firemen hurried through the glass door. Laurel had always thought of it as a glad thing when the firemen came, a promising thing. It had been the firemen who said it was common, it was fine, let's take her to the hospital anyway to be sure, when Shelby was three and had a febrile seizure. They'd arrived first again when David, who tripped over dust motes and should have known better, had gone up on the roof to clean the gutters himself and fallen off and broken his ankle. But when Laurel's daddy shot her uncle Marty, it had been the sheriff's men, dressed in light blue, and look how that turned out. They'd come from the direction of the cabin, ambling slow because Marty's blood had already cooled, setting like gelatin.

It heartened Laurel to see the busy rush of firemen now. There was a beat when the pinkest part of her fool heart thought seeing them meant Molly was fixable and could be woken and handed back to her mother, whole and safe.

Laurel bent and pushed a last breath into Molly's slack mouth, and then she knew it wasn't any good. Strong hands came down and lifted her away, like David had lifted Molly out of the pool, and she was passed backward to David as the firemen took over.

David walked with her to the patio, one hand on the small of her back as if Laurel were a touchstone holding him present, even as the fluid economy of his movements disintegrated.

Shelby stood hugging herself in front of the glass doors. As soon as she was close enough, Laurel's hands reached out for Shelby as if they had their own brains in the thumbs. She pulled Shelby tight against her chest.

Over Shelby's head, Laurel watched the firemen milling around and unpacking their vinyl bags, pulling out what she supposed was medical equipment, a jumble of tubes and long cords and boxes.

There didn't seem to be anything for them to do for the moment. They stood in a huddle on the patio, Laurel holding Shelby and David looming over them. Bet was off to the side, clutching her Hefty bag, so that for a single heartbeat there was no Bet, no firemen, no little girl gone too still in the yard. They were frozen, the three of them like a snapshot of Laurel's life for over thirteen years, since the day she'd gone to David's grungy student apartment with her eyes puffy and rimmed in pink. She'd balled both hands into fists before she'd knocked, ready to punch his guts out if he shrugged and said he'd pay for an abortion.

Now the child who had become Shelby was in her arms, and

Laurel held her daughter for that single beat, felt the pulse of Shelby's mighty heart doing its good work. She thought the word "safe," and she thought the word "finished." David watched over them, her sentinel, and she thought, "Our part is over now."

Immediately, she heard her sister, Thalia, say, "You're wrong."

"What?" she said.

She looked around, but Thalia wasn't there. Thalia was in Mobile, or Timbuktu, or hell, for all the good it did Laurel.

"I said you're wet."

Shelby's voice was muffled, her face pressed into Laurel's chest, but Laurel could hear a thin edge of hysteria in the normal words. Shelby tried to pull back, and Laurel felt her whole body contract, grasping Shelby too hard, keeping her.

"Ow," Shelby said, jerking away, and Laurel had to bite down an urge to yell, to demand that Shelby would forever be in the first place Laurel looked, safe and expected and perfectly unharmed. She forced her clamped arms to loosen and let Shelby turn sideways. Shelby bent at the waist, her shoulders hunching up and in, her head down, gulping in air.

Laurel put one hand in the center of Shelby's back. "I'm sorry," she said. Her voice came out too high. "I was so scared. You weren't in your bed."

Shelby, still hunched over, said, "I fell asleep in the rec room. Me and Bet were watching TV."

Bet's head jerked at the sound of her name, as if she'd been asleep on her feet, like a horse. "Do what?" she said.

Shelby looked up at Laurel and said, "Mommy, is that Molly?"

Laurel couldn't answer. She felt the irrational anger draining out of her. It flowed through her arm and into Shelby like a current.

Shelby's brows came down, and her mouth crumpled up into

an angry wad. "Now you say it isn't," Shelby demanded. "You say."

Laurel pulled her close again, and Shelby suffered it, stiff in Laurel's arms.

"I'm so sorry," Laurel said, and Shelby clamped her hands over her own mouth, her eyes wide and furious and too bright above her laced fingers.

A young fireman with apple cheeks and a clipboard stepped over the patio fence to join them in the spill of light coming through the glass doors. He asked how long Molly had been in the pool, what they had done to revive her, and how long they'd been doing it. His questions required short, factual responses, and David turned to him with something like relief, answering methodically.

Bet Clemmens stood by the glass doors, wearing a pair of the soft pajamas Laurel had given her. Her feet were stuffed into rubber flip-flops she'd brought from home, and she still clutched the trash bag as if it were her childhood lovey.

"You packed your things?" Laurel said.

Of course Bet would have to go home now, but it seemed strange that she had already packed. It was both too fast and too intuitive.

Bet said, "I heardat sarn goff. I thodda wazza far."

It took Laurel a few seconds to process through the thick DeLop accent. Bet's vowels stretched, taking up so much space that the consonants got jammed together, and her lips hardly moved when she spoke. Her words sounded swallowed, as if they came from her stomach instead of her lungs and throat. In DeLop, where everyone talked like that, Laurel's ears adjusted to hear those sounds as words, but here, Bet Clemmens's accent was an interloper. It took a moment to translate: "I heard that siren go off. I thought it was a fire."

"It was the burglar alarm," Laurel said.

Bet shrugged. Laurel's relatives in DeLop did not have burglar alarms. They were, for the most part, the people burglar alarms were meant to deter.

Bet squeezed the Hefty bag and said, "I didn't want them clothes you got me to get burned up."

Laurel dropped it. It didn't seem appropriate to talk about alarms or packing at the moment. No topic seemed appropriate. It simply couldn't be that Shelby's friend was dead in the backyard while Laurel talked about useless things with Bet Clemmens. In a few hours, she realized, she'd have to make her family breakfast. In two days, the pansy bed would need weeding. It wasn't right.

She heard Mindy Coe calling from the backyard next door. "Laurel? Are you guys okay?"

Laurel's mouth called out, "Yes."

It was a reflex, like the way her knee jumped when her doctor tapped it with his rubber mallet. She didn't want pretty Mindy Coe, her good friend next door, to see what was happening in her yard. If Mindy came over and saw, then it might be real. And they were okay, weren't they? There they all three were, alive and whole, and what else mattered?

Shelby pulled herself out of Laurel's arms altogether and said, "God, Mom," from behind her hands. "We're so, so not."

Mindy's head popped up over the tall privacy fence, her hands folded over the rounded boards like prairie-dog paws, her pointy chin hooked over the top between them. Mindy was barely five feet tall, so she had to be standing on a piece of her patio furniture, and still no part of her neck was visible. She was probably on tiptoe.

Jeffrey Coe's head and shoulders appeared beside those of his mother. He was a tall, good-looking boy, older than Shelby, already in high school.

The Coes looked like cheery puppets peering down over the slats, their disembodied heads concerned and friendly. Laurel thought that on their side of the fence, she'd find daylight, a garden party, a recipe exchange. She had an absurd urge to run for it, break straight through, leaving a perfect Laurel-shaped hole in the wooden boards. Her own backyard had become a foreign country.

"Ma'am, you need to get down from there," a fireman said, heading for the fence. But Mindy had already seen Molly.

"Oh, my dear God," she said. Her hand snaked up to push Jeffrey's head down. "I'll call Simon." Mindy's husband was a doctor. Then she got down.

Shelby was staring at the pool, her body curved away from Laurel. Laurel put one arm back around her, both to steady herself and to feel the simple living flesh of her. "Close your eyes, baby," Laurel said.

"I already saw," Shelby said. Tears spilled out of her eyes, and her nose was running unchecked. "It is Molly. It is." She pulled away again. "You're freezing me to death." The last word rose in an indignant adolescent lilt. Then she put her hands up to scrub at her eyes with her palms, a toddler move. Her mouth was still a cupid's bow, as unformed and generic as a baby's. Laurel wrapped her arms around her own middle, sick with not touching her daughter.

She could hear people tramping through her house. One of

them found the switch for the back floodlights. Her pupils had dilated in the near-dark, and the burst of light hit her like a flash bomb going off. The backyard was all at once awash in summer's colors, green grass, the last hot-pink azaleas, the bright peach-and-blue-striped cushions on the patio chairs. Only the yard's back corners were still dark. The bulb had died in the light above the gazebo, and no light reached the pet cemetery where David had interred Bibby, Shelby's first cat, and a childhood's worth of gerbils and the kind of short-lived goldfish won at fairs and the school carnival.

Bet Clemmens was watching the firemen with her blank, calm eyes. She seemed almost serene, and Laurel realized with a start that this was as comfortable as she had ever seen Bet in Victorianna. Sirens and flashing lights were a regular Saturday night for Bet. She was one of The Folks; that was Laurel's name for her mother's family in DeLop, though Thalia, colder and more dramatic, called them The Squalid People.

DeLop had once been a mining town, but the coal had run out seventy years back, and most everyone in town had moved on when the jobs dried up. The Folks were what was left. They lived squashed up on one another, three and four generations layered into one falling-down mobile home or trailer. Half of them were meth heads, the rest were drunks, and girls Shelby's age walked around dead-eyed with babies slung up on their skinny hips. At Christmas, Laurel went with Thalia and Daddy and Mother to deliver a ham dinner and a pair of shoes and some toys to every child in DeLop who had a shred of blood in common with Mother. Three years ago, Shelby began agitating to go along. She wanted to help deliver the toys. She'd picked most of them out, she argued. She'd kicked in part of her allowance every week to help buy them. Why should she be left at home with her dad?

The very idea of Shelby in DeLop chilled Laurel to her marrow. Guns or meth labs inside every other house, drunk men laid out bare-chested on their porches, Dixie plates of soft white food left moldering on the floors, every yard adrift in dog crap and broken glass and needles and Taco Bell wrappers and used condoms. Once, at Uncle Poot's house, Laurel had seen a dead animal lying in the middle of the driveway. It was about the size of a possum or a small raccoon. There was no telling, since the thing had been left there so long it had rotted down to bones lying in a nest of its own dark hairs. Shelby had no idea what she was asking.

Bet Clemmens was a compromise. She'd started as a pen pal whom Laurel had selected from the herd of vaguely related DeLop kids near Shelby's age.

"How touching. It's like you're bringing a tiny piece of shit mountain back to Mohammed," Thalia had said when she found out. "I assume you'll read the letters first and black out the bad words before Shelby's little eyes get tainted?"

But Laurel had chosen well. Bet was one of the few DeLop kids who hadn't dropped out before middle school. Even so, her handwriting looked like an eight-year-old's, and she wasn't literate enough to write much beyond "Hi, I'm Bet. I got me a dog name Mitchl. Do you got a dog?" The letters had tabled the discussion of DeLop until last summer, when Shelby, in a pen-pal coup, invited Bet to come visit her.

That first year had been a qualified success. Shelby and her friends treated Bet Clemmens with elaborate courtesy. At twelve, they'd been more impressed by their own kindness to The Poor Girl than they were interested in Bet herself. Bet Clemmens stood it the way she stood everything, phlegmatic and unsurprised, plunking herself down on the fringes of Shelby's gang. Laurel kept a careful watch, but Bet didn't instigate liquor-cabinet raids or bring the drugs she certainly had access to or relieve the gangly boys in Shelby's circle of their innocence.

Laurel had a cautious hope that the visits might do Bet some good. After all, Mother had gotten out. Sometimes it happened. Maybe Bet would finish high school, let Laurel and David help her get through college. Laurel had driven over to get Bet again this summer. She hadn't regretted her decision until now, as she watched Bet Clemmens stand rooted to the patio, practically dozing in the middle of the ugliest night Laurel had ever witnessed.

The young fireman finished questioning David and walked back toward the other firemen. Laurel, who had kept her profile to the pool as long as possible, found herself tracking him. The other firemen had stopped CPR. The group shifted, and Laurel caught a glimpse of Molly's face framed by black boots.

Laurel said to David, "Molly looks like herself, only she's not there. It's the hatefulest thing I've ever seen."

No one spoke for half a minute, and then Bet Clemmens said, "I seen my one uncle who got drowned." Shelby turned to look at Bet. They all did. "He laid out drunk in the crick. It was only five inches deep."

"Thank you, Bet," said Laurel, meaning "Stop talking."

"He was out there dead all night afore I found him," Bet offered. "The crawdaddies et his face."

"I don't think that story's helping right now," Laurel said much too loudly.

Shelby was looking at Bet with rounded eyes, as if her summer charity had shifted from a project to a person. "You're the one who found him?" she asked. "You saw his face?"

Bet Clemmens bobbed her head. "Et," she repeated, and Shelby took a step closer to her.

A flood of people, paramedics and policemen, poured through the glass doors, streaming around the four of them as if they were rocks in a river.

David hunched his shoulders, compressing as they passed him. He had his hands folded together, the fingers tucked inside, and he was compulsively bringing his palms together and then apart, as if he were doing that hand play for kids that went *This is the church, this is the steeple, open the doors, and see all the people.*

With no more questions to answer and his yard filling up with human beings, he was looking to Laurel for cues. People were Laurel's department. But Laurel was as lost in this crowd as David was in any. Laurel's mother had read the "Miss Manners" column aloud at Sunday lunch, reverently, in the same voice that she used to read the gospel. Laurel had been raised on Miss Manners and King James, maybe in that order; neither source had ever told her what was proper on a night like this.

She didn't know if she should offer to make coffee or start screaming until someone gave her medicine. Both options seemed equally obscene. She needed a script to tell her what words to say, what actions were appropriate to perform, and she found herself wondering if this was how David felt when she gave dinner parties.

Her only reliable instinct was to touch Shelby, to physically move her child two steps back from Bet Clemmens's story of the drowned uncle. She reached for Shelby's arm and saw a line of red and rust on the shoulder of her daughter's lime green T-shirt. It was shaped like a finger.

Laurel pulled her hands back and turned them over in the light to see the palms. Her right hand, the one she'd placed on the back of Molly's neck to tilt her head back, was streaked and flecked with drying blood. She rubbed at it, but she succeeded only in marking her other hand as well. She felt a scream building, and then a small, strong hand encircled her wrist, catching it before she could wipe her hand down her damp pajamas.

A brunette in a tailored brown pantsuit was standing beside her. Her hair was scraped back into a ponytail. "Detective Moreno," she said by way of introduction. "You touched the body?"

"I touched Molly," Laurel said. "We did CPR."

Moreno looked around and then flagged down a passing man in a jumpsuit. Laurel saw that the detective's ponytail was perfectly centered on the back of her head, and it narrowed evenly to a point at the end. It was such a mathematically exact ponytail that under normal circumstances, she would have pointed it out to David. Its symmetry would have pleased him.

"I need a tech to look at your hands, mm-kay?" Moreno handed Laurel's wrist over to the man in the jumpsuit as if it were an object. Laurel closed her eyes.

As Moreno walked away, Laurel heard her saying, "You need to get these people out of my crime scene. The skies could open up anytime."

But it wasn't her crime scene. It was Laurel's yard, where things like this were not allowed to happen.

She smelled the tang of rubbing alcohol and felt the cool tip of a swab running down her palm. She opened her eyes.

The tech said, "You can wash up after this," and his voice was kind. "We're going to take you over to your neighbors' house." He tilted his head toward the Coes'. "We'll need your daughters' T-shirt, too. She can change at your neighbors'. We'll take you there now, okay?"

"Who did this?" she said to the tech, but he was putting the swab into a little tube and labeling it.

Laurel wasn't sure what she was asking, anyway. She'd thought of waiting half an hour after eating, of signs that said NO LIFEGUARD ON DUTY and SWIM AT YOUR OWN RISK. She'd assumed Molly was here because of some violation of the careful, basic safety rules of childhood. But drowned people don't bleed. Blood meant bullet holes and violence. Blood was Uncle Marty on his last hunting trip. Her teeth buzzed, as if she'd bitten tinfoil. Time sped up, and too many people milled around, moving things. Her family became some of the things that they were moving. A uniformed woman was telling them all to follow her, please, and Shelby was looking down at her stained shirt, saying, "What? What?" to the tech.

"This won't come off," Laurel said, holding her bloody palm up to David as they passed through the wooden gate and crossed their lawn, walking toward the Coes' house. Shelby led the way between Bet Clemmens and the tech who wanted the T-shirt.

Out in the cul-de-sac, Laurel and David's neighbors stood in clots between the emergency vehicles. Edie Paintin, Laurel's other close friend, stood on the edge of Mindy's yard with her husband, and in between the cop cars and the wasted ambulance she saw the Simpsons, the Decouxs, and the Rainwaters in a huddle. The Prestons and another woman, maybe Julie Wilson, stood farther back, almost lost in the shadows.

Trish Deerbold, the thin lines of her overplucked brows raised and her mouth curling, was across the cul-de-sac in front of her house. She stared hard as Laurel passed, as if Laurel were an exhibit. Laurel saw Trish poke one elbow into Eva Bailey and then lean toward her, whispering. All her neighbors' eyes were on her. She hated being looked at this way, her stained hands held up like a confession.

Out of the corner of her eye, she caught a glimpse of another person standing across the street. He was well behind the crowd, all the way back in the Deerbolds' grass. The colored lights of the farthest cop car bounced off his curls, or else he would have been invisible. He had Percy Bysshe Shelley hair, the top rumpled into an artful tousle. It looked like Stan Webelow's hair, but everyone else she could see milling in the cul-de-sac was a close neighbor; Stan lived all the way over in Victorianna's phase one.

"Who is that?" she asked David.

"Who is what?" said David. He didn't stop.

Laurel craned her head back over her shoulder as David walked her forward. The Decouxs were blocking her view, so the person had to be short. Stan Webelow was built small and leanly muscled. When he jogged shirtless through the neighborhood, his lithe chest as dewy as if he'd oiled it, the mommy brigade paused to watch. Not Laurel; Stan Webelow had a pixieman face, and his hands were moist and soft, as if he'd deboned them. He should not be here now.

Mindy came running to her other side and threw an arm around her, saying, "Oh, honey!" She saw Laurel's hands and added, "Are you hurt?"

Mindy tugged her up the stairs and inside. Laurel peered through the crack as the Coes' front door was closing, but she could no longer see the man.

Thalia would have pulled away and run across the street. If it were Stan Webelow, she would have grabbed him by all his curls, squeezed him at both ends, demanding to know his business here on Chapel Circle. But her sister had not set foot in Victorianna for going on two years now; Thalia wasn't here, and Laurel wasn't her.

For the first time in her life, she wished she were.

CHAPTER 2

The last time Thalia came to Victorianna was in the dead heat of an endless September. The dog days made her torpid. She spent the weekend lounging by the pool with Laurel, watching Shelby and her friends leaping in and out of the water like seal puppies. That time she hadn't needled David much about being a robot or taught Shelby's crew how to say "fart" in nine languages or gotten rowdy with someone's husband back in Laurel's gazebo. She was lazy and easy, right up until the last night of her visit. Then she made up for all her good behavior: She let Laurel take a walk.

They stayed up too late, sitting hip to hip in front of the fireplace and drinking wine as Thalia pulled out pretty childhood memories for Laurel in a string, like Christmas lights. No one could tell stories like Thalia in a sweet mood; she'd gone to Chapel Hill's prime drama school on scholarship, and by her sophomore year, she'd had more than one West Coast agency courting her. But she'd fallen in love with the tiny laboratory theater in the basement of Graham Memorial.

"I can smell the audience's collective breath. That's intimacy. Television is for assholes," she explained. "And movies are for slightly smarter assholes."

She dropped out, married her gay boyfriend, Gary, and together they opened a nonprofit theater in Mobile that teetered on the desperate edge of collapse every time the electric bill came. They survived on grants, the yoga and acting lessons Thalia taught, and a small but dedicated fan base.

That night, long after David and Shelby had gone up to bed, Thalia had been on, and Laurel was an audience of one. Her stomach muscles hurt from laughing. It was after midnight when Thalia sat up straight and said, "Do you remember the Resurrection Snail?"

"I don't think so," Laurel said.

"He's a Gray family legend. You were little, though, maybe five or six. We were playing hospital, and I was going to do surgery on that doll you loved, Pink Baby. We went out to the garage to get something out of Daddy's toolbox. Maybe a screwdriver?"

"No," Laurel said. It was coming back. She pointed an accusing finger at Thalia. "You wanted the drill!"

"Lucky for Pink Baby, that big-ass snail was by the workbench to distract me. I almost stepped on him."

He'd been a huge fellow, larger than a silver dollar, making his slow way toward the door that led to their backyard. Thalia had pressed her cheek to the sealed concrete, her butt poking up, her arms draped flat at her sides, trying to mimic the way he moved forward, the upside of him sailing smoothly while his belly undulated.

Daddy had left a hammer sitting out by his workbench, and Laurel had picked it up.

"You held it over him," Thalia said, her fingers curling around an invisible handle as she made an instant shift. She was five-year-old Laurel, her head tilted, innocent of bad intentions, running a curious finger over a shell that felt invincible. Then she was Thalia again, intoning, "The tool of Damacles," with such high drama that Laurel burst out laughing again.

"The poor snail," Laurel said, wiping at her eyes.

Laurel had let the hammer tip and fall forward, no force behind it except its own weight. It seemed unlikely she would do more than shiver his fine edifice, but there was a crunching sound when the hammer landed like a foot on the gravel driveway. When Laurel had lifted it, the snail's cream and brown swirled house had mashed into a flat sliced pie. His middle had become a jelly filling, oozing up between the slivers, though his head had still been plump and his ball-tipped feelers had waved and quested, suddenly frantic.

"Holy crap, the weeping," said Thalia, unfolding from her mashed-snail pose. " 'Unbreak it, unbreak it,' you said. You ran to our room and flung yourself onto your bed. Mother came down on me like the very wrath of God, sure I'd done him in myself to make you sorrowful."

"Poor Thalia," Laurel managed to sputter out. "Although I'm sure you'd done *something* that day to earn a little wrath of God." Mother had appeared by Laurel's bed to pet her sweat-damp hair and tell her to stop crying. "Mother said that you had put that snail right back together again."

"With Super Glue. That was my idea," Thalia said, inclining her head graciously to an imaginary audience.

"That's right! She read the package to me, about how it could fix anything. She made it sound magic," Laurel said. "So I went to look, and it *was* like magic. He was gone, and there was a trail, like a greasy slug trail, all the way from the workbench to the door."

"Vaseline. Mother gave me two bucks to design the set and sell the story. Lazarus, take up thy shell!" Thalia reached for the cabernet.

Laurel covered the mouth of her glass with one hand and then stood up, unsteady. They were halfway through the second bottle, and her eyes felt grainy, as if they'd been salted. Outside the glass doors, lightning split the humid air, but the storm was still too far off for them to hear thunder.

"None for me. That was perfect, but I'm done, done, baked through."

Thalia stood and bowed extravagantly, flourishing her arm, putting one leg behind her and then bending deep at the knee. At the bottom of the bow, she nearly lost her balance, which sent Laurel into a fit of fresh giggles. She trailed up the stairs to her room. In her mild wine glaze, she tumbled into bed without putting the chain on the bedroom door, and her dreams came bright and fast. She heard calliope music and saw a boy with hair like wheat running with her childhood dog, Miss Sugar.

The storm drew closer, and by three A.M., Laurel was up again, barefoot, naked under her sheer blue nightie. She came down the stairs with David's Swiss army knife in one hand, the screwdriver attachment extended.

Thalia was reading on the sofa. She took less sleep than a cat and had trouble getting settled to do what little she liked, especially away from Gary.

"Tigers in the deer garden. We have to root them out," Laurel informed Thalia, then walked purposefully past her to work the locks on the front door.

Thalia punched in the key code before the alarm went off, and watched Laurel walk out onto the front porch. That night Laurel had seen Thalia be everything from their mother to their monstrous uncle Poot to a murdered snail, so it was easy afterward to reconstruct what Thalia did next.

Instead of helping her sister back upstairs to her safe bed or calling David, Thalia slipped on her shoes and followed Laurel out into the night. Followed her exactly, placing her feet carefully in Laurel's footsteps. She left one hand at her side, the fingers curling under, while the other held out an invisible pocketknife. She dogtrotted around to the front for a moment to observe and re-create the expression in Laurel's open eyes, as if Laurel were a subject, not a sister. Thalia learned sleepwalking until she owned it, until she learned and owned Laurel in her most vulnerable state.

The air was so thick with storm that the smell came into Laurel's dream, hot and electric. Victorianna was dense woods all around her. Thalia was slinking along behind her again like a predator. Laurel felt meaty breath on her neck. She sped up, winding her way deeper into her vine-lashed neighborhood.

They had passed the communal playground and the duck pond when a fat drop of rain came slicing down through the summer air and popped off Laurel's shoulder. Then water fell out of the sky in one solid sheet after another.

Laurel woke up drenched, her left heel bleeding where she'd stepped on something unfriendly. Her nightgown had gone transparent. She screamed and dropped David's knife, jumped back from its clatter and screamed again. The storm and darkness stripped the houses of their colors, and they crowded the sky around her, the turrets looming high.

Thalia said, "Laurel, it's me."

Laurel's head jerked back and forth as her eyes tried to focus. She put her arms out to catch herself, as if she were falling. Thalia tried to gather Laurel up, but she was lean as a greyhound, not built for comfort; her attempted pat felt like a slap on the slick wet skin of Laurel's back. Laurel pushed at her, her eyes rolling as she tried to find a landmark. She saw the lights of the clubhouse as Thalia came at her again, her long arms spreading to try to take her in. Laurel turned and limp-sprinted away from her, down the road home, her arms wrapped tight around her front to keep her breasts from bouncing.

She felt the invisible eyes of a hundred imaginary neighbors on her. Was Darla St. John peering out from her darkened bedroom windows, calling Mark over to see that Laurel Hawthorne had snapped like a June pea? Was Edie's teenage son peeking through the blinds, watching his mother's friend hobbling through the streets in a nightgown that the rain had rendered as sheer as wet tissue? She could have cried at the injustice of it. This was Thalia's fault! But Thalia was fully dressed in jeans, tank top, and shoes, running after a hollering, struggling, nearly naked Laurel. Thalia, who didn't give a crap what any human on God's green earth thought of her, looked like a Good Samaritan, arms outstretched, trying to rescue her shivering mess of a sister. Laurel, who had to face her neighbors at church and the PTA for decades yet to come, was a train wreck, calling all eyes.

Thalia yelled her name again, and Laurel stopped long enough to shush her sister. She waited, letting Thalia catch up, so at least it would no longer look like Thalia was trying to chase her down and stop her from streaking madly up Beeton Street. They walked back to the house together, quickly, in silence, both of them soaked to the skin. Once inside, Thalia stopped in the foyer, but Laurel kept walking.

"You be gone when I get up," Laurel said without looking back, and she stalked upstairs.

David sat up as she came in, turning on his bedside lamp and blinking in the light. He stared at Laurel for a long minute, his gears grinding.

"I forgot the chain," she said. "I took a walk."

"I thought I set the house alarm," he said.

Laurel turned her back and started rummaging through her dresser for fresh pajamas. She didn't want to tattle. David didn't notice her sister's good visits, but he kept a running tally of the days Thalia had left Laurel exhausted or furious or crying. Angry as she was, she already knew she would make it up with Thalia; David was less forgiving when it came to injuries against her person.

"Did you turn off the alarm?" he asked, and Laurel shrugged, carrying her bundle of dry clothes toward the bathroom. She hoped he would leave things there.

"Thalia turned it off, didn't she?" he said, making her sister's name sound like a dirty word.

He didn't wait for an answer. She heard him climbing out of bed and turned around in time to see him yanking the door open.

"David, no."

Assuming he didn't plan to either challenge Thalia to Rubik's Cubes at dawn or strangle her, David was no match for her sister in an argument. Delivering words was Thalia's forte, while David thought so strongly in numbers that English seemed almost his second language.

"I'm fine," Laurel called after him. "David!"

He didn't hear her. He'd transferred his considerable focus to the space around him, moving through it with an angry precision that boded ill for her sister. Most times David didn't pay attention to his limbs, but he went out and down the stairs with a scything grace that was almost beautiful. She let him go. Maybe Thalia was the one who should, this time, be worried.

Laurel had finished her good cry in the shower and was in bed by the time he came back up. He was pale and winded, and his eyes were round. He had a spot of red in each cheek, about the same size and shape as his eyes. His mouth was a lipless line.

"She'll be gone in the morning," Laurel said, her tone apologetic.

"She's gone now."

That was all he said.

Three months later, Laurel felt Thalia's absence like a lost tooth. She couldn't stop exploring the hole, and Shelby, who thought her bohemian aunt was the ultimate in cool, was agitating hard to see her. It wasn't unusual for Laurel and Thalia to stop speaking, but it had never gone on this long before. One night at dinner, Laurel talked around the idea of having Thalia back, and David's usual rapt focus on her changed into a charged, unhappy silence. Laurel decided to leave him out of it. She and Shelby went to Thalia's home turf, buying tickets for her latest production and driving to Mobile.

That night Laurel had walked out of the theater midplay, finished with Thalia. Period. Shelby was heartbroken, but Laurel was deaf to all pleas and whining on the subject. There was silence from Thalia's camp as well. Since then they'd seen each other only at the annual Christmas sojourn to DeLop, where Mother's presence ensured that all interactions would be muffled by a thick coat of good manners. Even when Thalia slipped in a dig, calling Laurel's neighborhood "Stepfordianna," Laurel took an egg from Mother's basket and refused to notice.

But Laurel could not stop thinking of Thalia now. She imagined her striding across their backyard, her gimlet eye piercing the chaos. Thalia would grab that brisk detective by the ponytail, yank it sideways off its perfect axis, and shake her until her head bobbled loose on her neck and she explained why there was blood at the scene of a drowning.

Moreno had questioned the Hawthornes for what felt like hours, but she'd avoided telling them anything. She'd directed most of her questions at Bet and Shelby. She'd started by asking Bet if she knew why Molly would have sneaked out and visited the Hawthornes' yard. Laurel had wanted to ask Bet that very question; Bet wasn't charismatic enough to be a leader, but Laurel had been worried about the DeLop influence ever since the day Shelby invited her. But Bet was genuinely clueless. She'd answered with a guileless "I dun know," then looked to Shelby. Shelby's cheeks had pinked, just barely, and her lids had dropped.

Thalia would have taken one look at Shelby's exhausted face, the lavender shadows under her eyes the size and shape of thumbprints, and stepped in. Stepped in hard. But Moreno's next question seemed so innocuous. She'd lulled Laurel, following up by asking Shelby if she had planned to meet Molly, perhaps to play a trick on someone?

That sounded plausible to Laurel. Only two months ago, she'd caught Shelby and Molly trying to sneak out during a sleepover with a bag of Charmin double rolls, bent on mayhem. But then Moreno had stepped it up, slowly, inching forward, and she'd focused on the girls more and more while David and Laurel sat silent. As it became obvious that Bet had not known Molly very well, Moreno zeroed in on Shelby. She pushed and bullied, asking if Molly ever talked about running away, if Molly was unhappy at home, if Molly was having trouble at school.

Shelby, shrinking into Bet Clemmens's side as they sat on Mindy's love seat, kept saying she didn't know in a scared, small voice so unlike her own that it sounded borrowed. Real Shelby trilled and yawped and gabbled dramatically and waved her arms around. She didn't fold herself up into an unhappy packet and stare at her feet. Thalia would have knocked that bitch Moreno into next week. But Laurel, shell-shocked, sat dumb and let it happen.

The police had released Laurel and David's house at around four A.M., and now only the backyard was wound in yellow tape. It might have been more proper to go to a hotel, but both girls were nodding off, and Laurel had wanted the comfort of her own things more than she had wanted to be proper.

Back in their bed, Laurel and David lay curled into S-shapes that faced each other, listening to the clatter and the voices of policemen and techs working in the yard. The CSIs were trying to process the scene before the rain came. They'd put huge floodlights all around the pool, and a hard white slice of artificial light came through a crack in the drapes. David watched Laurel steadily, but she felt her own lids drooping. She was sinking into sleep, drifting down, almost against her will.

From the surface, she heard David say, "I can't sleep. I'm going downstairs to do some work."

He got up, and it was as if he took the light with him. It reflected away before it reached her, as if she were deep under dark water. Somewhere, above her, in the safe, dry place she could not reach, David walked away. Laurel's lungs ached for breath, but she could not reach the surface. She realized she could kick only one foot. She looked down and saw her mother squatting in some water weeds, her fluffy hair waving in the currents. Mother had a calm grip on Laurel's other ankle.

She woke up halfway out of bed, both feet on the floor, choking for the air that was all around her. She had one hand on the phone beside the bed. She jerked her hand away as if the phone were hot. The clock told her she hadn't been asleep longer than a few minutes. She got all the way up, knowing she would not sleep again until she had checked on Shelby.

She walked to Shelby's doorway, and again, the bed was empty. Laurel's heart stuttered. She whirled and peered across the hall into the small guest room. Shelby was there. She'd moved to the trundle bed, one level down from Bet Clemmens. Laurel got a full breath at last.

Shelby was on her back with her arm flung up onto the daybed, her fingers loosely curled around a piece of Bet's sleeve. The veins of Shelby's arm glowed pale blue through her skin even in the hallway light. Freak veins, Shelby called them, and begged for tanning-bed sessions or those self-activating lotions that turned a person orange. "You're too young," Laurel told her, and that was true, but the secret truth beneath was that Laurel loved the prominent veins. When Shelby was a baby, Laurel would map them with her fingers, following the trail that spent blood took from Shelby's beating heart, heading to her lungs to renew itself.

The small guest room acted as a catchall. The overspill of Laurel's fabric collection and the stash of toys and shoes she collected all year for DeLop ended up here. Laurel navigated her way around the stockpiles and Bet Clemmens's Hefty bag. Bet's mouth gaped open, and her breathing sounded thick. Shelby was breathing through her nose, quick and shallow.

Laurel knelt by the trundle, taking Shelby's arm down and tucking it under the quilt. Her daughter's arm felt too light, as if it had a will of its own. As if Shelby were moving it with her.

"Shel?" Laurel whispered. "You awake?"

No answer.

"Shelby," Laurel urged, her voice growing louder, and then started when she saw that Bet Clemmens's eyes were open and glittering in the hallway light. "Sorry, Bet. I didn't mean to wake you."

"I dun care," Bet said. After a moment she added in a wistful voice, "Do I gotta leave?"

Laurel swallowed hard and said, "I think if Shelby were at your house and something like this happened, I would want her home."

Bet said, "Mama won't mind none. I only been here four days this time."

Bet stared unblinking into Laurel's eyes, her mouth turned slightly down. Bet's mother, Sissi, had the grayed-out skin of a longtime meth user and a mouth so chapped it cracked and bled at the corners. She'd waved one lazy hand and said, "Bye, then," when Laurel took Bet away, but blood was blood, and surely any mammal would want her child home under the circumstances.

"You can come back another time. Soon. I promise."

Bet nodded. Her rounded eyes had a downward tilt that matched her mouth. She looked like a little beef cow being led off toward an unfamiliar building. She hadn't blinked in so long that Laurel's own eyes began to itch.

"Good night," Laurel said, and Bet rolled onto her back to stare up at the ceiling. Shelby's eyes were closed and moving under her lids, as if she were dreaming. Maybe she wasn't playing possum. Moreno had obviously exhausted her.

No matter how many times Shelby said she didn't know whether Molly had been unhappy at home, at school, Moreno had come back to it. Moreno had also asked several times if Molly had a boyfriend. Shelby had been definite on that one, shaking her head, eyes down, shaking her head again when Moreno asked if there was a boy Molly liked.

But there had to be a boy she'd liked. Molly was a thirteen-year-old girl. She and Shelby had talked constantly about which of them liked what boy in an endless round-robin as Laurel ferried them from school to dance and home again. Yet Shelby had shaken her head, a definite no, no boy, and Laurel had seen someone who didn't belong standing in her cul-de-sac. He'd been short, but not middle-school short. An adult with curly, tousled hair like Stan Webelow's, and as always when she thought of him, her blood chilled and ran a little slower.

Stan had moved to Victorianna about three years ago, when his mother died and he inherited the house. Cookie Webelow had been a neighborhood fixture, always out digging in her flower beds. She kept gum in her apron pockets, and the neighborhood kids adored her, but she raised the hairs on the back of Laurel's neck.

All of Victorianna had turned out for her funeral. It was open-casket, so Laurel had left ten-year-old Shelby with Mother. She thought the funeral-home people had lost their minds; they'd put Cookie in a full face of makeup, though she'd never so much as powdered her nose in the decade Laurel had known her. Her hands looked white and strange without her gardening gloves.

Trish Deerbold had stood in line ahead of David, putting one hand dramatically over her heart and exclaiming, "She looks so natural."

The standard southern funeral response was "Lord, yes, she looks exactly like herself," but David hadn't recognized it as ritual, and his eyes widened at the blatant falsehood. He stared at Cookie's round brown face, powdered pale around the lips with a big red mouth drawn on, as overblown as a rose four days past prime.

He whispered to Laurel, "Natural? She looks like a sock monkey."

Trish gave him a fast glare, but his description was both so horrible and so accurate that Laurel had to quash an inappropriate spray of laughter that was rushing her throat. She forced herself to look away from Cookie, focusing instead on the small, dapper man in the black suit standing by the head of the coffin. He was passing out handshakes as if they were the prize a person won for viewing. Laurel assumed he was the funeral director, but as she reached the front of the receiving line, he took her hand and introduced himself as Stan Webelow, Cookie's son.

Laurel murmured her condolences, but her spine went all a-shiver in his oily presence. His fine-boned hand felt as waxy and inanimate as his mother's looked. Cookie had never mentioned a son, and in her house, there were only pictures of her late husband and her corgis.

The next week, Stan Webelow had moved into Cookie's peach-colored house. Laurel wondered why a young single man wanted to live in a four-bedroom, three-bath home in a family neighborhood. He had no visible means of support, though Mindy believed Cookie's estate was substantial, and Edie had heard he owned a Web-based business of some sort.

He'd stayed, and stayed unemployed and single. He'd never brought a date to neighborhood potlucks, but he had an unctuous, touchy-feely way with the ladies that made Laurel doubt he was gay. He was around thirty, and most of the neighborhood women considered him attractive, though he gravitated toward women a good ten or even twenty years older than he was. Laurel found it puzzling before it occurred to her that these women had something besides their age in common: They had teenagers.

Laurel watched him closely after that, especially with Shelby. Although she never saw him do anything untoward, she couldn't shake her uneasy dislike of him, so she'd warned Shelby to steer clear. Now she was pretty sure he'd been in her cul-de-sac, way off his turf, and Molly had led Laurel to her small body as if it were a message.

If so, Molly had chosen the wrong woman to interpret it. Laurel wasn't Joan of Arc, with a team of helpful angels to light her up a path to truth. She wasn't even a poor man's Nancy Drew.

Still, Molly had chosen Laurel to pull her from the water. She'd put her blood on Laurel's hands, and since the moment Laurel had seen it, she hadn't stopped thinking of her sister. She'd heard Thalia's voice, and she'd woken up with her hand on the phone. Now, staring down at Shelby's wan face, she knew the number she needed to dial.

She had to talk to David first. He thought of Thalia's name as a synonym for all hell breaking loose. He wouldn't want her. Laurel would have to make him see that Thalia could do no harm. Here on their pretty street, hell had broken loose already.

CHAPTER 3

David was down in his office in the basement, sitting in one of the two leather rolling chairs. He had three worktables set in an L-shape that he used like an enormous desk, and the monitor sat centered in the longer leg. His game was running, so looking at his monitor was like looking through the cockpit of a plane with the controls all at the bottom of the screen. He leaned in toward the flat-screen LCD he had hooked up to his multi-box system.

Laurel saw another plane flash by. David muttered, "Gotcha," and began firing. He spun after it, zooming through an endlessly unfolding blue sky. The sound effects were on low, but he still had no idea she had entered the room. He probably didn't know he was in the room, either. David was in the zone.

She could call him out of it. After thirteen years of marriage, all she had to do was say his name, and he would come to her, beaming himself in from the foreign place he lived when she was silent. When she first met him, in her freshman year at NC State, he'd seemed strange and closed, as if he lived buttoned up inside his brain. He was weird, and Laurel hadn't liked him. She had about enough weird to last her, thank you.

Growing up two years behind Thalia had been like going to Strange boot camp for eighteen years straight. By the time Laurel started ninth grade, Thalia had already infiltrated every nook and cranny of Pace High. She'd been a cheerleader and a stoner, and she'd made and dropped track team, student council, and the twirling majorettes in quick succession before joining—and as rapidly unjoining—debate squad, band, and chorus. Finally, she'd defaulted to hanging out with the five geek-lunatics who called themselves the Drama Club.

Thalia had entertained herself on Laurel's high school orientation day by spreading a rumor that she'd been diagnosed with Tourette's syndrome over the summer. Thalia calibrated her performance carefully, operating well below teacher radar, but her small, controlled twitches, head tics, and soft squeals and profanities were convincing. Even the most Thalia-jaded members of the student body became true believers, and kids Laurel didn't know kept stopping by her locker and her lunch table to ask about Thalia's "condition."

Laurel had gone shopping with Mother in August for Chic jeans with tapered legs, and strawberry lip gloss, and brown mascara. She kept her shiny hair in a thick French braid and was quiet and smart but not too smart. She should have been allowed to blend.

Instead, she found herself saying over and over, "I don't want to talk about it," while staring down at her pink Converse high-tops. Every third girl in her class had those same colored sneakers, but rather than easing her into the scenery, hers seemed to glow like bright and shameful beacons.

Thalia closed the show three weeks later by squawking, "Fuck-a-poo, birdy!" during bio class every time Mrs. Simon turned her back to write on the board. It earned her yet another suspension, and for the rest of high school, even after her sister had graduated, Laurel was known as "Thalia Gray's sister, poor thing."

Away at college, Thalia-free for the first time in her life, Laurel immediately took up with a group of bouncy-ponytail girls, mostly education majors, pretty enough, smart enough, but not too . . . anything. They looked like the pictures that had so entranced Mother in the college brochures. They had an equal and opposing bunch of boys whom they traded around, jocky business-major types, round-faced and cheerful and about as complicated as a bunch of puppies. Not one of them had ever met Thalia, and if Laurel had her way, they never would.

David was twenty and already a grad student at Duke, Big Brain on Campus. He was the star of the math and science hybrid classes, tall and skinny as a pipe cleaner, but cute enough, if he hadn't been so weird. He had the apartment across the hall from Laurel's friend Jeannie. Laurel never would have met him if he had lived anywhere else.

He didn't fit with her set, but when Laurel was a freshman, he kept happening into them. They'd be doing the kind of perfect-snapshot college things that had attracted Laurel to this crowd in the first place: plumping hot dogs on the grill in the apartment complex's pavilion, sunning on Jeannie's deck. He'd come up and say hello and then simply stay.

By the time Laurel was a sophomore, he'd grown on her. He was like Jeannie's bright orange paisley sofa, a strange hand-me-down that became so familiar it seemed like it belonged in the room. He sat through the games with them and paid his share for pizza, watching Laurel and her friends like Mr. Spock watched the humans. He didn't get a lot of the jokes or know the teams, and he once stood up and started out in the middle of a tight World Series game without saying a word.

"Where're you going, Lurch?" Jeannie called after him.

Jeannie's current boyfriend had named him after the silent butler from the Addams Family. David didn't seem to mind, or maybe he didn't get it. Laurel minded for him, though. She always called him David.

David pulled his watch out of his pocket, checked it, and said, "PBS has an all-night *NOVA* marathon starting at nine."

Jeannie managed to keep a straight face until he closed the door, and then she and her boyfriend both cackled like two of Macbeth's witches while Laurel said, "Guys. Be nice," and tried not to be the third.

His quiet presence was such a constant that she hardly noticed him, and he didn't truly become a person to her until the day he found her weeping in the hallway near his door. She was waiting for Jeannie to come home and let her in so she could cry far away from the fishbowl interest of the girls in her dorm; her boyfriend, Dale, had broken her pink heart that day.

When David saw her sitting in a miserable pile on the floor, he set down his grocery bags and folded his body into an awkward crouch beside her. Laurel had cried all her bones out and was too floppy to worry that she was red-nosed and puffy-eyed in front of a boy. It was, after all, only David Hawthorne.

"I'm having a bad day," she said.

"I see that. Come in out of the hall," he said.

He had some white wine in one of his grocery bags. It was the big-bottle kind, but with a real cork, the glass frosted because he'd bought it cold. In his apartment, he had real wineglasses, too, mismatched but pretty. They sat sipping with their backs propped against his futon, and if Jeannie got home, Laurel didn't hear her.

Laurel spilled out her tale of woe, and he kept his eyes steady on her. She'd never had a boy listen to her blather on about love troubles, but David acted like her every word was interesting and important.

Laurel wound down until she was whispering. David leaned in close to hear, so close that it seemed like he was going to kiss her. She leaned in, too, until she was kissing him, or maybe they kissed each other. Either way, it was a good kiss. A really good kiss. He didn't do the oil-drill thing with his tongue that the heartbreaker had thought was such a great idea. She talked more, and then they kissed again. Still good. Kissing turned into making out, and then they broke apart while Laurel talked. He listened, shifting closer and closer until they were kissing again. Every time it started up, it went a little further.

David was good at things. Different at things. Dale had been Laurel's first "serious" boyfriend, and the sex had been exciting mostly because it seemed like such a grown-up, college thing to do. It was bouncy and friendly and interesting, and Dale was made so helpless by it that Laurel felt proud, like she was pretty and necessary. But it wasn't something she would have missed *Melrose Place* for.

This wasn't like that. When David touched her, he did it like an experiment, bent on finding out what kind of touching worked. It was as if he had hypothesized that the female body had nerve endings in it, and his five-year mission was to seek all of them out. He woke something up when he slipped his hand under Laurel's shirt, drifting his fingers against the thin nylon of her bra. Laurel's previous boyfriends had always treated her breasts like knobs or squeezy bath toys. In high school, she'd let boys feel her up because it distracted them from trying to work her jeans off, but David made her *want* to take them off.

She didn't decide to have sex with him so much as, at some point, her body decided. Everything he did made her want the next thing without even knowing what the next thing was, but then they'd find it out. She didn't think they were going to have sex; this was something else, something she and David were inventing as they went. Her body got hungry, and her mind blanked itself into an animal place. She went blind with it, her panties tossed away, her hips pressing up toward him, thoughtless and asking, and he was there, answering. They gave themselves up to it.

Afterward he fell asleep like boys do, sprawled naked on his back with his head propped on a cushion he'd pulled down off the futon. Laurel lay beside him with her blood running through her veins all irregular but sexy, as if it were made out of jazz. She scooted down to align her hip with his and looked at their thighs together. His was a long line, mostly bone. Hers was curved, shorter and paler. She couldn't be still. Her eyes wouldn't close. She stood up and pulled on her panties and David's discarded T-shirt, liking the wood-smoke and cinnamon smell of him on it. She was dying to talk, and she thought about slipping across the hall, but she realized she didn't want Jeannie to know. She didn't want any of her friends to know. This thing with David, unpredicted and peculiar, didn't match them.

David's apartment had a breakfast bar between his den and

the minuscule kitchen. Laurel boosted herself up to sit on the low counter, resting her feet on one of the two stools. His phone hung on the wall beside her, and she picked it up and dialed her sister. Thalia was already living with Gary over in Mobile. They had dropped out of Chapel Hill and were trying to scrape together the cash to open their theater.

Thalia picked up on the fourteenth ring, barking, "What, Jesus Bug, what?" into the phone. She knew only Laurel would let the phone ring on and on past eleven, the same way Laurel knew Thalia would not be sleeping.

Laurel could hear a piano and raucous conversation, distant, from another room. She spoke barely above a whisper. "Dale dumped me, and then I had complete sex with David Hawthorne. On his floor!"

"David Hawthorne?" Thalia said. "I don't— Wait, is that Lurch?"

"Don't call him that. You've never even met him." Laurel's whisper had turned fierce. "Sex is an amazing thing, Thalia."

Thalia laughed. "Um, doofus, I know."

Laurel said, "But I didn't."

"Dale was bad in bed!" Thalia crowed. "Ha! Gary owes me five bucks."

"You bet on that? You've never met Dale, either." But Laurel didn't have the brain space to think about Dale, not an inch. She said, "This changes everything."

Thalia made a piffling noise and said, "An orgasm doesn't change things, Bug. It's just a nice way to end Friday night."

But Thalia was wrong. It did change everything. While Laurel was whispering with her sister, her body was already busy making Shelby.

Sex with David was a continuing revelation, even while Laurel was pregnant, even after. She'd always been body-shy, the girl who took her gym clothes to a bathroom stall while everyone else stripped off in the locker room. She didn't want to be like Thalia, who paraded naked from shower to closet and then stood there dripping and glaring at her clothes, saying, "Who do I want to be today?" Dale had visited Laurel's body briefly and by candlelight, like a tourist, and she had pulled up the sheet the second he rolled away.

With David, she left the lights on and kicked the covers back. Growing Shelby, she ballooned up to what felt like twice her normal size, but in their bedroom, he stayed innovative; she stayed shameless.

The sex held Laurel during that difficult first year when they had only each other and the mixed blessing of Thalia. Mother had dreamed of Laurel in a cap and gown, then a wedding dress. Laurel hadn't given her either, and she was aloof and overly polite in her disappointment.

David's mother and grandparents wanted him in tweedy jackets with suede elbow patches, getting paid for understanding string theory and marrying some physicist from Harvard. Instead, he'd taken some computer code, his hobby, to a company all the way down in Florida, near Laurel's family. He'd traded grad school for Laurel and a high-end corporate job that came with a fifty-thousand-dollar signing bonus and insurance rigged to cover her "preexisting condition."

David was working crazy hours, proving himself invaluable in the hope that the company would let him work at home, away from all the people. So Laurel was alone, learning to be a mother and the wife of a near-stranger who hardly ever spoke to her.

None of it mattered, not when she secretly felt they did sex different and better than anyone else in the world. And David listened to her. She could talk about sewing or their neighbors or her long, lovely baby days with Shelby or tell rambling stories about her childhood. He pricked up his ears and gave her the same attention that he would have given Albert Einstein, and sex was how he answered back. Sex was where Laurel knew she knew him, and talking was the way she called him to her.

Now she said his name softly, and he immediately glanced over his shoulder. His eyes were as empty as hollow glass balls, unseeing, but as she watched, they filled up with her husband.

He turned back to the monitor and depressed a button on his keyboard, saying, "Hold on. I need a couple of minutes."

His office took up most of the basement, with only the laundry room and a small bathroom walled off behind it. David's ancient futon was up against the wall behind his desk. Laurel sat down on it, prepared to wait, but almost immediately, he swiveled in his chair to face her.

"I thought you were sleeping," he said, concerned.

"I was. For a minute," Laurel said, one finger tracing the ghost of Molly's blood on her palm. "David, I need Thalia over here."

"Or for the house to catch fire. That'd be good."

David's answer had come so fast it seemed automated. Behind him, on the screen, his plane began spiraling downward. He hadn't paused his game properly, and the green and brown earth came into view.

"I mean it," she said.

He gaped at her and said, "Have you met Thalia?" He leaned toward Laurel, bracing his elbows on his knees, long hands dangling, oblivious as his plane hurtled down and crashed behind him. Laurel heard the faint rumble of the impact and explosion. "You can't be serious," he added.

"I am, though. This isn't a regular day. This is the kind of day Thalia is good at."

It was true. Thalia didn't fit inside the hours set aside for lawn mowing and trips to the grocery. She chafed against their edges, pushed until she burst their seams and ruined them.

David touched the pads of his fingers to his forehead. He sat up and dropped his hand, then pressed his forehead again, as if he had something stuck up there and was pushing at it, trying to manually make it drop down and come out of his mouth. At last he said, "I don't know how to respond to that."

"That detective. Moreno. She barely asked us anything, and she treated Shelby like a perp on *Law and Order,* bad-copping her. We sat there and let her."

"You think Thalia would have stopped her?"

"Yes," Laurel said.

No hesitation. After all, it had worked that way before. Daddy had shot Marty, and after, in the bitter dregs of that long day, Thalia had done all the talking. When the deputy had turned to question Laurel, Thalia had taken her thumb out of her mouth and said, "My dumbass sister had her eyes shut. She's scared of guns. She's probably scared of deer."

Laurel hardly had to say a thing after that.

Now Laurel said, "That detective kept saying we had to answer her questions first, but then there never was a turn for us to ask anything. Molly Dufresne is dead, and Moreno is treating Shelby like a criminal. Thalia would make her stop. She'd make Moreno tell us what's going on. Thalia would—"

"Thalia isn't magic," David interrupted.

Laurel had to bite the inside of her lip because she was about to ask him how he knew. There was a tiny piece of her that still believed her big sister had taken Super Glue and put that shattered snail right back together. Maybe he had gone creeping off the garden to live out his life, eating moss and making more snails.

David said, "They'll tell us what's going on when they know."

Laurel didn't believe that. On the monitor, the game reset, the plane's windscreen repaired, the controls restored. The view showed a red dirt runway that bisected a grassy field.

Laurel said, "What *was* Molly doing in our yard? After midnight? All by herself? That's not like her."

"It's not?" he said.

"Of course not," Laurel said. "What do you remember about Molly? As a person?"

He thought for a moment, his forehead creasing. "She was blond?" he said. "And not loud."

"That was the wrong question. Never mind. Molly wasn't a leader in that dance gang of Shelby's. She did whatever Shelby did. I'm not saying she wouldn't sneak out to TP a house or maybe even meet a boy, but she wouldn't do it alone." Laurel remembered the drowned girl's ghost landing beside the pool, changing into a moving shadow that faded into the darkness as Laurel's gaze found Molly in her pool. "What if someone else was there, David? I think I saw someone moving in our yard when I was looking out the window."

He shook his head. "You were sleepwalking. You could have seen dancing trees. It wouldn't mean our pines were sentient."

"There's more, though. After, when we were walking over to

Simon and Mindy Coe's, I thought I saw Stan Webelow. He was standing in the Deerbolds' yard."

"The creepy guy who lives all the way down Queen's Court? Are you sure?"

"No," Laurel said. "I only saw curly hair."

David thought about it. "Rex Deerbold has curly hair."

"It wasn't curly like that. Anyway, I think Trish said it was a travel week for him."

"Wait. Why didn't you tell that detective?"

Laurel lifted her hands and said, "I don't know. She didn't ask who was in the cul-de-sac, and I wasn't thinking very clearly. All she wanted to do was pry at Shelby."

The screen saver came up, fish swimming peacefully in an aquarium.

"You have to tell the police," David said.

"Tell them what? I saw suspicious hair? I was sleepwalking, and there was a shadow that might have been a dream or a fox or a . . ." She stopped before she said the word. Ghost. David knew the name of her every childhood hamster, every boy she'd kissed, every favorite teacher. But she'd never told him that her dead uncle Marty used to visit her at night.

She hadn't known David very well when they'd married, and since that day, Marty had not come. Not once. Of course, David had heard her family mention Marty's name. He knew that her daddy had been raised by his older brother and that Marty had died in a hunting accident. But that was all.

At some point early in their marriage, she began to believe that to talk about dead Marty would be to make him real for David, too, to reinvite him, perhaps to reinvent him. So she had tucked all thoughts of him deep away. She slept curled against her husband's long back with her face buried in the warm corner made by the mattress and his side, and Marty could not penetrate the high, hard wall of David's rationalism. David did not know her ghost, and she couldn't explain it to him. He wouldn't understand; he had never even set foot inside DeLop.

These things were connected; even though Marty had been Daddy's family, Laurel could see him because of Mother's people.

Laurel had a cousin just her age who had claimed to see ghosts, too. When he and Laurel were seventeen, he'd "gone all the way to odd," as Aunt Enid put it, by which she meant he stopped talking and had to be fed by hand. He sat in a rocking chair drooling his days away. Every now and again, he'd stand up and whirl in frenzied circles and then lope back and forth across the room, grabbing and smashing anything he could touch. His daddy or his brother would wrestle him to the ground and sit on him until he went limp and could be propped back in his chair. Then he had burned down Uncle Petey-Boy's shed and gotten arrested. He was diagnosed with schizophrenia and sent to a state home instead of prison. Petey-Boy had said, "I coulda tol' them he was ass-rat crazy a year ago and stilla had my shed."

Laurel had her own diagnosis; her cousin had gone with the ghosts when they wanted to show him things. He had looked too long, was all.

Her great-aunt Moff still read cards for The Folks, and she was spooky-right when she laid them. Hearts for love, diamonds for money, clubs for family and friends, and spades for death. Moff left the ace of spades out of her deck because, she said, "If I dun, that ace drops ever' time I lay. Shitfire, I dun need uh ace to tell that we're all gonna die."

In DeLop, death came sooner rather than later. People who were born there tended to stay there. People who stayed died young and angry. No health insurance, so cancer, when it came, ate them. Too many drugs around too many guns. No jobs, restless young men with knives, drinking in small packs. The walls of the rattletrap houses were soaked in ghosts, all with things to show, all wanting to be seen. They eased into the genes.

David had never seen anything like DeLop. He'd spent his childhood in affluent Cherry Hill, New Jersey, and he probably thought Laurel had grown up poor because her parents' house had only two small bathrooms and Mother believed Hamburger Helper and a salad was a nice family meal.

If David understood people, she could take his hand, lead him upstairs, and show him a piece of DeLop lying with eyes open, wide and dry, in the small guest bedroom. But people were one of her jobs, like balancing the checkbook was one of his. He couldn't extrapolate DeLop by looking at Bet Clemmens. Without DeLop, Laurel couldn't tell him about her ghosts, even though she'd been looking for Marty from the moment the drowned girl had appeared in her room.

A woman's voice came through the speakers that sat on either side of David's monitor. "Dave? Are you back yet?"

He turned his chair toward the keyboard and pushed that button again. "I need a few more minutes," he said into the air.

The voice said, "Okay. I'm going to go make a fresh pot of coffee. I'll yell when I'm back."

David swiveled back to face Laurel.

"Someone is talking in your computer," Laurel said.

"Yeah. That's Kaitlyn Reese, the coder from Richmond Games."

"In San Francisco?" Laurel said.

"Yeah. She's there this week. We're in TeamSpeak." At Laurel's baffled look, he explained, "It's a voice-over IP application. Gamers use it to coordinate attacks."

"The San Francisco people call you Dave?" Laurel asked. He shrugged, waving away the question. If they were calling him Dave, he hadn't noticed. "Can she hear us?"

"Only when I hold down the tilde key."

"That's so strange. If we lived in California, I'd be married to someone named Dave," Laurel said. San Francisco sounded crisply green and temperate, like a place where she'd have fruit trees in a tiny yard with no pool. Her head hurt. "It must be three A.M. there. Did you wake her up?"

David blew air out between his teeth, a quick, dismissive exhale. "She was up. She's a coder." He said it as if coders were some strange species of space camel that could walk through an airless desert of ones and zeros for days without water or sleep.

"Coffee's on," said the woman's voice. "Dave? Hello? We've got to demo these dogfights this week."

"Go ahead," Laurel said. "We can talk about it when you've finished."

Still he didn't turn away. "I can't take Thalia here," he said. "Not right now. It's too many things. There's too many things already."

She nodded. "I know it's a bad time. It was an awful night, and this week is huge for you at work. But I need help."

"I'll help you," he said. He sounded matter-of-fact, as if not helping her had never been a possibility.

"How?" she said.

"I don't know. I need to think about what you said. But I will think. And then I'll help you or get you help. Trust me, okay?"

"Okay," she said, but even to her, she sounded uncertain.

He leaned in closer and held his rough cheek against hers, turning his face to press his nose into her neck. If he was sniff-testing her for truth, then she passed. He leaned back, pushing with his feet to roll his chair toward his desk, and she had the sense of him moving again, that same underwater feeling; she was drifting down, and he was walking away. She caught his leg before he could swivel. Laurel looked down at her hand on his knee. Washed clean.

"Baby," he said, "you need to rest. I'll figure out what to do. Lie down, okay?"

There was an old quilt that Laurel had thrown over the back of the futon, three rows of identical Sunbonnet Sues watering flowers in a nine-patch garden. Mother had made it with her when she was a girl, teaching her to sew. Laurel put her head down on one of the throw pillows, and David pulled Mother's quilt up around her. Then he turned back to his monitor. He put on a headset and turned off his speakers, so she could no longer hear the shooting or the whoosh of the planes or the voice of the woman all the way across the country.

She lay quietly, listening to him telling the woman to bank left, to try upping the difficulty level, to switch to keyboard controls. The whole night felt like it had happened in pieces, so she was left with scraps, their edges shredded so she could not fit them into a seamless whole. She was sinking again, and still his voice went on, only this time it was sinking with her. He'd said he would think about it. Maybe he'd realize they needed Thalia after all. Through the thin film of her sleep, she heard it happening.

He was saying, "Sorry to wake you, but I do think you should come. Laurel needs you."

It was a warm invitation, issued in a tone she hadn't heard him use with her sister in years. Maybe not ever. Laurel found herself relaxing into a deep and peaceful darkness.

Thalia was on the way.

CHAPTER 4

Laurel dreamed her parents' house, half an hour away in Pace. It was in the center of the block, on a busy street lined with brick ranches that squatted low under the wind. The rain was falling, and Marty's ghost stood by the porch, lurking in the faint gray-on-gray shadows of a drizzling sunrise.

Marty tied his tether to her father's bumper, and then Laurel's parents were on the move. As their car pulled out, the warm backwash of air pushed Marty high, sent him rising up until the identical black slate roofs camouflaged the one that had been his. The small yards were brown with summer grass, perfectly square and all the same. The Buick towed Marty like a pale kite on an endless string toward Laurel's house in Pensacola.

The gargoyles in the eaves saw him coming, and the weathervane spun as he passed over. The Buick pulled in to the driveway, and Marty drifted down to settle by the backyard fence. He found himself a knothole in the wood and oozed inside it, seeping down into the buried part of the post until he was an abscess at the root of it.

He'd come to stay.

Laurel woke to the sound of her mother's low heels tapping across the hardwood floors above. The pleasant hum of Mother's voice drifted down the stairs. Laurel couldn't make out the words, but already the house felt blanketed, cozy with decorum.

She sat bolt upright, saying, "David, you didn't!"

But David was gone. There was a note duct-taped to the backside of his leather chair that said, *Had to get file from office. Back ASAP.*

He'd promised he would help her, and she'd heard him make that call. To Mother? She was dizzy with disbelief. She put her hands down flat on either side of her, pressing into the worn cloth cover, and tried to calm her ragged breathing. Mother and Thalia were not the same thing. Not even close. Even David should know that. When she watched her mother and sister exchange their ritual stiff kiss at Christmas, Laurel always held her breath, waiting to see if matter touching antimatter really would make the universe explode.

Then Laurel heard her daddy say, "Water can call a person."

Of course, Daddy was here, too. Whither Mother went, there Daddy was also. There was no mistaking the sound of his voice. It had a single blaring timbre, large and low. He dredged words up from the bottom of his narrow tube of a chest and sent them on a side trip through his nose before releasing them.

Daddy's voice came from up the stairs in the keeping room, and Mother answered him. Laurel recognized her tone, sharpness coated with sweet indulgence, designed especially to pull Howard Gray down off flights of fancy.

When Mother's voice stopped, Daddy said, "That's how stories about mermaids and sirens got started, Junie. Sailors know."

Mother must have passed close by the stairs, because Laurel heard her clearly. "I'll put that on my to-do list for today. Ask some sailors how mermaids got invented . . ."

Her parents' voices went back and forth, peppering the house with their own odd music. It was the soothing lullaby of Laurel's childhood, Daddy's trumpet blaring between long refrains on Mother's sweet viola, but Laurel didn't want to be soothed this morning. She had to be sharp. If Mother was David's idea of help, then she was truly on her own.

She got up, running her hands through her hair, trying to smooth it. She wished she weren't wearing silly green pajamas with pink umbrellas on them. She'd borrowed them from tiny Mindy Coe, and the bottoms fit her like capri pants, the loose hems flapping around her calves. She wished she had a toothbrush in the downstairs bathroom, and slim black pants to put on with her sleekest deep blue sweater. Even a hairbrush would help. Mother's hair would be immaculate, her clothes pressed, and her shoes would match her handbag.

Worse, Mother had come to Laurel's house blindly bearing more than familial support. She'd brought Marty, sailing him effortlessly over the gate that had kept him out for thirteen years. Laurel couldn't even yell at her. Ghosts, like family squabbles, bad manners, and other people's dirty houses, rendered Mother oblivious. She flat refused to see them, although she was the one who had come out of DeLop, a town so haunted that every tin shed and 'fraidy hole housed its own dark spirit.

Long before Uncle Marty began visiting, before he died, even,

Mother unwittingly introduced Laurel to her first ghost: Uncle Poot's foot.

Poot lived in DeLop with his common-law wife, Enid, his "no-account" brother, and two grandbabies whom his daughter had abandoned. She'd peeled them off her body and dropped them at Poot's like they were laundry the year that Laurel turned six. The babies added his house to Mother's Christmas route.

Poot was a spindly man with a big belly and a tittery laugh that made him sound like a girl hyena. He was sprawled on a cot in the den of his two-bedroom tract home. He'd angled the cot on the downslope of the sagging floor, so he could see the TV over his belly without having to sit up too much. His stump had been sticking out from under his blanket, covered by a thin and graying sock.

The foot was gone, but Laurel could still see the foot.

Not when she looked directly. But if she looked away, there was the foot in her peripheral vision, with an old man's yellowed toenails and calluses as thick as horn. The foot twitched from side to side as if it were listening to polka music. It was the happiest part of Poot, and Laurel couldn't blame it; it had escaped him. For months after that first visit, the sour smell of Poot and his cot and the dirty sock with no foot in it, the ghost foot bobbing cheerfully in the corner of her eye, woke her up screaming.

From then on, Christmas by Christmas, up until the year she turned ten, Mother smiled and nodded and passed out presents, unseeing, while Laurel and Thalia watched their uncle Poot get eaten.

The next year, when Daddy pulled up in front of Poot's house and shut off the engine, Laurel hung back in the car with him.

Daddy was more than willing to drive them all over DeLop, but he never went inside.

Laurel whispered, "Can I stay here with you, Daddy? For this one house?"

He didn't hear her. His bird eyes had already focused sharply on something invisible floating three feet above the solid roof of the car. "Visiting sprites in Daddy-land," Thalia called it.

Mother, arms already full of bags, bumped at the window with her elbow and called, "Laurel, come on now," through the glass.

The three of them picked a path through Poot's rocky yard, toe-stepping from one tip-tilty slide of gravel to the next: Mother, then Thalia, Laurel trailing behind. Aunt Enid had the door open before Mother knocked. Once inside, Laurel saw that the whole lower half of Poot's leg was gone, even the knee. Uncle Poot had his new, higher stump right there in plain sight, as if he were giving it an airing. It was a knob-shaped object with dry skin webbing the tip and curling off in little peels. Underneath the skin he was sloughing, the flesh looked waxy and wattled.

The stump had a long, curved scar on the end, and Thalia whispered, "Holy goats. It's *smiling* at us."

It was. Laurel couldn't look away. Part of her didn't want to, because she didn't want to see if the ghost foot had been joined by a ghost calf. Would it be attached? Or a separate entity? It was all she could do to keep her eyes from squinching shut entirely, but Mother looked Poot right in his face and said, "Merry Christmas, Uncle," in a firm voice, unmindful that another goodly chunk of Poot had left the building.

Laurel turned her back and found herself facing the broken end table with Poot's glass Christmas tree on it. The tree was hollow, and it had an electrical cord, so the cheap bulbs dotting its surface had probably worked at one time. An undisturbed layer of grime coated its green glass spikes, testifying that no one had moved it in years. Laurel snaked one hand out and pulled a red bulb from its socket, curling her fist around it, tight, tight, not looking.

The next year, Poot's other foot was gone, too, and the following year, the remaining leg joined it. A scant year later, Poot, his phantom foot, and even his sour cot had been taken away.

Mother told Enid, "I was sorry to hear of your loss."

Aunt Enid answered, "Yeah. I tol' Poot that the sugar diabetes would get him in the end if he didn't stop with the drinkin'. But he kept him a bottle of—"

"Please pass on my condolences to Doodle," Mother interrupted. Doodle was the no-account brother.

Nothing more was said.

Back at home, Laurel asked Thalia, "Do you think Mother's sad that Uncle Poot is gone?"

Laurel was plaiting a hundred tiny braids all over Thalia's head. When she finished, Thalia would wet her hair down in the sink and sleep on it, and in the morning, she'd take out the braids and have the Pace, Florida, girl's version of a hundred-dollar spiral perm.

"Are *you* sad?" Thalia asked, incredulous.

"No," said Laurel. "But Mother might be." Poot had let Mother sleep on his couch and had fed her some after her mama passed out holding a cigarette and burned herself up.

Thalia snorted. "Mother doesn't even know he's dead."

"Oh, come on, Thalia. She can't say condolences and not know Uncle Poot's dead."

"Sure she can." Thalia shook Laurel's hands out of her hair

and crossed the room to her bookshelf. She ran her fingers across the spines of her paperbacks and then pulled one out and passed it to Laurel. It was *Watership Down.* "Mother is Cowslip," Thalia said.

It was a thick book, intimidating, but Laurel had to know what Thalia meant, and once she'd begun it, she couldn't put it down. Cowslip turned out to be a fat healthy rabbit in a warren of equally fat and healthy rabbits. Laurel thought the whole bunch of them were smug. They had things the regular rabbits didn't have: feasts and poetry and art. But she ended up feeling sorry for Cowslip. The feasts, the poems, all turned out to be distractions. A farmer was putting out the food and, every now and again, setting a trap and having rabbit supper. Underneath, Cowslip knew, but he loved his peaceful life. So he willfully stopped knowing, and he made every other rabbit in the warren stop knowing, too. Laurel read that part of the book with a faint shock of recognition.

Thalia was right: Mother was Cowslip.

From then on, Thalia used it as a verb, whispering "She's Cowslipping" whenever they saw their mother's face blank itself, her closed lips stretching into a wide smile, quelling whole rooms into submission with her mighty blindness and her will.

And this was the person David had called in to help her. Laurel buried her head in her hands. There had been a day, just one, when Mother had taken a stand for Laurel, but she'd done it covertly, in her own sly way. Mother would not want to hear that Molly Dufresne had walked through walls to visit Laurel's bedroom. She would not be interested in getting Thalia to come over and soak that detective in words, then twist her and wring out answers. She wouldn't want Laurel to run around asking her neighbors if they could confirm the presence of a pervert lurking on the Deerbolds' lawn last night, and Laurel could not remember a single time in her life when she'd pitted herself against her mother's love of decorum and won.

Still wishing for a toothbrush, Laurel squared her shoulders and went on upstairs.

Shelby and Bet Clemmens sat side by side on the sofa, watching a movie. Shelby's mouth was turned down, and her eyes were tired. She had her feet tucked up and her arms looped around her legs, as closed up as a shoe box full of secrets in the very corner of the sofa. Bet slumped beside her, looking like Bet. Someone—Laurel's money was on Mother—had closed the drape over the glass doors, and Daddy was standing at the end, peering out at the backyard through a narrow crack. He glanced over his shoulder and said, "Morning, sugar," as Laurel came up.

Laurel's scrawny daddy looked like he never got fed enough when he was growing. He had a body that wanted to be strapping, but it had failed and dwindled on him. His arms, ropy with muscle and dark veins, were too long, and his head and hands were too big. He turned his head away to peer out again.

"Sweetie," Mother said, and came immediately to give Laurel a decorous peck on the cheek. "What an awful night you've had. Would you like coffee? Or an egg? I'm making lunch soon, but you could have an egg."

"Just coffee," Laurel said.

"Come away from there, Howard," Mother said. Her tart, fond tone was back. "And no more about mermaids or the water calling people. It's morbid." She sailed off toward the kitchen to get Laurel's coffee. Daddy stayed where he was.

"There was a detective. Moreno—" Laurel said. Daddy was nodding. "Is she still out there with them?"

He shook his head without turning around.

Fine. Maybe she could get Mother out of here before Moreno came back.

Shelby was walled in between Bet Clemmens and the sofa's arm. Laurel went and squatted on her haunches in front of her.

Bet leaned sideways, her eyes glued to the TV.

"Whatcha watching?" Laurel asked.

"Nothing, now," Shelby said. Laurel was blocking her view.

"That boy there wants to ballet-dance, I think," Bet said, pointing. "I can't hardly understand a word he says."

"It's *Billy Elliot,*" Shelby said.

She'd ordered it and *October Sky* from Netflix specifically for Bet's visit, as if the films would help her feel more at home. In Shelby's head, DeLop was probably as cinematic as the mining towns in those movies. She'd never seen the real DeLop, and Laurel's descriptions had been soft, to say the least.

"As soft as Dairy Queen cones, and just as fucking ersatz, Jesus Bug," Thalia had scoffed once. She'd overheard Laurel telling Shel how much her cousins had enjoyed the Tinker Toys. Thalia had amused herself by taking Laurel's gentling even further, telling Shelby long made-up stories set in a picturesque DeLop, one eyebrow cocked ironically at Laurel.

Thalia had peopled her purely fictional small town with big-eyed, delectably shabby orphans pulled straight out of velvet paintings from the seventies. They were watched over by Dear Old Aunt Enid, who, in Thalia's version, possessed both teeth and a kind spirit. Enid lined the orphans up in clean, well-mannered rows to get their packages each Christmas. "Oh, please, convey our deepest thanks to Shelby," Thalia's orphans warbled, tears moistening the red ribbons Shelby had curled with a pair of blunt-tipped scissors left over from her grade-school days.

Laurel didn't think Shelby had stopped to compare the real DeLop girl in her house right now with Thalia's version. Bet had never warbled in her life, but she was such a blank slate, it was probably easy for Shelby to mistake the mute endurance for shyness; she saw in Bet what Thalia's stories had prepped her to see.

"That other boy, that fag one, is about to get his butt beat," Bet said in a pleased voice. Scottish accent or no, she got this part.

Laurel and Shelby and Mother all paused and looked at her. Bet watched the screen, oblivious.

"Call Sissi," Mother mouthed at Laurel as she came close to hand her a steaming cup. Laurel nodded, taking the coffee. Mother tilted her head sideways, and her eyebrows came down. "Laurel, you're pale as bedsheets. You're supposed to take things easy today, David said. Now get up off the floor."

Laurel stayed where she was. "How're you doing?" she asked Shelby.

Shelby shrugged, pinching her shoulders up and then only half dropping them, so she stayed turtled up.

"You look tired. What time did you girls crash out up there in the rec room?" It was the most innocuous of all of Moreno's questions, but Laurel was still surprised to hear it coming out of her mouth.

"I don't know," Shelby said. She glanced at Bet but found no help there. Bet had turned her head to look at Laurel, her eyebrows creasing in as if she were slightly puzzled. Either the movie or the conversation had lost her, there was no way to tell which.

Shelby went on. "We were watching some stupid cartoon or

something. I fell asleep in my beanbag." Another glance at the inert Bet Clemmens, and then her voice got the slightest bit louder. "I think I fell asleep first. Isn't that right, Bet?"

Bet's gaze snapped back to the screen, and the faintly puzzled look was gone. She nodded, too vigorously, and Laurel's mom antennae, finely tuned to catch these things, vibrated. Shelby had silently asked Bet to back her up, and Bet had agreed.

Laurel's throat tightened, and her mouth went desert-dry. She stared at her daughter and realized Shelby was looking between Laurel's eyes, not into them. It was an old theater trick of Thalia's for doing love scenes with someone you hated, or hate scenes with someone you loved.

"It also makes lying a hell of a lot easier offstage," Thalia had said more than once, no doubt when Shelby was around with her little pitcher's ears wide open. It worked, too, but only from across the room. This close, Laurel could see the faint disconnect, and all at once she wondered if Moreno had been on to something. Molly and Shelby had been so close. If Molly had been somehow grossly involved with Stan Webelow, Shelby could not be entirely ignorant.

"Come and talk with me," Laurel said gently, gently, as if her insides hadn't all turned to ice. She turned one hand palm up, extending it toward Shelby.

"Grandma says I'm supposed to be taking it easy, too."

Shelby came down hard on the word "supposed," just as Mother had done, as if the gap between how the world should be and how it actually behaved were a grievous thing.

"We could go lie down together," Laurel coaxed. "You've had a hard night."

Shelby didn't move, but at least she was looking straight into Laurel's eyes. "Where is she?" Shelby asked. "Where's Molly?"

Laurel felt the question like a belly blow. "She's in heaven, sweetie," she said.

Shelby's mouth tightened. "I'm not four, and I'm not stupid. Daddy said the ambulance took her, they took the actual her, they took her—" She floundered, and Laurel realized she was trying hard not to say the word "body."

If Thalia were here, she would say, "At the morgue, babe. Somewhere across town, educated people are prowling around Molly's flesh for evidence, and why was she in our yard? What were you girls up to? Were you supposed to meet someone? Had she been spending time with Stan Webelow? Have you?"

Thalia would heat her up and pop her open like an oyster, because if Shelby broke, she might let slip things that would help Laurel protect her. Shelby was hiding something. She'd just looked Laurel right between her eyes and lied, and Laurel wasn't equipped to handle it. She rallied, readying herself to say these hard things to her damp-eyed, angry girl.

"To a funeral home, my darling." Mother stepped in before Laurel could make words come out. Of course Mother had a beautiful lie at the ready, horses and acrobats to soothe and distract. "They'll put her in fresh clothes and brush her pretty hair. They'll take good care of her."

Shelby nodded, looking down at her lap. "You're blocking the movie," she said to Laurel.

Laurel sank down, sitting low on the floor, waiting it out. She couldn't do this with Mother here. Mother was walking back toward the kitchen, trailing her hand along Daddy's shoulder as she passed.

"There are still places where sailors tie themselves to the ship, the call can be so strong," Daddy said, as if Mother's touch had activated him. "No one brought *me* any coffee."

Mother tutted at him. "Poor mister! No legs at all, and no thumbs for pouring. Come away from there and get you a cup."

Even now, when they were well into their fifties, Laurel was sure people wondered how her jug-eared, google-eyed daddy managed to catch a beauty like Mother. Mother had an elegant nose and lovely skin, and when she was younger, her hair was corn-colored. Only her teeth—crooked and still faintly stained despite whitening toothpaste—testified that she had grown up in DeLop.

But women liked to hear Daddy talk in his big voice. He had a slight distance in him, as if no one woman could ever quite get his whole attention. It made some women want to try. Also, he and Mother had common ground in that they were both orphans. Daddy had come to DeLop with his Church of Christ youth group when he was sixteen. They'd thrown a party in the abandoned Baptist church, passing out canned goods and hand-me-down shoes to every town kid who came.

Knowing the kind of dour, old-school C of C her parents favored to this day, Laurel pictured the DeLop kids sitting in rows, clutching brown-paper bags full of charity. A chaperone read the fifth chapter of Mark by a table with a few sad green streamers and a punch bowl full of bug juice on it. There would be no music, and certainly no dancing.

Even so, lightning had flashed between the two of them like an uninvited guest, illuminating Laurel's strange daddy and making Mother smile her geisha's smile, hiding her bad teeth behind her hand. Daddy, smitten, kept driving over to DeLop to see her, and when springtime came, they eloped. Mismatched as they seemed, forty years later, here they were, a solid unit in the living room.

"Shelby?" Mother called. "Why don't you girls pause the movie and run get showered and dressed? You'll feel better with clean hair. I'm going to start lunch now. Laurel, you should go get dressed, too."

The remote was on the armrest, and as soon as Shelby paused the DVD, Bet got up and headed for the stairs as if she were being pulled on strings. Shelby scooted around Laurel to follow Bet.

Laurel got up, too. Mother had made it easy. Once they were all upstairs, Laurel could send Bet Clemmens to shower first, and she'd have Shelby to herself.

Laurel had her foot on the first step when her mother said, "Wait, Laurel, can you help me find a few things? Honestly, I'll never understand your pantry system! What's soup doing down here with the beans?"

Laurel backtracked to the kitchen, impatient. Mother put a hand on her arm, her mouth widening into a close-lipped smile. She craned her neck, looking up the stairs to see that the girls were really gone, and then said, "You need to make today be as normal as possible. Don't go up there and pick at Shelby."

It was as if Mother had read her mind.

"This is not a normal day," Laurel said.

Mother raised her eyebrows and said, "I'm only saying it's not a good time to go prying. Get Shelby doing regular things."

"Regular things," Laurel repeated.

Regular was last week, Shelby and Molly bounding in after auditions, still wearing their leotards and tap shoes. They had clattered through the kitchen, David following, and Shelby had hurled herself at Laurel, spinning her once around.

"I got the ballet duo with Jimmy Brass," Shelby crowed.

Molly had grinned, hanging back with David. Molly, with her cheerleader's nose and curvy little figure, had been such a pretty thing. Shelby was still all knees and elbows, and her ears had grown ahead of the rest of her. But when the two of them were together, people tended to look at Shelby. Shelby, shining it on, was bright enough to blind people.

Laurel had taken Shelby's bun down for her, slipping out the hairpins one by one. "That's wonderful. How'd you do, Molly?"

"Okay." Molly had ducked her head and smiled at her toes. "It's not a big deal, not like—"

Shelby had interrupted her. "Is, too. Molly got a featured in the opening!"

"You girls will steal the show."

Laurel had released the last lock of Shelby's hair and kissed it. Shelby had been fresh-sweaty from dance, and Laurel had breathed in citrus and the smell that comes in springtime right before a light rain. The smell of things about to bloom.

Shelby had twitched the piece of hair away and said, "Don't get all mooky. It's only fall recital. Spring is the biggie."

David had hung back by the door, following the conversation intently, his dark eyes ticking back and forth between them. Shelby had those same eyes, a rich, bright brown like kalamata olives.

She had gazed earnestly up at Laurel and said, "I have to learn a new lift, and I better not grow any more, Mom. Seriously. I need to start drinking coffee."

"You don't even like the smell," Laurel had said. "I never broke five-five, and I didn't drink coffee until college."

"Five-five is practically a yeti." Shelby had spun away, clicking out of the kitchen with Molly on her heels, calling over her shoulder, "We need to go to Starbucks."

David had watched them pass and then grinned and said, "Don't look at me. I've been trying to put a book on her head since she was four."

That was normal. That was regular and real. It didn't look like a place Laurel could get to from here.

She stepped in closer to her mother, glancing back at Daddy. He was weaving, buzzing little hums to himself out of his nose. Laurel lowered her voice. "I have to know what happened, Mother." She looked right into her mother's eyes, willing her to remember, to acknowledge. A long time ago, Laurel had learned for sure and for certain that there was a place inside Mother where her love for Laurel trumped all her careful blindness, trumped silence. The day it mattered most, Mother had chosen to see and speak, if only in a whisper. "I have to know so I can protect her. Like you protected me."

Mother's eyelids dropped briefly, and her lips twitched up at the corners. When she looked back up, she was wearing Cowslip's face. "Laurel, I never once came digging at you like you were a dead worm in a high school biology class."

"That's not what I meant," Laurel said. "Shelby is—"

"Then have at her," Mother interrupted. Her voice was tart but with none of the indulgence she gave Daddy. "Pester and poke. But I never yet saw a dissection that did the worm a speck of good."

Laurel heard the faint echo of DeLop in Mother's accent. Most times Mother talked like a California TV actor trying to sound mildly southern. Her words came out breathy, with an unobtrusive lengthening of vowels, pre-formed into carefully constructed sentences. She'd had a subscription to *Reader's Digest* for longer than Laurel had been alive, and she had, God knew, paid to enrich her word power. But with Bet Clemmens in the house, the old DeLop speech patterns were infiltrating Mother's measured language.

Laurel spoke in a hard whisper. "You can't expect me to treat today like normal when my backyard is full of police and any minute that detective could come back and start questioning Shelby again. It's better if I—"

Mother held one finger up, waggling it back and forth to shush her. "Oh, sweetie, no!" she said. "I'm so sorry. You asked Daddy about the detective, so I thought David must have told you before he left. Here you've been worrying this whole time, and for nothing. They're all gone."

"Who's all gone?" Laurel asked.

"The police. The coroner declared it an accidental death this morning. They left over an hour ago."

"Accidental?" Laurel said. She couldn't stop repeating her mother's words. She looked down at her hands and shook her head. "No. I touched her. She was bleeding."

Mother said, "They think Molly was standing out on the diving board. Probably just being silly. We can't know. She fell, and she cracked her head open on the side of the board. They found the place. She knocked herself out. It's a tragedy, but it's all over, and the faster things go back to normal, the better for Shelby."

Laurel turned and walked as quickly as she could to where Daddy stood, still peering through the crack in the drape as if there were something to see. She pulled aside the cloth; her yard was empty. The tape was down, the lights were gone. Water mizzled down, rippling the pool's surface. It was as if nothing had ever happened.

But her yard did not look right. It wasn't only the dark skies and the rain damping the colors. There was a deeper darkness there, with the fence as a perimeter. The tops of the neighbors' trees and the roof of Mindy Coe's tower looked fine, standing in their perfect places, at ease in the world. But Laurel's trees and pool and patio furniture, everything, looked as if it had been shifted one tenth of an inch left. It was the same, yet infinitesimally wrong. Chill went trickling down Laurel's spine in a droplet, and she found herself tucking her hand inside her father's.

As a little girl, she used to stand like this with him on the porch, watching fireflies buzz around the yard. In the pearl-gray dusk, the bugs themselves were visible. They were ugly and busy, but their lights were deep tangerine, flashing in slow motion. As the sky got darker, the bugs disappeared onto the velvet black background of night, only the lights showing.

"Fairies," Daddy had told the girls once.

Thalia had stared up at Daddy's face as if it were more interesting than any thousand fairies, but Laurel had peered hard out at the fireflies and seen the curved body of a girl, slim as filament, glowing in the heart of every light.

"Stop your nonsense, Howard, before I end up with jars and jars of creepy-crawlies in my house," Mother had said from behind the screen door. "Come in and have cocoa before the mosquitoes eat you alive."

"Sec, Junie," said Daddy, and then asked Laurel and Thalia, "Do you see them?"

"No," Laurel said, and went inside with Mother.

Thalia had said, "I see them, Daddy," without even looking.

He had smiled down at her lying face, turned up toward his, as open as a morning glory.

Standing quietly now with her hand in his, watching the rain on the pool's surface, Laurel wanted to whisper that she had seen them, the fairies, that one time, and ask him what he was seeing as he peered into her yard.

Her yard was looking back at them with ghost eyes. Molly or Marty, she couldn't tell, so she couldn't ask. She never talked to Daddy about Marty. No one in her family ever did. She never so much as said his name in front of her father. Marty had raised him. Daddy had loved Marty best, and Daddy had held the gun.

"Come away," she said to him, tugging at his hand. She didn't want to look anymore. Perhaps Mother was right. She should pull the curtain closed and give her yard time to shift back into its normal self. It ought to.

If Moreno was gone, then Laurel wouldn't have to invite Thalia back into her peaceful life. Surely that sharp-eyed Moreno and her CSIs would not have missed a single trick, rain or no rain. Molly had come to Laurel, led her to the window, and then drifted down to model her own body as if she were Vanna White, showing Laurel what she'd won. But perhaps she'd wanted only to be found.

Marty on his kite string was just a dream, a reaction to seeing a ghost again after all these years. She'd been seeking him, so she'd dreamed him. Her yard probably looked wrong because the floodlights had been on stands and their bases had cut into the grass. She could feel the sleepy tug of Mother's will; she was sliding into it. She took a step back, trying to pull Daddy with her, but he stood fast.

"What's that?" he asked, pointing out into the yard.

The air got out of her in a long, soft braying ha-ha noise that sounded suspiciously like a laugh; Daddy was a middle-finger pointer. Thalia used to make Daddy point when she was in junior high. When she was angry with Mother, Thalia would ask Daddy where something was, an object in plain view that was close to Mother. Then she'd waggle her eyebrows at Laurel while Daddy gave Mother her bird-by-proxy.

It was genetic, because when Shelby was a toddler, she'd pointed like that, too. Laurel would read with her in the glider rocker, and Shelby would shoot the bird at pictures of dogs and dump trucks, lisping, "Awe you my muzzah . . ." Laurel would take her hand and gently fold the naughty finger away, uncurling Shelby's index finger from her tightly fisted hand. Now Laurel felt an urge to do the same for Daddy as he stood flipping off her yard.

Mother came up behind them. Laurel could feel her there. "What's funny?" Mother asked.

"Nothing," Laurel said. "They're really gone. I'm sorry. I'll go get dressed."

"But what's that?" Daddy insisted. His middle finger was aimed at the side fence that separated their backyard from the Coes'.

She looked. There was a dark spot marring the wood. It was deep and black, as if it had been there for years, part of the wood. It hadn't.

"It's nothing," she said, but she did not believe it. "It's just a knothole." Her voice shook.

He was still pointing, but it wasn't funny anymore. Mother pulled the curtain closed, as if cloth could keep out Marty.

"Normal day," she said to Laurel, and gave her Cowslip's smile.

CHAPTER 5

Laurel was eleven years old the first time she was allowed to go hunting. It was also the last time. It was her uncle Marty's last hunt, too.

Laurel and Thalia scuffled along the dirt road as they followed Daddy. Florida dirt was gray-brown and crumbly, but in Alabama, the dirt was black and rich as peat, staining the sides of Laurel's pristine Keds. Thalia, a veteran, had known to wear old shoes. Marty was in front, and both men had their rifles pointing at the sky. Laurel swung a small cooler full of sandwiches and fruit. Thalia carried the drinks cooler. It was heavier.

The pine trees made the woods glow green around them even though the leaves on the hardwoods had already gone gold and orange and russet. All the morning birds were talking. It was close to dawn, and a sheer mist was making that day's dew. Thalia was holding an imaginary cigarette with her free hand, sucking in on it and then puffing white breath into the chilled air. Laurel's clothes felt heavy with damp, and she could smell more damp decaying the fallen leaves and needles.

Laurel had told Daddy before they left the cabin that she didn't want to watch the deer drop, though Thalia had bagged her own first deer last year, using Daddy's gun. Hunting was what Daddy and Marty and Thalia did together, all three of them thick into their odd pretends, whispering made-up songs, Laurel left at home with Mother to cut up carrots for the Crock-Pot and fold the towels so they had even corners. Laurel had made up her own secret song on this trip, and it was running over and over in a silent loop inside her head: "No deer, anywhere near. No deer, anywhere near."

But they hadn't been hiking ten minutes when a young buck stepped out into the middle of the road ahead of them. He took tiny, picking steps, and his nose was up, searching the air for the flat tang of gunmetal. They were safe downwind. He gave them his profile and his brown rib cage, a target so broad and close it seemed like something he was offering them.

Uncle Marty put his hand back, motioning them to stillness. "Yours," he mouthed, stepping back.

Daddy began to lower the barrel of his rifle. His big voice muted to a mournful tremble, he whispered to Laurel, "Close your eyes, baby."

Laurel kept her eyes closed even when the echoing bark of the shot made her flesh jump, her whole skin trying to leave her bones in one shuddering, fast rebellion. She heard the rustle of leaves as the deer bounded away, and Daddy saying, "Get him."

Marty said something back, but she didn't catch it, and then the second shot rang out. She kept her eyes closed even after she heard Thalia's short, gulping scream.

When at last she opened them, the deer was gone, and Laurel saw Marty lying facedown in the dirt, a small hole going bloodlessly into his ruined jacket. Daddy had abandoned his gun on the dirt trail. Thalia was staring at it with shell-shocked eyes, her hands hanging limp at her sides, the drinks cooler tipped on its side by her feet. Daddy had already run to Marty and was turning him over. Low on Marty's chest, Laurel saw the same size hole, only bloodier, going out.

Laurel heard herself talking from far away. "It went straight through," she said to Thalia.

"Daddy says this kind of bullet doesn't spoil the venison," Thalia said, and then she lifted her right arm as if her hand were very heavy, pulling it up so she could jam her thumb into her mouth.

"Thalia?" Laurel's voice came out quiet but desperate. Thalia didn't answer. Her eyes were pointed at Laurel, but they weren't focusing. Thalia wasn't behind them. Thalia wasn't home at all, and that scared Laurel more than anything.

The shots had left a smell in the air, burned oil and sulfur. Daddy put his face by Marty's face and yelled his name over and over. Marty's eyes were open and empty of all things.

Later, back at the borrowed cabin, Laurel and Thalia sat with blankets around them, even though Laurel wasn't cold. The nicest deputy had put the blankets on them, as if Laurel and Thalia had been rescued from a shipwreck. Thalia's blanket was pale blue, and she had it draped over her head like a Bible-times girl. She'd come back to live behind her eyes again, stretching them wide open, the whites showing all the way around. Her face looked stiff, like Laurel's felt. Laurel couldn't tell if Thalia was making her face be like Laurel's on purpose, but she'd never heard her sister talk in such a thready voice.

Daddy told the sheriff's men it had been an accident. He'd tripped, he said, and the gun had gone off. When it came their turn to talk, Thalia backed him up.

"Daddy shot at a deer, bang, and it ran," she told them. "Uncle Marty ran after it, and Daddy ran after Uncle Marty. Daddy fell. I heard it go bang again, and then Uncle Marty was on the ground."

Laurel turned to stare at her sister. She'd seen Thalia act. Thalia was born acting. But she'd never seen her lie so poorly. She thought that this was what it might look like if Thalia tried plain lying as herself and wasn't good at it. Thalia's throat worked, swallowing.

"Where were you?" the deputy asked Laurel.

"My stupid sister had her eyes closed," Thalia answered. She spoke before Laurel could even get the sticky hinge of her jaw to open. There, Thalia had sounded sharper, more like herself, but then her voice went sweet and bland as whole-milk pudding, and she said, "Laurel? Come and have some lunch."

Laurel jumped. Mother's knuckles made a decorous ratty-tat-tat against the door. "Did you hear me?"

Laurel sat in her workroom, her latest quilt spread out on the table in front of her. Having a normal day.

It was a large room behind the kitchen, painted cream and accented with warm brown and caramel. Nothing pulled the eye. A chocolate leather office chair sat in front of Sylvia, Laurel's Bernina. She moved it over on the rare occasions when she wanted to work with her dear old Singer. There was a matching chair, ratcheted up higher, for the table where Laurel did all her cutting and embellishing. The side wall was covered with built-in cabinets where the bulk of Laurel's fabric stash was stored. The quiet room was usually filled with Laurel's presence and her work, but today she felt as neutral as its off-white walls, as blank, as easily overwhelmed, by anything with color.

"Did Shelby come downstairs?" she called through the door.

"I'm letting the girls take their plates to the rec room," Mother said. "They want to finish their movie."

"You and Daddy go ahead without me," Laurel said.

"Laurel," Mother called through the door, drawing out the middle vowel, long and reproachful.

"I mostly miss lunch when I'm working," Laurel said. Snapped, almost. "That's normal when I'm working."

She could feel her mother's hovering presence through the wooden door. She waited it out, and at last Mother's heels clicky-clacked away in an odd echo of her knocking.

Laurel had showered as Mother had told her to, then gotten dressed in soft jeans and a jersey pullover, combing her damp hair back in a ponytail. Mother had told her to use the time before Bet and Shelby finished getting dressed to call Sissi Clemmens, so she'd sat at her built-in phone desk in the breakfast nook and dialed. Sissi had not answered, and she didn't have voice mail. Mother had told Laurel to try again later, so she would try again later. Mother had told her to do what she would normally do, so here she sat, a good, good dog, embellishing the figure of the bride in the center of her latest quilt.

The bride's eyes were bright crescents, and she had smile lines embroidered in her cheeks, but she had no mouth yet. Laurel was hand-sewing slim red satin ribbon into rosebuds. They would form the bride's lips, a grinning, three-dimensional bouquet. The bride lifted the inverted bell of her skirt as she hurried forward pell-mell, showing boots with daisies on the toes. Her feet were huge and her head was very small, as if someone were looking up at her from the ground.

Laurel had already glued down lumpy oval potato pearls to make the daisies' petals, binding them with silver wire after they dried. The boots were the old-fashioned kind that buttoned up the sides, and the buttons on the front boot could be opened. Under the boot was a dark blue space deepened by plush velvet. Inside, Laurel had embroidered one of the eyes that served as her signature. The eye was looking toward one odd petal, too sleek and pointed for a freshwater pearl. It was a human tooth, an incisor.

When she'd first planned this quilt a year ago, she'd thought she would use one of Shelby's baby teeth. She kept them all upstairs in the false bottom of her jewelry chest. That small space was reserved for relics and remembrances that she'd imagined as the starting place for quilts she'd never sewn: an amber doll's eye, a broken plastic Christmas bulb, a mouse charm from an old bracelet.

But in the end, she couldn't bring herself to give up even one of Shelby's baby teeth for a quilt she planned to show and sell. They were too precious, these ivory mementos of Shelby at six, flashing a pink-gummed, gappy grin.

Laurel had put off the bride quilt, making others until she stumbled on a stash of teeth in an old bureau drawer at an estate sale. She didn't think they were for sale, or even there on purpose, so she bought the ugliest bureau she'd ever laid eyes on to get the teeth secreted inside.

The bride was already quilted in patterns that seemed random on the front but made pictures and letters and more of her eyes that showed up perfectly on the hand-dyed cotton she'd used to back. The quilt was bound in yellowed satin cut from a musty old wedding gown, another estate-sale find.

She wanted to enter this piece in the Pacific International Quilt Festival at the end of the month. She'd won first prize in Innovative Quilts last year, but this year she was gunning for Best in Show. Or she had been. It seemed stupid now. The mouthless bride leaned forward, eager, like she might step at any second into some big adventure in her high-buttoned boots. Laurel couldn't remember what had made her feel a connection to this piece in the first place.

The one picture Laurel had from her own wedding was a Polaroid taken by the clerk of the court. In it, David's chin was set and his brows were down, like he was planning to grab Mount Everest with his bare hands and pull himself straight up it. His father had taken a long walk when David was five, and in the wedding picture, it was plain that David had already decided he would never be that guy. Laurel looked trembly and puffy-eyed, Shelby faintly pushing out the skirt of her best blue Sunday dress.

Her busy fingers made red rosebuds one after another, doing their regular job on the regular day she'd been told to have. She wanted to believe it was over, but she couldn't catch her breath. The investigation might have ended, but it didn't feel finished.

She ought to be relieved that the policewoman would not be back to prod at Shelby. Instead, she felt an odd, strong urge to call the police back in. To lie. To say she'd seen Stan Webelow for certain, not his possible hair. They would find out if the moving shadow she'd seen by the pool had been a ghost, a dream, or something real and worse. They'd make sure Shelby was hiding nothing more than a silly girl plan gone awry. Then she'd know Shelby was safe.

Shelby seemed so closed, so soaked in guilt, sheltering herself near Bet Clemmens as if Bet were a wall, asking Bet to back her up when Laurel knew damn well her daughter was lying. If Shelby had planned to meet Molly or even Stan, had failed Molly in some way, was somehow culpable . . . It wasn't possible. Laurel would never believe it. But if Laurel could conceive it, consider it even for a second, Moreno could, too. Did Laurel really want to bring that woman's cold, assessing gaze back to her daughter?

Mother had told her to let everything be normal. Go to the funeral. Say goodbye. Grieve. Move on. But her house did not feel normal. It was silent and too large around her, as if it had been hollowed out. The wrongness in her yard had its nose pressed against her glass doors, and she felt something small and feral scrabbling in her belly. Every time she thought she'd lose herself in her work, the something would run one spiky tooth along her stomach lining. It was too quiet, as if Daddy had herded everyone together and they had crept out of the house and driven away, leaving Laurel alone with her ghosts.

She set down a finished rosebud and leaned over to press the listen button on the intercom system. She could hear the faint sounds of *Billy Elliot,* dancing his skinny guts out up in the rec room, but Shelby and Bet weren't talking. She supposed Mother and Daddy were eating in the dining room, where the intercom system had no receiver. The closest one was around the corner in the entryway. Laurel's kitchen table could fit a cozy six, but Mother preferred the pecan table in Laurel's formal dining room. She'd perch at the foot and survey the gorgeous antique china displayed in the built-ins. David's mother had given that china to them after Shelby came. A belated wedding present, even though—as she'd pointed out several thousand times—five minutes with a justice of the peace was hardly a wedding.

Laurel turned the volume on the intercom all the way up and caught the faint clatter of silver and Daddy buzzing air out his teeth, a sound he made between bites of food that really pleased him. The house ached with a grating silence. Laurel wasn't the only one bothered by the quiet; her daddy needed voices around him. He turned on a TV or talk radio in every room he walked through.

The intercom system had a radio, and Laurel flipped it on. It was already set to a jazz station. Daddy liked jazz and would be happier with background noise, though if he and Mother were to talk, she wouldn't hear, and the music couldn't take the hollow taste out of the air.

She started laying the roses out on the bride's face, shaping them into lips. When she sewed them on, she'd bunch them tight against one another. For now she wanted to get an idea of the mouth's shape. She made the smile wide enough to show teeth and tongue. She'd have to fill that space.

There was a tap on the office door. "Laurel?" Mother was back, as if summoned by jazz.

Laurel swiveled in her chair and rolled herself across the tile, close enough to the door to crack it open without rising. "You said normal day. I'm normally trying to do my normal work," she said. Her voice came out louder then she'd meant it to.

"I only came to see if you want me to bring you a plate. It's hot chicken salad, and it's getting stone cold."

"I can microwave it later."

"All right," Mother said, but she'd eased forward, insinuating herself into the door's rightful space so Laurel couldn't close it. "Did you call Sissi Clemmens again?"

"I tried her not an hour ago."

"You have to keep trying. You have to catch her when she's home. And awake. And . . . taking calls." She meant when Sissi wasn't high. It was a narrow window. "I'm not sure Bet Clemmens is a good influence to have around Shelby right now."

Laurel blinked. Bet Clemmens couldn't influence the butter from one side of the table to another, much less have an impact on a small force of nature like Shelby. If anything, the influence ran the other way—Bet chose the kind of jeans Shelby liked at American Eagle Outfitters and agreed to try foods that she saw Shelby eating. Until last summer, Bet had never tasted lettuce that wasn't iceberg.

"Bet Clemmens says strange things sometimes," Laurel said. "She's certainly a novelty, but Shelby doesn't find her glamorous."

"This is a time when Shelby might be more easily influenced than usual," Mother said. "She's been glued to that girl's side ever since I got here."

"I'll try Sissi again," Laurel said. She could hear impatience in her own voice, and yet her mother stayed.

"We're still having lunch day after tomorrow. Yes?" Mother said.

Laurel had forgotten. She took Mother out to lunch, just the two of them, once or twice a month. Someplace fancy, and Laurel had already made reservations.

"I guess. Unless I'm taking Bet home. Or unless Shelby wants me."

"Wonderful," Mother said. "I'll come here before. Daddy can

spend a little time with Shelby, or he and I can both stay with her if you get ahold of Sissi. Shelby shouldn't be alone right now."

Just talking about Bet, Laurel could hear the DeLop creeping into Mother's inflections. "Ahold" was not a typical part of Mother's vocabulary, and perhaps her desire to remove Bet had nothing to do with the girl's influence on Shelby.

"That's fine. Mother, I'm trying to work."

Mother stepped farther into the room and looked down at the quilt. She reached down and touched the rose mouth with one careful finger. "Why, that's pretty, Laurel. I like that."

"Really?" Laurel said, faintly surprised.

Mother didn't like Laurel's quilts, taking umbrage at the lift-the-flaps and hidden panels and found objects. Laurel had once made the mistake of asking her mother's opinion on a mermaid quilt she was particularly proud of. Mother had eyeballed the broken bits of shell and pursed her lips up and said, "Why stick all that mess on? It's not comfy." She seemed to think the value of the work rested on how cozy she'd feel if she wrapped it around her legs while she was knitting.

Thalia hadn't liked that quilt, either, for the opposite reason. "You've hidden everything that's at all interesting down in secret pockets until it looks like a freakin' blanket. Grow a pair. Drag out those dead sailors," she'd said.

Laurel had sent it off to one of the galleries that showed her work anyway. It had sold in under a week for twelve thousand dollars, so someone must have liked it.

"I'll let you get on with it," Mother said, stepping back. She pulled the door closed.

Laurel looked at the bride with fresh eyes. With the rosebud smile and the flap in the boot safely buttoned shut, it did look like a nice blanket.

Last year she'd entered an older piece called *Eye Bones*. It had multiple layers that could be unfolded and attached by hooks and Velcro tabs and buttons, so what was hidden and what was seen were changeable. No matter how it was arranged, the face of the woman at the center could never be symmetrical or whole. It was one of her more disturbing pieces. She almost didn't like it, although David had not been troubled by it. But he liked everything she did, more because it was hers than because of a personal aesthetic. David didn't have one of those.

It was more telling that Thalia had said she almost liked *Eye Bones*. This year Laurel had tried to pull back, but if Mother liked it, she might have pulled back a bit too far, all the way to *Sunbonnet Sue Gets Married*.

She dashed an angry hand across the bride's face, and the loose rosebuds scattered, flecking the dress in red. She stood to pick them back off, but the small splashes of red were both diffused and intensified by being scattered across the cream and gold and white.

It was interesting. This bride had secrets. With the mouth gone, only the shape of the eyes told the viewer she was smiling, and the invisible lips drew themselves in smug. There was an implied urge to search her, to find her out. Laurel stopped picking the rosebuds off and started moving them, repositioning them in random spots of color on the bride's hands, spattering up her arms almost to the elbows.

She snipped off a couple of lengths of scarlet ribbon, then twisted them and pinned them into streaks of vivid color, running down the bride's forearms. She stepped back and gazed down at the quilt for a long time.

It was exactly right.

It wasn't what she'd intended when she first began, but the displacement of the roses had reconnected her with the quilt. It was right for right now. Looking at her bride's soiled hands, Laurel was finished. She knew it the way she knew most things, down in her chest, not up in a tumble of wordy thinking.

She could do what Mother wanted, spackle this day over with normalcy and pile a host of other days on top of it, one by one, until the surface of her life was whole and seamless. But if Shelby had a secret, no matter how innocent, would she be spackling over a wound that should be aired? Beneath the pretty surface, a secret might eat at her child, fester and rot her and ruin her. Laurel would be complicit in her ruining. Worse, what if it *had* been Stan Webelow's hair that night? Surely the police could unearth the truth. But Laurel didn't want Moreno back here vivisecting her child.

She wanted Thalia. Needed her. She had needed her from the beginning.

David had said he would help, but his version of help had been bringing in Mother. Now Mother was grinding her down. By the time Mother left, David would be home, earnestly helping in all the wrong ways, not wanting Thalia back to stir around in the corners of their life. Laurel would forget what she knew in this moment, so true it felt like it was a glowing hole in her center.

She knew things best when she was quilting. In this room, she didn't follow patterns to please Mother, or let everything ugly out to eat up the image to please Thalia, or worry that David wouldn't like it, which would be tantamount to his not liking her.

The bride was right. She knew it. Inside these walls, that ended it.

Here in her quiet room, Laurel knew what was right for Shelby, too, and she understood what Molly had come to ask her to do. Molly hadn't really wanted Laurel, and she certainly had not come hoping for a path to Laurel's mother. Laurel looked at the phone. Fearless Thalia, the seeker, the digger, who looked at things hard and bald enough to learn them and become them, was only eleven numbers away.

Laurel reached for the phone before Mother could knock again, or before yet another neighbor or friend from church called, offering sorries and support and tying up the line.

The phone rang twice in Mobile, but Thalia didn't answer. Her husband did: "Spotted Dog Theater." Gary had a deep voice, rich and smooth, as if his throat had been coated in dark chocolate.

"Hey, it's me," Laurel said. "Is Thalia there?"

"Why, yes. She is," said Gary in a pleasant tone.

Then he hung up.

To fight with Thalia was to take on Gary, too. Laurel depressed the button to get the dial tone back, then hit redial.

"Oh, I'm sorry," Gary said, picking up halfway through the first ring. "Were we not finished?"

"May I speak to my sister, please?"

"Nope!" Gary said cheerfully, and hung up again.

Laurel took three deep breaths, then hit redial again.

Ethel Merman answered. "Whoopsy-doo!" said Ethel. "My hands are slippery!" and the phone banged down.

Gary's voice was extremely versatile for being set so low.

Laurel buried her face in her hands. Enough. It had to be now, or it would never happen.

She stood up and threw open the door. She walked through her kitchen with long strides, pausing to scoop her purse up off the little phone table and dig out her keys. She came around the corner into the dining room, saying in a loud, announcing voice that brooked no argument, "I'm going to drive over to Alabama and—"

She stopped. She'd been going to finish: "—pick up Thalia. Please stay with Shelby."

But David had come home. He'd joined her parents at the lunch table and was eating a large portion of her mother's hot chicken salad and chopped fruit. He looked up at her as her parents did, Daddy turning around backward. David's eyebrows lifted, listening, innocent of her intent, and she couldn't finish. She'd avoided calling Thalia in the first place because he'd asked her to.

Mother was rising, smiling her broad, closed-lipped smile. "Wonderful!" she said. "See, I told you to go ahead and try Sissi again. I'll just run up and have Bet pack her things."

Laurel blinked. Mother thought she meant DeLop. When she looked around the table, she saw David and Daddy thought so, too, swept up and carried in the current of Mother's assumption.

Laurel opened her mouth to say no, she hadn't reached Sissi, she was going to damn Mobile to get her damn sister, and then she closed it again. David had promised to help her, but he clearly had no idea how. Daddy had come, but he was Mother's right-hand man, not Laurel's. And most of all, there was Mother, who would pin Laurel down with Cowslip's blank gaze and sap her will with hot chicken salad and promises of normal days to come. Laurel couldn't fight them all.

She shifted her gaze a hair over so she wasn't looking Mother in the eye. Mother would see the lie there. Laurel focused on Mother's bottom lashes, and from across the room, Thalia's trick worked perfectly.

"Bet packed most of her things last night," Laurel said, and her voice sounded sure and steady.

First David and then Daddy offered to drive Bet Clemmens back. Mother demurred for David on the grounds that he was unfamiliar with the route and the houses. Beneath her approving smile was a wall of will; she'd worked for years to ensure her Cherry Hill son-in-law never saw the rotten taproot of her family in DeLop.

Laurel waved Daddy's offer away, saying, "I wouldn't want you driving this tired, Daddy. Anyway, I'll be back before you know. Before sunset, probably."

That was absolutely true. Mobile was an hour away.

Mother said, "It's an easy day trip. Good roads most of the way, and the sun so goes down so late these days, doesn't it? Dog days, they call them."

"Yes. Dog days," Laurel said. She tucked her hands inside her pockets and avoided David's eyes until he'd nodded and gone back to eating lunch.

Then Laurel went upstairs with Mother to round up Bet Clemmens. They found her in the rec room, hunched on the puffy love seat, holding her plate up near her face so she could scoop an outsize bite of hot chicken salad directly into her mouth.

Before Laurel could tap at the door frame, Mother said, "Bet, dear, let's go gather up your things. Laurel's going to run you home this afternoon."

Bet looked up at them and quickly shoveled in another bite and then another, stuffing them in on top of the food already there. Her mouth was so full she couldn't close it all the way, and flecks of thin mayonnaise bubbled out at the corners. She gulped down some of the half-chewed food, her fork already going back for the last of it.

"Don't choke yourself," Laurel told her. "There's time for you to finish your lunch."

"Are you serious?" said Shelby. She was hunched in her oversize pink beanbag, everything but her head tucked under a chenille throw. A plate of chicken and fruit sat undisturbed by the chair, the tines of the fork pristine. Laurel thought Mother would answer. When she didn't, Shelby looked back and forth between them. Finally, her gaze settled on Laurel. "This sucks," she said.

"Now, Shelby, there's no call for ugly talk," Mother said. "Sissi Clemmens is worried sick with all the goings-on here. Think how she must want Bet safe at home."

The only person in the room who believed that was Shelby. Laurel found her own expression mirroring Bet Clemmens's, both of them incredulous at the idea of Sissi lathered and pacing, desperate to get her baby home and lay hands on her. Laurel quickly dropped her head and blinked her widened eyes back to normal, for Sissi would be doing exactly that in the wholly fictional DeLop that Thalia had created for Shelby.

Shelby slumped down even farther in the beanbag, her hidden hands tucking up the blanket around her face. Only her eyes and the top of her head peeped out. "Fine. Get out, then," she said, not looking at Bet.

"Shelby!" said Laurel.

"Bye," said Bet, then added, "I wish't I knew what happened to thet boy."

On the television, Billy Elliot was auditioning at a ballet school.

"He dies," Shelby said in a sour voice.

"Shelby Ann!" Laurel said again.

But Bet was nodding. "I thought he might," she said.

"You can see the end when you come back," Laurel told Bet. "It's a nice end. He does not die."

"He does, too," Shelby said. After a grudging pause, she added, "Eventually."

Mother spoke up then, in the sweet-tart tone she usually saved for Daddy. "Yes, Shelby, and then a terrible war breaks out somewhere. And the world ends!" She turned slightly toward Bet. "That all happens years after the credits roll, you understand."

"I can't believe you didn't call and ask your mom if you *could* stay," Shelby said. Bet stood dumb and shrugged, and Shelby's eyes flicked over to Laurel. "Did you even ask if we could keep her? Or did you just call up her mom and totally freak her out?"

"Bet did ask to stay. She asked me," Laurel said. She stopped. She didn't want to lie directly, and while she picked her way through various constructions, trying to come up with a sentence that would convey to Shelby that Bet would be back sooner than Shelby thought, Bet spoke up.

"Mebbe you could come, too?" Bet said. "Just for a little visit."

Shelby began to sit up straighter, but Mother and Laurel both said, "No," so fast that Shelby's mouth hadn't even cleared the edge of the chenille throw before she was sinking back down again.

Laurel had almost yelled it, even though she knew she wasn't going within a hundred miles of DeLop. The very idea of Shelby shining in that dark place chilled Laurel down to her marrow. Who knew what Shelby's light would call?

In a gentler tone, she added, "I want you home, Shel."

"I wanna go with Bet," Shelby said, her eyebrows mutinous above the throw, and Laurel tried to ready herself for a battle that she didn't want to have over a trip that she wasn't going to take.

If only Mother weren't here, she would let Shelby come. It was Mobile and Thalia, after all. If Mother weren't here, Laurel would tell David she had to have Thalia, period, had to, and who had called Mother in, after all? David, that was who, and if she was lying, then that was on his head.

Mother's dulcet voice said, "Shelby, darling, if you go, you'll miss Molly's funeral," and just like that, Shelby's eyebrows went from battle-ready to wounded. The argument was over. Shelby pulled the blanket up all the way over her head.

"Bye," Bet said to the blanket.

Laurel said, "I'll be back in a flash, Shelby."

Shelby didn't respond. Laurel led Bet away to pack. She looked over her shoulder at her daughter, wanting to tell Shelby with her eyes and her smile that it would be all right. But Shelby was still slouched under her throw, an eyeless Halloween ghost made of hot-pink chenille.

CHAPTER 6

Bet Clemmens's Hefty bag was a deflated packet, too small and sad to need trunk space or even the backseat. Bet had packed only the things she'd brought with her from DeLop. The clothes Laurel had bought for her were stowed in the closet in the small guest room, tucked in among Laurel's Christmas stockpile of toys and shoes.

"I druther leave my new clothes lie," Bet had said. "You tole me I could come back real soon. You promised."

Laurel hadn't argued, loath to waste time when she knew it was moot. Bet *would* be back, sooner than she could imagine. Three or four hours. Laurel had thought it was sweet, even, Bet planting her Rainbow flip-flops and American Eagle jeans as proof of her faith in Laurel's promise and then stoically bundling herself into the Volvo, the Hefty bag at her feet.

But they weren't out of the driveway before Laurel heard a snuffling noise from the passenger seat. She glanced over in time to see a tear rolling unchecked down Bet Clemmens's face. It spattered on her bare thigh.

"Oh, honey, don't. I think there's been a misunderstanding," Laurel said, and then floundered, because there hadn't been so much a misunderstanding as an enormous load of whoppers.

Bet said nothing. Her tear ducts were functioning, and her nose had gone pink around the nostrils, but her body was relaxed and her mouth was slack. She seemed wholly disconnected from her wet eyes as they took care of the business of crying.

Still, it was the most emotion Laurel had ever seen Bet Clemmens display, and she gave the cool flesh of Bet's leg a pat. She had to fess up. Bet would know something was off when they stayed on I-10 instead of exiting at Highway 29. This could be Laurel's practice confession, the first of many, because when she returned home with both Bet Clemmens and Thalia, her lies would become obvious to anyone with a brain wave. There was no story that could explain the return of Bet and the presence of Thalia, except the truth: that Laurel had smiled and nodded and knowingly let Mother's assumption stand so she could get her way.

Mother would exact a decorous but grim revenge, Laurel felt certain. Worse, Laurel had allowed a lie to wriggle in between her and David, a tiny wedge making a space where there had been no space before. And he wasn't even wrong; she knew from experience that she and Thalia in the same house together would likely end in plague or famine or a rain of frogs.

Even so, if she had it to do over? She balanced the consequences against the gray feel of ghost eyes, the way her yard was shifted and wrong, Shelby gone silent and Molly gone for good. She would do it again just the same.

"I'm not taking you home, Bet. That was a big lie. I'm sorry.

We're going to Mobile to pick up my sister. Then we'll all three come right back here, okay?"

Laurel watched Bet in her peripheral vision as she drove. Bet blinked twice, slowly. Then she swiped the back of her hand across her nose and said, "Mm-kay."

That was all.

Shelby would have been wailing like an outraged howler monkey by now. Any Victorianna kid would have been. Shelby at thirteen was more sophisticated than Laurel had been at the same age—they had HBO, after all—but at her core, Shelby was still a child. She believed that the good guys triumphed in the end, that the universe ought to be fair and could be made so, and that her mother didn't tell self-serving lies.

Bet Clemmens wasn't outraged, though. She wasn't even surprised. She kicked at the Hefty bag on the floorboards, pushing it forward to use as a footrest, and settled back in her seat, done with it.

Watching her placid acceptance, Laurel all at once understood that Bet's nice clothes hadn't been left on the shelf as an act of faith. Bet didn't have any of that. She'd left them because at home, they would go the way of the rolling suitcase. Laurel should have known.

When Bet was here, dressed to blend and circling the edges of Shelby's crew, Laurel was lulled into forgetting what Bet's actual life was like. It was like her accent: hard to fathom when not standing in the middle of DeLop. When Laurel had driven over to pick up Bet last week, Sissi had been too stoned or drunk or both to stand unaided. Laurel had given her a hand, wincing at the zippery sound Sissi's blue-veined legs had made against the vinyl as Laurel had peeled her off the sofa.

Sissi had stared at Laurel, her gaze sliding into focus, and then she had slurred, "Laurel? S'it Cripmus aw'ready?"

She'd forgotten that Laurel was taking her child for two weeks. Sissi would be the first to steal Bet's eighty-dollar sandals for herself or to hock. A corner of Laurel's heart broke for Bet, but underneath that, a sly stray thought slid by: There was a fundamental disconnect between Bet's and Shelby's ideas of what should be hidden from mothers.

Bet Clemmens didn't have a curfew or a standard bedtime. She would no more need to hide a secret from her mother than Shelby would need to hide her Game Boy. If Laurel could ask questions aimed into the chasm between how Shelby's and Bet's lives worked, Bet might blandly answer, never thinking she ought not to.

"So I gather you girls had some plans last night," Laurel said. She tried to sound casual, like this was something she might well ask Shelby, if only Shelby were here. Thalia taught her students that acting started from the outside in, with physical control. She didn't hold with Method. "Make the body right," Thalia said. "The rest will follow."

So Laurel made her body relax, slump, loosening her shoulders and easing the muscles that had gone tense in her thighs.

Bet said, "I dun know. Shelby and her friends, they dun tell me all their stuff."

"But you think Shelby and Molly were planning something?" Laurel asked.

Bet said, "I dun know."

Dead end. They were almost to Victorianna's wrought-iron gate.

Laurel flipped her blinker on and turned right, circling through phase one, turning left to get to Queen's Court. She drove slowly down it. The houses here were smaller and a year older. Cookie Webelow had bought the peach house on Queen's Court twenty years ago, when the neighborhood was still in development.

"Do you know anyone who lives on this street?" Laurel asked.

Bet pointed up ahead and said, "That there is that redhead gal's house, that Carly."

"Anyone else?" Laurel said. They were passing Stan's house now, not going even ten miles an hour.

Bet didn't say anything, and Laurel stopped right in front of it. "Do you know who lives here?" she asked Bet.

"Mr. Webelow," Bet said. No hesitation.

"Have you ever been inside?" Laurel asked.

Bet said, "Naw, I wouldn't. Shelby said not to, even if he offered me a drink or a snack or if I needed to pee."

These were the rules Laurel had long since laid down for Shelby, repeated back almost verbatim, except Laurel had said "use the restroom."

"Did Shelby say why?" Laurel said.

"Naw," said Bet. "Why?"

Laurel said, "It's just a good rule, Bet. Young ladies shouldn't go off alone with a grown man they don't know well."

It occurred to Laurel that she should have given Bet those rules herself. Perhaps by not saying anything to Bet, she'd put her at risk, but looking at Bet, it seemed hard to believe that was the irresponsible act here.

Bet had changed into clothes she'd brought from home, cutoff jeans that were way too short and a ruffled plaid halter top from Wal-Mart. It was far too skimpy for a teenager. It was too skimpy for anyone who wasn't gunning for a career in the streetwalking industry, really, but Bet Clemmens was so inert that she rendered the outfit innocuous.

She had what Thalia called duck-body, a small head and narrow shoulders that sloped down, making them look even smaller. Frail collarbones, as delicate as bird bones, were probably her best feature. She had tiny flaps for breasts, set on a rib cage that spread as it went down instead of narrowing to a waist. Her hips were broader still, and the outside of her thighs was her widest point. Her legs narrowed sharply after that, tapering down to skinny calves and delicate feet that matched her shoulders. Her skin was waxy and seamless, like doll skin. Even in these clothes, she seemed sexless.

Laurel said, "Have you ever seen Shelby go in there?"

"Naw," Bet said again, but this time Laurel caught a gleam of something under the answer.

She waited, and then Bet peeped at her, a sideways sloe-eyed glance. Anyone who spoke teenager would recognize that look. It meant Bet knew something, but Laurel hadn't asked the right question. If Laurel came at her right, Bet would tell. Laurel's heart beat as if it were made out of a thousand little wings, all trying to fly off to different places. Then she had it.

"Who have you seen go in there?"

"Molly," said Bet promptly. "I saw Molly Dufresne go on in there once't."

Laurel's blood cooled and slowed. She stared past Bet, out the passenger-side window, at the skeletal remains of Cookie Webelow's fancy gardens. Stan came outside only to jog the streets in his tiny shorts and ankle socks. He had a yard service keep the front as neat as the neighborhood charter demanded, but it was nothing like when Cookie had wildflowers blooming around the mailbox and a proud gauntlet of tulips lining her walk.

Laurel forced her voice to stay casual. "Was Shelby with you when you saw Molly go in there?"

Bet shrugged.

Laurel said, "Did you ask Molly why she went?"

"Shelby's friends dun tell me all their stuff," Bet said again.

Laurel had noticed that herself. Bet was in Shelby's dance gang, but not of them. While they leaped in and out of the pool, Bet waded in carefully, no farther than her waist. Last year, especially, Laurel had kept a watchful eye on them, not only because Bet was an unknown influence. Twelve-year-old girls were not the world's most empathetic creatures, and Bet Clemmens wasn't like them. For a preteen, not being like was a cardinal sin.

Instead, they had adopted Bet, treating her like a backward mascot. They may have been patronizing, a little superior, but they didn't tease her or make her the butt of jokes. She went along happily enough to see their movies and wander the mall with them. But when a pair or trio of them clumped up to whisper, they used the deep end of the pool, as far as they could get from where Laurel lay in the shade playing lifeguard, and Bet was never included. They didn't even glance at Bet, so it wasn't that they were whispering about her. They were talking about boys Bet didn't know and teachers Bet would never have. Bet stayed in the shallows, swishing her arms back and forth in the cool blue, and it wasn't only because she couldn't swim.

"Shelby didn't see her go in?" Laurel asked. Bet's brow furrowed like she was thinking, but she didn't answer. It was getting harder to keep the casual tone. "How long did she stay? Did you see her come out?"

"I dun remember."

Laurel backed down and said as calmly as she could, "When was this, Bet?"

"Last summer," Bet said. "I seen Molly go in there. Maybe Shelby and I was walking to the Tom Thumb? But I dun think Shelby saw. She didn't say nothing if she did."

"Why didn't you tell anyone?" Laurel said. Bet looked at her, mystified, as if she had no idea why she didn't tell or no idea that she should have. "Shelby told you not to go in there . . ."

"I thought that was because Shelby didn't want us to hang around with a fag."

"Please don't use that word, Bet," Laurel said automatically.

"You dun think he's a fag?" Bet said.

"That's not the point," Laurel said.

Maybe Stan Webelow was gay. Laurel's friend Edie thought he was. More than once Edie had watched his tight body as he ran past, glossy with sweat, and had said, "There goes a sad waste."

But Trish Deerbold and Eva Bailey always had their hands on him, patting at him as if he were their lapdog, and he preened and basked under their touch. Eva was always trying to set him up with some divorced friend or another. Trish and Eva would gag on their Valium if he showed up to a neighborhood association potluck with a seven-layer salad and a male date. Laurel would feel a thousand times more comfortable with him if he did. With a sister in theater, she had been around gay folks all her life; she worried that Stan Webelow was something else.

Laurel saw the drapes moving in the big bay window. He was home, watching her as she watched him. She took her foot off the brake.

"It isn't a nice word," Laurel said to Bet as the car eased forward. "I know several gay men you might meet today at Thalia's. They're nice people, and how do you think they'd feel if you called them an ugly name like that?" She didn't bother explaining that one of the gay men was Thalia's husband. It was too complicated to get into.

Bet asked, "What's it nice to call fags, then?"

"Well, nothing," said Laurel. She decided to circle the block instead of turning around. She didn't want her car to pass through Stan Webelow's sea-green gaze again. "You call people by their names. Or you can say someone is gay."

Laurel wasn't really listening to herself. There was no good reason why Molly would have gone into Stan's house last year. Laurel had warned Shelby off, and if Shelby had passed the rules on to Bet Clemmens, she must have said something to Molly, a much closer friend. Maybe Molly's mother had sent her to borrow something? No. Stan lived blocks and blocks away. People went next door for a cup of sugar, not to the other end of a large community. And what twelve-year-old girl would knock on the door of a single adult man and announce that she needed to use the facilities, especially with Carly's house only four doors down?

Molly last year had looked a lot like Shelby now, the tiny buds of breasts beginning to poke themselves forward, hips as slim as a boy's, the rush of estrogen giving her a little podge at the tum. This summer Molly had filled out her swimsuit perfectly. She looked three years older than Shelby, not three months, and Laurel remembered thinking that the Dufresnes would need to dress their daughter in flour sacks and padlocks when Molly hit high school, with all those older boys with cars.

Bet said, "What about 'queers'? Can I call 'em queers?"

Laurel turned to tell her no, of course not, and she caught that little gleam hiding behind Bet's flat gaze again. "Did you just make a joke?" Laurel asked, surprised enough to say it out loud.

Bet quirked one shoulder up in a shrug, a Shelby move that meant, "Guilty as charged." It wasn't the world's nicest joke, but the kid was trying.

Laurel reached out and gave Bet's narrow shoulder a squeeze. Bet leaned in to the touch, a light and cautious shift, like that of a barn cat who wasn't used to petting but could maybe get to like it. Laurel had a sudden strong memory of holding Bet one Christmas when Bet was just a baby.

Laurel had been so heavily pregnant that her doctor hadn't wanted her to make the trip. The baby—Laurel was almost certain it had been Bet—had stiffened her fat naked legs and braced her feet against the top of Laurel's big belly, her round eyeballs focused and intent on Laurel's face. Shelby had kicked upward exactly then, so that Laurel felt four small feet pushing at her, inside and out. Laurel had fought an urge to clasp Bet tighter and make a run for the car. She'd leap into the backseat and yell to Daddy, "Drive. Just drive."

It wasn't a new impulse. She'd wanted to steal the babies every year since she was six and met the little ones Uncle Poot's daughter had abandoned. Laurel had walked over to the playpen and stared down hard at them, mostly to keep from looking at the foot that wasn't there. They'd been sleeping, curled up together like dirty puppies in a ratty old playpen. There was a stuffed dinosaur lying on the floor outside the pen, and its one remaining glass eye was hanging by a thread. It was what Laurel's mother called "a chokey." Laurel had pinched off the eye and slipped it in her pocket, then tucked the doll back in, close beside the older one.

Laurel had been a child herself, but she'd already known that babies belonged in clean yellow pajamas with feet, sleeping in a house that smelled like her own: of Pine-Sol and Mother's cooking. Babies shouldn't be left behind with Poot. Poot's growly voice and the salt-and-pepper bristles on his face made Laurel think of trolls. His eyes were sunk so deep into his skull that their color was a mystery. The glass dinosaur eye went home with her, safe in her pocket, but the babies stayed in that playpen, stayed in DeLop, and every year when Laurel came back, she found them bigger and more blank-eyed and more broken.

There had been a lot of babies she'd had to leave there. More, it seemed, every year. Now, paused at the iron gate that led from her neighborhood out into the world, she wondered what Bet would be now if Laurel had been allowed to take her.

Without thinking it through, without thinking at all, Laurel said, "I have to call Sissi, Bet. You're her kid, and it would be wrong not to let her know what's going on. But if she doesn't insist you come home early, we'll take you back the weekend before school starts, like we planned. Okay?"

Bet gave a curt nod. A wait-and-see nod with no trust in it. Then she ducked her head down as if embarrassed. "Can I put thet radio on?" she asked.

Laurel's nerves weren't up for a solid hour of the Shelby-inspired girl-bop pop Bet had decided she liked this year. "Check in the glove box," she said. "Shelby left her Nano in the car, and I think I stuffed it in there."

Bet fished out the iPod, a hot-pink object that Laurel couldn't work. Shelby must have given Bet a tutorial, because she popped in the earplugs and worked the front buttons with her thumbs like a pro. Laurel could hear a pounding bass and the tinny voice of Pink or maybe Christina Aguilera. It wasn't loud enough to be distracting. Laurel pointed the car at Mobile in the blessed relative quiet, ignoring the tribe of running bugs that had decided to have races in her belly.

She was off to get Thalia, if Thalia would allow herself to be gotten. If Laurel had to eat crow pie, then someone should pass her a fork. She was ready. Her real problem with needing her sister's help was always only this: In order to get it, a person had to talk to Thalia.

CHAPTER 7

Laurel pulled in to the lot attached to the Spotted Dog. It was a converted firehouse, taller than it was wide. Thalia and Gary lived in the old barracks on the top floor. They'd turned the truck bay into a black-box theater, the outsize garage doors kept closed unless they were loading a set out or in. A huge podlike storage trailer was slowly rotting into the ground behind the theater. It was stacked floor to ceiling with the Spotted Dog's in-house set pieces, a fire hazard behind a building no longer equipped to deal with such a thing.

Thalia's Pacer was near the people-sized glass door that led into the lobby. Laurel pulled in beside it and shut off the engine. The glass door had a rusty burglar grate over it; the Spotted Dog wasn't in the best area. Its neighbors included a liquor store and the most frequently robbed Starvin' Marvin in the state. Laurel put the emergency brake on, and Bet pulled off the headphones and sat there. Laurel hadn't made a move to get out of the car, so Bet didn't, either.

The last time Laurel was here, she'd come to see one of Thalia's plays, an olive branch of an outing if ever there was one. It was *A Doll's House,* so Laurel had gotten Shelby a ticket, too. She'd had a vague memory of reading it in AP English back in high school.

She'd forgotten the play, something about a letter, something about a party, but if conservative Pace High had allowed it on the curriculum, it was sure to be suitable for Shelby. Still, Thalia had been known to "adapt" the classics, so Laurel had asked when she'd called to order the tickets if it was okay to bring her kid.

"It's Ibsen. Of course bring Shelby. She should probably get school credit," Thalia had said. After a small pause, she'd added, "I'm glad you're coming to this one, Bug."

Laurel had taken that to be an acceptance of terms, an indication that Thalia wanted peace, too. All Laurel had to do was bring David around, and things could at last return to queasy normal.

Then she actually saw the play. Most if it, anyway.

Sitting in the dark, watching the story unfold, she'd begun to wonder if Thalia hadn't meant she was pleased Laurel was coming to this play specifically. It seemed like Ibsen had written each scene to spit in Laurel's soup. It was mostly about how dreadful and unfulfilling it was to be a wife and mother. Thalia's character, Nora, was more her husband's mindless little pet than a person.

Laurel kept her temper, even when Nora began chewing at the side of her thumb exactly the way Laurel used to as a kid. She kept her seat when Nora told her servant, who was mending a dress, to leave the room so her husband wouldn't have to be offended by the mundane sight of a woman sewing.

That dig was so direct, Laurel couldn't help but wonder if Thalia had added the line. It was Thalia, after all, who gleefully referred to her sister as a "sewer," pronouncing it as if it rhymed with "truer."

But Laurel took a deep cleansing breath and whispered, "Peace. Make peace" to herself on the exhale. This was nothing new. Thalia always needed to get in a last little prang. Laurel stayed right up until Thalia showed her butt.

During the scene where Gary-as-Torvald was giving Nora a patronizing dance lesson, Thalia began to spin out of control. Torvald protested, but her dancing became even wilder and stranger, until she finally flung her dress over her head, ripped off her underpants, and began using the old fireman's pole in a manner Laurel didn't think the firemen—or Ibsen, for that matter—had intended.

She'd let Shelby watch Thalia channel a hateful parody of her mother, and now Thalia's bare buttocks, gyrating suggestively, were practically churning in a primal and thrusty sort of way at both Gary and the audience. Laurel had jerked Shelby up by the arm and marched her right up the aisle to the door. Shelby had craned back around as they went, her mouth a wide O, and Laurel had manually turned her head to face front. She'd let the door bang as loud as she could on the way out.

In the lobby, Shelby had said in an outraged whisper, "I want to know how it ends!"

Laurel had replied much louder, "Then you can read it. But you'll be reading it without the naked part, because that was strictly your aunt Thalia's interpretation."

"That doesn't really happen?" Shelby had asked.

Laurel had shaken her head, pulling Shelby along through the lobby. "I'll get you the book."

Shelby had muttered, "Forget it. It was boring till the naked part anyway," then sulked all the way home. Laurel had added a long drive with a hyperdramatic, palpably suffering preteen to Thalia's considerable tab, and she hadn't tried to make peace since.

Now Laurel glanced at the marquee. It was an old freestanding, changeable sign, the kind churches used to spell out messages like GOD ANSWERS KNEE-MAIL AND THE BEST VITAMIN FOR A CHRISTIAN IS B1. Calling it a marquee was more of a courtesy. Right now it said NEXT EXIT, A PLAY BY ALLEN MALLORY and listed the dates of the run. The play had closed last week, ending their summer season. They were on hiatus until September.

Laurel said, "Bet, I'm going to need to talk with my sister alone, with no mice ears. She's mad, I'm mad, and in the making up, there might be some language you don't need to hear." Bet looked slightly incredulous, and Laurel realized she was doing it again—forgetting where Bet came from. "It's personal. Sister stuff. They've got some good magazines in the lobby, and I won't be long. You can bring in Shelby's iPod."

Bet reached for the door handle, but Laurel put a hand on her arm, stopping her. She sat for another scant minute, gathering herself. For about the thousandth time in her life, she needed Thalia's boldness. She tried to make her skin feel thick. She tried to make her heart beat slow and steady.

"Okay," she said, and opened her door. They got out of the car and walked up to the glass door. Laurel pushed the discreet button that sounded the bell in the loft upstairs. Then they waited. No answer came through the intercom, and they didn't get buzzed in. The padlock wasn't on the metal grate, so Laurel gave the door an experimental push. It gave under her fingers, so she went through it, Bet stepping in behind her.

The Spotted Dog smelled like every other small theater Thalia had dragged Laurel to, a dry must stuck to air that had been waxed with greasepaint. The lobby had a ticket booth and a concession stand and an old red velvet chaise longue and matching love seat. Behind the concession stand was a doorway hung with a once plush velveteen curtain, also dull red. The doorway led to the dressing and costume rooms, and to the stairs up to Thalia and Gary's quarters.

Laurel walked to the counter and called, "Hello?"

After a minute, Gary poked his head from behind the curtain, his mouth turning down when he saw Laurel. He wasn't drop-dead handsome, exactly—he had regular features set in a flat face—but a low hum of energy seemed to leak out of his skin. Laurel could always feel him as a presence in a room, even when he wasn't speaking.

"And here you are." He said it like Laurel was a cold sore he was resigned to having show up every now and again. Then he saw Bet standing behind her. "Good God," he said, eyeballing the ruffled Wal-Mart halter. "What's this?"

"This is Bet, a friend of Shelby's," Laurel said, and when Gary's eyebrows went up, she added, "Actually, she's Shelby's third cousin."

Laurel could see him make the connection to DeLop. His expression softened. "Right. Pleased to meet you, third-cousin-in-law." He tipped her an imaginary hat and turned back to Laurel. In a far more baleful voice, he said, "I didn't think you and herself were speaking."

She could feel his dislike for her rolling off him in salty waves, but it didn't bother her. She'd stopped liking him first. That had baffled him, because Gary didn't think it was humanly possible for a person not to like him. He was smart and funny and talented on top of his generic good looks, the whole package, and in truth, she had liked him fine initially. Right up until the day he married her sister and the two of them moved to Mobile to live out the most elaborate conceit that Laurel had ever seen.

They pretended Thalia had no idea that he was gay. He sneaked around having thrilling, forbidden trysts with multiple men who thought they were hiding from Thalia, which allowed Gary to hide them more easily from one another. He clambered out of whatever bed he'd been tumbling around in and came home to Thalia every night. They slept cuddled up like kids at a slumber party, enough created drama swirling around them to make life as interesting as anything in Noël Coward.

Thalia claimed it was the perfect marriage because they both were first and forever in love with theater. "Gary keeps the lonelies away," Thalia told Laurel once, after a five-martini birthday lunch. The birthday and four of the martinis had been Thalia's. "You let yourself get lonely, then you want to be in love, and love is an illusion, Jesus Bug. A delusion, even. It leads to marriage and monogamy. M&M's—the candy that kills art."

Not that Thalia lived celibate. "Wronged, chaste wife" was casting her too far from type. Thalia's idea of a perfect marriage included running out and getting some sex the way Laurel went to Albertsons to get celery, but she always came back home to Gary.

Laurel couldn't fathom whatever it was Thalia and Gary had, but Thalia couldn't seem to fathom her marriage, either. More than once Thalia had tried to shock Laurel with wild tales of the delights of catting, as if sex were something Laurel was missing out on. She used words Laurel had never heard to describe acts that sounded perfectly filthy.

After one particularly foul-sounding and one-sided conversation, Laurel had gone to Urban Dictionary online and looked up all the phrases she hadn't known. All but one turned out to be things she and David had figured out for themselves long ago, and Laurel felt she could limp along through the rest of her life and be completely happy without ever once experiencing that last one. All she was missing was Thalia's vocabulary, which did not come from *Reader's Digest,* and Thalia's delight in sharing every intimate detail.

Now Laurel gave Gary a smile that felt cool even on the inside and said, "Thalia and I always make up, one way or another."

"Yet every time I keep my fingers crossed." He put one hand to his forehead, overacting to make it seem like he was kidding. "Foolish, hopeful me."

He wasn't kidding.

"Is Thalia upstairs?"

"Nope. In there." He gestured toward the doors that led into the theater.

"Will you be all right, Bet?" Laurel asked.

In answer, Bet plopped down on a corner of the red velvet love seat. A puff of dust swirled around her hips as she landed. She stuck the earplugs back in and then grabbed an old copy of *Interview* magazine from the end table. She furrowed her brow, puzzled, peering down at what looked like a photo of Kirsten Dunst licking a kitten. Gary was looking at Bet with an almost identical expression. He shook his head and disappeared back behind the curtain.

Laurel left Bet there and walked into the theater proper. The doors opened at the top of one of the aisles. The Spotted Dog didn't have an actual stage. Seating was on three sides, the chairs all angled slightly to face the acting area. It was a very flexible space, Thalia said, because they could build risers and make it multi-leveled, or leave it flat and shape the audience chairs around the demands of the play. Right now the acting space was empty. Either *Next Exit* had used a minimalist set or they had already torn out. Once the doors closed behind her, Laurel was in the dark, but the acting area was lit up in a circle made sunshine-warm with pale orange and gold gels.

Thalia was on a black yoga mat that she had centered in the middle of the ring of light. She stood on one bare foot with her other leg extended behind her and curled up, so her left foot was hovering practically over her face. Her spine was bowed back, her neck extended so she could look up at her foot, and her arms were stretched back over her head.

She wore a long-sleeved black unitard that covered her from ankle to neck, but it was so sheer and fitted that it looked more like naked than naked did. From where Laurel stood, her sister was in perfect silhouette, and her silhouette was pretty damn perfect.

Laurel looked like a slightly faded version of Mother. She had regular features, the default of pretty. Thalia had similar features but in very different proportions, and she could be brutally ugly and then stunning half a minute later. She had Laurel's short, straight nose, but much smaller, set in their father's flat, wide face with his full mouth and a pair of long, slitty sloe eyes that were all her own.

The first time Laurel saw the blond Bratz doll in Target, perched in its box with one boy-skinny hip cocked, trashy beyond

Barbie's wildest imaginings, she'd been struck dumb. The doll was whippet-thin, big-eyed, fat-mouthed, and all but noseless; Laurel had wondered who on earth had modeled a doll on her sister. Shelby had been absolutely forbidden from bringing Bratz dolls into the house. The trashy clothes would have assured that anyway, but a truer reason, one she could not share with Shelby, was that Laurel didn't want tiny Thalias scattered across her floor in abandoned poses, wearing hooker shoes and staring at her with dead plastic eyes.

Thalia, poised on the mat, either hadn't noticed Laurel or was pretending she hadn't. Maybe Gary had told her that Laurel had called. Laurel could imagine Thalia waiting here, holding this impossible position for hours, so that by the time Laurel made her entrance, Thalia would have already pre-stolen it.

Thalia released a slow exhale and then uncoiled herself in a movement so fluid it was almost slithery. She kept moving, planting both feet and easing her spine until it was curving the other way. She put both hands flat on the floor, ending in the shape of an upside-down V, her butt pointing straight up at the ceiling. As she moved, it was as if her lean body displaced more air than it should have, cool air that came wafting up between the rows of chairs to touch Laurel's skin with gooseflesh.

Marty was here.

Not his ghost, though. What she felt was his memory, coming to cold life in the space between Laurel and her sister. Mobile's humidity went crystalline in his chill. A long shudder worked its way down Thalia's spine, as if she felt it, too, an unseen hand passing down the length of her, cool and strange. She sighed and arched her neck and stilled herself.

Laurel walked down the aisle between the rows of chairs. She stopped on the edge of the lighted space. "Hey, Thalia."

Thalia turned her head to peer out from behind her arm and said, "Hey, Jesus Bug."

"I wish you wouldn't call me that."

Thalia had been calling Laurel "Jesus Bug" since they were teenagers. It was Daddy's word for the little skating beetles that zoomed over the surface of ponds and puddles, never looking down.

Thalia pushed off with her hands and stood upright. "Is it Christmas already?" she asked, unwittingly echoing Sissi Clemmens.

"Still August," Laurel said.

"Zounds!" Thalia said, affecting an overblown Shakespearian accent. She moved her right foot forward, as if stepping into ballet's fourth position, and put one arm out dramatically to her side while her other hand twirled at an invisible cruel mustache. "What hath summoned thee, good my lady, so fucking prematurely?"

Laurel wasn't sure she'd felt Marty at all. The cold might have been only Thalia's anger, thick and icy.

"Please don't be like this," Laurel said.

"How should I be, then?" Thalia said in her regular voice, cocking her head to one side.

Laurel said, "You have to know, for me to come here, that it has to be pretty bad. And it is, Thalia. So bad that I lied to David. Sort of lied. Almost lied. To get to you."

And she had. She had let the truth march purposefully out the door with her and Bet Clemmens, then blamed him for it because he'd called Mother in. She couldn't think about that now. She kept her eyes steady on Thalia's face.

"Really," Thalia said, drawing out the E sound. She dropped the invisible mustache and the pose and said, "Trouble in paradise. Who could ever have imagined? Bug, don't you get *Woman's Day*? Look in between the recipes and the hundred fun rainy-day crafts. There'll be something about meeting him at the door naked except for some Saran wrap, or scented candles, or K-Y warming massage crap, whatever it is your kind of people think is all sexy. Go home and make it up. Your domestic disputes are not my problem."

"I'm not here because I lied to David," Laurel said, holding her voice steady with effort. "David's not the problem."

"So you keep saying," said Thalia to the air. "Come back and see me when you've figured out that yes, in fact, he is."

Her fourth wall came down with an almost audible bang. Laurel stopped existing, and Thalia was alone in the center of the stage, playing Beautiful Woman Doing Yoga. She coiled down into an easy lotus position and tilted her head back to begin slow breathing.

Laurel backed up until the light wasn't touching her, and then she stopped. In the safety of the darkness, she sat down in one of the chairs and watched her sister's body curl into impossible shapes, ropy muscle shifting under skin. She made her breathing match Thalia's and found it was a calming way to breathe. She quit watching Thalia after a while because it was easier not to be angry when she wasn't looking.

When she was ready, she said, "Remember Molly Dufresne? Shelby's friend? She's dead. She fell in our pool and drowned."

Thalia stilled, one ankle folded back behind her neck. She

brought her leg down and put her foot on the floor, her eyes trying to find Laurel in the darkness. "How's my girl?" she said quietly.

"Not good," Laurel said.

"Right. Let's get this part done quick, then," Thalia said, and stood up with abbreviated grace. "Bitch, you walked out in the middle of Gary's best transition. You banged the door and wrecked his third act."

"You sent thong underpants whizzing out into the audience. Right past Shelby's ear."

Thirty seconds ticked by.

"Call it even?" Thalia said.

"Yes," Laurel said.

"Even, then. What's going on with Shelby?"

Laurel took another one of Thalia's cleansing breaths and said, "Molly drowned in the middle of the night. Her ghost came and woke me up and showed me where to find her body. The police are calling it an accident, but Shelby wasn't in her room when Molly died, and Molly came to see me for a reason. I need to know what it is."

Another thirty seconds ticked by, and then Thalia said, "You know I don't believe in your ghosts."

"I know," said Laurel, and yoga breaths or not, she could feel herself heating. She wasn't angry, exactly. More like exasperated. "You don't believe in ghosts, or God, or marriage or country or that puppies are really that damn happy. You don't believe in anything."

"That's not true," Thalia said automatically. "Come back down here. I want to see you."

Laurel got up and joined her sister on the mat. They sat cross-legged on opposite ends, facing each other. Thalia stared hard at

Laurel, as if trying to see past her tired eyes, all the way into her brain.

"I'll tell you what I believe. I believe you mean it," Thalia said. "I believe seeing ghosts is your way of telling yourself something is bad wrong. I believe you're smart. If you feel it this strongly, then I believe it's true. That's a pretty long list."

"That's really only one thing," Laurel said. "You're saying you believe in me, and that's the only thing that matters right now, Thalia. Please come home with me."

Thalia didn't answer for a solid minute. Then she said, "I remember Molly. Even at eleven, she looked to me like she was going to grow into a beauty."

"She did," Laurel said.

"Lay it out for me, Bug," Thalia said. "Like Aunt Moff lays the cards."

"Hearts for love, diamonds for money," Laurel said.

"Don't leave out the ace of spades. Not this time," Thalia said.

So Laurel started at the beginning, trying to think of the events as cards she was turning up, and it was better that way. It came out clearer than when she'd tried to explain to David in the basement. Thalia listened, not speaking at all until Laurel had wound down to the end: David calling Mother to the house, and the lie she'd let stand to get to Thalia.

The first thing Thalia said was, "Typical David, but at least this time you see it."

"You're missing the point," Laurel said.

"Am I? Fine. You have a ghost, Shelby's empty bed, and you think you saw a creepy, dateless man's hair. It's not much, Bug. I don't suppose the creepy-hair guy wears pink Izod shirts and rooms with some genial tanning-booth godlet that he introduces as 'Sean, my life partner'?"

"No," Laurel said.

"If he's gay, I'll probably be able to tell right off. All these years with Gary, I've developed a nose for it. You need to get me in a room with him."

"We can do that," Laurel said, ready to agree to anything. It sounded like Thalia's scales were tipping in her favor.

"Stan Webelow," Thalia said. "Are you sure this isn't you—you know—projecting?"

She'd said Stan's name. Not Marty's. But now Laurel was certain that it was Marty's memory in the room with them. They sat quietly, both thinking of Marty Gray, and of all the bad things that can happen to young girls who are shy and good and obedient. The secret keepers. The easily led.

"I don't know," Laurel said honestly. "It's possible, but I can't gamble. Not when it's Shelby."

"If he's not in love with God, nor man, nor woman, it has to be going somewhere," Thalia said. She quirked up one eyebrow. "Does he keep goats?"

"Thalia!"

Thalia stretched her arms up over her head. "Bug, this could all be in your head. You think he dragged Molly through the neighborhood all the way to your pool and then banged her in the head with a brick and drowned her? The forensics would have shown that."

Laurel shrugged. "What if he was just . . . there? Maybe Molly was going to tell. Say she has plans to meet up with Shelby and she's going to spill their secret. She's threatened Stan? Or she's just left his house? Somehow he knows. So he comes to stop her. The pool light's the only one on in the backyard, so Molly waits for Shelby there. She's sitting on the diving board. He sees her, she sees him. She's startled. She jumps up, misses her footing, falls, and hits her head. And he does nothing. He watches. He's the shadow I see slipping away, thinking his secret has taken care of itself."

Thalia was nodding. "Okay, that works. Criminally negligent homicide." Laurel raised her brows, and Thalia went on. "What? I watch *CSI.* Your scenario is possible, but it's not the most likely one I can think of. We're predisposed to look for perverts in the bushes, you and I. On the other hand, the world is full of predators. If you even slightly suspect you had something toothy in your own backyard, not thirty feet from where your own baby lies at night, then you can't put your nose down and graze all sheeply and stupid and hope it passes into another yard next time. Neither can I. I'd best go throw some panties in a bag. You wait here or in the lobby so I can smooth it with Gary. He's not going to love me going off with you, of all people, especially since we've got company auditions set for Monday week."

Thalia stood up and walked out of the circle of light, over to the curtained entrance on the left that the actors used. Laurel could barely make her out as she slid her feet into her shoes and unfurled a long strip of weightless cloth from the floor.

"Little Shelby and your weirdo neighbor, what a list of suspects," Thalia muttered to herself.

"Shelby's not a suspect," Laurel said, so hard and loud that the good acoustics picked it up and amplified it, setting the words ringing in her ears.

"Oh, relax, Mother Bear. I'm coming home with you mostly because I'd burn down Paris for Shelby, and you know it," Thalia said.

"I meant that Stan-Webelow-gives-you-the-wig and Shelby-has-a-secret shouldn't be your whole list. You've missed the obvious."

The heels of her black slides clicked on the wood as she walked back to the edge of the light. Thalia shook out the cloth she'd picked up, a sheer scarf in leopard print, and wound it around her body. The addition didn't make her look less naked. It only made her look accessorized. "You didn't lay clubs, Bug. When Aunt Moff lays the cards, clubs are for family. Maybe things are ugly inside the Dufresne house. You ever notice Molly having bruises, anything like that?"

"No," Laurel said.

"Still, a young girl goes running out into the night, coming to her best friend's place, you have to ask what happened in her house to drive her from it. Statistically speaking, it's more likely. It's almost always people in a family who kill each other."

Thalia stepped back out of the light, turning away and walking toward the door that led backstage. "No one knows that better than you and me," she added, and exited stage left.

CHAPTER 8

Uncle Marty had the short eyes.

That's what they would have called it if he had ever gone to prison. He didn't. Instead, Laurel's daddy took them hunting in a county where he and Marty knew the sheriff so well they were borrowing his cabin. Marty had the short eyes, and Daddy shot him.

Put that way, it didn't seem like murder. Laurel had seen similar stories on late-night cable, one with Clint Eastwood, and she thought maybe Charles Bronson had done one like that, too. Clint Eastwood had been the hero. It was a good story, but Laurel couldn't claim it as her own. In spite of what had happened between them the day before Marty died, Laurel's uncle never laid a hand on her that wasn't proper. Laurel didn't even know which way his tastes ran until his last day on the earth.

Laurel was eleven years old, and Marty came, as he did every year, for the first weekend of deer season. He brought a real silver charm bracelet with a starter charm each for Laurel and Thalia.

Laurel's was cutesy kidsy, a mouse with obsidian chip eyes, but Thalia got a high-heeled shoe with gem flecks set to make a flashy daisy on the toe.

When Laurel and Thalia got home from school on Friday, it was obvious that Marty and Mother were already skirmishing. Marty was the closest thing Mother ever had to an in-law, and they fussed over Daddy like those squabbling ladies who came before King Solomon with one hapless toddler pulled so tight between them he was probably spread-eagled.

Marty sat on one end of Mother's faded cabbage-rose sofa, and Mother held court at the other end. Both of them were drinking coffee and not looking at the other. Mother smiled a cream-filled cat's smile, clearly well ahead on points. The air around Marty fairly crackled with electric anger.

Thalia rolled her eyes and whispered, "Want to take a long-odds bet over who'll get to cut up Daddy's meat tonight?"

Laurel stopped in the doorway, but Thalia said a quick hello and then meandered down the hall toward the room she shared with Laurel. Halfway there, out of Marty and Mother's sight, she turned back to face Laurel. She grabbed her blouse on either side in a pinch, then pulled cloth tepees out over her small breasts. "Nice rack," she mouthed at Laurel, grinning.

Laurel flushed. She'd forgotten to take out the cotton balls she'd stuffed into her training bra that morning.

"Would you like a snack?" Mother asked.

She hadn't yet noticed the sudden sprouting of Laurel's fluffy bosom, so Laurel shrugged her backpack off and hugged it to her chest. Down the hall, where Mother couldn't see, Thalia laughed silently, giving Laurel a double thumbs-up. She went into their bedroom and closed the door with elaborate gentleness, Thalia's signature anti-slam.

Laurel kept her backpack clutched across her front and nodded at Mother, who got up and wafted through the swinging door into the kitchen. Laurel blew her air out in a relieved sigh and let the bag slide down until she was holding it by one strap, the heavy book-filled bottom resting on the floor.

"Tell Mother I went to change out of my school clothes," she said to Marty.

"Hold up," he said. He was wearing faded jeans that had been washed baby-soft and one of his loungey flannel shirts, but his body language did not match the comfort of his clothes. His long torso was folded stiffly at the waist, his spine not touching the sofa back.

As the swinging doors came to rest, he tipped his head to one side, appraising her, until Laurel wished she'd kept her backpack in her arms.

"Little Laurel, are you finally growing up?" he asked.

She flushed and turned her back, looking out the windows as if she'd suddenly become fascinated by the view into her own backyard. The bird feeder was empty.

"I need to go change," she repeated.

"You've already changed," he said. "You're getting to look exactly like your mother. I never noticed till now." His tone had an unfamiliar edge. He didn't sound like Laurel's redneck, drawly uncle, the one who called her Peapod and brought her packs of Juicy Fruit. "Are you turning into a lady?" He made "lady" sound like a dirty word, not a thing a girl would want to be.

Laurel let the backpack drop entirely and crossed her arms,

even though her back was to him. She felt the cottonballs flattening, and underneath, she felt her heart thump, hard and fast.

"Little Lady Laurel. Want to see something?"

She didn't move, didn't answer, uncomfortable and not sure why. Then, in her mother's tidy family room, she heard the unmistakable rasp of a zipper being drawn down.

"Want to see?" he said, wheedling-like.

Her stomach turned, went sour, as if she had eaten something that was beginning to go rotten. She knew what he'd unzipped. His flannel shirt had pearl snaps on it. His leather jacket was beside him, but it had buttons.

"Want to see, Lady Laura-Lee?"

It was so dead quiet she could hear the muffled rasp of his calloused fingers on the denim. She stared at the empty bird feeder until her eyes ached from not blinking. The worst part wasn't the nasty undercurrent in his voice. It wasn't even that she'd loved him her whole life. The worst part was that a piece of her had a hard time not looking. She was eleven years old and had only a sister. She had never seen one.

Laurel heard the kitchen doors swing open again, heard Mother's low heels tapping one last time against linoleum before she stepped onto the carpet.

There was a tiny silence, and then Mother said, "Laurel, honey, I told you to go change." She spoke sweetly, in her normal dulcet voice, as if Marty's cock weren't loose in the room.

Laurel headed back to the hallway that led to her bedroom, careful to turn around by going right, so that she never looked at Marty or Mother. She walked down the hall to the room she shared with Thalia.

Thalia sprawled on her stomach on the floor. Her gutted backpack was beside her, and she had three open books, a notebook, and a yellow folder scattered across the floor. Laurel could hardly see a speck of carpet.

When Thalia saw Laurel, she sat up and said, "What happened?"

Laurel said, "Uncle Marty," like his name was a complete thought.

Thalia made one of Daddy's faces, that fierce kind of bird-looking, foreign and intense, as if she could see straight through Laurel to something beautiful and strange three feet behind her. Then she blinked and said, her voice matter-of-fact, "You still have your fake tits in."

She picked up a pink highlighter and pulled her history book into her lap. All at once she was playing Studious Girl, and Laurel's presence didn't register. Laurel grabbed her play clothes and carted them off to the bathroom to change and throw out the cotton balls. She did her homework and ate the granola bar Mother brought her, exactly like she did after school every other day.

Uncle Marty was his normal self at dinner, pretending Mother wasn't there and joking with Daddy, calling Thalia "Madame Pigtail." Laurel's tomato soup was bitter, and her grilled cheese went down in waxy lumps. Marty was in all ways ruined for her. But at the same time, he barely existed. His colors ran, the blue and rust of his shirt bleeding into the yellow wallpaper, and he blurred into the other shapes around the table. The only object in the kitchen with a sharp outline was Mother. She sat at the foot of the table, closest to the stove, spooning up mannerly tastes of soup.

"May I be excused?" Laurel said.

"Me, too," said Thalia.

Mother nodded, and they scraped their chairs back in tandem, grabbing their plates to drop off at the sink. Uncle Marty tugged Laurel's long braid as she tried to slide past without letting even his chair touch her. His eyes on her were his regular plain eyes, as if he were the same Marty he had always been. Mother kept her seat, allowing him to look at Laurel, to touch her braid with the same calloused fingers she'd heard rasp against his jeans.

"Thalia, you'd best get to bed," Marty said. "We got to get to Alabama before sunup if we're going to catch them deer."

Laurel stayed by Marty's chair. It was as if her braid had nerve endings in it and she could still feel the imprint of his fingers. Mother's expression was bland as she heaped Daddy's plate with more fruit. She wasn't even watching.

Cowslip, Laurel thought, but that wasn't the word. She knew the real word now. She'd seen it months ago in one of Mother's *Reader's Digest*s. The real word was "complicit."

Mother hadn't been surprised. That was the part Laurel couldn't forgive. Mother hadn't gasped or taken in a hard breath. She must have known before that he was one of those. Early in the year, their gym teacher had shown a film, girls only, like the one about getting a period. Pervos, Laurel's friend Tammy had called them. She'd made Laurel giggle all through the movie by whispering suspicions about the male math teacher with the enormous mustache. But here was one for real, her own uncle at her table, and Mother must have known. Mother had let Laurel have friends over with Marty there, knowing. Last month Thalia had tried oral sex with a high school boy.

"Tastes like chicken," she'd told Laurel in a gleeful whisper.

Was that "acting out," like the film had said, or only Thalia being Thalia? Had Marty ever asked Thalia if she wanted to see?

If he had, if Thalia was acting out, then Mother was complicit.

Now he wanted to show Laurel, Mother's favorite, and Mother stayed blind and bland and unsurprised.

Laurel stood as if rooted by Marty's chair, the dirty plate still in her hands, waiting until the waiting was obvious. She was giving Mother time to get up and put out Marty's looking eyes with her thumbs, to come after his braid-touching fingers with her dinner knife. But Mother only sat. Laurel waited so long that Thalia stopped by the swinging doors and Daddy set down his fork and looked up at Laurel, eyebrows raised and questioning. Marty craned his neck back, with Daddy's expression on his similar features. Only Mother kept right on eating.

"I want to go along on y'all's hunt," Laurel said.

Mother's hand stilled with her spoon half dipped into her bowl.

Daddy chuckled and said, "You're too little."

"I'm in sixth grade now," Laurel said. "You let Thalia go in fourth."

"Sixth grade?" Marty said. "Already?"

"Ugh, please. She'll wreck it," Thalia said, speaking over Marty. "She gets dizzy looking at a scraped knee."

"I want to go. It's safe," Laurel said, looking right at Mother. "If Daddy and Thalia have to run a deer down, I'll be fine. I'll be with Uncle Marty."

Laurel watched her mother's eyes harden, saw her throat move in a dry swallow.

Daddy said, "No shooting until you've spent some time on the range with me and Thalia."

By "the range," he meant an empty field where he spent a few hours every Saturday. He and Thalia would take boxes of bullets, all three of his rifles, and his pistol for good measure. They'd shoot and shoot and shoot, lining up two-liter bottles and Coke cans, blasting away until the cans and bottles were shredded strings of metal and twisted plastic that could no longer stand.

Laurel had tagged along a time or two, but she hadn't liked how Daddy's eagle gaze was so fierce on the bright cans Thalia lined up for him. Last time she went, Daddy had started shooting with the pistol, so focused that he hadn't been able to stop when he was out of bullets. He'd dry-fired four or five times before he'd caught himself and offered Laurel a turn.

"I've been to the range," Laurel said now.

"Not enough to try to bag you a deer," Daddy said. "But you can come along and watch."

Mother cut a bite of honeydew in half, speared it, and put it in her mouth, chewing carefully and not speaking.

"Would you let me go off with them?" Laurel asked, her eyes trained on Mother.

Thalia said, "Mother, you promised you guys would bake us cookies for when we got home."

Laurel said, "Will you? Let me go off with him?"

Thalia was still griping. "Hunting means we're going to shoot things until they die. There's guts, did you know that? We cut the guts right out, Jesus Bug, and spill them on the ground."

"Don't take the Lord's name in vain, Thalia," Mother said.

Thalia went on. "Look, she's going green just hearing about it."

Mother cut another piece of fruit in half and said, "Fair is fair. Your sister is almost twelve, and she can go if she wants to." She paused and then said, "Do you want to?"

She might as well have looked right at Laurel and said, "I don't much love you."

"Yes, Mama," Laurel said. "If you let me, I'm going."

"Don't say 'Mama,'" Mother said. "That sounds trashy. Say 'Mother.'"

That night Laurel went to bed in a bleak world where the person she most belonged to sat quiet and smiling and let her go trip-trapping off, wide-eyed, into danger.

But Laurel had underestimated her.

Mother was so mindful of propriety that she still had single beds in the master bedroom. Thalia called the space between the beds "the Great Divide," and said her own existence proved that someone must have bravely taken a single crossing. Her money was on Daddy.

"He went back at least one more time," Laurel had protested the first time Thalia put this theory forward.

Thalia had shown Laurel all her big white teeth at once and said, "Nah. I suspect Mother budded you all on her own."

That night Mother must have turned in her own bed to face Daddy's, must have whispered things across the void. Perhaps she didn't say anything about Laurel or that afternoon. After all, Thalia was older and had bloomed earlier. If Thalia had been interfered with, then it explained a lot about her that surely needed some explaining, and Thalia was Daddy's very heart.

Whatever Mother said, it was enough. Her words must have echoed in the space between their beds for hours, growing louder. They had gotten inside Daddy, gone banging through his veins from brain to heart and back again, circulating that whole long night into the morning. Out in the woods, Marty had said something and then moved into Daddy's line of sight as the deer ran off, and Daddy had twitched his finger hard against the trigger.

It wasn't planned. Daddy never would have thought ahead to

shoot down his brother in front of his daughters. It was the work of a moment, and Laurel believed that if he could have, Daddy would have called that bullet back before the sound of it rang out. Daddy had turned Marty over with such careful love. He'd put his hands over the hole to try and stop the blood, and with all his will, he'd tried to make his brother not be dead. Daddy was sorry to this day, and even though he had pulled the trigger, Laurel knew it was Mother's whispers that had saved her.

Mother had blinded herself to ugliness early; growing up in DeLop made blindness a survival skill. But for Laurel's sake, Mother had seen. She'd gone against everything in her nature to protect Laurel.

That was all Laurel was doing now, protecting her own child. She had to keep reminding herself of that. It got harder and harder to remember as the car rocketed back toward Pensacola. The trip home was happening at warp speed.

Thalia was playing with all the remote controls, adjusting and readjusting the seat. She found the heater button and stabbed at it, watching the amber light flash on. "It's got a butt warmer?" she said, scornful.

"I guess," Laurel said.

"You have too much money," Thalia said. She looked into the backseat, where Bet Clemmens and the Hefty bag and Thalia's own three suitcases sat in a row, all equally silent. Bet was still listening to Shelby's Nano, so loud that Laurel could hear Justin Timberlake blasting directly into Bet's ears.

"You know what she reminds me of?" Thalia said, turning back around and jerking one thumb over her shoulder at Bet.

"Who? The girl right here in the car with us?" Laurel asked.

"Yeah. The one with the headphones in," Thalia said. "Remember, right after you had Shelby, you wanted another baby."

"No, I didn't," Laurel said.

"Yeah-huh," Thalia said. "They'd brought Shelby to your room, and you were still zoned from the epidural. My God, fifteen hours of that. You looked straight up at the nurse and asked how long until you could, you know, mount up and ride your mechanical bull again—"

"I would never say that!" Laurel said, risking a glance over her shoulder. Bet's head bobbed slightly, and her eyes didn't seem to be focused on anything.

"Not in those words. I'm sure you said 'make beautiful love with the robot,' but it was the same basic idea," Thalia said. "There you sat, holding the seven-pound baby I'd just watched you push out your wing-wang, which, by the way? looked like it hurt like a sumbitch. I said, 'Don't tell me you are feeling romantical now, Bug. What are you, a hamster?' David was purple."

"I don't remember this at all," Laurel said, and then she stopped. Because she did remember it. "Oh, Lord. The spare baby."

Shelby, brand-new, had been so alert in the hours just after she was born. She had stared up at Laurel, swaddled in a roll of receiving blankets, a solemn expression on her scrunchy monkey's face. Laurel couldn't look at anything else in the room. Shelby had dark, serious eyes, and she was completely innocent of hair. Laurel couldn't believe this was the person she'd had inside her not an hour ago, the person she and David made, out here blinking in the harsh light, so floppy and helpless and perfect and beautiful. She couldn't hardly stand to have Shelby breathing hospital air that might have a baby-killing germ in it, or drinking breast milk already poisoned by the Cheetos Laurel had eaten right before her water broke.

A crazy thought had wandered through her exhausted head: "I need a decoy." Without thinking, she had asked the nurse when she and David could try again. She wanted an extra. A faceless, rubbery baby who was not Shelby. She wouldn't love it very much. It would be a howler, a loud distraction, something she could offer to the ravenous world while she hid Shelby away, safe and secret.

"That was postpartum crazies," Laurel said. "I didn't really want a spare baby."

She hadn't wanted any other baby at all. The way she loved Shelby had been so huge, so inadvertent. She hadn't chosen it. It was something that had happened to her, and she couldn't imagine taking that kind of risk again on purpose. If she had another, it would smell like Shelby smelled. It would make the same helpless breathy noises. Even before it was born, it would spin and kick inside her with Shelby's vigor, and Laurel would be lost to more enormous, boiling love.

As Shelby grew, changed, took her first faulty steps, Laurel sometimes imagined a brother or a sister, but then she'd see Shelby and the new baby toddling in different directions. She couldn't be right behind both of them, couldn't stretch herself thin enough to stand between them and all the ugly things on earth.

David had asked every so often, "Want to try again?"

Laurel had said, "Not yet. Not yet," every time, until he'd stopped asking.

"I thought it was brilliant," Thalia said. "We could have named the spare Puppethead. I think Puppethead would be the most awesome baby name."

"I'll pass," Laurel said. "If you wanted a kid named Puppethead, you could have married yourself a straight man and had one."

Thalia laughed. "Now, now, kitty cat, don't scratch. I only brought it up because when I looked in the backseat, I found myself thinking about that spare baby, all made of rubber, and how here, thirteen years later, damned if you didn't go to DeLop and get you one."

"Thalia!" Laurel said, more shocked than she ought to be, mostly because there was a tiny ring of truth to it. "That's hateful."

Thalia shrugged. "So, what's new. Wake me when we get to Tara." She fiddled with the buttons again, working the seat until it was as far back and low as it would go, and then she closed her eyes. Thalia slept like a soldier, in short bursts anywhere it was convenient. In two minutes, she was out.

That left Laurel to fret the wheel with her hands and try to think of exactly how she should present her lie of omission to David. She deliberately slowed, setting her cruise control lower, but it seemed like time was going by so fast that the drive became a slide show: the bridge, the state line, her exit, Victorianna's wrought-iron gate. Then Laurel was pulling in to her own driveway.

Thalia's eyes clicked open the minute the engine cut out. "We're here?" she said, sitting up straight and making a grunty noise. "Shit, look. We're here. I never sleep that hard."

"Language," Laurel said, tilting her head back to indicate Bet, who was pulling off the headphones.

"Yeah, right," Thalia said, and made the grunty noise again. "Sorry, Bet, I forgot you existed for a second." She tumbled out of the car.

Laurel and Bet got out, too, and the three of them hauled the suitcases up the front walk. Laurel unlocked the door and opened it, but then she stepped back and let Thalia and Bet go in first, cursing herself for a coward.

They trooped through the foyer, past the formal living room and dining room on into the keeping room. David was in the kitchen, loading the dishwasher. Shelby slouched at the breakfast bar, the remains of some kind of sandwich on a plate in front of her.

David's face changed as they came in, first a little flash of puzzled; then he made thinking eyebrows as he did the math. His face became unreadable as Shelby caught sight of Thalia and Bet and made the happiest noise Laurel had heard out of her in two days. She got up off the stool with something like her old Shelby bounce and hurtled into Thalia's arms. Thalia had to drop the suitcase and catch her.

"Shelbelicious," Thalia said, and put a round smacking kiss on her face.

"And Bet, too!" Shelby all but crowed, her arms still looped around Thalia's waist. She turned to Laurel and said, "How, Mommy?"

"You seemed to really want Bet here, so I decided she should finish out her visit. And I wanted Thalia here, the same way you want Bet." Laurel looked at David as she said that last part. His face was still carefully blank.

"Thalia," he said, giving her a brief nod.

"David," Thalia said, and returned the nod exactly, same degree, same angle.

"Can I see what happens to thet boy? In the movie?" Bet asked Shelby.

"Sure you can. Can we unpack for you, Aunt Thalia?"

Thalia's closet held nothing but Levi's jeans and T-shirts and stretchy unitards, but she packed for trips out of the costume room. Shelby had always loved digging through her suitcases.

"Absolutely. Help me get these bags upstairs, girls. Bet, I hope you're in the little guest room, because I am planting a flag and claiming the one with the queen-size bed for France. And I am France."

"Do what?" Bet asked.

"Yes, she's across from me," Shelby said.

They began carting bags up, but Shelby paused to look over her shoulder and mouth, "Thank you, Mom!"

Then Laurel was alone with David. They stood on opposite sides of the low counter that ran between the kitchen and the keeping room. David spoke first. "I get it," he said. "I really do."

"Please don't be mad," she said.

"I'm not mad," he said. He sounded mad.

"Do you understand why?" she said.

David played with unreal numbers, so this simple math was not a problem for him. It was obvious that she'd let Mother's assumption stand and gone to Mobile. He'd probably also gathered that she hadn't really spoken to Sissi Clemmens, because David could have outsolved Sherlock Holmes any day on questions of who and when and how. But motive was not his forte.

"You need to know why," she added.

"It doesn't matter," he said. "Really. I told you I needed her not to be here, and you got her anyway. So. It's clear that you need her here more than I need her not here."

It took Laurel a moment to sort through the grammar and see

what he meant. "Exactly," she said. "It's like when Shelby came, remember?"

Fourteen hours of hard labor with little progress, and her doctor had said it was time to think about a C-section. Laurel had sent David to the waiting room to get Thalia. He'd been so nervous that he hadn't wanted to leave, but she'd begged him. He'd come back with her sister and then stood off to one side. Laurel had held his hand, squeezing so hard she felt his bones grinding, but it was Thalia who had called her a pansy and told Laurel it was time to "man up and push." That had made Laurel so angry—being told to give birth like a man, of all things—but it had worked. She'd rallied, cursing her sister as she pushed Shelby out into the world.

"I remember," David said, and his hand flexed, an involuntary movement, like it was remembering her grip.

"Are we okay?" said Laurel.

He waved that away and said, "We're always okay. But I'm working at the office for the next— How long? Few days?"

"Maybe a few days, yeah," Laurel said.

"Because that's a lot of bags she brought."

"Thalia packs that much for an overnight," Laurel said.

"True enough. Okay. I see what happened. It's fine." Now he was saying it to himself more than to her. "I've got to get back to work. I'm supposed to meet the Richmond Games coder online for more dogfight tests."

"Okay," she said. "Go be Dave."

He walked toward the basement stairs, and his gait was stiff, as if his legs were sore.

"You are mad," she said.

"A little mad, yeah," he said, his back still to her. His voice was loud. Then he stopped and took a deep breath, and he did turn around. He spoke quietly. "But I'm right downstairs if you need me, okay?"

"Okay," she said, and she watched him walk down. His head glided lower and lower with each step he took, as if he were setting. He'd said he was close enough to call if she needed him, and it felt true, right up until the moment when she couldn't see him anymore.

CHAPTER 9

Thalia's long body was sprawled out on the hardwood floor of Laurel's dining room. She was on her back, her legs together, her back arching up as she stretched in the spill of late-morning sunshine that came in through the big bay window. It lit up her hair, two shades lighter than Laurel's. Pure corn-colored, like Mother's when she was younger. Laurel knelt near her feet, keeping watch through the sheers.

Thalia was all but naked again, this time in a Lycra sports bra with barely enough of a strap to credibly be mistaken for a shirt. She had on low-cut Lycra boy shorts, too, the kind Laurel had called "creepers" back in high school. They rode up as she moved, and showed the undercurve of her butt. She didn't have one bit of cellulite there, and her breasts looked like unripe plums, set hard and high.

"I kind of hate you," Laurel said, looking at her sister's flat abdomen.

"Yoga," said Thalia. "And clean living. See him yet?"

"Not yet."

Thalia sat up, her feet still together, and bent at the waist, stretching down to touch her toes. Her long feet flexed. "God, who runs at noon in Florida?"

"He doesn't work. I think this is first thing in the morning to him," Laurel said.

"Is Data down in the basement?"

"*David,*" Laurel said, "is working from his office today. Does it matter?"

"If Stan Webelow takes me up on my offer, we'll need a place to go," Thalia said, and showed Laurel all her teeth at once.

"Oh, gross," Laurel said, her lip curling as she got a vivid mental flash of Stan Webelow's moist golden body, slick in its running shorts. "You wouldn't."

Thalia laughed and stood up, stretching her arms high toward the ceiling. "Get a grip, Bug," she said. "If he's gay, I'll pick that up in three minutes. If he's straight, I bet I can pick *him* up in two. Either way, we can cross him off the list and look where we need to be looking. It's always the family." She finished stretching and knelt down beside Laurel. The two of them peered up over the windowsill, watching the street like crocodiles. Even through the sheers, Laurel could see low waves of heat shimmering off the asphalt.

"Barb and Chuck Dufresne seem so . . . regular," Laurel said.

Thalia snorted. "Even our family seems regular from the outside. As I remember, Chuck Dufresne is an ass. What's that he calls her? Rabbit?"

"Bunny," Laurel said.

"There you go. And she drinks like a Trojan soldier."

"Lord, she does drink," Laurel admitted. "I was always careful to be the one to drive the girls. Even in the daytime. Just to be sure. But I can't imagine they had anything to do with this."

"Then you need to work on ruling them out while I dry-hump Stanley in the road and see if anything rises—"

"Thalia!"

"Just calling a duck a duck, Jesus Bug. I bet you have funeral casseroles in the freezer, don't you? Good to go?" Thalia turned her face like a bird would, to look at Laurel out of one fierce eye, and when Laurel didn't answer, she laughed and said, "It was a sucker bet. Pull one out to thaw. We need to talk to Bunny, at the very least. Unless you're up to cat-burglaring through the Dufresnes' window in the dead of night with our eyes blacked out like quarterbacks and searching Molly's room for her Mommy-hits-me diary?"

"No. Absolutely not. Never."

Thalia had said it like she was mostly kidding, but with her sister, it was better to be clear. For that matter, Thalia hadn't definitively stated that she wasn't going to ravish Stan Webelow in the basement. Laurel made a mental note to deadbolt the door after Thalia left, just in case.

"I thought not, you pansy. That means we have to get invited in like blood-fat, darling flies, so who is Miss Spider? Who feels every little twitch in the neighborhood web?"

Laurel thought for a moment. "Trish Deerbold. But we're not friends."

"Bah, no. I don't mean which rich bitch has the gossip. I mean who's down in the trenches? Who runs bunko and calls around to coordinate the dinners whenever one of these cows drops a calf?"

"Oh," Laurel said. "Thalia, that's me."

Thalia looked at her, nonplussed, and then dropped her face into her hands. "Some days I wonder how you don't drive hard into a wall, just to make your life stop," she muttered into her palms.

Laurel, who sometimes wondered the same thing about her sister, had to bite her bottom lip hard to keep from saying so.

Thalia put her head up again and said, "Okay, if you're Kirk, who is your Spock?"

"Spiders, cows, *Star Trek.* You're exhausting me. Can't you ask plain?"

Thalia shook her head. "Sorry, Bug, but plotting requires figurative language."

"Something is bad wrong here, Thalia," Laurel said. "This isn't a game."

Thalia stilled. She kept her eyes on the road, watching for Stan Webelow, but when she spoke, her voice had gone toneless, cool as dead water. "I'm not playing. A child is going in the ground soon, and Shelby loved her. Shelby's not herself. I see it. It's like a light's gone out. If any righteous bastard helped that happen, we will find him out, and we will make him sorry."

They knelt side by side, quiet together, and Laurel believed her. She wished David would appear right at that moment. She would point to Thalia, who was watching the street as dead-eyed as a veteran sniper, and say to David, "This is why I lied to you. This is what I went to get."

Then Thalia said in her regular voice, "But we're going to treat this part like a game. We have to, or I'll get sick with mad, and you'll cry, and we'll be worthless. Don't think about the whole thing. We do this one small piece at a time, and we pretend each piece is the whole of it. Today? I'm playing snuggles with Stan

Webelow, and I'm going to win. You're on the Dufresnes. So. Name your Spock."

"Mindy Coe," Laurel said. "Next door."

"Call her and find out when the funeral is. I bet you anything it's set, if the police have released th—" She stopped speaking abruptly, and in the quiet, Laurel heard footsteps.

Shelby and Bet Clemmens came shuffling into the foyer. Shelby carried a long, thin game box. Bet loomed behind her. "Can me and Bet—" Shelby began, but then she stopped and asked, "What are you doing on the floor?"

"Stretching," said Thalia. "I'm going running. What do you need, Shel?"

"We're bored," Shelby said. "Can we play this game?"

"Sure," Laurel said. "Take it up to the rec room."

"I was talking to Aunt Thalia," Shelby said. "It's hers. We found it in her suitcase."

"Don't lose any of the pieces," Thalia said. She'd turned back around to watch the road again.

Laurel looked at the game box in Shelby's hands, then really looked at it. It was an old box, so old that the cardboard side had buckled in and she couldn't read it, but the pattern of the small writing that covered the back looked familiar.

Laurel stood up so fast her knees cracked. She walked toward Shelby until she could see the sepia box top, which was a picture of the game board. All the letters of the alphabet were in the middle in two rows, bent into a rainbow shape. The font was old-fashioned, with curls and flourishes on every letter. A pale sun guarded the word "yes" in the upper right-hand corner, while a black moon showed the word "no" its grim profile. Along the bottom, the word "goodbye" stretched itself out between two all-seeing eyes.

Laurel snatched her old Ouija board from Shelby's hands. It was the most ill-conceived Christmas present Thalia had ever given her, and that included the water bra eight years ago. "No, you are not playing with this," she said.

She'd never even played it. She'd known better, although she'd sat on her bed, her back to the wall, and watched Thalia and her friends mess around with it. The spirits Thalia drummed up were always foulmouthed and dirty-minded, and Laurel had never once wondered who was controlling the planchette. "Go play Xbox."

"We already played Xbox," Shelby said.

"Go play Xbox some more," Laurel said, staring Shelby down.

"Can we go running with Aunt Thalia?" Shelby said.

"No," Laurel said even louder. Whatever Thalia was planning to do with or to Stan Webelow, Shelby didn't need to see it.

Shelby's eyes widened. "Mom? Are you okay?"

Laurel took a deep, calming breath and stepped back, the game board clutched to her chest. "Maybe you could . . ." She stopped, horrified. She'd been about to suggest that they go lie out in the backyard by the pool, and she would come in a few minutes and watch them swim. Most of their summer days past had been spent in and around the pool. Now the curtain was drawn over the glass door in the keeping room. The whole room seemed darker; its gold and green colors, so warm in sunshine, had gone unfriendly. ". . . play Xbox?" she finally finished.

"You said that already. We're not boys, you know," Shelby said. "We're tired of Xbox. Why can't we go running with Aunt Thalia?"

"You'll get heatstroke," Laurel said. It was all she could think of.

Shelby shrugged. "Then let me have that Ouija thing."

Before Laurel could answer, Bet Clemmens said, "It's not a 'Ooh-ja,' Shelby. You say it like 'Wee-gee.' "

Shelby looked at Bet, surprised. Even Thalia turned around to look at her. Bet flushed and shifted her weight from one small foot to the other. "I know because of Della's got one," she said.

That made sense; Della was Aunt Moff's girl. Laurel turned back to Shelby and said in the softest voice that she could muster, "Why don't you change and let me take you to your dance class this afternoon? That might be good, huh? See your friends. Get some endorphins going."

All expression left Shelby's face, until it was as blank and plain as a closed door. "We'll go play stupid Xbox," she said.

She executed a smart little turn on her heel, abrupt and precise, and walked away. Bet started to follow her, then paused.

"Yes?" Laurel said to Bet, but Bet waited until Laurel could hear Shelby stamping up the stairs.

Then Bet said, "I'm not sick of Xbox." She was almost whispering. "I'm not sick of nothing here."

"That's sweet, Bet. Thank you," Laurel said, but Bet was already scurrying away. They heard her clattering up the stairs after Shelby.

"That little thing is getting all rooted in," Thalia said.

Laurel barely listened. She thrust the Ouija board at Thalia and said, "Seriously, what the hell?"

Thalia shrugged and turned back to peer out the window. "There he is," she said. She backed away from the window and stood up.

"Crap!" Laurel said, and slammed the game down on the pecan table.

Thalia was already trotting through the archway to the front door.

"I'm not done with you about this," Laurel said, following.

Thalia peered out of the peephole. "As soon as he gets past the curve, I'm going out. I'll head the other way, sprint up to the intersection, and get myself winded. Work up a good fresh sweat. Men like a good fresh sweat."

Laurel ignored that and said, "You brought that thing to get at me." She waved one hand back at the Ouija board, even though Thalia had her back turned.

"Not true," Thalia said.

"You said you'd help, but you're making fun."

"Great timing on the nervous breakdown, Jesus Bug. Really," Thalia said, finally facing Laurel. "The short version is, you sleepwalk. With your eyes open. I've seen it. I brought the board because I thought pretending to talk to one of your little mystic essencey friends would let your subconscious tell you what that shadow was you saw moving in the yard. What or who. I brought it to help, and meanwhile, your potential perv has already passed the house. You want me to go after him, or you want to stand here and fuss about the Ooh-ja?"

Laurel wavered and said, "Go."

Thalia opened the door and slipped through it. "Call Missy Coe," she said, and closed the door after herself before Laurel could get out the words "It's Mindy."

Laurel started to walk away but then reached out and twisted the deadbolt closed with a little more force than was strictly needed. She ran lightly back through the dining room to the swinging door that led into the kitchen. It opened beside the small built-in desk. She snatched the cordless phone off its charger and hurried back toward the window. The Ouija board lay where she had left it, the dark letters standing out, stark and black; the all-seeing eyes at the bottom corners seemed to be looking at her. She flipped the box over and left it where it lay. For now.

She knelt in front of the window again, down low. Thalia was already out of view; she would sprint to the corner and back. Laurel was going to call Mindy while she waited, but when she hit the on button, she heard the broken dial tone that reminded her she had messages waiting. Probably quite a few: She'd been avoiding the phone.

The automated voice-mail robot told her she had six. The first three were concerned messages from Mindy Coe and Edie and another friend from church. The next was from a reporter with the *Pensacola News Journal*. Laurel deleted it after the first sentence.

Through her wide window, she could see a long piece of her street. Thalia came into view from the right. She was moving along at a good clip.

The phone was playing the fifth message. Laurel recognized Trish Deerbold's voice saying, "Oh! Laurellll . . ." She hit delete before Trish had gotten through the long pity-filled L.

Stan Webelow appeared, running around the curve that led back past her house from Chapel Circle's cul-de-sac end.

The last message was Mindy again. Laurel listened while she watched Thalia and Stan Webelow running toward each other on a collision course, down the wide white strip of sidewalk.

"Sweetie, please call me back," Mindy was saying. "Anything I can do, you name it. I wanted to let you know that they've set

Molly's viewing. Day after tomorrow, at Fernwood, from seven to nine. They'll have the funeral there the next morning at ten."

Laurel jogged those same sidewalks three or four times a week in fall and winter. Weather like this, she used the treadmill up in the rec room. But she knew the etiquette. Stan Webelow would go onto the grass when they met. Men moved for women, always, and younger women moved onto the grass for older ones. Thalia and Stan were going to meet right in front of the house, it looked like. Both of them were sweating so hard Laurel could see their skin gleaming through the sheers.

On the phone, Mindy was still talking. Laurel had only been half listening, watching her sister jogging inexorably toward Stan Webelow, who was now lifting one hand in a polite wave as he prepped to move to the side.

But then Mindy said something so odd, it jerked Laurel's attention back.

"No one is blaming you," Mindy Coe's recorded voice said. "No one. Not even the Dufresnes. In fact, I think Bun—Barb, I mean, would especially like to have Shelby at the viewing. No one is blaming you at all, Laurel."

It hadn't occurred to her that people might be blaming her. Why would they? She hit save and looked back out at the street just as Thalia and Stan Webelow came together on the sidewalk. As expected, Stan moved onto the grass. He hadn't slowed, and neither had Thalia. Before he could pass, Thalia tangled her feet together and pitched forward and sideways, directly at him. Her hands and face smashed into his chest. Laurel found herself on her feet, before common sense told her Thalia was doing this on purpose. Stan Webelow was falling, and Thalia was falling, too, sliding down the slick length of his sweaty body.

He landed on his back in the grass, and she landed half on him, her face pressed into his belly just above the waistband of his tiny shorts. She'd caught herself with her hands—Thalia had practiced all kinds of safe falls for theater—but her elbows remained bent so that her throat and collarbone rested against his crotch. Stan Webelow froze, then scuttled backward on his feet and hands like a startled maiden crab. Thalia sat up.

Laurel found herself looking around to see if any other neighbors were watching, and when she looked back at the two of them, she was surprised to see Stan doing exactly what she had done: darting his head around, looking to see if anyone had seen them. It struck Laurel as an odd reaction; she was looking around because she knew Thalia had done it on purpose. But why was he? Then he spotted her and boggled at her, while Thalia stood up and leaned down, offering him a hand.

"Crap!" Laurel said, and dropped the phone.

It went clattering to the floor. She dove after it, getting her head below the sill on all fours, feeling ridiculous, a poor man's secret squirrel. Stan had already seen her.

"You fixing to run, too?" Bet Clemmens said behind her, and Laurel screamed. She scrambled sideways, out of the window, and didn't get up until she was safely through the archway that led to the foyer.

She got to her feet and turned around to look at Bet, who had come through the swinging door from the kitchen in her sock feet. Now Bet scooted silently forward across the hardwood, heading toward the window.

"Come here," Laurel said, her voice urgent.

"You was stretching?" Bet said, looking doubtfully at Laurel's linen slacks and sandals.

"Come on, over here," Laurel said.

Bet took one more dubious glance out the window and then joined Laurel in the foyer, saying, "Shelby sent me to come ast, could we have Cokes?"

"Yes," Laurel said, her mind racing. What would a person who had witnessed the fall be doing? A person who happened to see it, not one who was spying?

"That's him in the yard, huh?" Bet asked, her eyes dark and serious. "That one what had Molly in his house?"

Laurel blinked so long it was more like closing her eyes. The person, she concluded, would be going outside to check on the sister she'd seen take a tumble.

"Don't say anything about this, okay? Not to Shelby," Laurel said. "Not to anyone."

"Okay," Bet said, and shrugged.

"Go get Cokes," Laurel said, shooing at Bet, and then opened the front door and stepped out onto the porch.

Thalia and Stan Webelow were standing on the grass, talking. Thalia was too close, easing her hips forward, well inside his personal space.

"Are you okay?" Laurel called, and Stan and Thalia both turned toward her. Laurel saw a flash of exasperation on Thalia's face before she smoothed it away. Stan Webelow was red-faced, but that may have been only the heat. The moment he saw Laurel, he began jogging in place.

"We're fine! Mostly," he called. "Can you come give your sister a hand? I think she's hurt her ankle. I'd help her, but here you are, and my heart rate is dropping . . ." He smiled the even white smile that Edie thought was so damn charming, and Laurel had to force her curling lips into a return smile.

She walked across the lawn toward Thalia as Stan Webelow got back on the sidewalk and took off like a rabbit down Chapel Circle.

"Dumbass!" Thalia mouthed at her.

Laurel pulled Thalia's arm around her and walked toward the house. "He saw me at the window," she whispered. "It would have looked weird if I hadn't come out."

"Shit. We're nowhere," Thalia said. Together they began crossing the yard slowly, Thalia pretending to limp in case Stan Webelow looked back. "I didn't have enough time. A gay guy probably would have found it funny, me face-planting practically in his crotch, but he was all weird and guilty. More like a married man, but . . . he's not. It was truly odd. Those are some shorts, though, huh? Satin piping."

"Now what?" Laurel said.

Thalia shook her head. "I was hoping to rule him out today, but all I can tell you is that I don't think he's gay. Gary would know better. You want me to call him over and let him take a whack at it? So to speak?"

"God, no," Laurel said, aghast.

Thalia grinned. "I don't think Gary wants to do you a solid anyway, Bug."

They had reached the porch. Thalia tried to move past Laurel, but Laurel stopped her. "Stay out here a sec. Bet Clemmens is skating around the hardwood spooky-quiet with her shoes off."

Thalia nodded, stopping by the steps. She dropped her arm off Laurel's shoulder and took a step back. "Did you call your friend?" she asked, and when Laurel nodded, she asked, "So are you allowed to come to the funeral?"

"Of course," Laurel said. "Mindy was saying she thinks it's

important to Bunny that Shelby go, although I'm not sure how I feel about that. Then Mindy said the strangest thing. She said no one was blaming me."

"Shit," said Thalia, and she sat down hard on the porch steps, her long arms dangling between her legs. Laurel sat, too, one step lower than Thalia.

"That means something to you?" Laurel asked.

"Yeah," Thalia said. "Their kid is dead, Bug, and unless they know damn well it's their own fault, they are going to blame someone. You're a good target. It was your pool. They ought to be saying to themselves, why didn't that bitch wake up, how could she not know this was happening in your own yard?

"If Bunny isn't pointing a finger at you, we need to find out which way she's pointing. If she's not pointing anywhere, she's guilty as all hell. Her or Chuck. I was hoping to rule out either your pervo or the family today, but I've got dick, and I don't just mean sticking my face in your creepy neighbor's limpy. We'll have to get to Bunny tomorrow." Thalia paused and then added, "As for tonight, there's always the mysteries of the Ouija."

She said it correctly this time, so it sounded like "Wee-juh."

Laurel looked away, her insides cooling, her blood slowing, though it had to be over ninety on the porch. She didn't believe in submerged memories any more than Thalia believed in ghosts, but Molly Dufresne had already come to Laurel once, uncalled. She wanted to be heard. If Laurel's moving shadow had been Stan Webelow, this was one way to confirm it.

"We could try," Laurel said, and her stomach felt like a small, cold stone, dense and heavy at the very pit of her. "Tonight, after dinner, after everyone else has gone to bed. We could try."

"There's my brave little testicle," Thalia said, and Laurel

turned and knuckle-punched her in the arm, fast and hard, before she could think.

Thalia chuckled. "Ow! That's quite a right, Buglet."

Laurel wasn't laughing. She felt sick and trembly and had to fight the urge to hit Thalia again on pure principle. Thalia was right; they might get answers. But Laurel had spent the second half of her childhood rolling away when Marty came, closing her eyes, wiping his footprints from her rug.

Given a tool, Molly might speak. But Molly had left a door open somewhere when she came, and Mother had used it. Molly Dufresne was not the only ghost in Laurel's yard.

CHAPTER 10

It was going on eleven when Thalia slipped back into the keeping room through the glass door.

"We're set up out there. Those candles stink," she said.

"They keep the bugs away," Laurel said from the kitchen. "Anyhow, I like how they smell." She wiped her damp hands on the dish towel. The kitchen was clean, the dishes were loaded, and the girls had gone to bed. Shelby had asked to sleep on the trundle bed again, so they might well be awake, whispering back and forth. Laurel hoped so. Better if Shelby talked to someone, even if it was only Bet Clemmens. She was certainly not talking to Laurel. She'd hardly spoken at dinner. "Maybe we should wait. Give the girls time to fall asleep."

Thalia stared right through Laurel in a way that let Laurel know she saw all the way down to the cowardice at her roots. "Shelby's in the guest room. That window faces the front yard."

Laurel nodded, squaring her shoulders. "I saved one of the brownies out for David." The rest were packed into a Tupperware for the Dufresnes. She peeled the Saran off the dessert plate. "Let me run this down to him, and I'm ready." Ready as she would ever be. Though she'd just wiped her hands, her palms felt damp again.

"David's home?" Thalia said. "When did that happen?"

Laurel raised her eyebrows. "A couple of hours ago. While I was making the brownies? You were reading on the sofa. He came through the room and said hello to you."

Thalia shook her head slowly back and forth and said, "Are you sure?"

"Yes," Laurel said. "I'm positive. He's been working in the basement. I took him his dinner down there."

"The invisible husband," Thalia said.

Laurel cocked her head to the side and said, "You don't get it. He's being nice, Thalia. He's got a deadline at work, and the last thing he needs is more stress, but I went and got you anyway. He's making room and not fighting with you. It's like a present he's giving me."

"Big man, eh?" Thalia said. She cocked her head, too, same angle, mirroring Laurel. "Give me that brownie."

"No," Laurel said. She was already walking toward the stairs down to the basement, but Thalia intercepted her, gripping the other side of the plate. Laurel didn't let go of her side.

"I can be a big man and give you a present, too." Thalia tugged gently at the plate, and when Laurel still held on, she stopped tugging and spoke in a voice so subdued she hardly sounded like herself. "I've missed you, Bug. Let me make peace."

Laurel let go, but as Thalia started down the stairs, Laurel couldn't help calling after her, "Please be nice."

Thalia paused on the top step and said, "I'll be fluffy as a bunny tail, sweet as cotton candy. Head on out. I won't be a minute."

She went down with the brownie held in front of her in both hands, as if it were a shield or a sacrifice.

Thalia had said to go on out, but Laurel didn't want to. Not alone. She crossed the room, intending to close the curtain and wait, but paused with her hand on the cloth, peering out at her yard. She hadn't set foot in it since the police had escorted her whole family over to the Coes' house. She hadn't looked at it, even, since she'd stood by Daddy, staring at that knothole.

The patio lights were turned off, and the bulb was still out in the light over the gazebo, but Thalia had lit all the citronella candles around its railing. She'd set up the card table in the gazebo, too. It had been Laurel's idea to do this outside. Out there, it already felt like something gone rotten, and she didn't want to invite that rot into the house. But she'd meant the patio, not way out in the corner between the knothole and Shelby's small pet cemetery. The gazebo glowed in the candlelight, and she could feel the presence of the board there like a pull.

She slid open the glass door and stepped out as gingerly as a cat, as if she weren't sure that the tile was solid and would hold her. She could feel a wedge of sweltering Florida air shoving its way through the open door into her keeping room. She closed the door behind her.

The opening in the curtain let a narrow rectangle of yellow light spill onto her patio. The pool lights were out, all of them, but as her eyes adjusted, she could see a faint pale mist rising off the water.

She wrapped her arms around herself, tight, hands clasping her own shoulders. The night air was thick with heat and moisture, but her skin felt clammy, and gooseflesh broke out down the backs of her arms.

She stepped over the low fence, Shelby's dammit, onto the grass. The board waited for her under the gazebo, and she walked toward it as if she had been beckoned. She could smell chlorine and, under that, the musk of Florida in late summer. It was a green and mossy smell, faint and familiar. The cicadas and frogs and crickets were all talking to one another, a night sound that was such a constant that from inside the house, it was white noise, like the hum of the air conditioner. Out here in the dark, it sounded louder, a buzzing chorus underscoring a larger silence. There were no human noises except her own: her feet bending the grass, the thump of her heart, her own hard breathing.

She skirted the pool's high iron fence. The flickering candles perched on the gazebo's rail made an evenly spaced circle of light. With the card table set up on the wood floor, there was just enough room for Laurel to sit down on the bench and then slide past the corner of the table until she was sitting, her feet under the table, staring down at the Ouija. The planchette rested near the bottom, the dangling needle pointing at the B in "goodbye."

Thalia had given her the board back when they were in high school. Laurel had never set it up, never once touched the planchette. She reached out with one hand, her fingertips hovering, and then she set them on the edge of the thing. The plastic felt cool under her fingertips. She felt a tug of energy from it, as if it were drawing heat out of her, an electric current running from her core down into the board. It was an open circuit, and she felt instinctively that another hand on the other side of the planchette would close it. Even incomplete, the energy it took from her was gathering, shaping itself. Something was coming. Or someone.

She didn't know who. She snatched her hand back, then tucked both hands under the table, clenched together in her lap. "This is a bad idea," she said.

Thalia wasn't there to hear, but Laurel could not shake the sense that she was not alone. She started to stand, but light flashed in the corner of her eye. She looked back toward the house. Thalia had thrown the curtain half open and then shoved at the door, sending it shooting down its track. She stepped through and reached for the curtain. She paused there, her long form a silhouette against the gold light, and then she pulled the curtain closed with elaborate gentleness and the light was gone, rendering her invisible. Laurel searched the darkness, but her eyes had to readjust before she could see Thalia prowling across the lawn toward her.

Thalia scooted past the table corner, sitting down and sliding along the gazebo's built-in bench until she was directly across from Laurel. She smiled then, but it was her too-big, wolfy smile. Laurel could see all her teeth gleaming in the candlelight.

"Your husband is kind of an asshat," Thalia said softly, and plopped one hand on the closest side of the planchette. "Grab the other half, and let's get going."

"What happened to bunny tails and being fluffy?" Laurel asked. She kept her hands tucked under the table, even though the energy she'd felt a moment ago was gone, eclipsed by Thalia's crackling anger. "Please tell me you didn't go down there and pick a fight."

"I didn't pick anything. He didn't even notice I'd come down." Thalia took her hand off the planchette, too, and stared down at it, as if she expected the intensity of her gaze alone to move it.

"If he had his headset on, he probably couldn't hear you. He listens to music really loud, or he gets in this TeamSpeak thing where there are other people talking," Laurel said in a propitiating tone. Thalia could stomach anything but being ignored.

"Can I ask you something?" Thalia said, but she didn't wait for permission. "Hypothetically, what would it take for you to leave him?"

"Please don't let's have this conversation again." The night outside the pale flickering ring of light was pressing in on them. Laurel could feel it, so warm and dense with moisture that it was like they were sitting inside the hot breath of something awful. "Not out here, Thalia."

"But if he hit you, say," Thalia insisted. "Or got addicted to heroin. Or cheated on you, or—"

"Those things won't happen," said Laurel.

"Hypothetically," Thalia said, and ignored Laurel's exasperated sigh. "What if he had some redheaded slutty thing down in your basement right now, making the beast with two backs. Say I told you, and you went down and saw it with your own eyes. Then would you leave him?"

Laurel felt a headache starting low at the base of her skull, a tingling as if the buzz of cicadas were gathering there. "I wouldn't even go look. There is no redhead in our basement. There never will be," she said. "Thalia, we're happy."

Thalia snorted and then said, "So *this* is what happy looks like. I'd always wondered."

The buzzing at the back of Laurel's head got louder. "I'm not happy today. Obviously," she said. "This is the worst week of my life, and that's another great reason to skip this conversation."

"You don't even know what happy means," Thalia said. She scooted back, pressing her spine against the railing, and then drew her legs up, knees to chest, careful not to bang the table.

She boosted herself up to rest her skinny bottom between two candles on the railing. All the light was below her, hollowing her eyes as she looked down at Laurel. Her voice was matter-of-fact, a cool thing in all the heat. "This is a low point, and you came to get me because you had no idea how to handle it. You don't have lows, or highs, either. You sleepwalk straight through the middle of things, mucking around with secret pockets. You make art for rich, spoiled people who love to button their own ugly parts shut, and here's a blanket they can put over their sofa to mirror their protected lives. You could be one hell of an artist, Laurel. The way you understand color and the shapes of things, and God knows, you'd have a lot to say if you let yourself. But instead, you play with lift-the-flaps and macaroni, safe and tidy. You stay in half a marriage with a human-robot hybrid who does not love you. With just the one kid, so you never have to look away and let her take a single unsupervised breath."

Laurel squeezed her eyes shut, pressing the pads of her fingers tight against her lids, and said, "I'm not having this fight right now. You don't have a real marriage, Thalia. You don't have a kid. So don't give me advice on mine." She rubbed her hand along the base of her skull, opening her eyes so she could look up at her sister.

Thalia leaned forward, looming over her. "Because I chose theater. I chose it wholly and fully, and I'm happy in a way you'll never be."

"Highs and lows," Laurel said.

Thalia nodded, a vigorous jerk of her head, up and then down.

"I get it," Laurel said, and she did. Thalia churned up the waters around her; she'd walk into a potluck and know within ten minutes who was sleeping with whom and who was thinking about it, who was nursing secret grudges, where the female rivalries were. Laurel thought a potluck was good if someone brought twice-baked potatoes, but that was never enough for Thalia. She'd put a word here, a whisper there, and in minutes a friendly dinner was vicious chaos and civil war. Then she'd get a cocktail and a good seat and watch it all play out. "You don't know how to have things that aren't highs or lows. Anything regular and nice, you know you'll never have it, so you have to wreck it."

"This is not about me," Thalia said. She sounded angry. She flung one leg over the railing, then the other, and dropped to the ground outside the gazebo, standing up on the edge of the ring of light.

Laurel actually laughed, feeling a small surge of ugly triumph. "It's always about you, Thalia. You're mad because I'm right, and you don't like to be seen through."

"You're full of shit," Thalia said. "This is about you, holing up with David and your pretty accident—which, okay, you made the right choice there. Shelby's amazing, but you're trying to squash her into your half-life, and she's like me, Laurel. She's not scared. Shelby wants to live big. You have her wrapped up tight, tucked away in that private school. You screen her friends and choose all her activities. She's never seen DeLop, even though she's begged to go, because you won't put something that real in front of her. Why not go ahead and poke her eyes out? Blind her. Save yourself some trouble."

Thalia was pacing around the gazebo where Laurel still sat, circling it like a predator, moving along the edge of the light. "Shelby wants to see ugly. She wants to see ugly and see truly, truly beautiful, both. You may be some flaccid version of happy in all this muffled gray, but your daughter wants bright colors and then midnight, and you want to know what I think? What I really think?"

"No," said Laurel, but Thalia bulled forward, circling behind Laurel, becoming part of the buzz at the base of her skull.

"I'm checking in to Stan Webelow on the off chance he's depraved. If he is, I'll dearly enjoy flaying the skin right off him and showing the world his ugly insides. I'll check Chuck 'n' Bunny, too, in case they did something to send that girl running off into the night. But you know what I think happened? I think that Shelby and Molly were planning to run away—"

Laurel cut in, "That's ridiculous."

Thalia didn't even pause, at last moving out from behind Laurel, coming around to face her again. "I think Shelby feels crushed and watched and stifled, so they were meeting up in the yard to hit the road. But Shelby fell asleep and didn't show. Shelby's blaming herself, because if she had come, she and Molly would be famous actresses or hookers in New York by now, or more likely, down at the bluffs in a tent, sharing a single stolen beer, because at their age, running away is a half-assed thing, a call for attention, a 'Hey! Look, Mom! I can't breathe under your big, fat thumb and—' "

"Shut up."

Laurel almost screamed it, so loud that Thalia obeyed, her eyes widening in surprise. The closest crickets and frogs obeyed, too, and the night went still.

"I'm sorry, Bug," Thalia said. Her voice had lost all its fierce intensity. She came back to the gazebo's opening and slid herself in behind the table again. "But that's what I think. You need to ask Shelby. Directly. You say she's not talking, but you aren't asking. You don't really want to know that the most likely cause of Shelby's silence is guilt. Because she meant to run away from you, with Molly, and it all went bad."

"Shut up," Laurel said again, but her voice was small and lost, and she heard no conviction in it.

"You know I could well be right," Thalia said. "But I do apologize. I didn't mean to slap your face with it in a middle of a fight about C-3PO down there."

Laurel half laughed, an odd, sad little bark of a sound. "You meant to say these awful, awful things in a nice way. I get it."

"I didn't mean to say them at all. I thought I'd let *you* tell you," Thalia said. She tilted her head down toward the board, then lined her fingers up on one side of the planchette. "With this."

Laurel took one hand out of her lap and set her fingers up in a row of four on the other side. The planchette was dead plastic now. The only energy she felt coming through it was Thalia's.

"You think you're haunted, Laurel?" Thalia asked. "The only ghost in this yard is the ghost of my sister. I packed the board, hoping that it would let me talk to you. I thought you would move it and tell yourself these things. But David pissed me off, and I said them myself. Oops. It's not too late. You should try it. Ask yourself the hard questions, not just about Shelby. Ask the board. Is Laurel happy?"

The planchette jerked, carrying Laurel's hand with it, moving swiftly and decisively to the black "No" in the corner.

"That was you," Laurel said, tired and scared and irked all at the same time.

"Maybe," Thalia said. She tried out her most engaging smile on Laurel. "But maybe that was your spirit horse guide. Or maybe it was you, trying to tell yourself a truth you already know but can't admit."

"Every time I've seen that planchette move, it was you, Thalia," Laurel said. "What really happened in my basement?"

"David was making the big sex with a redhead?" Thalia gave Laurel a long assessing gaze and then said, her voice quieter now, "Nothing happened. That's just it. Nothing ever happens here. He didn't say one word to me. Like you for the last two years. Don't tell me that's not because of him."

"It couldn't be because of you, right?" Laurel said. She wanted to say more, but the heat was leaking out of her. She didn't have the time or energy to settle thirteen-year-old arguments, not when Shelby's safety was at stake. "I'll talk to Shel, okay? I will. But not tomorrow. Let's check these other things. To be sure. Stan Webelow and Bunny. If they didn't do anything, then I'll ask Shelby, like you said."

Thalia nodded, but Laurel wasn't done yet. "You can't see into my marriage, Thalia. It's closed to you. Stop knocking, even." They each still had a hand resting on the dead plastic of the planchette. "Are we done?"

Thalia pulled her hand away. "I am. I'm going to bed."

She scooted out from behind the table and walked out of the small ring of candlelight. The dark yard swallowed her. Just over the fence, in Mindy Coe's yard, Laurel heard a clatter and a muffled curse. It sounded like Mindy's son, Jeffrey, had stumbled into a piece of lawn furniture. A few seconds later, she heard the splash as he dove into his pool. The sounds of normalcy were right next door, but the wooden fence between that life and her own felt miles thick and unfathomably high.

The crickets had started up again without Laurel noticing; the night buzz was back in full force. Gold light spilled from the house as Thalia slipped inside, then it vanished as she closed the door behind her. Thalia was gone, Jeffrey was underwater, and the rest of the neighborhood was sleeping, but Laurel sensed that she was not alone.

She could feel the beginnings of that tug of energy again. Her fingers still rested on the planchette, and it was drawing something from her.

She knew how the game worked. She had seen Thalia play it with her friends. She should ask a question. Back in high school, Thalia's friends had asked which boys liked them and who was a slut and who was still a virgin. The spirits always knew because Thalia knew, and Thalia ran the board.

But Thalia wasn't here now.

Laurel pulled the planchette back to the middle, resting it in the plain space under the curved alphabet. She took a deep breath, and then she set her other hand on the opposite side.

She felt the connection close, like something clicking shut. The planchette came alive under her hands, waiting, but she didn't know what to ask. She was too tired to formulate a proper question.

Finally, she said quietly, "That night when you died, Molly—I hope to God this is you. Tell me what I need to know about that night. Tell me what I need to know to protect Shelby."

The planchette was moving before she'd said the last word. She wasn't moving it. Her fingers rested lightly on it, and the felted pads of its feet skated over the board so quickly that she had to hurry to keep her hands from slipping off.

Six times it moved, to six letters, and then Laurel jerked away her hands.

"That's not true," she said.

The board sat dumb, the planchette dead again. She scooted out from behind the table and stood, then picked up the planchette. She dropped it onto the gazebo's single wooden step, and then she stamped on it. Four times she brought her foot down, until the base was in shards, the needle lost, and the lens had skittered off into the grass. She picked up the board and methodically snapped it in half over her knee. She threw the pieces in the yard and then walked around the gazebo once, blowing out the candles. The ring of light got smaller and smaller, until she was almost in total darkness. The last candle she kept, picking it up by the cool bottom of its pottery base. She used it to light her way back to the house.

She would believe what Thalia had said before she believed what the planchette had spelled. It wasn't possible or true, and she would never think on it again.

Six letters. She would go upstairs and lie down and close her eyes, and sleep would wipe them from her mind. She would wake up tomorrow innocent of them, unknowing. She could do that. God knew she'd seen Mother do it often enough.

She had asked what she needed to know about that night, to protect Shelby. She meant from Stan Webelow, or from an ugly truth about Bunny, or from Thalia, or even from herself. But this was closer to what that hateful detective had been angling after, pestering at Shelby. It could not be.

Shelby had not been the moving shadow. Shelby had not been out in the night with Molly when she died. Laurel would not let it be so, and she would not ever again think on or remember those six small letters that the planchette had given her. *What do I need to know to protect Shelby?* she had asked.

The planchette had spelled two words for her:

She saw.

CHAPTER 11

Morning pressed against her closed eyelids, but even with her eyes shut, she could feel the absence of David. He must have already fled the Thalia-infested house for his office, but she wasn't alone in her bed. A slight weight dented the mattress, and she smelled her sister's gingery shampoo.

"Are you awake, Miss Possum?" Thalia asked.

"No," Laurel answered, her voice grainy with sleep.

She cracked an eye and looked at the bedside clock. It was past ten-thirty. Not surprising. Last night she'd crept in beside David's sleeping body and stared at the ceiling until the crickets had packed it in for the night. Still her eyes hadn't closed, and after an airless silence, she'd heard the first cheerful twitters of the morning birds. She'd watched the way sunrise shifted the shadows in the room, trying to Cowslip the entire night away, but those two words lingered in her head like small obscenities.

She saw.

If they were true, if Shelby had seen, she would have yelled the house down. She would have waded in and pulled Molly out herself. How could Shelby see Molly in the pool, dead or dying, and slip back inside? Laurel could not fathom Shelby resetting the house alarm, cool as a reptile, then hiding herself in the long curtain or behind the low counter in the kitchen when Laurel had come screaming past. Not possible. So why couldn't she forget those words?

"Where's Shelby?" she asked.

"Off with Bet Clemmens," Thalia said, sounding smug about it.

The depth of Laurel's immediate relief shamed her. She rolled to face her sister, turning in place because there wasn't much bed left that Thalia hadn't draped a long, skinny limb across.

"What do you mean, off with Bet? The park?"

"Bug, I'm a genius," Thalia said. The smugness was growing. "An evil genius? Perhaps. But we can't choose our gifts. Did someone have a lunch date with Mother today?"

"Oh, crap," Laurel said, her hand automatically reaching up to smooth her hair. "I can't manage it."

"You don't have to. I told her you were sleeping the sleep of the mentally deficient. Or maybe I said 'the emotionally devastated.' No matter. I asked her if she and Daddy wouldn't be so sweet as to take the girls to the mall, maybe go to Wendy's for one of those delightful Asian salads; perhaps they might even spend the night. She was all over it, so I pressed a warm credit card—one of yours, by the way—into her hand and packed them off. Now I can vivisect the Bunny at my leisure."

"You *are* an evil genius," Laurel said in shocked admiration.

She'd meant to aim Thalia back at Stan Webelow today; if Stan were to blame, they could leave Molly's damaged family alone. But now she was willing to give Thalia her head and let her unleash any kind of hell she chose. Laurel would tear Bunny open herself, right down the middle, and go digging in her insides, if that was what it took. She had a day's reprieve, one day, to find out where blame should fall. The Dufresnes or Stan Webelow, she didn't care, as long as the truth they uncovered wiped away those little words. When Shelby came home in the morning, Laurel didn't want to look at her girl the way Detective Moreno had, didn't want to pry at her, seeking Thalia's theoretical unhappiness, or worse, a monstrous coldness at her center.

She spoke again to make herself stop thinking. "Lordy, Thalia, Mother didn't even know Bet was still here."

"I know," Thalia said. She threw her hands over her head and arched her back, stretching herself like a long, lolling cat. "Shelby came in trailing Bet Clemmens like a pull toy. Mother positively gaped. It was as if I'd poured sour milk into her Froot Loops. Then she forced this ghastly, gracious smile. I knew she was about to pick up her spoon and choke down every freakin' fruity, curdled bite.

"You know the weirdest thing? Beyond weird, but this is Mother. When she said she'd take the girls, I think she meant Shelby and Molly. She's already managed to forget the kid died."

Some of Thalia's hair was draped across the pillow, tickling Laurel's nose. She pushed it away. "You know we'll both pay later."

"Oh, yeah," Thalia said, laughing. "Mother only lets DeLop exist at Christmas, and now I've walked her through a big steaming pile of it and sent her off with it stuck to her shoes."

Laurel sat up and swung her legs down off the bed. "So we're going to see Bunny today? At her house?"

Thalia didn't answer immediately, and the pause stretched out so long that Laurel stood up and turned around, looking directly down at her sister. "Thalia?"

Thalia closed her eyes and took a deep breath in through her nose. "Why does your bedspread smell like lavender?" she asked.

"I put sachet in the batting. Quit smelling my bed and tell me what the plan is."

"I'm the plan, Suzy Homemaker," Thalia said.

"I don't know what that means." Laurel's eyes narrowed. "That's my new blouse. Three suitcases, and you're wearing my new blouse?"

"It's a Bunny costume," Thalia said. "With this blouse and your casserole and brownies for props, I bet I can get invited down the rabbit hole."

"You mean *we* can get invited," Laurel said. "*We,* Thalia."

Thalia sat up, too, the laziness dropping out of her body. She was suddenly all business. "Not to regress to junior high, Buglet, but may I remind you that Bunny likes me best?"

That was true. Thalia had always been a big hit in Victorianna, mostly because Laurel had asked her to be.

When she and David had first moved in, the homeowners' association had assigned Trish Deerbold and Mindy Coe to stop by with the traditional muffin basket. Laurel, freshly married, hadn't started dressing David. It hadn't yet occurred to her that he wouldn't mind or even notice if she threw out most of his clothes and replaced them. That day he'd been wearing the big black shiny clodhoppers that Laurel called his grampa shoes and a frayed pair of khaki high-waters he'd probably had since high school. His hair had stood up in wild tufts. He'd wanted to carry in his computer equipment himself, but the movers wouldn't let him on the truck. Something about insurance. He'd practically yanked himself baldheaded, watching them unload his components. The moment one of his boxes had cleared the ramp, he'd made the movers hand it over until he had them all piled up on the driveway. When Trish and Mindy had arrived, he'd been toting them down to his basement lair one by one. Laurel, nervous and slightly queasy, had to physically step in his path to get him to stop long enough to say hello. He'd hardly spoken three words, but it had been enough for them to hear New Jersey in his accent. Then he'd gone back to muttering and dragging boxes.

Laurel, pregnant, tired from the long move, had meant to say, "Those are for his job. He wants to move them himself," but she'd accidentally said "hisself," like Daddy did. She'd blushed and corrected herself.

Mindy had put a friendly hand on her arm. "Pregnancy brain! I remember those days. How far along are you?"

Trish Deerbold had leaned all her weight onto one hip and eased herself back a step, as if bad grammar might be catching. She couldn't get away fast enough to tell her friends about the new neighbors, the Autistic Yankee and his wife, Illiterate Trash.

After, Laurel had been rolling the word "bitch" around in her mouth, readying to release it the moment Trish Deerbold was out of earshot.

David had spoken first, saying, "Nice neighbors. Do all the muffins have nuts?" with no irony.

So she'd swallowed it and then ended up crying, only for a minute, that night on the phone with her sister. Thalia, who already had plans to come over and see the new house, immediately wanted to escalate. "I'll black out one of my front teeth and put up pigtails. I can mow your lawn in Daisy Dukes and high-heeled sandals. We'll see how Trish the Dish likes that," she'd said.

Laurel had scrubbed at her eyes with her free hand and made a noise halfway between a sob and a giggle. "I almost wish you would. But don't. I think that other woman could become a real friend, and she's right next door. Try to blend, okay? You can make people like you when you try."

"Do you want me to make them like me? Or do you want to make me like them?" Thalia had asked, edgy, but Laurel had been too pregnant and too weepy to suss out double meanings and snipe back. She'd sniffled into the phone, and Thalia had at last said, "You win, Pitiful Pig, but only because you're breeding. I'll blend."

Being Thalia, she'd perversely set out to dazzle the very woman who'd been unkind to Laurel. She'd gone to neighborhood bunko costumed in elegant sandals and a clingy knit dress that made her look like a length of dark ribbon. She'd stationed herself by Trish Deerbold's elbow and tossed off sotto voce one-liners about every other woman in the room, cruel but accurate and blackly funny. Trish Deerbold and her coven had eaten Thalia up with spoons. Watching Thalia shine them on was like seeing a devious peacock peck and coo its way into the center of a smug flock of fat-breasted pigeons.

Barb Dufresne wasn't part of what Thalia had dubbed the "Deerbold Bitch Triumvirate." Barb wasn't close to anyone, as far as Laurel knew, not unusual for a closet drinker. At neighborhood socials, Barb tended to take her cues from Trish's set, orbiting them without ever truly being part of them, so she had eaten Thalia up with a spoon, too.

Now Laurel said, "Maybe she used to like you best, Thalia, but she hasn't seen you in a couple of years."

Thalia shook her head and said, "Do I think she's going to take your chicken divan like a ticket and bare her scary soul for me to oogle? Probably not. But if you're along, she'll take the food, say thank you, and close the door. It will be yesterday all over again: Stan Webelow, the remix. This is my kind of thing, Bug, and no offense, but you suck at intrigue. Apparently, you didn't spend a lick of time canoodling with the Ooh-ja, or you'd be too busy putting a divorce lawyer on retainer to get in my way. But if you didn't learn a damn thing last night, learn it this morning. Go make PTA flyers or a pie, and let me handle this."

"Don't start with the David stuff again," Laurel said. "That's not going to distract me, and you are not going to see Barb without me. Period."

Thalia got up on Laurel's side, rising in front of her. She had over three inches on Laurel, but Laurel held her ground until Thalia said, "Fine. But I can't wing it with you along. Get dressed, nice, and then you can take me out and feed me Mother's rightful lunch. I'm picking the place. We'll eat too many shrimps in butter sauce and plot it out. Every single word you say to Barb, I'll script in advance. Got it?"

"Yes, ma'am," Laurel said.

"But I'll make a bet with you, Buglet. In the end, I'll go see Bunny on my own. You won't even try to stop me."

She was still trying to stare Laurel down, but Laurel didn't even quiver.

"Now you're taking the sucker bet," Laurel said. The words were back in her head again. *She saw.* Laurel was ruthless in the wake of them. "Maybe you don't know everything I know."

Thalia's mouth turned down, and she said, "You are brave, little tin soldier. But you may not know everything I know, either." She sounded faintly sorrowful, but then she seemed to shrug it off. When next she spoke, she was all business. "Get dressed. We leave in thirty minutes."

Laurel took a shower so hasty it was more like a rinse, and scrambled into a sherbet-colored sundress with darker orange tulips cascading down the skirt. She threw on makeup while Thalia stood outside the bathroom door, pecking at it with her nails and alternately calling out "Bored!" and "Hungry!"

"That's not actually helping me go faster," Laurel yelled back.

By the time she came downstairs, Thalia had hooked Laurel's spare keys out of the phone-desk drawer, and she led the way to Laurel's Volvo and climbed in on the driver's side without asking. Laurel had no idea where they were going, so she got in the other side and buckled up.

Thalia turned left out of the neighborhood, driving down past the bluffs. "You're awfully quiet, Bug," she said.

"And you're heartless. You rushed me out so fast I didn't even get coffee," Laurel answered.

She didn't feel like talking. She didn't feel like lunch, either. She wanted only to make a plan and then execute it. Time was moving forward. Shelby would be home in the morning.

Thalia, for a wonder, actually let it go. She drove in silence until she pulled in to the parking lot of a place called Scampi's. It was new, and Laurel hadn't eaten there yet. It was housed inside a beige stucco building with a blue awning and a bulging dome for a roof. It looked like a Middle Eastern temple and seemed out of place on the edge of downtown Pensacola.

Laurel reached for the door handle, but Thalia put a hand on her leg, stopping her. Thalia looked strange, for Thalia. She had an expression on her face that Laurel didn't recognize, her lips thinning and pressing slightly together, as if she were summing Laurel up.

Thalia said, "I'm not heartless."

Laurel smiled and said, "I only meant I need caffeine."

"Let's skip this," Thalia said. "I'll drop you home and go see Barb myself."

"Go to hell, Thalia," Laurel said, her tone mild. "Coffee. Shrimps. Plotting. Barb. In that order."

She got out of the car and walked across the lot, not bothering to see if Thalia was following. By the time she reached the front door, Thalia was beside her. The odd expression was gone, and Thalia opened the door for her with a flourish and a half-bow.

Inside, there was a modern bar off to their right, and ahead, an older woman with a sleek bun stood at a hostess stand. Laurel hardly glanced at them. She was staring up at the dome. The whole ceiling was a mosaic of the ocean floor, with shells and starfish and red crabs scuttling. Mermaids lounged down low, near the walls, and Triton himself coiled on a sea serpent's tail in the center. On the deep blue walls, bright fish swam, shimmering and quick-looking. Laurel's feet were planted on a sky-blue floor.

"Holy cats," she whispered to Thalia.

The hostess was asking Thalia for the name on the reservation, but Thalia said to her, "Oh, I see the rest of our party." She took Laurel's elbow and marched her past the stand.

Laurel, still looking up at the ceiling, let herself be led, but then she stopped and said, "What rest of our party?"

Thalia said, "I'm sorry, Bug." She sounded like she meant it. She tilted her head, indicating the diners.

"You didn't," Laurel said, all at once sure that Thalia had called Mother. Somehow, Thalia had read the Ouija's small and ugly words out of Laurel's mind, and she'd made Mother bring Shelby here for crab legs and interrogation.

The restaurant had two levels, with a circle of sky-blue stairs leading down to a round dining area directly under the dome. Upstairs, businesspeople lined the walls, a blurry border of black and gray and navy, the men in ties, the women in sensibly chic pumps. Laurel dismissed them and searched the lower circle. It was filled with women sitting in brightly colored pairs and trios and whole gaggles, chatting and drinking chardonnay or Pellegrino. Laurel looked from table to table, seeking Mother's fluffy topknot, Shelby's bright braids. "I don't see them," she said.

She realized she was gripping Thalia's arm hard. Too hard. It probably hurt. She hoped it hurt, a little. Today was supposed to have been a reprieve.

"There," Thalia said. She thrust her chin to the right.

Laurel looked again, all the way to the far-right wall this time, to the dull-colored edge of business diners. Her gaze caught. It was David.

He was sitting at a two-top, wearing his usual khakis and a blue chambray button-down shirt. Scampi's had loaned him a jacket. It was an awful checked rusty thing, no doubt crawling with the filth of a thousand sweaty-necked businessmen. There was a woman with him, a brunette, but Laurel hardly glanced at her.

"Oh, for the love of Pete," Laurel said, turning to her sister, not sure if she was irritated or simply relieved. "You brought me here to see this?"

No doubt Thalia expected her to snatch a steak knife off a passing surf-and-turf plate and go scrabbling toward David, leaping over other diners, going for his throat. Thalia would have already stabbed him by now. But Thalia didn't know David. He couldn't manage an affair unless Laurel dressed him for it and made the hotel reservations and put all his assignations into the BlackBerry he toted around in his pocket and called Dr. Theophilus.

But Thalia was nodding, looking at Laurel with that same strange expression, her lips thinned and pressed. This time Laurel recognized it. It was simple pity, a tourist of an emotion; it hadn't ever lived on Thalia's face long enough for Laurel to know it when she saw it there.

"Are you insane?" Laurel asked. "David wouldn't do that to me and Shelby. He couldn't. He never has."

Thalia said, "You don't know what I—"

"Yes, I do," Laurel interrupted. "When you took the brownie down, you heard them planning lunch over that TeamSpeak thing in the computer. Redhead in the basement, my aunt Fanny. It's a business lunch for the game he's making." She glanced at the woman at David's table again, then back at her sister. "She's not even wearing lipstick, Thalia. Who has an affair without lipstick?"

"Laurel," Thalia said, and the sound of her sister saying her real name was enough to make Laurel pause. "Stop looking at me. Look at them."

So Laurel did. She turned and watched them across the room. The sleeves on David's borrowed jacket were too short for his long, spidery arms, and his wrists jutted out as he gestured. He was gesturing a lot, Laurel noticed, and that was because he was talking to the woman. David. Talking.

Her husband disliked social situations so much he'd once sent Laurel alone to represent him at his office's mandatory Christmas party. But here he was at a lunch, happy and lathered up, his mouth going a mile a minute and his brain switched to the on position. His bony hands waved around and then grabbed his head and crunched up his dark hair, then let go to wave some more.

The woman—girl, really, she couldn't have been over twenty-five—leaned toward him, her elbows shameless on the table like a frame for her Neptune salad. She didn't seem go to with either the ladies or the businesspeople. She was wearing a filmy blouse, a hippie-girl-looking thing with bandanna sleeves, and her long hair was smoothed back by a headband. She looked breathless and glossy, like he was saying the smartest thing. It was David, so he probably was, and she was pretty, lipstick or no.

"She's a colleague," Laurel said, but even to her own ears, her voice sounded thready.

"Really?" Thalia drawled, drawing the E out long in that hateful way she had. "Then we should go meet her."

She set off across the restaurant, and part of Laurel felt like she should walk out now, go sit in the car and let the scene play out without her. It had nothing to do with her, she was almost certain. But Thalia was bearing down on David, intent on mayhem, so Laurel followed her sister down the stairs, weaving through tables of women.

Going back up the three steps on the other side, she felt like she was crossing a border, bringing her tulip-covered dress out of Ladies' Lunch Land to the wall, where the conversation was low and the colors were serious. Laurel could hear the conversation now. The girl was talking, and she knew the voice. It was the woman from California, the one who had called him Dave over TeamSpeak.

"—actuality always precedes potentiality, and an egg is merely a potential chicken," she was saying.

David's arms were moving again, holding an imaginary oval

over his soup plate. He shook it at her. "No, an egg is an actual egg. The chicken has the potential to make eggs, just as eggs have the potential to make chickens."

"Fine. Chicken first." The girl flipped her long hair off one shoulder, chuckling. "Quantum me no more physics, please. Let's talk about dessert, like sensible people."

It didn't sound like business, and as Laurel and Thalia reached the table, neither David nor the girl looked up, even though Laurel felt like she was looming over her husband, and Thalia was practically on top of the girl.

"Hi," Laurel said.

David started, and immediately, his hands came together and folded themselves into a single still object that he set down on the table. He looked surprised to see her, but not too surprised. He gave Thalia a brief nod, and then he said to Laurel, "Hi back. What are you doing here?"

Thalia's smile was out, the big wolf smile that took up half her face and made her odd brand of beauty look feral. She spoke before Laurel could. "Better question. What are *you* doing here?"

The soup plate held the dregs of what looked like gumbo. He glanced at it, puzzled, as if the bowl should have answered the question for him. "Eating," he said.

He didn't sound like David, Laurel's personal mad genius. He sounded clipped and very formal. Laurel raised her eyebrows at him, tilting her head in a short nod toward the girl, who was waiting to be introduced with a polite, bored smile on her face. David either missed the cue or ignored it, and the pause stretched itself and grew into a gap.

Thalia filled it. She ran her pink tongue around her lips and spoke to the girl in a tone of faint, lascivious surprise. "You're beautiful. Across the room, I was thinking you were pretty, but when I come right up on you like this"—Thalia leaned down—"and get really close, wham! Gorgeous."

"Oh. Um, thank you?" the girl said. She turned toward David, which proved she didn't know him very well. Looking to David for social rescue was like asking the Sahara for a cocktail.

Still, Thalia was right. The girl had gotten prettier as they'd come closer. Even with no makeup, her skin had a creamy glow, and her dark eyes were wide-spaced and liquid over molded cheekbones and a lush mouth.

A waiter zoomed smoothly over to them. He was a young man with a single eyebrow that was shaped the way Shelby had drawn birds back when she was in kindergarten. "Will you ladies be joining the party?" he asked Thalia.

"God, I *hope* so," Thalia said, not taking her eyes off the brunette. The girl blushed, and the waiter's eyebrow lifted up until Laurel thought it might take flight, zooming up to the ceiling to hang like an unflapping black M beside the closest mermaid.

"Give us a minute," Laurel said, then gave him a belated smile to temper her curt tone. After a slight reluctant pause, he backed away.

Meanwhile, Thalia had put one hand over the girl's arm and leaned in even closer. "Can I maybe get your phone number?"

The dark-haired girl pulled her arm away, setting her hands under the table in her lap. "Who are you?" she asked.

At the same time, David said, "Stop it," to Thalia. He looked back at the girl and added, "This is my sister-in-law, Thalia. She's not a lesbian."

Thalia straightened and said to Laurel in a fake loud whisper,

"Denial. It can be so powerful. But you wouldn't know about that, would you?"

"I'm sorry," Laurel said, her cheeks burning. "My sister is a small bit mentally ill. I'm Laurel. By the way."

The girl looked blank, as if the name meant nothing to her.

"Oh. Right," David said. "Laurel, this is Kaitlyn Reese, from Richmond Games. She flew in this morning for the dogfight demo. Kaitlyn, this is my wife."

The minute David said the word, said "wife," Kaitlyn's expression changed. Once Laurel had found four-year-old Shelby standing in a glass-shard sea of what used to be a favorite vase. Shelby had immediately peeped, "I didn't touch it!" with her eyes round and wide, caught. Kaitlyn had that same look on her face now.

Laurel's world tilted and reversed, and she felt slightly sick.

"Nice to meet you," Kaitlyn said too brightly. She bobbed up, gave Laurel's hand a quick squeeze, and dropped back into her chair. Her palm was damp. Laurel saw her glance at David's left hand. It was the slightest flick of her eyes, but Laurel caught it.

She angled her body toward Kaitlyn and leaned across Thalia, speaking softly. "It's in his pocket."

Kaitlyn pinked faintly.

"What?" David said.

"Kaitlyn was wondering where your wedding ring is," Laurel said, and David's eyebrows came together.

"I missed that." He reached in his pocket and pulled it out, along with a jangle of change and his bandless watch. "I don't like things on my hands," he explained to Kaitlyn.

"I think I'm done here," Thalia said. She held up Laurel's keys and jingled them, a merry sound that struck Laurel as wildly inappropriate. "Still want to come to Barb's with me?"

Laurel shook her head. She wouldn't walk away from this table now even if it caught fire. Thalia turned on one heel, crisp and smart as a Buckingham Palace guard, and then marched off.

Kaitlyn said, "Should you let her go off by herself?"

"She's not that kind of crazy," Laurel said. "She's not a danger to herself or others."

"Says you," David muttered. "Where is Shel?"

Laurel closed her eyes. He'd been working on this project for weeks, working endlessly, to the point where she had hardly seen him. He'd been with this woman, virtually and in the flesh, day and night. The team from Richmond Games had flown out here more than once, and how had Kaitlyn Reese gotten all the way across the country, several times, without knowing David was married?

"Shelby's with Mother," Laurel answered. Her hands gripped the table so hard that her knuckles were turning white. To Kaitlyn, she said, "Shelby is our daughter." Invoking Shelby was pretty close to peeing around David in a circle, but Kaitlyn had recovered her composure.

"Dave's little dancer," she said, her eyes hard. "He talks about her all the time," and there was a subtle emphasis on the word "her." Kaitlyn was damn sure making it plain whom David didn't talk about.

"Are you okay?" David asked Laurel, but she wasn't. The world was upside down.

"I hate that ceiling," Laurel said.

"Your sister walked right out the front door," Kaitlyn reported. "Is she allowed to drive?"

"She's fine," Laurel said, and it came out angry, like a bark.

Kaitlyn was sizing Laurel up. All traces of her blush had faded.

"Well, if you two came together, then she's stranding you. Can you catch her? Dave and I have the dogfight demo in less than an hour." She turned to David, resting her elbow on the tablecloth so her body became a wall, enclosing the table and leaving Laurel on the outside. "We ought to head on over to the office."

Laurel had a strong urge to grab David's hand, pull him to his feet, and say, "You come on with me, Dave."

She could peel the jacket off his lanky frame and lead him out, sticking Kaitlyn Reese with the bill. He'd been readying for this demo for weeks, but his job could go to hell along with Kaitlyn. Laurel longed to tug him through the parking lot and find his SUV. They could climb into the back, and he would kiss her and touch her while she whispered to him about regular things, what to have for dinner, should they paint the bathroom, until he remembered who she was. Who they were together.

But David had pulled out his bandless watch to check the time. "How'd it get so late?" he asked. He signaled the hovering waiter for the check. "Did she really take your car?"

"I don't know," Laurel said. "Probably."

"Typical Thalia," David said, his nostrils flaring.

The waiter came over with the bill on a tray, and David glanced at it, then took out his wallet and set money down, his movements precise and spare. He had cooled and slowed the way he did in a crisis, but this wasn't a crisis. This was lunch. Lunch was not a crisis unless Thalia was right.

"I don't have time to run you home. I have to get to this meeting," David said.

"Let her take your car," Kaitlyn said. "You can come with me in the rental."

"Good." David stood up. He dropped a kiss onto the corner of

Laurel's mouth, and she had to physically stop herself from jerking back. "You have a key for the SUV?"

"Wait, David. How will you get home?" she asked, a stopgap measure that paused him only for a moment.

"I'll bring him back to you," Kaitlyn said. She gave Laurel a tight smile and then added, as if joking, "When I'm done."

David didn't seem to hear. He shrugged off the ugly jacket and hung it on the back of his chair. "I'll call you, tell you how it went," he told Laurel. "Sorry about—" He waved one hand around, and Laurel didn't know if he meant Thalia, or Kaitlyn, or leaving her here.

"Dave," Kaitlyn said, impatient, already walking down the three steps into the basin full of Trish Deerbold clones.

"Sorry," he said again, and then he followed Kaitlyn Reese.

He left Laurel standing there, the world reversed, her feet on a sky-blue floor and what felt like the whole weight of the ocean pressing down on her.

CHAPTER 12

Laurel wove the SUV through traffic, hurrying away, with no other destination. She pulled in to Albertsons but left after circling the parking lot twice, even though there were plenty of spaces. She couldn't stop picturing David leaning across the table, words pouring out of him in torrents for a girl who wasn't Laurel.

With his old cronies from Duke, David could yawp endlessly about quarks and how to bend space. Computer talk with other engineers made his long torso stiffen and still itself, while his arms did their odd, controlled flailing, drawing diagrams in the air; he could be so excited about a code string that his eyes bugged out. But the hard-core coders at his job were all men. He never talked to Laurel like that, and he never talked to her in the regular way people do, to say how he was feeling. If David ever began a sentence with "I feel," Laurel could rest certain that the next words out of his mouth would be "like eating another piece of chicken."

He didn't talk to women; he hardly spoke in words to his own mother. Until Laurel had seen him waving his arms and all but hollering, so excited, back and forth with Kaitlyn Reese, she would have said it wasn't possible.

Kaitlyn was such a pretty girl, and with David's brand of smartness. Laurel knew how the male-female thing worked. Words forged connections in the brain, and then the body followed. She'd learned that lesson at nineteen. Her husband had been giving that girl who called him Dave something he'd never given Laurel, and Kaitlyn Reese was giving him something back that Laurel didn't have.

She drove around the lots at Eckerd and the farmer's market before she realized she wasn't going to get out and buy shampoo or fruit, or even stop and pick up the dry cleaning through the window. She didn't want the eye contact or to say "Did the grease spot come out of that skirt?" like everything was regular.

She drove back to Victorianna, punching in the code so the hydraulic gate swung wide to let her in. As she wound through her neighborhood's clean streets, the absence of ugly plaster geese or gnomes or even pink Florida flamingos began to grate on her. The neighborhood charter forbade yard art, at least in the front. There was an exception clause for Christmas; and on December first, the sudden invasion of herds and herds of light-up wire statues in tasteful white always made Laurel feel like God had sent Victorianna a plague of reindeer. Here at the end of the summer, there were only the stone mailboxes, beds of late flowers, well-watered lawns, and house after lovely pastel house. Everything sat perfect in its perfect place, except for Laurel. There ought to have been a cracked window somewhere, she thought, a roof missing some shingles, a small decay she could use as a landmark, but instead, the seamless lots blended one into another, and she was lost.

Thalia had wanted her to ask the Ouija—*Is Laurel happy?*—but it was the wrong question. She was happy. She had been happy. She should have asked if Shelby was happy. Thalia had said she wasn't, and Laurel had Cowslipped it away until it came to this, Molly dead and Shelby sealed up full of secrets. *She saw.*

She'd assumed David was happy, too, but now she saw that if he wasn't sleeping with that girl, he soon would be. Laurel had heard them talking over TeamSpeak, and she should have clued in when Kaitlyn called him Dave. Dave was a stranger, someone who didn't belong to Laurel, but she'd Cowslipped that away as well.

How could she protect Shelby if she refused to see danger coming? She hadn't seen it in her house when it was rising all around her, filling up her shoes, soaking her.

She drove slowly and aimlessly through her streets, winding her way into phase two. If she took the next left, she'd be on Chuck and Barb Dufresne's street. She stopped at the intersection and peered down the road. Her Volvo was not in front of their house. Thalia, even armed with casserole and brownies, must have failed.

Laurel started driving again. It was after lunchtime, and heat shimmered off the pavement. The streets were deserted. She turned another corner, and there, up the street, jogging toward her, was Stan Webelow. She stopped the SUV, grateful for David's tinted windows, and watched him coming. He loomed larger and larger as he trotted up the sidewalk. He couldn't see into the car, and she doubted he recognized it, but as he approached, he lifted one hand in a neighborly wave. His wide smile unfurled over his knoblike, elfin chin, the corners of his mouth pulling back so far toward his ears that he looked carnivorous.

All at once, she couldn't stand to let him pass. If Thalia was right, if she was Mother, then she would damn well be like Mother. Mother was Cowslip, but she had leaned in to the void between her bed and Daddy's and spoken, going against everything in her entire nature to keep Laurel safe. Laurel could do that now for Shelby.

She leaned on the horn. Her own car's horn was a contralto beep, polite as a throat clearing. David's blared like a foghorn, bisecting Victorianna's genteel afternoon silence. Stan Webelow's step faltered, and he peered at the SUV as he approached, as if uncertain that the blaring horn was for him. She banged out another blast.

Stan slowed to a walk as he drew even with the front windows. He came hesitantly toward the passenger side, picking his steps like a nervous horse. He was wearing minuscule shorts, a tank top, and running shoes. His brown hair, shot with copper highlights, was a boyish mop, as if he'd spent half an hour and ten dollars' worth of products tousling it into artful disarray before leaving the house for his jog.

Laurel's breathing sounded loud and ragged over the purr of the engine—the SUV's mechanized autonomic functions ran more smoothly than her own tense body's—but she managed to hit the button, and the passenger-side window scrolled down.

Stan Webelow did a double take when he recognized her. Whomever he had been expecting to find blowing the horn of a big-ass SUV, calling him over like a high school boy impatient for a date, it hadn't been Laurel.

"Mrs. Hawthorne?" his mouth was saying, polite and surprised, but she spoke over him.

"I saw you," she said.

"I'm sorry?" he said. His eyelids moved in a flurry of puzzled blinking.

"The night Molly Dufresne died. I saw you on Trish Deerbold's lawn."

His mouth dropped open as if her words had unhinged it, but then she saw his widened eyes go sly and secret. His body stilled, and he deliberately closed his mouth. His eyebrows came together as if he were confused, but it was a polished emotion, manufactured and glossy. He wasn't half the actor Thalia was. "I don't know what you're talking about," he said. He got the tone right; it was a single note higher than his usual speaking voice—but he couldn't control biology, and his cheeks flooded with ruddy color.

"Yes, you do," Laurel said, her voice steady now. "You were standing back out of the crowd, behind everyone. They were all looking at my house, facing away from you. But not me. I was looking back at them, and I saw you."

"You couldn't have," he said. It came out sounding truthful, genuine. But he wasn't saying he hadn't been there. He was only saying that she could not have seen him, and the round spots of color in his cheeks ripened.

"You thought you were too far back, safe in the dark, but you have highlights," Laurel said, touching her own bangs. "They're meant to catch the light."

His eyes narrowed. "You saw some hair glowing in the dark? And that makes you think it was me?"

"I know it was you," she said. Her heart was pounding itself against her rib cage, moving the blood through her so quickly she could feel it pulsing at her wrists and in her throat. But her voice came out strong and certain.

All at once the pretense dropped away from him, and his skull seemed to bulge under his skin. "This is not your business," he said quietly, but so fiercely that he was practically hissing. He came at the car, darting forward, his hand reaching for the passenger-side handle.

Laurel took her foot off the brake and stomped down on the gas. The SUV screeched forward, and then she jammed on the brake. She stopped six feet beyond him. He'd come all the way into the road, following her, so he was directly behind her. She could see him in her rearview mirror, that hectic color still staining his face. She had a terrible urge to throw the car into reverse, tear backward over him and crush him, and end this. Her foot trembled on the brake. She stabbed the button for the driver's-side window and leaned out, looking back at him. "Pervert," she yelled, loud enough for anyone whom the horn had called to hear.

He held up his hands, a propitiating gesture, his lips pursing as if saying "shush." He peered all around as if checking for witnesses.

"I know you," she yelled.

Stan Webelow's chest heaved as if he had already run his five miles; fresh sweat was popping out on his forehead and his shoulders. He started forward almost involuntarily, as if his body had decided to rush the SUV without his consent.

Laurel whipped around and hit the gas, lurching forward, then smoothing out and speeding away. She kept glancing into the rearview mirror to make sure he was growing properly smaller.

Her hands gripped the wheel so tight it was hard to tell how badly they were shaking.

Her blood sped through her, thinned and quickened by adrenaline. She'd done something real, the way Mother had once, the way Thalia always did. It wasn't enough to take to the police, not yet, but she had been right. He had been there the night Molly died, and he was hiding something ugly. She could pull Thalia off of Molly's poor family and sic her on Stan. Thalia would find a way to prove he'd been there, something solid that they could take to Moreno. They needed only enough to turn the detective's calculating, clever eyes on him. Moreno would root him out, and then Molly could rest.

Laurel drove directly home, but when she opened the garage door to put away the SUV, she saw that her side was empty. Thalia and the Volvo were both still MIA.

Laurel pulled into the garage and then hit the button to close the garage door. She stayed in the SUV until the door had closed all the way. She hadn't expected to be alone. What if Stan Webelow came here? She'd baited him, and she wasn't sure how dangerous he was. She hurried inside and locked the door behind her, but the house felt big and far too quiet. Her adrenaline faded, leaving her shaky and a little sick at the pit of her.

She paced the house, too nervous to be still. She was afraid Stan Webelow would show up, and under that, she was afraid that if he didn't, she'd have to start thinking again. David and Kaitlyn Reese. Finally, she went to her workroom and spread her quilt out on the table. The bride stared up at her, a mouthless witness to whatever came next. Laurel turned herself deliberately to the task of sewing on the pinned rosebuds and lengths of scarlet ribbon. It required enough concentration to slow her racing thoughts, but she still felt herself tensing every time she heard a car come down the quiet street. She wasn't sure whom she was more afraid of seeing—Stan Webelow or David.

Each car passed right by the house, continuing on its business without even slowing. The afternoon shadows lengthened outside as she worked, and still Thalia was not home. Laurel attached the final rosebud and stood back to look at the completed quilt. She couldn't tell if she liked it or not. She left it out on the worktable and went back to the kitchen.

She opened a cold bottle of Chablis and poured herself a generous measure, then sat on the sofa and sipped it, too sick to be hungry. She finished the glass and poured herself another. She drank some of that, too, until she realized it was making her dizzy. She hadn't gotten lunch. Now here it was, almost time to start dinner. She took the glass back to the kitchen and set it by the sink.

She heard another car coming and stood up straighter, her ears straining. This one slowed, pulling in to her driveway. She went into the dining room and peered out of the sheers. It was her Volvo, at long last. She hurried to the front door and undid the locks, swinging the door wide.

Thalia was coming up the walk, but she wasn't alone. She had one long arm draped over Bunny Dufresne's shoulder. They were tilted in, leaning on each other. A wave of spiced rum and coconut rolled onto the porch before they did, and as they got close, Laurel could see that Barb's lipstick was askew.

"Buy a girl a drink?" said Thalia, and lurched inside, carting Bunny with her.

CHAPTER 13

Barbara Dufresne was a barb in the morning, sharp and pricking. Her husband always called her Bunny, but Laurel thought of her as Bunny only in the afternoon. By three P.M. each day, she would be blurred to fuzziness, her eyes as pink-rimmed as any rabbit's. Bunny was crafty and she functioned, but DeLop was full to bursting with every shade of alcoholic, so Laurel had recognized her colors by the second time they met.

Since their daughters had become fused at the hip, Laurel was familiar with both of Bunny's incarnations, but the woman Thalia was half carrying over the threshold was a stranger. Laurel had never seen Barb blatantly intoxicated. Barb and Thalia swayed past Laurel like dance partners, sweeping through the foyer and into the keeping room.

Thalia called back over her shoulder, "Barb says she's ready for some coffee." She slurred a merry path through all the S's.

Laurel got her mouth to work and said, "Dear God, what have you been doing?"

Thalia paused and rotated her head as far as it would go, peering close to backward at Laurel like a sloppy-drunk owl. "Just make the coffee, Buglet." Thalia pulled Bunny onward. Laurel followed them into the keeping room. They navigated around the coffee table and plopped onto the sofa, Thalia first and then Bunny, like an echo. "Coffee," Thalia demanded.

Laurel stalked toward the kitchen, and Bunny blinked at her as she passed, slow, like sleepy babies blink.

"Let's have it Irish-style," Bunny said. "You got whiskey and Cool Whip?"

"No," Laurel said, vehement. "I don't have anything like that."

Thalia swallowed a burp and said, "You make that rum cake with the nuts every Christmas. That cake is soaking in it."

Bunny lifted one wise finger. "Palmolive," she intoned.

Thalia said, "We can put milk and rum and sugar in."

"Rummish coffee," said Bunny.

Laurel glared at Thalia. This was worse than useless. It was downright awful. They needed Stan Webelow here, drunk and helpless, sprawled out on the sofa while Laurel and Thalia worked a version of good cop/drunk cop on him. Not poor Bunny. Laurel grabbed the coffeepot and started running water into it.

"Where's Shelby?" Bunny said, peering around.

"She's at my parents'," Laurel said, thanking God for small favors.

"Oh," said Barb, and she released a mournful exhale. "She's a sweet girl."

"Finest kind," said Thalia.

"We could put the rum in fruit juice and not wait. Be easier," Bunny said. "Or we could just put the rum in some rum."

"It's perking," Laurel said, pressing the button. "I think the coffee is a great idea."

"I could sure use a drink," Bunny said, and drifted her eyelids down into another of those painfully slow blinks. "Chuck went back to work today. Can you fathom? Sent the boys to camp and then to their soccer. Like normal. And me all by my own self. Doing not so well."

"Come get the rum down for me," Laurel said to Thalia, her voice tight. "It's up in that little cabinet over the china hutch in the dining room. I'm not tall enough."

Thalia boosted herself carefully off the sofa and came around the counter that separated the kitchen from the keeping room. They walked single file, leaving Bunny in a sodden heap on the sofa. Laurel held her tongue until they were through the dining room's swinging door, but the second they were out of Bunny's sight, she wheeled on Thalia and hissed, "I can't believe you drove in this state."

"Oh, please," said Thalia. She twitched her shoulders, and all that drunk went slithering down off her to puddle at her feet. "As soon as Bunny went to break the seal, I got the bartender to stop putting any gin in my G and T's. I've had so much tonic, I bet my next pee comes out carbonated. I snatched the tab so Bunny wouldn't see I'd pulled that old dance-hall-girl trick on her and paid it—or rather, you did. When I got the Amex out of your purse for Mother, I may have nicked your Visa, too." Thalia pulled Laurel's credit card out of her pocket and handed it over along with a receipt. Laurel's eyes widened at the total. "Blame Bunny. She was drinking nine-dollar tropi-tinis. For a scrawny lady, she sure can pack it in."

"You've got to get her home," Laurel said, still angry.

"Not yet," said Thalia. "There was this window between mighty-drunk and oops-too-drunk when she was talking. Did you know Chuck moved into a guest room? He's threatening divorce. Because of the drinking, I suspect, though she didn't pony up to that. I was right, Bug, there was some kind of fresh hell starting at the Dufresne house. We've got to sober Bunny back up to lucid." Thalia opened up the high cabinet and felt around until she found the rum bottle. "We can pretend to put this in and try and get as much coffee down her gullet as possible in the next hour. You need to make her a damn sandwich." She pulled down the bottle and then turned back to Laurel. "Why are you still glaring at me?"

"Take Barb home," Laurel said. "You're playing in her life now, for no reason. We need to focus on Stan Webelow, like I told you and told you. I saw him, Thalia. I confronted him, and he ran at me. He was there that night. He admitted it."

Thalia, for once in her life, looked surprised, her mouth pursing into a small O. "Bug, when exactly did you grow a pair? I didn't get the memo."

Laurel said, "We need to get Bunny out of here and safe home. Now. Before David comes home."

"David's not here? I thought after we so flagrantly interrupted his delicto, he—"

"We interrupted lunch, Thalia," Laurel said, her voice gone icy.

"Oh, are we still pretending to believe that?" Thalia asked, quirking an eyebrow. "His car is here, I thought—"

"He gave me his car because you stole mine," Laurel said.

"Right. So he got a ride on Kaitlyn?" Thalia said.

"Stop it," Laurel said, her voice kept low but so fierce it rasped in her throat. She grabbed Thalia's upper arm, hard. "I'm not discussing David with you. Ever. Stan was there that night. It's him. We have to take poor Barb Dufresne home and put her to bed. I don't want David to see what you did here. What I let you do."

Thalia said, "Did you not hear me? She's feeling guilty as all hell, and right now she's in a state to tell us anything."

"It's Stan," Laurel insisted. "God help me, I am not going to let you dig at that poor woman."

Thalia's mouth bloomed into its widest, most hateful grin, and she said, "I think God knows you never could stand Bunny."

"Take her home," Laurel said. "Now."

Thalia lifted one shoulder and then turned away, rum bottle in hand. Laurel couldn't tell if her sister was capitulating or ignoring her. Meanwhile, Thalia went from sober to dead drunk in the single step it took her to get through the door back into Barb Dufresne's line of sight.

The drunk dropped back off her in the next heartbeat, and she said, "Dammit. Now look."

Bunny had melted down into the sofa, head resting on the back, faint snores coming from her throat.

Thalia thumped the rum bottle down on the kitchen counter. "Barb? Barb?" she called, but there was no response.

"We're going to hell," Laurel whispered, staring at Barb's slack face.

Thalia waved hell away with one hand and said, "She's not going to remember this in the morning, Bug. Help me get her up."

"No, Thalia," Laurel said. "I won't be part of this."

Thalia looked Laurel up and down, as if appraising her. Then she gave Laurel a short, sharp nod, as though she had decided. "Fine. I'll handle it myself, then. I always do." She glanced at the sleeping Bunny, and then she shaped her hand into a gun. She pointed her index finger at Laurel. "Close your eyes, baby," she said. She cocked her thumb and shot Laurel in the chest.

All the air went whooshing out of Laurel, as if she'd been hit, as if Thalia's hand had actually been loaded.

Thalia was already turning away. She poured a cup of coffee and headed back into the keeping room toward Barb.

Laurel stared after Thalia and felt herself sway and tremble, all at once undone. She'd left her half-empty wineglass sitting by the sink; she picked it up and drank deeply. The Chablis was room temperature and tasted much too sweet. Laurel swallowed with an effort, leaning on the counter.

It's almost always people in a family who kill each other, Thalia had said at the theater. They'd been thinking of Marty. Both of them had been, perhaps for the first time in years. Now Thalia had quoted Daddy exactly, had shot Laurel with her finger. It was more than a reminder. It was an invocation calling something up. Laurel could feel it rising. The hair at her nape prickled, and her skin felt charged, electric.

Thalia said, "Wakey-wakey, Barb. Let's have a little coffee."

Barb didn't so much as twitch, even when Thalia sat down beside her on the sofa.

Laurel drank the wine down to the warm dregs. Did Thalia mean only that Bunny was a deer? That Thalia was taking her down, and if it was too ugly for Laurel to watch, then now was the time to look away?

I'll handle it myself, then, she had said. *I always do.*

"Thalia?" Laurel said, but her voice was small and seemed to come from very far away.

Thalia was patting Barb's hand, getting no response. Outside,

Marty uncoiled from his knothole. He was coming. Thalia had awakened him, and Laurel knew if she pulled back the curtain that covered the door, she would see his pale face pressed against the glass.

Want to see, Lady Laura-Lee?

She didn't. She really, truly didn't.

She opened the junk drawer in the kitchen, sifting through peelers and melon ballers and teaspoons and strainers until she dug out a metal jigger. The rum bottle was still out on the counter, and she grabbed it, pouring the big end of the jigger full. She drank it off in a single open-throated swallow. It smoked a molten-hot trail from her mouth to her stomach, dumping into the wine, combining and igniting. She had to stand very still and concentrate hard on not sending it right back up. She gulped air, trying to hold it, even as her unsteady hands were pouring another. She curled her hand around the refilled jigger, waiting out the burn.

From the sofa, Thalia said, "Laurel?"

Laurel made a shushing noise. She didn't want Thalia's voice coming at her from the outside. Thalia was already talking so loudly inside her head.

Close your eyes, baby.

Laurel felt her body cross a threshold, accepting what she'd put into it, and immediately, she lifted the jigger and downed the next shot. It was like being punched in the gut with a fist made out of blue flame. She coughed in two short barks, sounding like their old cat, Bibby, with a hairball, and then she concentrated on breathing short and slow, in through the nose and out, lips clamped shut.

"Ka-boom!" said Thalia. She stood up off the sofa, abandoning the snoring Barb, and came toward Laurel. "What was that for?"

Laurel poured another, her hands shaking so hard that rum splashed out of the jigger, running over her fingers and puddling on the counter.

She waited for that threshold again, not speaking.

Thalia leaned across the low counter toward Laurel. She had one of Daddy's expressions on her face, that bright, foreign bird-eyed look, her head cocked sideways. "You're doing Uncle Petey-Boy," she said in a tone of wonderment.

Laurel put the next shot down her throat. This time not throwing up was an act of superhuman will. She bent at the waist, coiling around her flaming center, turning her head to press her cheek against the cool, rum-wet tile.

Under the burn, she felt a faint shock of recognition: She *was* drinking like Petey, truly the most dedicated alcoholic in DeLop. He drank raw brush whiskey with a bored efficiency that implied putting home brew into his stomach was his job. Now Laurel felt like sending him a thank-you note, and a giggle escaped her mouth at the thought of one of her monogrammed linen cards wending its way to DeLop in a wax-sealed envelope. Inside, she'd have written in her tidy hand, *Thank you so very much! Without you, I never would have known how the business end of necessary drinking should be handled.*

"It's a pretty good Uncle Petey-Boy," Thalia said, her voice gentle. "But I think you need to stop now."

"Don't talk," Laurel repeated. With Thalia talking, it was harder to keep picturing Petey-Boy, shirtless and pounding back shots, reading her note with his man breasts hanging down in small, sorry triangles.

"Bug. Set the jigger down and back slowly away."

"I said please don't dammit fuck fuck talk."

Laurel heard herself from such a distance that she could not be sure, but she thought she might be yelling. She was so loud that Barb DuFresne made a snorking noise and stirred without waking. It was too late. Thalia had spoken again, and that thing Laurel was trying so hard not to look at was coming through the glass, coming right at her, coming as if called.

I'll handle it myself, Thalia had said. *I always do.* Then her hand made itself into a gun. Point and shoot. *Close your eyes, baby.*

What if it had been Thalia, all those years ago, in the deep green woods of Alabama? What if Thalia had been "handling it herself"? Had Thalia shot Marty?

And still Thalia was talking.

"Did you say the very bad F-word, Buglet? You? Twice? What's happening?"

Laurel, her face pressed into the cool counter, closed her eyes. She saw the deer step out into the road.

Yours, breathed Uncle Marty, moving out of Daddy's line of sight. He also moved out of Thalia's. They could sit in the blind all day and not have a deer amble up and hand them such an easy shot. Maybe Marty meant to give the shot to the least experienced hunter, their favorite girl, the one who'd bagged her first buck only last year.

The gun was moving in Daddy's hands.

Close your eyes, baby.

Laurel's lids dropped obediently, so she had no way of knowing if Daddy was bringing the gun down to aim, or passing it to Thalia. They kept a necessary quiet; they were upwind, where scent would not betray them, but sound could set the deer running.

Had Daddy held his gun out to Thalia, silently asking? Her answer would have been a nod, a reaching. Laurel could imagine the gun cradled properly in her sister's thin arms. And there was Marty. Ahead. Standing by the road.

Laurel heard the first shot. A miss. The deer crashing away. She kept her eyes closed. *Get him,* Daddy said, and then Marty said something back. Was he speaking to Daddy? Or to Thalia? The gun went off again, and still Laurel waited. When at last she looked, the gun was lying on the dirt trail, abandoned, and Daddy was bent over his brother's body, trying to call him back.

Laurel watched her sister fight to lift her heavy hand and stuff her thumb into her mouth: the unbreakable Thalia, wiped down to toddler level.

"It shouldn't matter," Laurel said now, out loud. Daddy or Thalia, her family's complicit silence would have been the same. Marty had the short eyes, and they'd shot him. But it did matter, and she was desperate to unsee the reason.

"What shouldn't?" Thalia asked.

Keys rattled against the front door. Laurel heard David's baritone in the foyer and then a softer voice, female. She welcomed the instant rage that filled her from her deep gut to the top of her throat, welcomed it like a lover. Her eyes met Thalia's, and she said, "Tell me he did not just bring that whore into my house."

Thalia instantly went feral, her eyes slitted and as avid as a hawk's as she breathed out. "You're doing Uncle Petey-Boy because of David?" The worry was gone, replaced by something uglier. "Excellent. Go get him."

Laurel was already moving, barreling around the counter and

across the keeping room toward the foyer. She felt tipped forward, overbalanced, like she couldn't have stopped moving even if she wanted to, not without falling flat on her face. That didn't slow her. She didn't want to stop. She was leaving something behind in the kitchen with her sister. She wanted it left behind.

She tore through the doorway to the middle of the foyer, and then she stopped as if she'd slammed face-first into a wall of glass bricks. She'd come ready to breathe out the fire she had stoked up in her belly, to burn Kaitlyn Reese down, but Kaitlyn wasn't there.

David stood just inside, holding the front door open for her parents. Mother was ushering a sober-looking Shelby and Bet Clemmens forward, one hand on Shelby's waist.

"—thought she'd want to sleep at home, what with Molly's viewing tomorrow," Mother was saying in a reverent hush to David. She glanced up as Laurel came charging in and said, "Hello, dear, I—" Mother's voice cut out as Laurel stopped, bracing her arms in the doorway. Then she said, "Why, you're bone-white, Laurel. Are you sick?"

Behind Mother, on the street, a dark sedan pulled away from the curb. Kaitlyn Reese's rental, no doubt. Mother and Daddy's blue Buick was parked at the bottom of the walk, the engine running. Daddy, dreaming at the wheel like always, missing everything that mattered.

Laurel's gaze pulled inexorably back to Mother. Whatever she'd tried to leave behind in the kitchen, it was here, meeting her at the door. She drew in a ragged breath, and the air was made of razors, filling her throat with a wash of burning red.

"You okay?" David asked. He came two steps toward her, and Laurel couldn't back up because Thalia had followed her. Her sister blocked the way back into the keeping room, a thin wall of heat at Laurel's back. Laurel pivoted, keeping him in view, and backed up toward the dining room instead. She stopped in the large archway, one hand grasping the frame to steady herself.

David looked from Laurel to Thalia. In the sudden quiet, Barb Dufresne snored and muttered. David looked past Thalia into the keeping room, where Barb was laid out on the end of the sofa. Laurel watched the cogs in his brain start churning; he couldn't make what he was seeing add up.

"Mommy? What's happening?" Shelby asked in a quiet voice, but she and Bet were standing beside Mother, and Mother eclipsed them both.

"Is that Barb Dufresne?" David asked. His voice pulled Laurel's focus, and looking at David was better, a relief. Anything was better. David asked again, "Laurel, are you okay?"

"No," Thalia said. "She's not okay, and she's beyond drunk."

All of David's attention switched to Thalia. Laurel felt it like a loss, felt the room receding as Mother said, "Laurel! Have you been drinking?"

Laurel blinked too long and saw the deer step out into the road. Her eyes flew open, and she said, "You're a liar."

She said it to the air, to all of them. Mother looked affronted, David puzzled. Shelby's lids dropped, shuddering closed over her big eyes. Only Bet did not react, standing placidly at the back of the bunch. One woman passed out in the next room, another screaming drunken accusations: For Bet, the scene must be familiar. She didn't even twitch.

"I'm sorry," Laurel said, this time speaking to Bet and to her daughter. Shelby grabbed Bet's arm, hard, and Bet suffered that, too, in the same uncomplaining silence.

David's hands burst into motion, one moving up to crumple and release a fistful of his hair, the other rising up by his shoulder and unfolding in a baffled star. "What's happening here?"

"I think that's the question Laurel wants you to answer," Thalia snapped.

"You tell him," Laurel said to her. "Shoot him, Thalia. Shoot him with your finger."

Thalia prowled forward until she'd taken Laurel's place in the center of the small room.

Mother said, "Shelby, honey, come upstairs."

Shelby's cheeks flushed hot pink. "Why is Molly's mom here?" she asked.

Mother put one arm around Shelby, herding her toward Thalia and the keeping room, but that path brought them closer to Laurel. Laurel moved fast, backing around the pecan table, putting it between her and Mother. She stopped by the built-ins where the antique china gleamed, framed in rich wood.

Mother paused with Shelby still huddled underneath her arm. She stared as Laurel stumbled backward. David loomed behind Mother. Thalia stood nearest the keeping room, all four of them neatly framed for Laurel in the archway.

"Close the front door, Bet," Mother said.

Laurel couldn't see Bet anymore, but she called, "Yes, close the door, Bet. If no one sees it, then it isn't happening."

Laurel heard the door swing shut and catch, but Bet stayed by it, out of Laurel's view.

"This isn't like you," David said to Laurel.

"Maybe you don't know her very well," Thalia returned.

"It's like you," David said to her.

"Shelby. Upstairs. Now," Mother said in a voice that brooked no argument.

"What's happening?" Shelby said, her voice high-pitched and close to hysterical. She was staring at Barb Dufresne. "Why is she here? Is she mad at me?"

Part of Laurel longed to go to her daughter, but Shelby was sheltered under Mother's arm, and Laurel's body balked. She could not make her feet take even one step toward her mother.

"Enough," David said. His color was high, but he sounded cool and decided. "Shelby, Mrs. Dufresne is going home now. You can talk to her tomorrow. Go upstairs with your grandmother."

Shelby said, "Does she know I'm sorry?" Her voice was pitiful and small.

David turned to her and said, "I'm sure she does, honey. Okay? Go upstairs now."

Shelby shook her head in an emphatic no, her widened eyes glossy with gathered tears, but she let Mother lead her around Thalia. They passed out of Laurel's sight, and every step Mother took, every inch of distance put between them, was precious to Laurel.

David stepped into the archway, standing across the table from Laurel, Thalia at his left shoulder like the very devil. Bet Clemmens, silent and unseen by the front door to his right, was all the angel he was going to get.

"You. Get Barbara up and take her home." He used the same firm tone that had just worked on Shelby, only louder and much angrier. It was clear he was speaking to Thalia, even though he'd turned away from her.

"Don't yell at her," Laurel said. "Lord, I need another drink."

David said, "That's the last thing you need," at the same time that Thalia said, "You definitely double damn do not."

"You don't get to yell at me, either," Laurel said to David. "I get to yell at you. You're the one who's cheating."

David did a double take, eyes wide. "I'm whatting?"

"Cheating," Laurel said. "With Kaitlyn Reese."

David blinked. "What put that in your—" He stopped and turned, slowly and with great deliberation, toward Thalia.

"Don't look at her," Laurel said. "Look at me. I saw you. If you aren't sleeping with her yet, you're working up to it. You're— I don't know what to call it. You're talking on me with her."

"What does that mean?" To Thalia he repeated, "Take Barb Dufresne home. Then come back here and pack, because you are getting the hell out of my house."

"It's not your house," Laurel said.

"Then I want her out of our house," he said, loud and angry. "She's a poisonous . . ." He couldn't find the word. Finally, after wagging his lower jaw up and down, seeking it, he gave up and spat out, "Poison thing."

"If you keep yours," Laurel said. "I'm keeping mine."

"Keeping my what?"

"Your other woman," Laurel said. "Your talking buddy. Kaitlyn."

"I do not have another woman," David yelled. His hands were up by his face now, open but curled toward each other, as if the truth were an invisible ball he was trying to hold up for Laurel to see.

"Keep talking," Laurel said. "You will."

David took in a long pull of air, and when he spoke, his voice was deliberately quiet. "Baby, you're drunk," he said.

"Were you happy here at all?" she said. "That's what I should have asked the Ouija. Were you happy, or were you only ever here because of Shelby?"

He went pale, a spot of color in each cheek, as if Laurel had slapped him twice. "You're saying things you can't take back. And you don't even mean them. That's Thalia talking."

"Do you see my hand up her ass?" Thalia said. "She's moving her lips all on her own."

"Girls!" said Mother in a quelling, haughty voice straight out of Laurel's childhood. She came back into Laurel's view, stopping beside Thalia. "You think Shelby can't hear you? You will stop. Immediately."

Laurel did stop. Mother was back in the room, and not even tearing her marriage into little tiny pieces could distract Laurel now. The thing she'd been running from ever since her sister had cocked her hand and shot her was there. It was simple and palpable and true and ugly.

If Marty had interfered with Thalia, and Thalia had handled it herself by way of a bullet, then Mother had not saved Laurel. Daddy, visiting his sprites in Daddy-land, hadn't even known she was a breath away from needing to be saved. Mother had never turned to Daddy in the dark, had never whispered the truth into the space between their beds. She'd let Laurel go off with them into the woods, knowing full well what Marty was. What Marty wanted. Complicit.

Laurel had nothing left. Thalia had told her how unhappy Shelby was, how unhappy she had long been, and Laurel hadn't seen it. Now Shelby seemed terrified of Molly's mother, asking if Barb was angry with her, and Laurel thought the words: *She saw.* Perhaps there was a secret Shelby she'd long refused to see, one who could stand by in a fit of teenage rage and let it happen, maybe saying, *God, Molly, quit it already*, not really believing Molly wasn't horsing around until it was too late, and then running. Hiding. Not understanding how very final this would be, choosing not to see or understand. Shelby would have learned not to see, not to understand, from Laurel, who had learned from her own mother.

Thalia had shown Laurel that David was less hers than she had ever thought, and the pieces of him she did own were being taken. Now Mother, the only rock remaining in Laurel's foundation, was sandstone, crumbling under the light touch of Thalia's pointing finger.

Mother hadn't saved Laurel, a bullet had, so how could Laurel, the daughter formed in her own image, save anyone or anything? Not Shelby. Not her marriage.

Laurel's body was a dead thing under her. A voice came out of the body, and it said, "Get out of my house."

"There, you see?" David said to Thalia.

"She's not talking to me," Thalia said, but she looked confused. "Who are you talking to, Bug?"

Laurel closed her eyes, but she could still smell Mother, talcum powder over a pale green scent like celery. The ghosts of the thousand times that Laurel had been sweet and blind and silent for her mother's sake came crowding in, riding that scent like a wave, and then ten thousand more ghosts came. They pushed in around Laurel. Laurel had believed her mother's love was stronger than all the ways she had been broken, stronger than DeLop. She knew better now.

"Laurel, I think you need some help," Mother said, dulcet and overkind.

Close your eyes, baby, Laurel thought, but she opened hers.

Mother's gaze was fixed slightly left, over Laurel's shoulder. Laurel thought of that as Thalia's move, a theater trick, but perhaps Thalia had learned it earlier, from Mother. Mother had always had a genius for not looking at things directly.

"You need to pull yourself together, go upstairs, and reassure your child."

Laurel glanced over her shoulder to see what Mother had focused on. The pretty dishes.

Mother snapped her fingers. "Laurel. Do you hear me?"

Laurel reached around and opened up one of the glass doors on the built-ins. She took out a delicate teacup. She turned it sideways, holding it up for Mother to see.

Mother opened her mouth to speak again, but before she could, Laurel threw the teacup down against the hardwood floor. It shattered into a thousand satisfying pieces.

"Get out of my house," Laurel said softly.

"Laurel!" Mother said.

At the same time, Laurel plucked out the saucer and sent it hurtling down to smash in the remains of the teacup. "Get out," she repeated.

Thalia and David stared, both shocked into silence.

Mother didn't move, so Laurel stuck her arm all the way into the cabinet, reaching behind a row of delicate wineglasses lined up like good soldiers behind the stacks of salad plates. She shoved them all out. Gravity grabbed them and pulled them down. They detonated in a huge initial clash followed by a symphony of crystal shards ringing off the smashed china and jangling away across the wood.

"Stop it!" Mother yelled, and Laurel drowned her out by sending a double stack of dinner plates hurtling to the floor. David was dead silent, but Thalia started making a strange choking noise, as if she might at any second break into hysterical laughter.

To David, Laurel said, "Get that bitch out of my house."

David took one step toward Thalia, then paused and looked at Mother. He went still again.

Laurel grabbed a heavy crystal pitcher and held it up. To Mother, she said, "Get out, or this one's coming at your face."

Mother's head wagged back and forth in small negation. Her eyes had not one safe place to land. David went to her and took her shoulders, his face grave and serious. He looked oddly disappointed. "Come," he said.

He led her toward the front door, out of Laurel's sight. Bet Clemmens must have still been pressed against it. She came scooting out of their way as Laurel heard the door open, coming to stand by Thalia in the middle of the foyer. Her blank, calm gaze hurt Laurel's skin.

Laurel heard Mother's heels tapping out the door and away, to where Daddy was waiting. All at once, the pitcher weighed a hundred pounds. Laurel set it down carefully, back in the cabinet, and started toward her sister.

"Laurel, no," Thalia said. "Your feet are bare."

Shattered glass was all around. Laurel stood on a tiny island of safe floor, blinking and uncertain.

Thalia held up one finger and then disappeared from the doorway. David had left the front door open, and Laurel could feel August push its way inside, a wave of heat that rolled across the room. It wilted her in one blast.

Thalia came back with the hallway runner rolled up in her

hands. She bent into a deep bow and unfurled it as if laying out a red carpet. It made a bridge across the glass.

As Laurel walked over it, Thalia straightened up and put her hands together, once, twice, then faster and faster, until her hands were a blur. Bet stood behind her, uncertain, looking back and forth between them. Thalia clapped and clapped, calling, "Brava! Encore! Encore!"

Laurel kept moving, passing them both. She ran through the keeping room and up the stairs. She could still hear Thalia's hands banging together, a one-woman standing ovation that went on and on and on. Laurel could hear her even when she ran into the bathroom. She fell to her knees there in darkness and threw up until there was nothing left at all.

CHAPTER 14

Laurel dreamed the boy with hair like wheat again. This time he was running through her own backyard with that same dog. The dog wasn't Miss Sugar after all. It only looked like Sugar, with a lot of beagle in the mix. Laurel was below them, looking up the length of the boy's string-bean body. She could not see his face, only the curved underside of his pointed chin. He was tinted blue, and his limbs were curved, distorted. Around him, her backyard was a wonderland, shimmering, filled with blue-washed stone angels and flowers in full bloom. She realized she was down deep in the pool, looking through the water as the boy ran past her and away.

She wanted to follow him, but Shelby's familiar hand was curled in hers. She squeezed, and Shelby did not squeeze back. Shelby's eyes were open, but they did not register the boy, and her limbs shifted gently as the pool water lapped. Her body had no will, no movement of its own, and she was stiller than Shelby ever was. Only her hair seemed alive, tendrils of it coiling and swaying upward, reaching toward the sunlight like yellow petals. Laurel tugged on Shelby's hand, tried to swim them both to the surface, to the boy, but firm fingers gripped her ankle.

It wasn't Mother. This time it was Thalia's hand holding her under. Laurel could see Thalia's big teeth gleaming, pearly and iridescent, from the thatch of water weeds that had grown up over the concrete floor.

"You can't get there from here," Thalia said, then shrugged, nonchalant, like she wasn't all that sorry about it.

"Watch me," Laurel said, and her own voice woke her.

The world flipped. She wasn't looking up from the pool's bottom. She was standing by her window, looking down at the pool. She grabbed the sill to steady herself. She must have taken a short walk, going to the window and opening the curtains as she slept.

The pool was empty, an innocent clear blue. There was no boy in the yard, no dog, only Bet Clemmens sitting on the gazebo steps in her pajamas and sifting a fistful of what looked like twigs back and forth, hand to hand.

Even from the second-floor window, Laurel could see the dark knothole, feel the wrongness like a living thing in her yard. She'd tried to keep it all outside, but it was inside now, too, in this pretty bedroom. The colors were wrong. The air tasted flat. It bothered her a lot less than she would have thought; she'd broken everything that she could find to break last night, and this morning, she'd awakened empty.

"I'm sorry," she said to Molly.

She'd come close. She'd started something with Stan Webelow that she doubted she could finish alone. And she would be alone in this soon. She couldn't have Thalia in her house any longer.

She turned away from the window toward the bed. David's

pillow was dented. He must have come up sometime in the night, after she'd finished throwing up and had passed out on her side. It would have been more heartening if he hadn't left again while she was sleeping. She pulled off her pajamas and let them lie where they fell, then went to the bathroom to dry-swallow some Motrin and get in a hot shower. She let the water beat down on her head until the ache faded and she felt something like herself again. It had been a while.

She dressed in a pair of jeans and a pale green tank top, and then she tidied up out of sheer habit, putting her pajamas in the hamper. As she made the bed, the ghost of lavender rose around her. She'd made the quilt that served as their comforter five years ago, and she'd never thought the sachet would last this long.

When everything was put in order, she looked at herself in the mirror on the back of the door. She'd pulled her damp hair back in a ponytail, and she wore no makeup, no shoes. She saw only Laurel, with no plan and nothing whole left to throw. Downstairs, she would find the scraps of things she'd shattered, waiting to be sorted through, and she would see what could be salvaged.

She opened the door, ready to go down, and there was Bet Clemmens. Bet's hand was raised to knock, so it looked like she was about to punch Laurel in the face. Laurel's heart jump-started, and she involuntarily stepped backward.

"I'm sorry!" Bet said, almost a yelp, and she lowered her arm.

"It's okay," Laurel said, putting one hand to her chest. "You've got little cat feet, you know that?"

Bet tilted her head to the side and said, "You give me a pitcher book oncet. For Christmas. It said the fog come in like that."

"I remember," said Laurel, though she didn't specifically recall giving that book to Bet. Shelby had loved it in preschool, so Laurel had taken quite a few copies of it to DeLop over the years.

Laurel looked past Bet, down the hall. The door to the little guest room was closed. Bet glanced over her shoulder, following Laurel's gaze. "Shelby's still hard sleepin' in there," she said.

"Let her," Laurel said. "She's not going to have an easy day."

"Because of they're laying out Molly this evening," Bet said.

"That, too," Laurel agreed, but she'd meant what must happen when Shelby woke up. She thought of Mother saying, *I never yet saw a dissection that did the worm a bit of good,* but she'd tried to handle this like Mother already. All she had learned was that Mother had failed her. "Did you need something?"

"Naw. He saved you the downstairs, because of he said you like the chunks of things," Bet said. "So I went and got you these."

Laurel blinked, not following even a word of that, and then Bet held out a sandwich bag. Some shards of beige and clear plastic were jumbled up in the bottom. Laurel took it and spread the bag flat on one hand, petting the pieces into a single layer.

She recognized what she was holding, and she pulled her top hand back, as if the broken shards of plastic had gone hot. "It's the planchette?" she said, and it came out high on the end, like a question, even though she knew the answer.

"Naw," said Bet. "It's that pointer thing. From thet broke Ouija in the grass."

"Yes, that's called a— Never mind. You picked up all the bits?" Laurel said.

Bet nodded. "I even grubbed around the grass some till I found that nail."

Sure enough, in the bottom of the bag, Laurel saw the silver needle that had pointed out the letters, one by one, while the planchette moved willfully, alive under her hands.

"Why on earth," Laurel said.

The feel of it, even in pieces, made her spine shudder so hard she felt her vertebrae clacking together.

Bet shied back a step, her dark eyes widening. "I did wrong, didn't I? I thought you might could want it for a blanket."

Laurel suppressed another shudder and stepped toward Bet so she could look close at the girl's face. "You thought I'd want to use these pieces in a quilt?" she asked.

Bet bobbed her head in a shy, ashamed affirmative, and Laurel found herself smiling in spite of everything.

"That's really very thoughtful, Bet. I might one day."

"Naw," said Bet. "I can see I fussed you."

"No, really," Laurel said. "Look, let me show you."

She carried the bag over to her dresser. Bet followed her across the room, taking such timid mouse steps that Laurel had to wait at the dresser for Bet to finish sidling over.

Laurel opened up her jewelry box. Her rings were lined up in a tidy row in the holder, and her necklaces and bracelets were each inside its own small velvet box. She didn't own a lot of good jewelry, and what she had, she'd mostly picked herself. David wasn't adept at buying jewelry. Even if he had been, he wasn't the sort to remember it was Valentine's Day. He wasn't the sort to remember it was February, really.

Shelby reminded him when Mother's Day came, but he had yet to remember their anniversary. It was hard to hold a grudge when he also forgot his own birthday. If he didn't hate parties, Laurel could have given him a surprise one every year, and he'd be probably the first person in history to be genuinely startled when friends came leaping out from behind the sofa with a cake. Candy hearts and flowers and diamond anniversary bands weren't part of the life they'd built together. She hadn't thought she minded, but today she wished she had pearls from their fifth anniversary and a tennis bracelet from their tenth. She wanted something hard, something tangible and valuable he'd given her that she could put on her body like a touchstone. Something like a proof.

She lifted the tray out of the way and set it aside. "There," she said, and pointed into the secret space in the bottom. It was fuller than the jewelry compartment, brimming with strange objects of no value to anyone but Laurel. From the center, between the cork from the outsize bottle of white wine David had opened their first night together and a broken pocketknife of Uncle Poot's, the plastic dinosaur eye stared up at them. Laurel laid the sandwich bag over it like a blanket. "This is where I keep important things, the ones I'm not quite ready to use in a quilt yet. I'll keep your planchette here."

Bet reached in with one finger to touch the mouse charm, then the small velvet bag that was full of Shelby's baby teeth.

Laurel held herself still until Bet withdrew her hand, and then she put the tray back, covering up the flotsam from her life. Bet's dark eyes were shining, proud and pleased. On impulse, Laurel reached out and touched Bet's cheek, and Bet immediately leaned in to the touch, closing her eyes and pressing against Laurel's palm.

Thalia had said, *That little thing is getting all rooted in,* but Laurel hadn't noticed. She'd brought dinner and shoes and a toy or game to Bet every Christmas, from her first to the one last year. This was Bet's second long visit to her home, but Laurel felt she'd never truly looked at the girl before.

"Can I ask you a question?" Laurel said. It was what she should have asked David, or Shelby, or even the Ouija, and it wasn't a fair question for Bet. Not really. But Bet nodded, so Laurel asked, "Are you happy here? Do you think this is a place where people can be happy?"

Bet pulled away from Laurel's hand and turned away, so that Laurel saw her in profile. Her nose had pinked. "I like it here fine," she said. She tried to shrug off her answer, but her voice was trembling.

It wasn't a fair question because Bet came from hell. Who wouldn't like it in Victorianna, if DeLop was all they had for a comparison? But Laurel hadn't come from hell. She'd come from Pace, and she'd liked it here fine, too. Loved it, even, every minute and molecule, no matter what Thalia thought. Thalia couldn't imagine anyone being happy in a house and a life that were both so tidy, making chicken and quilts in between toting Shelby from dance to drill team. Laurel had been.

But that was when she'd thought that David loved it as well. Her good life was a thing they made up, made together, almost by accident, the same way they'd made Shelby.

If she'd left pieces out, then she'd done it for her family. She'd only been buttoning shut the ugly parts. The things she'd buried were better left that way. What would David and Shelby want with ghosts and family skeletons and her criminal relations and the ugly face of true and abject poverty in DeLop? She'd left those things buried, and good riddance. It had never occurred to her that David also left parts of himself outside of this house. Now that she'd seen him in excited conversation with a girl who was his intellectual equal, Laurel knew the pieces of him that she didn't have weren't awful. They might be his best and favorite things, buttoned up because she couldn't share them.

Bet Clemmens had turned farther away, so that all Laurel could see of her face was the curve of her cheek. She said something else, softly, but Laurel couldn't make out the words.

"What, honey?" Laurel asked, and it was as if the casual endearment undid Bet.

She turned toward Laurel, and her voice came out in a whispery rush. "I am happy here. Everything smells real good. You even smell good, like what I think them moms on Shelby's Nick at Nite must smell like."

It was nothing short of a declaration, naked and desperate. Bet flushed a deep wine red, and her throat moved as she swallowed. She ducked her head, not able to meet Laurel's gaze in the wake of her words.

It shamed Laurel that she couldn't say back to her, simply, *I love you, too, kiddo.*

She didn't love Bet, and no one had a finer nose for insincerity of feeling than a DeLop kid. Laurel had never tried to love Bet, nor even thought to try, but she imagined that she could. If she spent any time at all looking at Bet like she was looking now, she could find this unexpected sweetness, this hopeful core, and come to love her back.

"We're going to think about things, you and me, okay?" Laurel said at last, gently. "I don't know what will happen, but there are opportunities for you that we can find. I haven't been good enough with that. I haven't been good enough to you, period. I'm sorry. But I promise I'm going to try and do right by you. Righter, anyway."

Bet bobbed her head. It might have been a nod, but it was

noncommittal, a wait-and-see movement. Words were cheap, and Laurel knew it would count more if she showed Bet. Over time.

"Have you seen Thalia?" Laurel asked.

"She's in her room, doing thet yoga," Bet said.

That was good. This morning, hollowed out and staring down at the dark spot of the knothole in her yard gone wrong, she had realized that she wanted David, this marriage, their troubled child, this life. She wanted it on almost any terms. If David left out pieces of himself, so be it. She could work with what she had of him, even if he was here mostly for Shelby's sake. That was a starting place. She would sit him down in the soft ashes of last night until they found a way to work together. Shelby needed them both, badly. Of all the broken things, Shelby was the one that must be salvaged.

Laurel would send Thalia home as a gift, a yielding to what David needed. She would call Detective Moreno and state definitively that she'd seen Stan in the cul-de-sac the night Molly Dufresne drowned. That might be enough to get Moreno looking at him, but even if it weren't it was the best she could do. She wanted Shelby safe and her marriage intact. Everything else was negotiable.

She turned to go downstairs, but Bet put out a hand and touched Laurel's arm lightly, stopping her. "I'm sorry I give you the shivers with them pieces."

Laurel shook her head. "It's a great present."

"Naw. It fussed you. You're like Aunt Moff, aincha? You see things."

Laurel smiled, rueful and a little sad. "Sometimes I think I don't see anything," she said.

Bet's eyebrows crumpled inward, worried or curious. "You ever see anything about me?"

Laurel shook her head. "No. But you have a good future, Bet. I know it. So maybe I should look."

"Naw," Bet said, hanging her head. "I am sorry I got you fussed."

Laurel said, "Don't be. Not everything under my jewelry is a happy memory. They're things that matter to me, good or bad. The planchette belongs there because I'm the one who broke it. I asked a question, and I didn't want to know the answer."

"What'd you ask it for, then?" Bet said.

Laurel shrugged. She didn't know why she had asked that question, of all the things she could have asked. She'd seen Thalia use the Ouija enough when they were kids to know that it worked best when you kept it simple, asking yes-or-no questions in a series. Otherwise, the Ouija's answers could be ambiguous. Could haunt a person.

"What did you ask, anyways?" Bet wanted to know.

She stood a little too close to Laurel, as if trying to get inside the circle of Laurel's body heat. A strange sweetness had sprung up between them; it was like that moment in the car on the way to Mobile. Bet would tell her more than the Ouija had, if only Laurel could ask the right questions.

"Shelby confides in you a little, right?" Laurel said.

"What's a confides?" Bet asked.

"Talks," Laurel said. "I asked that Ouija what I needed to know about the night Molly died. What I needed to know to protect Shelby."

Bet's eyes were dark, unfathomable. Her gaze fixed on Laurel's face, and her mouth turned down. "What'd it say back?"

"*She saw,*" Laurel said. "It said *She saw,* and then I broke it."

"You know what it meant?" Bet said. Her eyelids dropped; she was staring at the floor by Laurel's feet.

"I hope I don't. I hope to God," Laurel said. "But this morning, I'm done with being too scared to find out."

"Aunt Moff woulda known straight off. But maybe you're more like Della. It always takes Dell time to sort things into sense." Now Bet was looking sideways out the window. "*She saw* don't mean what you might come to think."

Laurel leaned toward her, drawn in, and said, "If you know something—anything—I wish you would say it."

Bet muttered something under her breath. Laurel couldn't make it out, but it seemed like Bet was talking to herself, deciding. Laurel's hands trembled a little, and she squeezed them together, hard.

"Don't be afraid. Whatever it is, Bet, you can tell me," Laurel said. "I won't be angry."

Bet looked up at Laurel, wary, but she had come to a decision. "I tole a story on you." That was DeLop-speak for a lie.

"That's okay," Laurel said, keeping her voice calm, not too eager, trying hard not to spook the kid. "You can tell me the truth now."

Bet's voice dropped to a whisper. "I tole that I saw Molly go in that orange house? I said I didn't know if Shelby saw, but that was the story. Shelby saw, awright. She made me swear not to tell no one. That's what that Ouija meant, I bet." Bet's whisper fell lower, so it was little more than breath. "Shelby saw Molly with that man, going in his house. I think that there is a real bad man, and I done seed me enough of 'em to know."

It was the last piece Laurel needed, the one she'd thought she'd have to do without when she sent Thalia away. She saw the pattern come whole and all the pieces fit. She'd known since the first day she'd touched his soft, moist hand that Stan Webelow was something wrong, unwholesome. She'd felt it in her gut, where she knew all the things that were truest.

Now even the Ouija's message made a kind of sense she could accept. Shelby had seen Molly with Stan Webelow, and she was feeling guilty for keeping Molly's secret, strong friendship mated with piss-poor teenage judgment. No doubt Molly had sworn her to secrecy. For Molly, Stan Webelow was probably a cross between a father figure and a forbidden love affair; Molly would be wholly unaware of all the damage that was being done to her. Thalia had learned that Chuck was filing for divorce; who knew how long the DuFresne marriage had been in ugly trouble. If Chuck Dufresne had been threatening to leave, then Molly would have been especially vulnerable.

Laurel could say for certain that Stan had been in the cul-de-sac the night Molly died: He'd admitted as much in the street. Shelby knew about the relationship, and Bet could back that up to some extent. Forensics would have shown if Molly had been pushed, but there were all kinds of pushing. Stan Webelow had pushed the girl, all right, pushed her out into the night and to her death.

It was as Laurel had always believed. Molly had been coming to see Shelby, that was obvious. Maybe she'd been with Stan already, and he had followed her. Waiting for her friend, Molly had been drawn like a moth to the lit pool, and Stan Webelow had found her there. He'd startled her, and she'd slipped, fallen. Banged her head on the board as she fell. He'd stood by and watched. Stan Webelow had been the shadow Laurel had seen moving in the yard when she stared down, someplace between sleep and waking. He'd been what Molly wanted her to see.

"Means, motive, opportunity," she said on a breath out.

"What?" said Bet.

"It's enough. It's enough to take to Detective Moreno. That's a real thing you told me, Bet, not dreams or Ouija boards. I can't thank you enough." She put her hand on Bet's arm, but Bet pulled back, staring at her with her dark eyes wide and panicked.

"You cain't tell nobody."

Laurel said, "Don't worry. Shelby is not going to be mad at you."

"She's sleepin'," Bet said.

"I know. I need to talk to her dad first, anyway. Don't worry about a thing, Bet, okay? You did the right thing, telling me. That's a big deal. You could have kept that secret, kept Shelby in danger, and you, too. That's what Shelby did. She kept secrets from the people who could help her longer than she should have, and you made a better choice. I'm really, really proud of you right now."

On impulse, she leaned in and gave Bet a quick hug. Before she could pull back, Bet latched on, winding her arms around Laurel and gripping her so tight and hard that Laurel's breath was squeezed away.

"I wish't you was my mother," Bet said in a fierce whisper, burrowing her face down damply into Laurel's neck.

"Oh, Bet," Laurel said, "I'm going to—"

Bet pulled away. Her face flamed red. "Don't say nothin'," she said. "Please."

She pulled herself out of Laurel's arms and fled, scurrying fast down the hall to the small guest bedroom. She slipped inside and softly closed the door after her.

Laurel got up and went to the window again, looking down at the bright blue pool.

You can't get there from here, Thalia had said in the dream. Laurel had been helpless, held under.

"Betcha I can get there from *here,*" Laurel said, and was surprised to hear how strong her voice came out.

CHAPTER 15

Thalia's yoga mat was laid out on the only floor available in the big guest room. Laurel had done the room in crisp pale blue and white with touches of daisy yellow to warm it, but now it looked like a color bomb had gone off in the center. The floor, the chaise longue, the small desk, and the dresser were strewn with bits of Thalia's real clothes and a ton of outfits she'd brought from the costume room. There were filmy blouses twining with silk underpants, drifts of pants and skirts dotted with shoes. In one corner, a haystack of gaudy silver feathers lay heaped, a marabou jacket or a long boa of some sort, Laurel supposed. The quilt she'd made was on the floor at the foot of the bed. The shams and throw pillows were wound in it, and Thalia's favorite lace-up boots stood at attention on top. The white down pillow top and duvet and bedsheets were so scrambled that Laurel could have found a thousand pictures in the humps and creases, reading the bedding like clouds.

It could not have been more different than the bare, clean lines of the emptied black-box theater, but there was Thalia, wearing a sheer sleeveless unitard, twisting herself into shapes more complicated than the ones she'd kicked the sheets into. And here was Laurel, watching. Last time she'd come to call Thalia home with her, a supplicant, needing favors. This time she didn't wait to be noticed.

"Time to pack up," she said, her voice gentle. "We're done."

Thalia was on her back, slowly raising her legs until her toes pointed toward the ceiling. She didn't pause when Laurel spoke. Always aware of an audience, she must have felt the air shift when Laurel came into the room.

"Mystery solved, Velma?" Thalia asked. "Is it time to pack up the Mystery Machine and say the part about 'if it wasn't for those meddling kids'?" Her legs kept rising until her hips lifted off the floor, and then she slowly lowered them, still straight, over her head. Her toes touched down on a single lace-topped stocking by the edge of the mat.

"I've got enough to turn things over to the police now," Laurel said. "Bet Clemmens knew more than she'd been saying."

"Mmm," Thalia said. "Septic waters run deep."

"Look at me, Thalia," Laurel said. She waited while Thalia unrolled herself and sat up, cross-legged. "I know you didn't come here to help me put Molly to rest. That was all set dressing. You came to root me out of here."

Thalia cocked her head to the side and said, "That's not entirely true."

"It's true enough," Laurel said.

Thalia shrugged. "I face-planted in a pervo's crotch for you, Bug, so don't make the big bruisy wound eyes and say I wasn't playing for your team. Yes, I'll kill the fatted calf the day you call me up and ask me to come over in a U-Haul and get you, but it's not like I've been covert about that. And I told you from the start, I don't believe in ghosts."

"You said you'd come because you believed me," Laurel said. "But this whole time, you were here to wreck me."

Thalia stood up and took a step to the left, centering herself by instinct so that the mat framed her. "You weren't that hard to wreck, Bug. That should tell you something."

"I'm still here," Laurel said simply and quietly. Shelby was sleeping one door down, and Laurel was past yelling. Past smashing things. Past dramatic exits up the center aisle.

"It wasn't to hurt you," Thalia said. "Never that, Bug. It was to get you free. You're half the artist you could be, all because that cyborg down the stairs forgot to bag it one night when you were barely nineteen. You're living our mother's god-awful smiley life, just in a better neighborhood. I see you going under for the third time, and I'm supposed to stand by and hum and watch? When the hell have I ever done that?"

"Not once," Laurel said.

Thalia wasn't a sideline kind of girl; no one knew that better than Laurel, who had spent her childhood being "Thalia Gray's sister, poor thing." Her classmates had meant she was the sister of the most notorious reprobate in school, but it was more than that. They had all wanted, on some level, to be Thalia. Maybe only for a day, but surely they had wondered what it must feel like to draw every eye, to not give two good damns what other people thought, to be made purely of appetites and bold enough to feed them all in turn. Laurel was Poor Thing because she lived in the chaotic churning of Thalia's mighty wake, but also because she would never be Thalia. Even Thalia pitied her for not being Thalia.

Laurel picked her way across the littered floor to stand in front of the mat. She came close enough so that Thalia could not look beside her eyes or between them. Close enough to speak in a voice barely above a breath and still be heard.

"Who shot Marty?" she asked.

Thalia backed up a step. "You know who, Bug. You were there."

Laurel followed, feeling her feet sink into the dense mat as she stepped up on it. "Your stupid little sister had her eyes closed," she said. "She was afraid of guns. She was probably afraid of deer. But I'm not her."

Thalia tried to stare her down, her expression inscrutable. Laurel stood fast, expecting nothing, waiting her out.

At last Thalia spoke. "I'm not sorry."

"I know," Laurel said. "It's okay."

"If you brought him here right now, I'd shoot his ass again," Thalia said, but there was a tremble in her voice.

"I understand," Laurel said.

She did. Perfectly. She'd been Mother's, and Mother hadn't saved her. Daddy hadn't saved Thalia, either, though she'd always been his girl. What's a daddy's girl to do when her father isn't Clint Eastwood or Charles Bronson but only a daydreaming plumber with a willfully blind wife? There was no one to come in, larger than life, and save Thalia. Thalia, born larger than life, had stepped up and saved herself.

"I don't blame you," Laurel went on. "But you're not rescuing me from anything here. I'm not you, Thalia. I never wanted to be, and you're blowing holes in everything I love." Laurel looked at Thalia for a long time. Again, it was Thalia who backed up a step, Thalia's eyes that dropped first.

"Pack," Laurel said. "I'll take you down to Hertz and rent you a car so you can get home."

"We're really done here, huh?" Thalia said. "Bet Clemmens gave you the goods?"

"Yes," said Laurel. "We are."

She was all the way across the room, in the doorway, when Thalia said her name. Her real name.

"Laurel?" Thalia said. "You and me, are we square?"

"No," Laurel said as kindly as she could. "I meant we're really done."

She closed the door behind her almost gingerly. The guest room door was still shut, too. Behind it, her sleeping child was lost, not even a trail of bread crumbs to lead her home again. Laurel would have to go and find Shelby, but she had to find a way to David first.

David must have heard her coming, because he was pouring coffee into her favorite mug as she came down the stairs into the keeping room. She sat down on one of the bar stools and leaned her elbows on the counter. He put in milk and one Splenda, then set the cup in front of her. "Want some aspirin?" he asked.

"I took Motrin upstairs. Anyway, I don't feel too bad," she said. "I think I threw most of that rum up."

He cocked an eyebrow. "I think you threw most of your liver up."

She had a sudden flash of memory. Last night David had come into the bathroom after her. She remembered a cool rag on the back of her neck, his hands holding her hair back. She flushed.

He was still in pajamas, although in deference to Bet and

Thalia, he had found the top to the set and pulled it on. The bottoms had faded from dark royal blue to a muddy, pilled navy, but the top was bright, the cotton stiff, like new.

On the long counter by the sink, she saw her black vinyl camera bag. Her digital camera sat beside it, charged and ready.

"What's that for?" she asked.

He picked it up and said, "Come and see."

He went around the counter, and she got up and followed him. He ushered her through the keeping room to the foyer and then waved one long hand at the dining room.

There was a band of duct tape running like crime-scene ribbon across the doorway. In black Sharpie, David had written DO NOT SWEEP DO NOT SWEEP across the front of it in his spiky print. What Bet had said about him saving the chunks of things for Laurel made sudden, glorious sense.

The shattered dishes lay where she had hurled them, the shards of china and crystal glowing in spectacular circular patterns, like fireworks going off against the dark hardwood floor. A couple of the plates had broken into diffused round shapes; she could see how each had once been something whole. The crystal dust of wineglasses caught the sunlight coming through the windows, so the chaos had a hard white glow.

She reached for the camera and found David already extending it to her, trading it for her coffee cup. She ducked under the tape, stepping onto the carpet runner Thalia had unfurled. Laurel took several shots of the plate that had broken most perfectly; then she took other shots, more patterns emerging as she spun on the carpet and framed pieces with the lens. She dropped to her knees to get some close shots.

She could see one quilt already, a big one. It would be a banquet table, people sitting down to eat, but the quilt would cut off just above their shoulders. No human heads, no faces. The fruit and meat would be on the green grass, dumped down for some happy dogs. The diners would each have a cunning silver knife or a set of tile nippers. Their plates would be in shatter patterns before them, and they'd be lifting up spoonfuls of glass to their unseen mouths.

She'd have to use a lot of sturdy fabrics to support the weight of the china. Upholstery fabric, maybe, but for the detail work, she'd need glossy things, raw silk and polished cotton, and a print that mimicked the pattern of tiny climbing roses around the edges of the real china. She'd make the plates out of a mix of glass and fabric or the piece would be too heavy to hang right.

She needed to bag the pieces of each plate separately, as much as was possible, so they'd be easier to puzzle into wholes later. She snapped a few more pictures, getting close to a plate that had broken into seven large pieces, and discovered a dark hardwood star created in the space between. She snapped it several times; she'd re-create this pattern over and over, quilting it into the coats of the happy dogs and diners' clothes.

At last she lowered the camera and looked up at David. He was standing in the foyer, his bare feet flat on the floor, a yard or so back from the shrapnel.

"I am sorry about your dishes," she said.

"These are mine?" David said. "Why do I have dishes?"

"Your mother gave them to us. They were— Never mind. Thank you."

"You want Ziploc bags?" he asked.

"Yes," she said, surprised. "The big heavy ones for freezing things."

He was already leaning over and setting down her coffee cup on the floor, exchanging it for a box of the right kind of bags. He'd had them set out by the doorway. He tossed the box to her across the glass. She caught it and stared at it, this solid cardboard rectangle in her hands, the proof she hadn't found upstairs in her jewel box.

She set it down unopened, looking from the box to him and back again. He'd known what she would see when she looked at this room. He'd saved it for her, and he'd known what she would need, down to the bags. It was a declaration, bald and obvious, though almost as inarticulate as Bet's had been.

"You love me," she said for him. He'd never been good with the talking parts.

His hands came up by his shoulders, and he flicked his fingers sideways in an "of course" gesture.

"Then what the hell are you doing with Kaitlyn Reese?"

"Not a damn thing," said David, vehement.

"She's pretty," Laurel said. "And she likes you." He flicked his fingers again, dismissively this time, and she added, "Oh, but you didn't notice."

"Of course I noticed," David said. "So she's pretty. So's Famke Janssen."

"Who?"

"Movie actress. She looks like a little deer in the face."

Laurel trailed her fingers along the plush carpet and said, "You don't have lunch with Famke Janssen. She's not real."

"Okay," David said. "Your friend Mindy next door is pretty. I notice. I notice that Eva down the street."

"But you don't—" Laurel said, and then stopped. "Eva Bailey?

Trish Deerbold's friend?" David nodded, and she said, "Her hair doesn't even move!"

He flushed and said, "But the body," and then he waved one hand back and forth as if erasing Eva's body from the conversation. "We're off topic. I'm a man, Laurel. I notice how women look."

"It's not the same," Laurel said. "Body aside, you can't stand Eva Bailey. This is the first time I've ever heard you use her name in a sentence that didn't have the word 'vapid' in it. I saw you, David, with Kaitlyn. You talked to her like—I don't know what. Like you've never talked to me."

That was the heart of it. Saying it out loud, she felt every inch of distance between them. The line of duct tape was a wall. She could feel how uneven the floor was under the carpet runner; she was kneeling on crushed glass. He put one hand over his mouth, thinking. Then he dropped it away, and his hands hung by his sides.

"I didn't like it when you asked me if I was only here because of Shelby. I wanted you before that, when we first met. I wanted to get you a different way, with dinners. Flowers. All that stuff girls like. I didn't know how to do that. Then Shelby happened. You remember how scared you were when you came to tell me? I wasn't. It was a shortcut to someplace I was heading anyway."

She stood up, feeling the glass shift under her feet, breaking down further. She said, "You never told me that."

"Maybe not," he said. "But I used to sit around while your friends yakked about that TV show with the people who slept with each other and then had fights about it. I'd work on proving that week's extra-credit theorem in my head while they talked.

They sounded like white noise, and they looked like . . . whatever the visual equivalent of white noise would be.

"I'd stay, though. Because I knew you'd come. You'd be in color. You would talk about—I don't know. Nothing special. But you made everything around you be in color, too. You'd light up the most ordinary things and make me see the shape of them. Most times it's all white noise, except the numbers. It's like in my head, numbers are green, say. A green I've never seen in real life. I see that color when I talk to other math people like Kaitlyn. Yes, I've noticed from time to time that she's pretty. I've got a pulse, Laurel. But when we talk, she could be anyone. I see green. I don't see her. Not like I see you."

She was already moving toward him, fast, glass crunching under the runner as she ran. She broke the tape as if it weren't there and hurled herself into his arms. He caught her.

"What—" he said, but she wound her arms around his neck and whispered in his ear, "I'm answering you."

She pressed into him, pulled his mouth down onto hers, responding to him in a language he was fluent in. His mouth was still, almost inanimate, but Laurel was electric. She shocked his body into movement, filled him with current. His hands came to her hips, pulling her to him, and the new pajama top crackled between them.

"Where can we go?" he said.

Upstairs, Shelby slept, Bet Clemmens drifted, and Thalia, thank God, was packing.

"Down," Laurel said, kissing him and kissing him, and they moved in tandem to the basement door.

David fumbled it open and pulled her through, slamming it and shooting the deadbolt lock. Then his hands were back on her body, his mouth on hers, and they slid lower, stair by stair, tumbling and thumping down into the darkness of the basement. They left pieces of their clothing as they went. By the time they hit bottom, they were together, fast and savage, like a series of jolts. At the end, she said his name so many times it lost its meaning and stopped being a word. It became a sound, the syllables of how they were together. His face was buried in her hair, he breathed her in and said "Laurel" once, as if he were naming her.

Then they lay beside the futon, legs intertwined, in David's plain white space. It was cool in the basement, and David pulled the Sunbonnet Sue quilt down around them, her bonnet hiding her face. Laurel suspected that Sue might be blushing. Laurel was, her cheeks pink and overheated even in the chilly basement. David pulled a throw pillow down as well and propped his head on it. Laurel rolled in to him, putting one arm on his chest and bracing herself above him so he could see her face in the dim light from his monitor.

"Thalia's going home today," she said.

"Awesome," he answered, heartfelt. His eyes were sleepy.

"Don't sack out," she said. She lay her head down on his chest, pressing her cheek against him to hear the good thump of his heart. "I'm not done answering you."

She felt his chuckle like a rumbling against her ear. "I'm thirty-four, Laurel," he said. "I need a minute before you answer me some more."

She smiled into his ribs, giving his side a good whack with the flat of her hand. "I'm serious," she said. She turned over, and he put an arm around her so she was lying with her head propped up on his chest, both of them facing his desk. On the monitor, bright fish swam back and forth in an endlessly repeating pattern.

"Thalia couldn't have gotten in between us if there hadn't been a crack already. A big one. I think I put it there."

"Okay," David said.

There was no easy way to break thirteen years of silence, so finally, she said, "Our backyard is full of ghosts."

He said "Okay" again, this time drawing the word out slow, and she realized that she couldn't start there. It wasn't Molly or even Uncle Marty. It was DeLop. She should have taken him to see DeLop years ago, one Christmas, Mother's wishes be damned, to see the place where all the hidden pockets in her quilts came from. The place of her first ghost.

"Tell me," he said, and she was glad the lights were out. The time for lights was over.

"My mother grew up in DeLop, Alabama," she said.

"I know," he said, but she was rolling her head back and forth along his arm, back and forth, a tactile "no."

"I have to take you there sometime. Very soon, David. You should see it. And we should go back before Christmas anyway. To visit Bet. She's a whole 'nother thing, Bet Clemmens. She's going to matter more to us when this is done."

And then Laurel told him everything that she could think to say, dragging out ugly things for him as if they were prizes, and then stacking them, one on top of the other, so they were building a place where Molly's ghost could stand. She told him how DeLop looked in the winter, when ice sealed the peeling paint to the tract-house walls. She told him about the letters to Santa that Enid sometimes forwarded to Mother. Her little cousin Jase last year had asked for nothing but a piece of tarp. He didn't say why he wanted it, but when they got to his house with the ham dinner and his shoes and a perfectly useless Mr. Potato Head, Laurel had seen a hole in his bedroom ceiling big enough to see the moon through. God only knew how long it had been there, letting the rain in to puddle and freeze by the cot where he slept head to foot with his little brother.

Next door, eight-year-old Leslia didn't want a damn thing for herself, she told Santa. She sounded mad about it. Her letter said, *I was want a mattress. My broter turn three, and he don't fit good now in mama's burro drawer.*

David hadn't moved past the hole in Jase's roof. "Why didn't someone climb up and nail a board over it?"

"Because they didn't," she said. "No one ever would. Daddy drove in closer to Birmingham and got tarp, and Thalia climbed up on the roof and nailed it down. That was last year, and if the tarp has held, you'll see it's still there when we go back this December."

David went silent again, and Laurel kept laying it out for him, ghost by ghost. Aunt Moff with her cards. Poot's foot. Marty wanting to show her things, things he had already shown Thalia, and the deer picking steps into the middle of the road with his careful feet. She told David how, later, long after Marty had been buried, he would come to Laurel's bed at night with moonlight shining slim as a pencil through the hole that Thalia had put in him. How here, in this good house, he never came.

"It wasn't secret," she said to David. "I wasn't lying to you. I truly thought that it was something over, and it didn't belong here. I didn't want it all between us, but not telling you left a gap. Thalia got in it."

"Baby, I'm not angry," he said. "You're not mounting a defense, here. You're telling me a story. I've always liked it when you tell me stories."

"This one isn't pretty," she said.

"Who said they all have to be?" he asked, and Laurel smiled because she had. She and Mother had said so, and that had brought them here, to all the ugly stories coming out at once.

"Go on," he said, and she was finally to Molly, to bringing Thalia back into their lives, to everything she'd done the past three days to try and put her ghosts back to rest.

By the time she finished, her throat was bone-dry. She'd been talking over two hours, and her voice was tired and drooping down into a whisper. But she felt cracks closing and pieces sealing themselves together. She'd tried to create an airtight home that ghosts could not enter, but they'd come in anyway, through the secret spaces, through the blanks she'd left in all the things she'd left unsaid to David. She felt her words tying them together with a new, strong seam. He listened like he always did, his arm around her, his hand playing with the ends of her hair.

Then they lay together, silent. Laurel was so exhausted she almost dozed. The fish on the monitor seemed to slip the boundaries of the screen, swimming out into the air itself, closer to her, shimmering and small.

She shook her head to wake herself, pulling her eyelids wide. "Do you think I'm crazy?"

"Little bit," he answered. "No more than before."

She elbowed him. "I guess I mean do you believe me?"

He didn't answer for the space of a long minute. Then he said, "I believe the universe, everything that exists, is made out of thousands of billions of infinitesimally small rubber bands. The bands vibrate in a variety of ways, and those vibrations create matter and every kind of energy."

She turned over again, bracing herself up on his chest and peering down in the dim light, trying to read his face. "Seriously?"

"Yes. That's the nutshell version of string theory," he said. "You believe me? You think I'm crazy?"

"Little bit," she said. She dropped her face down onto his chest. "But no more than before. So now what?"

"Now, please God, you go get Thalia a rental car," he said. "Then it sounds like we need to take Shelby and Bet down to talk to Detective Moreno."

"Yes," she said, relieved. "But I meant bigger than that. What happens after today and tomorrow? What happens next?"

"For the rest of our lives, that kinda thing?" David said.

Laurel nodded.

"I don't know. We go on, step by step. We get through today, talking to Moreno, going to Molly's viewing. Next week, when you take Bet home, I go with you. To DeLop."

"Mother will have a cat," Laurel said, and realized she was done caring about that. Mother could have twenty cats. "Good, then."

"Right now the important thing to focus on is the part where you take Thalia to get a rental car."

"All right, already," Laurel said. "There's a load of whites in the dryer back there, and some of your jeans are hanging up by the ironing board."

David kissed her and said, "Let's get this day started. It's going to be an ugly one, but on the bright side, we're already halfway through it. I'm going to take a shower down here real quick, okay?"

He got up and walked naked back toward the laundry room and the little bathroom. Laurel dressed as she went back up the stairs, picking up her panties from the bottom step and pulling her bra down off the banister a few steps up from that. She found her jeans in a heap near the top step and pulled them on. Her shirt had caught on the doorknob and was hanging by a single strap, waiting for her.

In the keeping room, Thalia's bags were lined up in a row by the stairs. Laurel found Thalia back in her workroom, behind the kitchen, walking around the worktable to look from every angle at the bride in Laurel's quilt. Laurel had forgotten that she'd left it out.

"You ready?" she said.

Thalia started. "I didn't hear you," she said. "God, Laurel, this is really good."

Laurel blinked, surprised, and then said, "You're kidding, right? Because Mother liked this one, too."

"Really?" said Thalia, with that long-drawn skeptical E stretching out in the middle.

"She did," Laurel said. "I hadn't done the arms yet, though."

"Mm," Thalia said. "This is the best thing I've ever seen you do." She reached out with one finger and traced the place where the bride's mouth should be. "Is it you?"

"I don't think so," said Laurel. "Not anymore."

They stood quietly together for a moment, feeling the end of something long and living pass between them.

Thalia said, "Shelby's still bagged out. Teenagers, eh? Do you mind if I go poke my head in and say bye to her?"

"She'll be heartbroken if you don't, and she needs to get up anyway."

Thalia nodded. It seemed like she had something else to say.

Whatever it was, Thalia, for a wonder, let it pass. She went on upstairs.

Laurel waited by Thalia's bags. A minute passed, and then another. She didn't hear Thalia talking, or Shelby's wailing protest at her aunt's abrupt departure, and she felt unease run up her spine on little mouse feet.

Then Thalia called, "Laurel? Shelby's not here."

Something in Thalia's tone set Laurel's heart pounding. She took the stairs two at a time. "She slept in Bet's room," she called back as she climbed.

Thalia appeared at the top of the stairs. "I mean, she's no place up here."

Laurel pushed past, going straight to the little guest room.

"Maybe they went out in the yard? The park?" Thalia said.

"I don't think so," Laurel said.

The nice clothes Laurel had bought Bet had been stripped from the shelves, and Bet's Hefty bag was gone from the spot beside the bed. Laurel ran across the hall to Shelby's room, Thalia following. Shel's closet was open, and on the top shelf was a blank space where her black-and-silver overnight bag usually sat.

Shelby was gone.

CHAPTER 16

Thalia navigated Victorianna's streets, fast and precise, as if she were on a closed course. She had to stop because two small boys were racing a dog straight up the middle of Gaskell Street. They were deep in some pretend, flailing their arms and zigzagging back and forth, and they didn't hear the Volvo coming up behind them. Thalia leaned on the horn, and they looked over their shoulders and then stopped and sauntered out of the way with such maddening slowness that Laurel, sitting in the passenger seat, wanted to leap out just long enough to spank them. She couldn't even roll down the window and bless them out; she had Carly Berman's mother on the cell phone. She'd met the woman about a hundred times at dance recitals and school carnivals and neighborhood potlucks, but now she couldn't remember her name to save her life.

"No, she hasn't been here," said Carly's mother, sounding completely unconcerned. "Yvonne Feng is over playing, though. Want me to go ask?"

"Yes, please," Laurel said. She could hear Carly's mother clip-clopping away, calling, "Girls!" as if the word were two syllables.

In the backseat, David was on the phone with the Pensacola police department, saying, "No, she didn't leave a note. But you don't pack a suitcase to go get a Slurpee."

"Breathe, Laurel," Thalia said. "Ten to one they aren't with Stan Webelow. They're probably at a friend's house, hiding out and being stupid."

"I know," Laurel said. Through the phone, she could hear the high gabble of Carly talking with her mother. "Why don't we own a gun?"

"I wish you did," Thalia said. "Hell, I own two guns, and I'm a registered Democrat."

David said into his phone, "My wife is checking with her friends right now." Then he put his hand over the mouthpiece and said, "Stop saying the word 'gun,'" in a low, emphatic voice. "The police are sending someone to the house. We need to be there to meet them."

"We'll be back at your place in ten minutes," Thalia said. She turned in to Stan Webelow's driveway.

Carly's mother was back. "No, they haven't talked to Shelby—"

Laurel snapped her phone shut and tossed it on the floorboards. She was out the door before Thalia had come to a complete stop, running for the front door with David hard on her heels. She took the front porch steps two at a time and jammed her thumb into the bell.

David reached around her and tried the door. It was locked. Laurel hit the bell again, and they waited twenty endless seconds. David pounded the door hard five times, in a motion that was somewhere between knocking and punching it with the side of his balled fist.

Thalia came bounding up the steps, saying, "He's home. His car's in the garage."

David pounded the door again.

Laurel took three ragged breaths, one after another, and then said, "Call the police back. Have them come straight here."

"Screw that," Thalia said. "You really think she could be in there?"

"We know he had Molly here before," Laurel said.

Thalia said, "Okay, then," and stepped back, thinking.

Stan Webelow's porch was painted crisp white and trimmed in gingerbread. A large window overlooked the yard; Stan still had Cookie's pair of wrought-iron sweetheart chairs sitting in front of it, one on either side of a matching tea cart. In Cookie's day, the tea cart had been loaded with potted plants, but it stood empty now. Thalia picked up the closest chair. It was heavy; Laurel could see the sinews shifting in Thalia's arms as she tested the weight.

Thalia got a good grip, one hand on the heart-shaped curl of the back, one on the base, and then swung the chair hard at the window, feet first. The panes shattered inward, the chair legs sending the drapes swinging, but the frame held. The chair stopped with its base still outside, braced against the wood.

Thalia let go of the chair, and it fell to tilt down at a crazy angle. She leaned in to yell, "Shelby! Shelby Ann!" through the hole.

David took two strides and grabbed Thalia's arms just below her shoulders. He had them pinned to her sides as he moved her out of the way like more patio furniture. Thalia kicked outward and yelled, "Hey!" But he was already setting her down by the rail.

He swung around to pick up the tea cart in one smooth, fluid motion. He smashed it into the hanging chair, putting them both all the way through into the house, splintering the wooden window frame. The chair shot through and banged into something solid with a muffled thump, while the tea cart caught in the drapes and jerked them off the wall. It wrapped the drapes around itself as it rolled into Stan's house.

"Holy shit!" said Thalia, impressed, but David was already following the tea cart through the hole, folding himself almost in two and stepping carefully over the spikes of smashed glass jutting up from the bottom of the window frame.

Laurel followed him. Inside, she could hear running feet upstairs, pounding across the ceiling.

They were in Stan's formal living room. He still had Cookie's old furniture in there, plush pink chairs and an overstuffed sofa fraught with climbing roses. The furniture was sprinkled with glittery bits of glass and splinters of wood. The drapes and the tea cart lay in a heap, and the sweetheart chair had slammed into an ottoman and tipped it over into the coffee table. It looked like a small bomb had gone off in the center of the room.

"Shelby!" Laurel called as Thalia clambered inside after her.

The living room was open to the foyer with the main staircase. Stan Webelow came bounding down, holding a baseball bat. He was naked except for a minuscule pair of black underpants. He recognized them and stopped on the bottom stair, lowering his bat and staring at them, his jaw hanging open, eyes wide. "What the hell?" he said.

David stepped forward and, with the same economy of

motion, put one arm out, fast, in a straight line. He had a fist at the end of his arm, and it smacked neatly and decisively into Stan's cheekbone. Stan went down, making a surprised yelping noise and dropping the bat.

Laurel could still hear someone moving around above them, so she pushed past David. Stan lay where he had fallen, holding his face, and she scrambled over and around him, tearing up the stairs. David and Thalia pounded up stair by stair behind her.

"Shel?" Laurel cried.

She knew every floor plan in Victorianna; in this house, the master bedroom was upstairs, opposite the garage, above the living room. The door was shut, and as she ran toward it, the hall seemed to get longer and longer.

She cried out Shelby's name again but got no answer.

Thalia passed her on the right and got to the door first, flinging it open.

"I'm calling the cops," Stan Webelow yelled below them.

Thalia was already in the room, but she'd come to an abrupt stop inside the doorway. Laurel hurried in behind her, running into her sister's back, and David pulled up short right behind Laurel. Laurel grabbed Thalia's shoulders to steady herself.

On the other side of the bed, Trish Deerbold, makeup smudged, hair humped up into wild tufts, was struggling into her lime-green bra. She had on a matching pair of lacy panties, and the rest of her clothes were scattered on and around Stan Webelow's bed. The bed was a leftover from Cookie, too, high white wicker, but Laurel was willing to bet Cookie had never put black satin sheets on it.

All four stared at one another, speechless.

"Oh," said Laurel.

All the adrenaline went draining out of her, and her legs became rubbery and worthless underneath her.

Trish Deerbold yanked up her bra straps and grabbed a pillow, holding it in front of her body.

They could hear Stan Webelow stamping down the hall. "Are you people insane? You broke my house," he was yelling.

David stood boggling at Trish, and the strange, immediate grace that took over his body in a crisis leached out of him in two heartbeats. Then he didn't seem to know where to look.

Stan muscled his way past all of them to the back of the room, where his pants were lying in a crumpled heap on the floor. Laurel let go of Thalia's shoulders and took two steps back. There was a chair coated in peach and yellow check fabric by the door, and she sank down into it. Thalia stepped back the other way, over by the wall, where she leaned insouciantly against the wicker dresser.

"You're paying for my damn window," Stan said.

"Sure thing," Thalia said as Stan fished his pants off the floor and started easing into them. His cheek was already swelling up under his eye. It looked like he was winking at them. "Although, once we heard that screaming, we had to bust in."

"What screaming?" Trish said.

Thalia turned to Trish and continued, her voice earnest. "Well, it was a little muffled by that black leather zipper mask you're wearing, Trish, but still, we heard you."

Trish clutched her pillow, outraged. "Mask?"

"Give my sister any crap about this, and a zipper mask will be the least of it," Thalia said to them, unfurling her widest smile. "Trish'll be suspended from the ceiling, getting spanked with a live monkey, before I'm done telling what we saw here. Still want to call the cops?"

The pillow still clutched across her front, Trish rounded on Stan. "Don't you dare call the police. Not until I get out of here."

"Shel's not here," Laurel said to David. She was relieved, of course she was, but so confused. She couldn't reconcile all the objects in the room. She looked from Trish's pale buttocks, hanging out the back of her fancy Victoria's Secret underpants in two sad dewlaps, to Stan, coiffed and with a sheen on his bare skin as if he'd been oiled, to the garish sheets on Cookie's girlish bedroom furniture. David looked equally at sea, but Laurel asked him anyway: "Do we go home now?"

David shook his head. "I don't think we're done here. This makes no sense." He turned to Stan. "What was Molly doing in your house?"

Stan gaped at him. "Her name is Trish," he said, jerking a thumb at her. "She's here bungee jumping. Obviously."

Trish had turned back around to face them. She picked up a Lycra jog top and tried to get it on over her head without dropping the pillow.

"Looky here!" Thalia said. She sounded purely delighted. She'd picked up a small blue rectangle of paper off the dresser. It looked like a check. As Thalia read the front of it, she let out a low whistle. She glanced at Stan with something akin to respect and said to Trish, "He's worth four hundred bucks? A go?"

Trish stopped trying to get the top on and turned crimson, staring at Thalia. "Don't be repulsive. That's just a tiny loan. Between friends."

"Really?" said Thalia. Laurel had never heard the extended E go quite so long before.

"Answer David's question," Laurel said to Stan, but Stan was stalking back across the room toward Thalia, his pants up but still undone.

"Give me that," he said.

David stepped in as Stan tried to pass him. He was almost a foot taller, and Stan paused, one hand moving involuntarily to touch his swelling cheek.

"Focus, Stan." David waved one hand at Trish and went on. "I know who that is. I meant Molly Dufresne. Why did you have Molly Dufresne here?"

"That little girl?" Stan Webelow said. He was staring at David, confused. "The little girl who drowned?"

Thalia, meanwhile, turned and slid open the top drawer of the dresser, peering at the contents. She jabbed one hand in, stirring around what looked to Laurel like socks and underpants, and then closed it.

Stan said, "That little girl has never been in my house."

Thalia moved on to the next drawer, quick-searching it.

David took one stalking step toward Stan. "Our daughter saw her go in here. Bet Clemmens saw her."

Stan shook his head.

"I was so sure," Laurel said.

Thalia closed the second drawer, and then a jewelry box on top of the dresser caught her attention. She opened it. A small pink ballerina popped up and began spinning. A tinkling version of the theme from *Ice Castles* filled the room.

"What are you doing?" Stan was trying to push his way around David. David stayed in his path.

"Whoopsie," said Thalia. "Haven't made it to the bank yet, have you, Stan?" She pulled out what looked like another check.

"Dated today. Quite a busy morning!" To Laurel, she said, "Who's Jamie Gold?"

Trish's eyes narrowed. "What do you mean, Jamie Gold? What is that?"

"Another tiny loan," Thalia said. "Between friends."

"Jamie lives in phase two," Laurel offered. "They moved in last year. Her husband is a naval officer."

Thalia chuckled. "Navy, huh? All those lonely months of him at sea. We've been hunting the wrong game, Bug."

"Jamie just turned fifty-four," Laurel said. "You can't mean—" She broke off and waved her hands at Thalia, trying to push it all away.

"Your creepy guy is creepy all right," Thalia said. "But I'm afraid he's your basic garden-variety whore."

"Get out of my house," Stan said.

Trish scrambled over the bed in her jog top and underpants, bypassing Stan and David. She came at Thalia, reaching for the check, and Thalia relinquished it with a flourish. She leaned against the dresser again, watching Trish's face. "A cool six hundred," Thalia said. "I wonder what you get for that?"

Trish stared from the check to Stan, then back at the check. "You make me sick," she said. She ripped it in half and threw the pieces to the dresser top. She sat on the bed, spine curving, head down. She looked as if she had run a very long way and could not catch her breath.

Stan Webelow had gone practically purple. He stood shirtless in the center of his mother's bedroom, his fly gaping open. "You break my house open, hit me in the face, start asking me questions about some kid I never spoke to. What the hell?" he said to David. "That kid was never in my house."

"Then where is Shelby?" Laurel said, mostly to David.

"Your Shelby? Why would your kid be here?" Stan Webelow said. He looked from Laurel to David, and then his lip curled under. "You're twisted. She's a child."

"Excuse me," said Thalia, still grinning. "You're getting paid to sex up married ladies in your mother's bed. I'd say you've got the edge on twisted, here."

Trish was muttering to herself. She got her Lycra pants off the floor and then felt under the bed, pulling out ankle socks and tennis shoes. She jerked on the pants with an angry economy of movement. Laurel could see a lime-green bra strap poking out from the top. Trish had jogged down here, fancy underthings hidden beneath her running suit, and slipped inside, no one the wiser.

Trish pulled her socks on one by one. She said, "If you dare tell anyone any single bit—"

"Blah blah blah," Thalia interrupted. "Shut it, Trish. We've got bigger problems than deciding who to call first on the Victorianna gossip phone tree."

"You believe him?" David said to Laurel.

She nodded. Stan's runs made sense now. He wasn't jogging in the dead heat of the day. He was making rounds, tapping on back doors while husbands were at work, his incriminating car never parked in front of anybody's house. Laurel's stomach did a slow roll inside of her. She put her head down the way Trish had and took in a deep breath. She said to Thalia, "Do you believe him?"

"He wouldn't have been messing with Molly," Thalia said. "A teenager couldn't afford him." To Stan, she said, "Sorry about the window," but she didn't sound a bit sorry. She sounded interested.

"How long will it take you to earn enough to fix it? In your line of work, I mean."

Stan picked up his shirt and stuffed his arms through the holes. "Not long," he said. His spine was stiff with anger as he jerked at his shirt, straightening it, but his voice had the edge of a smug, professional pride.

"How many clients have you got here?" Thalia said.

"In Victorianna? Three, but it's not the only neighborhood I run in." He glanced at Trish. "Maybe two now."

"I feel ill," Trish said. She was trying to tie her shoelaces, but her hands were shaking.

Laurel stood up and took David's arm, pulling him toward the doorway. "We need to go home," she said. "Start an AMBER Alert."

"One sec," Thalia said. She turned back to Stan. "I have to know. How come you never hit up on my sister?"

Stan was buttoning his shirt, but he paused long enough to dismiss Laurel and David with a glance. "That's unbreakable. I can smell the ones who still like each other a mile off."

"No, really?" said Thalia.

Laurel said, "We need to go meet the police."

Trish said, "Oh, God! Who called the police? I told you no!"

The bedside table was cluttered with a clock radio, a teeny pink lamp, tissues, candles, and a grouping of blown-glass angels playing instruments. Trish rifled through the clutter, knocking over the flutist, muttering, "Where are my damn keys?"

"Relax," Thalia said. "The cops are coming to Laurel's, not here. We've misplaced Shelby."

Trish stopped and looked up, puzzled. "Why the hell are you looking for her here? She was just at the duck pond."

Stan kept stuffing his shirttail into his open pants, but everyone else in the room froze and stared at Trish.

"When," David said.

"Not even an hour ago," Trish said. "I passed her on my way over here."

She was still hunting her keys. David took two strides toward her and grabbed her arm. "Where?"

"Ow! Watch it!" Trish said. She jerked her arm away. "By the duck pond, like I said, with that . . . relative you have staying with you. I need to go home."

"Bet Clemmens," Thalia said. "You didn't think it was weird to see two thirteen-year-old girls at the duck pond with suitcases?"

Trish shrugged. "Shelby had a suitcase, but that other one didn't. It looked like she had a bag of trash, except she put it in the car."

"That is her suit— Wait," said Laurel. "What car?"

"An ugly car," Trish said. "A car I wouldn't let my kids lean on, much less ride in, but Shelby threw her case in the trunk and jumped into the backseat. The woman driving and your little cousin thing seemed like a matched set, so I didn't think twice about it."

"You have to be kidding me," said Thalia.

"What did the car look like?" Laurel said.

"It was this boxy sedan, mostly red," Trish said. "But the bottom was rusted out, and the driver's-side door was a completely different color."

"Blue," Laurel said, and she didn't need Trish's curt nod to confirm it.

"What does it mean?" David asked Laurel.

"That's Sissi Clemmens's car," said Thalia. "Everybody's favorite meth head came and picked up Bet and Shelby."

"DeLop," Laurel said. Her every bone felt brittle and cold, as if they'd been flash-frozen. Even so, her body was already moving, grabbing Thalia, pulling her back across the room, and herding David out the door ahead of them, hurrying them toward the stairs, the front door, the car, the highway, her daughter. "Shelby's headed for DeLop."

CHAPTER 17

The phone at Sissi Clemmens's place rang for the fifteenth time, and Laurel snapped her cell phone shut. She wished she were driving. Every red light, every pedestrian, every poky Honda Civic waffling its slow way into a turn lane was a personal affront. Behind her, David was back on the phone with the police dispatcher, answering questions in a low, deliberate voice.

All the pieces were falling into place, making a pattern that Laurel didn't want to see. The night Molly Dufresne died was unspooling in her head, over and over in an endless loop.

She stretched her eyes wide open and told Thalia, "You drive faster than this going to Albertsons to get milk."

Thalia said, "Once I get to the interstate, I'll open it up. There's about fifteen speed traps between Pensacola and the state line."

She sounded so calm, so reasonable, that Laurel had a sudden vision of reaching across her sister, opening the door, and pushing her out into the street. She'd scoot into Thalia's place and floor it. If only her hands would stop shaking. She doubted they would close around the wheel. "Just drive," she said.

David lowered his phone and said, "They want us to meet an officer at our house. One of us has to sign the report."

"No," Laurel said.

"They say it will take fifteen minutes, tops."

"We're not going back." Laurel's voice was fierce and loud. "We'll lose time driving back home, and then who knows how long they'll keep us there. Tell them we're on the way to DeLop already and to meet us there. They can take the report over the phone."

David subsided, and Thalia settled herself deeper into the driver's seat, one hand on the wheel. They were coming to an intersection, and the light ahead turned yellow. Thalia slowed and stopped.

"Oh, dear God," Laurel said, not sure if she was praying or only cursing her sister.

Shelby, somewhere on the highway with Sissi and Bet Clemmens, already had at least an hour's head start. Laurel dialed Sissi's number again, listening to the phone ring over and over. It was still ringing when the light turned green.

Thalia said, "They haven't had time to get there."

Laurel closed her eyes and let it ring anyway. She understood now, and the parts she couldn't know filled themselves in seamlessly, like a movie projected onto the back of her lids. She saw Molly Dufresne alive, thirteen, immortal, safe in her own bed. Molly waited for the quiet part of night to come, secreted under her covers with a book and a flashlight, still wearing her sundress and tennis shoes.

She'd put her brothers to bed, reading to them until they'd

settled into that deep sleep known only to little children, mouths open, hands flung up over their heads. Molly had put herself to bed after. Now she heard fierce, low voices downstairs, battling back and forth. Chuck sounded clipped and hard. Bunny, soused, slurred and hissed her words, so from this distance, they sounded like the ranting of an angry snake. Molly waited it out. This was what normal sounded like in her house right now, and when Shelby had asked if she wanted to slip out, meet up in Shel's backyard, the usually timid Molly had said yes, yes, hell yes, a thousand times yes.

At last Chuck made his angry way to a guest room. Molly heard him rattling around in the attached bathroom, and then he got quiet. Bunny had already passed out in the master bedroom, the click and stumble of her bedtime routine covered by his.

Molly Dufresne clock-watched. The house had been silent for a good hour before it was time to throw back the covers and go creeping down the staircase. She knew the third stair creaked, and she bypassed it. She knew the alarm code, and she punched it in. She paused by the back door, her heart beating fast and light. She wasn't afraid of getting caught. The bottle of wine Barb had opened to have with dinner rested empty in the bottom of the trash. Molly could have stomped across Barb's body singing the Gloria and then dived out her bedroom window without waking her mother. Though Chuck was a heavy sleeper, Molly half wished he would wake up and catch her. Maybe he would stop sniping about lawyers and look at his daughter for a change.

Then Molly was outside, closing the back door gently behind her. She waited on the lawn for a light to go on, for her father's voice to call her back, but her house stayed dark and silent. She'd done it, this bold thing that was more like something Shelby would do. It had been Shelby's idea, sure, but Molly was the one who was out alone in the good, dark night, and she found herself picking up speed as she left her yard.

She wasn't afraid. She was behind Victorianna's wrought-iron gates, as comfortable inside them as she was in her own skin. She spread her thin arms like airplane wings and ran, in silent, joyful rebellion, through the dark yards, liking the feel of the slick grass under her feet. The streets were lined with old-fashioned lampposts, and now that she was out, she didn't want to be seen or stopped.

She ran toward Shelby's, ready for all manner of nonsense. Shelby always made the best plans. Maybe, when they were finished, Shelby's mom would catch them. She could imagine Laurel calling her house, the shrill of the telephone waking her parents up. Laurel would say, "Barb, do you have any idea where your kid is?"

Her mother would be shamed, and serve her right. Molly could be anywhere. She was practically flying, up to no good, and thrilled about it. Served them all right.

David touched Laurel's shoulder, and she jumped. He said, "They need a street address for Sissi Clemmens. Either of you know it?"

Thalia said, "I'm not sure she has one."

"Her trailer is at the dead end of Harold Street," Laurel said. "It's the right-hand lot, a double-wide with a blue awning and about seven big pinwheels and some wind socks lined up in front of it."

David sat back, repeating that dubious address to the dispatcher.

Thalia merged onto U.S. 29, a double-lane freeway that would take them to the state line.

"I can't figure out what Molly and Shel were doing," Laurel said. "Everything else makes sense. I can see Shelby sneaking out and going to get Molly, but this is backward. Why did Molly come to our yard?"

"Oh," Thalia said. "Maybe I know."

"Did Shelby say something?" Laurel said, rounding on her as best she could with the seat belt holding her.

"No. That boy next door, Missy's kid? Apparently, he likes a late-night swim. He prefers to swim . . . freely, if you follow me," Thalia said. "I saw him from the window the other night, while you were still out in the gazebo. He was very much worth seeing, in a *The David* kind of way."

"God, Thalia, Jeffrey Coe is a kid," Laurel said.

"I'm not saying I want to paper-train that puppy. But he's what? Seventeen? And beautiful? And naked? If I were Molly, I'd pay good cash money to peek at that, all sneaky-like. Hell, I did exactly the same thing at that age."

Laurel was nodding. "That makes sense. I'd told Shelby no sleepovers while Bet was in town."

It explained why Shelby had lied, too. At first she hadn't wanted Laurel to know only that she and Molly had plans to peek over the fence at Jeffrey Coe. Later, when Laurel came to Shelby while she and Bet were watching the movie, she must have been tearing herself to guilty bits inside. Moreno's endless needling would have made her connect dots and ask herself, over and over, why she had fallen asleep when, if she hadn't, she would have been there to pull Molly out. So she had lied, first insisting to Moreno that there was no boy, because the latest crush was naked

Jeffrey Coe. Then she'd said she never planned to meet Molly and that she'd been watching TV with Bet in the rec room. Bet, with much more to hide, had backed her up.

Thalia took her eyes off the road long enough to look Laurel up and down, assessing her. "You're about to stroke out, Bug," she said. "Chill. We know where she's going."

David closed his phone. "They've sent out a dispatch. Cops along the highway will be looking for Sissi's car. Also, they're sending a Teletype ahead to the police in DeLop—"

Thalia snorted. "There are no police in DeLop."

"To whoever has jurisdiction there," David said, impatience coloring his voice.

"Are they calling in the feds?" Thalia said, perking up. "Federal agents are very often hot."

"No," David said. "She called this 'interference with custody,' not kidnapping. A sheriff, I would guess. He'll keep driving past Sissi's place until they show."

Thalia was moving at a good clip, weaving around the big trucks that used 29 as an access road to 65. The highway was lined on both sides with strip malls and gas stations. Every four or five miles, Laurel knew, there would be another Waffle House.

"Surely someone will see the car and stop them," Laurel said.

"It's a P.O.S. red lemon with one blue door," said Thalia. "It's not like it blends."

"They'll call my cell when they have her," David said, and he sounded as calm as Thalia.

Laurel could have clubbed them both. They were acting like they were going to pick Shelby up at the movies. Laurel dialed Sissi's home again. She listened to the phone ring and ring.

"You'll run your battery down and not have it when you need it," said Thalia.

Laurel snapped the phone shut. Sissi had both girls in the car with her right now. Assuming Sissi wasn't stoned to the gills and didn't plow them into an embankment, Shelby would be fine until they got to Sissi's house. It was the hour that followed that was making the pit of Laurel's stomach feel like a clenched fist. Even if they made good time, there would be half an hour, forty-five minutes, maybe more, between the time Sissi got home and Laurel's car pulled up.

Shelby would be loose in DeLop with Bet Clemmens, close to alone. Laurel didn't count Sissi as any sort of supervision. She imagined the blue-tinged flesh of Sissi's pale legs resticking itself to the vinyl of the sofa as her body sank into the custom groove she'd worn in its cushion. Laurel imagined Sissi's bleary eyes drifting shut. Shelby would be on her own. With Bet. It could not happen.

Laurel said, "What if Sissi doesn't get stopped?"

"If she scoots through, would it truly be the end of the universe?" Thalia asked. "You're being overly dramatic. Coming from me, that's quite a damnation."

"Leave her alone," David said. He spoke with almost no inflection, but it came out ice-cold. "Why did you come?"

"To drive, David. So you two could make your calls. You're welcome."

"I have a Bluetooth," David said. "And *it's* not being a jerk to my wife."

"Stop it," Laurel said.

Thalia said, "I haven't started. All I said was half an hour in DeLop might do Shel some good. She needs to see that not everyone in the world lives in a place where they genetically engineer the pansies to match the mailbox trim."

"I said leave her alone," David said. "This isn't the time to . . . be you."

"Go to hell," Thalia said without rancor.

"You're both missing the point," Laurel said. She couldn't blame them. She'd missed it, too, for days, her eyes focused only on Stan Webelow. But who had kept her focus there? Every time her gaze had strayed from him, Bet Clemmens had been there, saying she saw Molly going into Stan's house, saying Shelby had seen Molly with Stan, too.

David and Thalia were sniping back and forth at each other, Thalia's voice winding around his, while his curt responses were like punctuation, periods and exclamation points that ended her sentences before Thalia simply started on a new one.

Laurel stopped listening, closed her eyes as they passed yet another Krispy Kreme. She was seeing Molly Dufresne again, waiting in the Hawthornes' backyard.

Shelby was late.

A couple of hours ago, Shelby and Bet had gone to their separate bedrooms, supposedly to sleep. Shel had waited in her room for the appointed hour, but her eyelids had gotten heavy. Her alarm clock might wake Bet, asleep across the hall. Bet was not privy to the plan.

Not surprising, really. It was probably not pure teen-girl meanness. Shelby simply hadn't thought to include her. After all, Laurel had never gone out of her way to truly weave Bet into their lives. She'd made sure that Bet was behaving and that Shelby's friends were being kind to her, but she'd kept Bet separate, buttoned away in her own little pocket. She'd never made Bet integral and equal, so it didn't occur to Shelby and Molly to do so, either.

Shelby had tiptoed all the way down to the end of the hall to the rec room, which was farther from Bet's door and at the opposite end of the house from David and Laurel's room. She'd closed the door and put the TV's volume on so low that it was barely more than a murmur. She'd sprawled out in her beanbag, pinching her arm every minute or so to make sure she was still awake. Her eyelids had drooped lower, and the television conversation had blended into a lullaby of empty conversation. Shelby had fallen asleep.

Down in the yard, Molly got bored. She could smell rain coming. Clouds hid the moon, and the night was dark and hot. With the storm getting this close, Jeffrey Coe would not be coming out. Her elation faded. She wished Shelby would come so this would feel like fun again. It was dark near the gazebo, but she went back there anyway, dropping to her knees to feel around the base where she knew she could find round stones and pebbles. She gathered a small handful.

She picked her way across the blackness of the yard to Shelby's dark window. Molly tossed rocks at it, one after another, pinging them off the glass.

Nothing happened. Molly decided to give Shelby five more minutes, then she would go home. The only light in the backyard came from the underwater pool lights. Molly was drawn to that blue glow. She walked around the pool's edges, her toes pointing ballerina-style with each careful step, like a gymnast on a balance beam. At the far end, she shuffled lightly down the length of the diving board, sliding her feet along because it was so springy. She reached the end and sat down, dangling her tennis shoes over the glowing water.

Inside, the rocks hitting Shelby's window had woken up Bet Clemmens, who got up and went across the hall to Shelby's empty room. Shelby's window overlooked the backyard, so Bet had a clear view of Molly in her light-colored dress, noodling around on the end of the board.

Bet went downstairs. The alarm was set, so Bet put in the code and waited until the light went green before she slid open the glass door. Molly, at the far end of the pool, heard the door. She didn't know if it was Shelby or one of Shelby's parents coming out to bust her. She peered across the yard, trying to see. She scrambled to her feet, but the soles of her tennis shoes slipped on the board's damp surface. Molly tumbled backward, banging her head, and then splashed into the water. Bet saw the water contract as it accepted her, saw it splash up after. Ripples spread to the edge from the place Molly had fallen, but she did not rise. Under the surface, Molly had gone still, rolling facedown as the water filled her and cooled her.

Bet started forward on instinct, stepping over Shelby's dammit and coming all the way to the taller wrought-iron fence around the pool. There she stopped, her fingers curling around the latch on the gate. She was thinking. Her hands dropped to her sides. She didn't go down into the water, and she didn't yell for help. She simply stood and waited. She watched Molly die, and then she watched Molly be dead. She stayed that way for a long time, her flat unchanging eyes on Molly's body as it drifted.

She saw, the Ouija board had told Laurel, and Laurel, focused on Shelby's lie, Shelby's palpable, unhappy guilt, hadn't seen nor noticed the quiet girl sheltering her daughter in her shadow. Bet was so affection-starved that Laurel's wary caution and vague kindness seemed a feast to her. Laurel hadn't understood or seen the growth of Bet's awful love, so she could not imagine Bet stepping a little closer, a little closer, all the way to the edge of the pool, to look down at the small body drifting silent for an endless span of time.

It must have been hypnotizing, so powerful, to do nothing, to watch water fill Molly and emptiness take the place she used to occupy. Bet stood there until she heard Laurel howling from the window, banging on the glass.

All at once, Bet felt terrified. She was the shadow Laurel saw melting into the darkness as she ran for the house. She scurried inside to reset the alarm with trembling fingers. There wasn't time to get upstairs. She scuttled into the kitchen, crouching behind the low counter. She peered over the top to watch first Laurel and then David go tearing out into the night.

As soon as they were out, she dashed upstairs. She'd seen Laurel at the window of a dark room, hollering. Surely Laurel had seen her, too. Bet began frantically stuffing her clothes into her Hefty bag, readying to run. But then Shelby was there, at her door, Shelby's little living paw on her arm, pulling her down the stairs to see what was happening. Shelby went outside and Bet trailed behind, her Hefty bag clutched to her chest, numb. She was dreading the moment when Laurel's gaze would come to rest on her face.

Laurel's finger would point, and she would say, "It was her. By the pool. She saw. She saw."

"I fell asleep in the rec room. Me and Bet were watching TV," Shelby lied, and Bet, surprised, could say only, "Do what?"

Then Laurel looked at Bet, and her eyes barely focused as they skimmed over her body, her bag, her flip-flops. That must have felt like Laurel's normal look to Bet, and she'd relaxed into a passive state, adrift, waiting to see what would happen next.

Later, when Laurel was hell-bent on getting Thalia and digging up what really happened that night, Bet ghosted around on her cat feet, listening. Bet, Laurel was certain, had her ear at every cracked door. No doubt she eavesdropped when Laurel went downstairs to tell David that they needed Thalia. Laurel imagined Bet pressing down the intercom listen button and leaning one ear against the speaker. At the theater with Thalia, Bet must have taken off the headphones as soon as Gary went back upstairs, sneaking to the door to hear Laurel tell Thalia all her theories.

Bet had been covering her tracks ever since. She'd seen. She'd let it happen. Now she'd finagled Shelby into going with her to DeLop, the least safe place on Planet Earth.

Thalia and David were still volleying harsh words back and forth, but Laurel heard none of them. She willed David's phone to ring, for the police dispatcher to say they had Shelby at a rest stop off 65, not half an hour away, waiting for Laurel, safe and angry.

This far down 29, the strip malls had given out. They'd left Pensacola. Flat Florida grassland dotted with loblolly pine trees filled the long spaces between BP stations and truck stops. The phone didn't ring. Her child was still moving headlong into danger.

Out of the wash of hard words, Laurel caught this sentence: "Until you gave her that big 'you light up my life' speech in the foyer—"

Laurel's head jerked around to stare at her sister. "You heard that?" she said.

Thalia paused. She had the rearview mirror angled so that she could glare back through it at David, but she glanced at Laurel and said, "Yes, Bug. Bet's not the only one who can glide around the house in sock feet," and Laurel blanched. It was as if Thalia had been reading her mind. But Thalia wasn't finished. "I wasn't eavesdropping, per se. I came down to talk to you, and he was in the middle of it. I'm glad the whole 'you make me want to be a better man' thing worked for you, but then after, in the glow, in the endless hours the two of you were secluded in David's pit downstairs, I have to know, little sister, what fleas were you putting in his ear?"

Laurel shrugged, already losing interest. She leaned forward in her seat, pressing her hands in to the dashboard as if pushing the car forward. "Let it go."

"What did you tell him?" Thalia asked.

"It doesn't matter."

Maybe she should try Sissi's house again. Sissi must have a cell phone, too, or maybe Bet had gotten her at a boyfriend's house. Bet must have had a way to contact Sissi Clemmens that Laurel didn't know about, because Sissi was on the road to Pensacola not half an hour after Bet pulled her final snow job. Bet had overplayed that one badly, and Laurel had panicked her by saying it was time to bring the cops back in.

Thalia knuckle-punched Laurel in the arm, hard, claiming her attention again. "There's that whole 'no statute of limitations' thing that does make it matter, a tiny bit, to me."

"You should thank her," David said. "You make more sense to me now. In a way. You're almost forgivable."

"Wait, what?" Thalia said. "I make sense to you? Good God, I think the earth's polarity just reversed."

"David's not going to tell anyone. He understands why you felt driven to do what you did, and it's okay," Laurel said.

" 'He understands'? I don't like the way you said that. It was very moist and hand-holdy. I am not cattle, Bug. I drive. I don't get driven," Thalia said. Her gaze was back on the road, but then her sloe eyes narrowed into long angry slits. Her hands clenched down on the wheel so tightly it looked like she was trying to strangle it. "Wait a sec. You have to be kidding me. So Mr. Math here thinks he's solved for X, huh? You told him Uncle Marty gave me the bad touch and turned me into Crazy Thalia. How nice for the both of you, to be able to reduce me to such a simple two plus two. Is that what you told him, Jesus Bug?"

Thalia had let her foot grow heavy on the gas pedal. The Volvo wobbled over onto the shoulder, and Thalia jerked it back to the middle of the lane, so mad she was panting.

"It's not your fault," Laurel said.

"Is that what you think, metal man?" Thalia whipped her head around long enough to take David's measure in the backseat. She said, "Cause and effect. Incest in, actress out. God, I wish people really were so simple. If they were, acting would be a hell of a lot easier. Spare me. I don't want you to excuse me, David, and I sure as hell don't need you to explain me." Thalia laughed, an abrupt burst of angry sound. Then she said, "Marty never laid a hand on me. You assholes."

Finally, Thalia had Laurel's full attention. She turned in her seat to stare at her sister. "Yes, he did."

"No, he didn't," Thalia said.

"Sometimes," Laurel said carefully, "people don't want things to be true, so they stop remembering. I've read about it."

Thalia laughed again, this time in a glorious peal. "I bet you have. In *Family Circle* or *Reader's Digest,* no doubt. I bet those are the articles that always caught your eye in the pediatrician's waiting room. Did you angle the magazine carefully to the wall, so the other mommies wouldn't see what ugly story had you so engrossed?

"And what did *Reader's Digest* teach you? Do I need to go to hypnotherapy and retrieve my sad past? Please. I've *had* hypnotherapy and past-life regression. Gary and I once did a womb workshop where they tied us up together in a long canvas tube so we could struggle our way out and be rebirthed as twins. It's the sort of thing we do on date night, while you two share a Diet Coke and hold hands at the movies.

"What do you want, Buglet? You want some tidy cause and effect like Mr. Science back there? Then here's a double scoop of logic for you both. One: If Marty made me who I am, tell me when. Show me the day when the fairies took your sugar-mouthed angel sister and left you a wild nixie. If you can, I swear I'll go right back to the hypnotherapist and ask if it's possible my uncle diddled me when I wasn't looking."

There was no such day, and Laurel knew it. Thalia had always been Thalia, sly and mighty, a changeling only in her ability to slip her own skin and tuck herself inside a character. She'd been born with that. One of Laurel's earliest memories was Thalia at about six, weeping fat tears with Laurel's pony doll in her hands. When Laurel had asked what was wrong, Thalia's tears had stopped instantly, and she'd glared at Laurel, irked at the interruption.

"*I'm* not crying," she'd said. "I'm being your pony. He's the one who's sad."

"Why is he sad?" Laurel had asked.

"I don't know," Thalia had said. And then she'd peeped at

Laurel, her mouth expanding into the baby predecessor of her wide wolf's smile, and added, "Maybe he's sad because he's yours. I bet he wishes he was my pony."

She'd embellished on that theory until Laurel was the one who was crying and running to tell Mother.

Now Laurel said, "You were always you, but—"

"Thank you," Thalia said. Her anger receded slightly. She leaned sideways toward Laurel, intent on proving her case. "Scoop two: Have you ever noticed the mouth on me? I'm not the vulnerable secret-keeping sort. I was born a pedophile's worst nightmare, and if Marty had tried any crap with me, I'd have set up a sting and tried to catch his ass on film. The closest Marty ever came to getting out of line with me was when I was eleven or so. He showed me his dick."

Laurel's breath caught. In the backseat, David had gone quiet, observing the two of them.

"What did you do?" Laurel said.

"I put one hand on my hip, and I looked that thing right in its eye and said, 'I've seen better.' "

A squawk of laughter escaped Laurel. "You didn't!"

Thalia slowed. They were in Century, approaching the Piggly Wiggly. It was set on the Florida side of the state line to avoid Alabama taxes. On Marty's last hunting trip, they'd stopped there to buy beef jerky and Coors and bags of honey-roasted peanuts.

"I was losing my crap inside, Bug. Don't get me wrong, but I would have ripped out my own kidneys and cooked them up with eggs before I'd have let him see that. Plus, you know, by then I *had* seen better."

Laurel blinked. "You had not."

They crossed over into Alabama, the town changing from Century to Flomaton in the space of a blink.

"Oh, yeah. A couple of months before, I gave Lisa Cartwright a dollar to let me climb the sycamore tree in her yard. I could see straight into the back bathroom. You remember her older brother, Lewis? He was fifteen and could not leave himself alone. He had this monstrous appendage that turned purple when he made it angry. That kid was hung like a Trojan soldier."

"Thalia, stop," Laurel said. "When Marty showed you, why didn't you tell anyone, if you had such a mouth?"

Thalia peeked at Laurel, then returned her focus to the road. "You know why I didn't."

Laurel started to shake her head, but then she did know. "Because there was no need to tell. Mother walked in on it."

Thalia was nodding. "He set it up that way. I think I knew even then that it had very little to do with me. Marty had known me since I was a fetus, and his kind cherry-pick the kids who won't tell. He had to know I wasn't that kid. When he flashed me, it was something he was doing to Mother, part of their endless war over custody of Daddy."

"How do you know?" Laurel said.

There was a pause, and David said, "Why did—"

Thalia overrode him, talking only to Laurel as if he had stopped existing. "Lots of ways. It's amazing what you'll see if you're paying close attention. I watch people. It helps me later in my work, when I have to pretend to be one. What I don't understand is how you could tell *him* all this. You sat down there feeling all squishy-sorry for poor little Thalia, no wonder she's such a freak. Well, screw you. I won't be judged like that."

Now Flomaton was behind them. They were in Alabama

proper, and the grass was greener here as they drove north, away from the sandy soil. This was the last road Marty ever drove down in his life.

Finally, Laurel said, "It's what you do to me all the time."

"I do not," Thalia said, an instant dismissal.

"You do. I don't see how you can be happy, living hand to mouth in your weird, gross marriage. Maybe I did try to explain that with Marty. I hate your life, and if I knew how, I'd rip you out of it and make you do right. That's exactly what you did to me. You came here, sure I must be all oppressed and miserable, so you tried to root me out. But you were wrong. You were wrong about every damn thing there was to be wrong about."

"So were you," Thalia said. "Well, except Stan Webelow is extraordinarily creepy. I'll give you that one."

"And my husband wasn't cheating on me," Laurel said.

"Okay," said Thalia. "But Shelby's run away, just like I told you she would."

"She's not running from me, Thalia. She's running from Molly's funeral. I think seeing Barb so blatantly destroyed on our sofa the other night messed her up. She's gone with Bet because she feels so guilty for falling asleep and not meeting Molly—she thinks it's all her fault. The poor kid didn't want to go to the viewing."

"No," David said, and Laurel jumped. He'd gone so quiet that, driving down this old road with her sister, she'd forgotten he was there. "She would have left a note."

"I bet she did," Laurel said. "It's probably behind the bed or under her dresser, tucked barely out of sight so that it looks like it fell naturally. But Bet moved it.

"Bet can't let me talk to Shel. She doesn't know we already

went down to Stan's. She only knows Shelby will say that she never saw Molly going in there. If I talk to Shelby, Bet's whole house of cards falls down. And Bet can't bear that. She can't bear for me to know the awful thing she did. Don't you get it?"

Thalia and David shrugged in tandem, and Laurel said, "God, can't you see? The reason I kept going on so hard about Stan Webelow is that every damn time I started to look in other directions, Bet Clemmens pulled me back to him. She told me when I came to get you, Thalia, that she'd seen him with Molly. She's the one who said Shelby saw Molly going in his house."

"Yeah, and?" Thalia said.

"She saw," Laurel said, giving Thalia the same small words the Ouija had given her. "She saw, and she decided. She stood there and let Molly drown."

Thalia shook her head. "What did she have against Molly?"

"Nothing. She couldn't care less about Molly. It's me. My life, the one you think is such a nightmare, looks pretty damn good to her. Bet loves me."

"That makes even less sense," David said.

"It was dark outside," Laurel said. "The porch light was off. A storm was coming." She could see them, first David and then Thalia, groping their way to her conclusion.

Kneeling on Shelby's empty bed, Bet looked out the window. The only light came from below, diffused and softened as it shone up through the water. Shelby wasn't in her room, and Bet had not been privy to her plans with Molly. Bet saw a slim little blonde sitting out on the diving board. Bet went downstairs to join her and saw her slip and fall, saw her roll into the water and sink.

Bet didn't see Molly Dufresne. She saw Shelby, the girl who lived in the space Bet wanted to occupy. Laurel's life was so full, she never really looked at Bet. As Bet watched Shelby drowning, she must have seen it as an opening she could slip inside. She could find herself forever in that lovely place, take the seat beside Laurel, who smelled like Bet knew mommies ought to smell.

"Bet can't afford to let me talk to Shelby," Laurel said. "Not ever."

The temperature in the car seemed to drop three degrees.

Thalia said, "I'm not going fast enough," and jammed her foot down on the gas.

CHAPTER 18

They were close. The Burger Kings and Wal-Marts fell away, replaced by pawnshops and check-cashing outlets. They passed a final Piggly Wiggly, and then the only chain stores were three different places that would take a car title as collateral on a small high-interest loan.

The last of these was on the end of an otherwise boarded-up strip mall. After they passed it, there were no businesses at all, no buildings, nothing on either side of Highway 78. No trees, no kudzu, even. The trees had been ripped out for their wood, and the land had been peeled back to the shale for its metals. They had entered a wasteland.

It looked uglier to Laurel than it had at Christmas when she came with her family. Even with the distant trees providing a line of color on the horizon that was absent in winter, it looked immeasurably worse. Bleaker. The only difference was that her mother wasn't here. DeLop looked softer when Mother was along, as if it were being filmed through cheesecloth. Mother's blindness was so powerful, so catching, that Laurel hadn't seen DeLop this baldly even when she'd driven here alone to check out and return Bet Clemmens. It was as if she were seeing it for the first time, through David's fresh, shocked eyes as well as her own. Her daughter was somewhere up ahead, unprotected in the badlands.

Thalia exited onto a narrow two-lane road that hadn't had a street sign for so long Laurel had forgotten its name. Here, there were new woods, the trees six and eight feet tall, each as slender as a forearm. Choking brush grew up around them, and in most places, they were already heaped high with kudzu in summer's full, deep green. Had they ventured out of the car, they couldn't have walked four feet off the road without a machete.

The road forked, and Thalia banked right on Arnold Street, heading uphill. The asphalt was so old it was the soft gray of cigarette ash. On the right, almost grown over with brush, stood the familiar sign that had once said WELCOME TO DELOP. The edges had rusted away long before Laurel was born, and the right third of it was folded over and rusting down the seam. The ghosts of its red letters showed through a coating of thick grime: WELCO TO DE.

They passed it, and Laurel felt it like a border crossing. They had left behind America, even the disposable Wal-Mart culture of regular American poverty. In DeLop, nothing was disposable, because nothing was ever replaced. Everything was saved and stored and kept in decaying heaps. Shelby was here. Laurel could feel her heartbeat traveling through the ground, coming up through the tires, reverberating so strongly inside Laurel that her hands, when she held them up, look palsied.

There was no commercial building or store of any sort for over seven miles. They passed an access road that led down to a played-out strip mine. With no one to dredge it, it had filled with stagnant green water that raised and lowered itself depending on the rainfall. A long rusted chain hung between two metal poles, blocking vehicle access, as it had for over half a century. There was another, larger mining gash almost in the center of the town. It was a deep scar, the size of a small football stadium. The houses and mobile homes in DeLop were clustered in small pods, mostly south and west of the strip mine. The Folks still called it the mine, though no coal had come out of it for seventy years. Aunt Moff, who lived closest, called it the Frog Hole.

The first building they came to after the access road was Billy Eaver's single-wide. He was Mother's half brother; the Eavers and Clemmenses and Foleys were all Mother's people. Billy's place sat in a dirt patch with the scrub trees and brush rising around it, the kudzu leaning in, looking for a toehold on the heaps of trash and the skeletons of stripped cars that rested in the yard. Two flat-eyed pit bulls with alligator mouths and heads as big as boot boxes stared through Billy's front gate. He'd chained about four different types of salvaged fencing into a makeshift barricade with barbed wire laced through it and running along the uneven top. Faded signs hung along the fence; three said No Trespassing, and one said Beware of Dog.

David pointed at the last sign and said, "No kidding." His voice sounded thick. "Is it safe up here?"

"Safe-ish, for us," Thalia said at the same time Laurel said, "No." Then she glanced at Thalia and agreed, "Yes, for us."

"I meant Shelby," David said.

Neither Thalia nor Laurel had a good answer for that, so they said nothing.

"I didn't expect the fences," David said as they drove past another mobile home so hemmed in by split rails and barbed wire that it looked barricaded. "I can tell by looking, they don't have damn all to steal."

Now that they were here, Thalia had slowed. Laurel was looking back and forth, searching the yards and the roadside for Shelby.

"Some of them have drugs," Laurel offered. "But even the ones who don't are very territorial. They live in their own world. They don't like people from down the hill. I'm scared Bet is going to get Shelby out somewhere, here in the middle, and then leave her."

Thalia nodded. "That's what I'd do."

They were passing between two more double-wides, both so decayed that they looked like they were melting slowly into the landscape. Moff's girl, Della Foley, lived on the right with her sister and her sister's man and his mother; they had three babies between them. Della had cobbled together a playground out of scrap. She'd hung a tire swing, and beside it, she'd buried a length of rusty sewer ladder deep enough to stand upright. An old metal slide was soldered onto it.

In front of the left mobile home, Raydee Eaver and his brother, Louis, were messing around in the guts of an old truck. It had no hood, and they were bent over the exposed engine. Louis had a wrench and was jerking hard at something. Neither had a shirt on in the late-afternoon heat, and with their flossy blond hair, narrow torsos, and long sinewy arms, they looked like young male Thalias. They raised their heads and stared as the Volvo came even with them, their matched-set green gazes as flat as the dogs' had been.

"Do you know them?" David asked as Thalia braked to a stop.

"Yes, but they don't recognize this car," Laurel said.

At Christmas, Daddy drove them in the Buick, and last week Laurel had picked up Bet in David's SUV. An unknown car in DeLop was something between an event and an invasion. Strangers nearly always turned out to be either someone from the sheriff's office still-hunting, or a parole officer, or some churchly good-doer, coming up to save them with tracts and blankets and canned peas. A while back they'd "caught a social worker," as Enid had put it, making the poor woman sound like a rash. She'd wanted to track the children, the ones with Social Security numbers and school records, anyway, and try to get them back in a classroom. "Took her most of a damn year to peter out," Enid had said.

The Eaver boys were walking toward the car. Raydee led from the hip with his center of gravity so low Laurel knew immediately that he was stoned to his gills. Louis swung the wrench lightly back and forth as he walked, as if it weighed nothing. The sunlight gleamed off its silver. There was something in the set of his muscles that seemed coiled, his body readying itself for violence.

Thalia scrolled down the window and leaned out, calling, "Hey, Raydee. Hey, Louis."

Louis slowed a hair, and the springy, ready way he'd held the wrench changed in some subtle way, rendering it innocuous.

"That you, Thalia?" Raydee called.

"Who's that with ya? Larl?" Louis asked.

That's how everyone said Laurel's name up here, one compressed, gargling syllable that had hardly a vowel in it.

"Yeah, and her husband," Thalia called. "Her daughter's up here, too. You seen her?"

Thalia didn't bother to describe Shelby. There were maybe

sixty mobile homes and trailers and another ten or twelve actual houses in DeLop. The remains of what had once been a company store stood near the middle, a cinder-block building that had been stripped of every detachable piece of itself, so it no longer had even wooden windowsills or doors. A place this small, everyone knew everyone else, and most of them were interrelated. Strange to think that when Mother was Shelby's age, she had belonged here. She'd walked down these streets knowing no others, part of the landscape, but Shelby would stick out as brightly as a new penny. If Raydee or Louis had seen her, they would know.

"Naw," said Louis.

Raydee said, "You brunged Bet home already?"

Thalia said, "Yeah. You seen Bet?"

She looked at Raydee as she asked, but he only knitted his brows, puzzled. Louis stepped in and answered, his tone cool. "Naw, but Sissi's car come by a while back. Afore that, the sheriff's deputy been driving through. Aunt Shirl said he got out at Sissi's and banged her door. You know why's that?"

"Nope," Thalia said, but Louis's gaze did not warm, and he cocked a skeptical eyebrow. Thalia went on. "Listen, you see Miss Shelby, can you bring her on to Sissi's? We got to start the drive home."

She was echoing his diction and his accent, structuring her sentences the way they all did here. Raydee had gone easy in his body as she talked, watching his brother have a conversation with Junie Eaver Gray's girl. But Louis, sober, or at least less messed up, knew better. If Mother had been with them, he would have invited them in, maybe offered them a cold drink. Mother had been born here, and she was a part of this place in a way that her daughters, raised with television and indoor plumbing and fresh milk down in Pace, had never been.

"Sure thing," Louis said.

Raydee added, "I'll tell her she's gon' get her behiney paddled, she don't get home."

He tipped his baseball cap at Laurel and then stretched his arms up over his head, his torso elongating so that his ribs stuck out. Louis turned away, and Raydee followed him back toward the truck they'd been messing with. Thalia drove on.

"We should have asked how long ago they saw Sissi's car," David said.

Thalia released a scoffing chuckle. "He said 'a while,' David, and it's not like either of those boys owns a watch."

She drove the most direct route to Harold Street, leaving the paved roads twice to scoot through narrow gravel paths between mobile homes. Laurel scanned the lots, looking for Shelby's bright hair.

Sissi's trailer was one of the few places in DeLop that didn't have some version of fencing. Her broad-shouldered brindle dog, Mitchell, was on a chain by the door. He was lying under one of Sissi's raggedy pinwheels. The afternoon was so still that none of the gaudy wheels moved, and the wind socks hung limp. Mitchell lifted his head and stared at them as they pulled up.

As they were getting out of the car, Sissi opened the door and stood framed in it, glaring at them.

"She said she had alla y'all's permissions," Sissi said, preemptively defensive. "Bet and her both looked me in my eye and tole me. Now Shirl and Ruby come over, tellin' me the sheriff done drived by twice'd now, pullin' into my yard. Why's that, is what I'd like to know."

"Are they here?" Laurel said, striding angrily across the stretch of dirt and trash and gravel Sissi had instead of a lawn. Mitchell stood in a single fluid motion. He was probably eighty pounds, with a deep chest and a back end so skinny she could see the cut, lean muscle under his dirty coat. She felt his gaze, yellow and assessing, on the skin of her bare neck. She forced herself to stop and turned to him. "Hey, Mitchell. There's that good boy."

"Down, Mitchie," Sissi hollered at him, and he sank to his belly, shoulders still tensed.

"Is Shelby inside?" Laurel said.

"Is that sheriff coming back?" Sissi countered. "Do I need to maybe pick up a little?"

Laurel felt her hands clenching. "Sissi," she began, but Thalia interrupted, talking smoothly over her.

"I'd tuck things away, Sis, but I don't expect there's any need to go getting rid of anything. We weren't sure Shel had come up here until now. We've got people looking all over Florida, not just up here."

"Well, she ain't inside," said Sissi. "Bet's showing her around."

"Oh, God," Laurel said. She needed to sit down. Her blood had gone thin and cold, and it couldn't get good oxygen to her. David had come up behind her, and now he put one arm around her, shoring her up.

"How long ago?" Thalia asked.

Sissi shrugged and said, "They can't have got far. No place to go, anyways. Bet wanted Shelby to get her cards read over to Moff's. Try there."

"This is my husband, David," Laurel said. "He's going to stay here in case the girls get back, okay?"

"Well, I don't know about that," Sissi said. She and Mitchell stared David down together, equally suspicious.

Thalia said, "If the sheriff comes again, he'll be wanting to talk to David, not you. If David's here, he could go on out and square the sheriff away. Sheriff wouldn't even need to come inside."

Sissi's eyes narrowed, but she nodded. David opened his mouth to speak and then closed it again.

They'd decided in the car who would do what. Without Mother along, Thalia could do a better job of blending here. She could mimic posture and speech patterns, and The Folks were often more at ease in her company than in Laurel's, so Thalia would go to their relatives' houses. Laurel would do a circuit of DeLop, hitting all the small back roads and dead ends, looking for Shelby outside. David was to stay at Sissi's. He hadn't been happy about it, but nothing else made sense. He didn't know the landscape or the people.

"Call me as soon as you find her," he said, and walked slowly past Mitchell. The dog watched his every step.

Sissi scootched over a molecule to let David get past her into the trailer. "Don't you feed him any?" she called to Laurel.

"Throw me your keys, Sissi," Thalia said. "Be faster to drive to Moff's."

DeLop was small, but the houses were spread thinly around two sides of the Frog Hole, with close woods and wilderness between the clumps.

Sissi leaned into the trailer to grab her keys, then threw them across the yard in a bright arc that came nowhere near Thalia. They landed in a heap in the dust, and Sissi cackled as Thalia went to retrieve them.

"Go," Thalia said to Laurel.

Thalia had left the Volvo running, so Laurel got in on the driver's side and backed up onto the road. She wound her way through DeLop's warren of streets, a mix of gravel and old asphalt and dirt, all crisscrossing and doubling back. The paved ones had common names, like Alice and Janet and Jasper. The others were homemade and nameless. Laurel kept her windows down, moving slowly and looking side to side.

The late-afternoon heat was keeping most people inside. She saw a young woman she didn't know well, not part of her family, sitting out in the square of dirt she'd fenced around her trailer and watching a filthy baby grubbing around. The baby was shirtless and probably getting sunburned, and looking at its fat belly and the sag of the heavy diaper pulling at its legs, Laurel remembered the feel of Bet in her arms at that age. She'd felt that tightening urge to pick Bet up and run and keep her. Why hadn't she? They wouldn't be here now if she had. Bet would be in Shelby's school, her narrow calves poking out from under a plaid uniform skirt.

About a third of the kids in DeLop had never seen the inside of a school building. Some had parents or older siblings who would take them two miles to the highway, as close as the bus would come, so they could glean a meager education from the county school. The kids who did go almost universally dropped out before getting through middle school. Bet, still registered in seventh grade, was an anomaly, and her dogged attendance was the main reason Laurel had chosen her to be Shelby's pen pal. If Bet made it all the way through eighth grade, she'd be one of the best-educated people in the whole town.

Every now and again, one of them made it to high school. Laurel knew of only two kids who had graduated, and both of them had stopped being DeLop kids. They had gone out into the larger world and hardly ever came back.

Laurel couldn't blame them. Still, she should have known she couldn't pull Bet out of DeLop, drop her down in Victorianna, and not have the child feel the knife-sharp cut of difference. Of course she would long for a place to sit down in Laurel's world, but Laurel had not made room for her. The spare baby, Thalia had called Bet, rubbery and unreal, offered as a sacrifice.

The Volvo crept down the middle of Lance Road, and Laurel peered hard in all directions. DeLop's colors had washed out, a collage of rain-faded gray wood hung with shreds of clinging paint and metal so rusted it had no shine. Little flashes of the colors she associated with Shelby pulled her eye, shining in the dull landscape. Her heart leaped at a flash of bright pink, but it was only an overturned toy baby carriage abandoned by the road. Lime green caught her attention: a plastic bucket. A glimpse of neon orange was only a stolen traffic pylon peeking out from behind a pile of trash waiting to be burned. None of the colors were Shelby.

Was Shelby afraid? It would be so unfamiliar here. There was no trash service, and litter dotted every surface, scraps of food boxes and bottles and chicken bones. Most of the mobile homes had no indoor plumbing. Had Shelby ever seen a tin roof? They were everywhere here, some silver, some green; on rainy Christmases, they'd had to yell over the drumbeat of rain on tin. There were rusted propane tanks in almost every front yard. The Folks used propane for heat when they could pay for it. Would Shelby even know what those tanks were? Would she know to be quiet and cautious, or was she dashing about, bold as Thalia but not a third as worldly, poking her nose around, not paying attention to her surroundings, while Bet backed off and then slipped out of sight around a corner. The dogs here didn't know Shelby, and almost everyone kept dogs that were as territorial as the people were. The people didn't know her, either, and they were far more dangerous.

Laurel wished she had brought Shelby here before, the way Thalia had wanted her to. When Bet had urged her to come, Shelby would have been thinking of Thalia's Disney version of DeLop, freshly stocked with clean-scrubbed orphans and friendly old Aunt Enid.

Laurel had gone around in almost a complete circuit without seeing any evidence of Shelby's passing. She checked her cell phone and saw that she had two bars of reception. If Shelby had returned to Sissi's, David would have called. He hadn't, and neither had Thalia. It was tiny here. There were no businesses, no public buildings except the church where the older Folks still gathered to sing most Sundays. There were only so many places Shel could be.

Laurel was on her mother's old street now, Jane Way, approaching the burned ruin of the house where Mother had spent her early childhood. Laurel stopped the car and shifted it into park. Would Bet have brought Shel here? Surely Shelby would want to see this place.

Laurel got out, leaving the door open and the engine running. There wasn't much to see. The house had burned to its foundation and was nothing but a concrete slab and three scrolled wrought-iron posts that must have been part of a porch.

She stepped up onto the concrete, breathing deep, as if trying to catch a scent. The filth seemed undisturbed. If Bet and Shelby had passed this way, they'd left no indication. There was no sign of the years Mother had spent here, either. That genteel lady who spoke in a TV southern accent had once called this place home. That seemed important somehow. Laurel was missing something, some obvious clue, but anything the fire had not destroyed had long since been stripped away and carted off for use in other places. Mother had lived mostly at Poot's until Daddy had come with his church youth group in their old bus, bent on good works, bringing ham and brown bags full of hand-me-downs.

Laurel saw it then. She went to her knees on the concrete as if she'd been knocked there. Mother came back here Christmas after Christmas, bringing all the same things Daddy once brought her. To Mother, it wasn't a Christmas trip. It was a rescue mission. Once a year, she left her ordered life, the one she had created and kept peaceful at all cost, to foray here, into squalor, the enemy territory. It was more than the high school graduates who had gotten out had done.

But Daddy had come back to DeLop because he'd fallen in love with Mother, not to bring her ham. He had been warm and avid, coming out of Daddy-land to look at her. Mother could not see the difference. A cold offering of shoes and good manners was like throwing bricks to drowning people, thinking they were ropes. Still, it was the very best she could do. Laurel put her hands flat on the filthy concrete and accepted it. Everything. Looking at this place baldly, seeing it for what it was, Laurel knew: Mother had done the very best she could.

This had once been Mother's town, but she had left it, and she no longer chose to understand it. She had made herself an outsider, and she had raised Laurel to be one as if it were a gift. Laurel had been thinking like an outsider ever since they'd gotten on the road. They all had. But now, hands on the filthy slab, knees aching, Laurel saw inside DeLop.

Thalia had said if it were her, she'd wind Shelby around in the streets and leave her. But to Bet, these people weren't scary. They were as familiar and regular as the kudzu pressing in around this lot.

If Bet meant Shelby harm, she wouldn't expect it to come in the form of Raydee and Louis or even dogs like Mitchell. They weren't dangerous to Bet. But she had brought Shelby here for a reason. There was something here that Bet must think was dangerous. Something she could use.

Laurel remembered the drowned uncle Bet had found, his face "et" by the crawdads. Remembered Molly floating in the center of the pool. And then Laurel knew.

She was already up and running, leaving the car where it was parked, because she couldn't get there by car; there was a chain over the access road that had once let the coal trucks come and load. But there was still a footpath that was open, up behind Enid's house, two hundred yards or so down the road. Laurel was fumbling her cell phone out of her pocket as she ran. She thought she would call David, but her fingers were wiser. They hit the code for Thalia's cell.

Thalia answered by saying, "At Della's. Haven't found her."

Laurel yelled, "I think Bet took her to the Frog Hole. Get David. He doesn't know the way," and then she hung up and saved her breath for running.

She circled the perimeter of Enid's fence, going back to the familiar place between two trees where it was possible to slip sideways into the brush-filled woods. The slim trail led up, and Laurel hurtled along it, running flat out with the branches catching at her clothing and scraping her bare arms.

The strip mine's sides were so sheer it looked like someone had taken an enormous bread knife and cut a slice out of the earth. The stagnant water, a fathomless green, crept up its sides and then evaporated out in an endless cycle with the rain. This year had been damp, so the water would be high, emerald green and unmoving, so deep that the sun could warm only its surface.

Laurel saw a flash of color: the familiar hot pink of a Justin Timberlake T-shirt. There Shelby was, forty feet up the path, close to the edge of the quarry with her back to Laurel. Bet was right beside her, standing in profile. Shelby had a big piece of brick held up over her head, high, in both hands. As Laurel cleared the rise, rushing forward, Shelby hurled it in. It arced out over the water, plummeting fast, and Shelby yelled, "Ka-boom," as it splashed down.

Bet Clemmens was fiddling with something, and once the brick had sunk, Shelby took it from her. As Bet leaned down to pick up her own chunk of brick, she saw Laurel, fast and breathless, racing up the trail behind them.

Their eyes met, and Bet's mouth dropped open in silent surprise. Laurel skidded to a halt, her hands lifting, palms facing Bet.

Bet glanced down at the chunk of brick she'd just scooped up, then her gaze flicked back at Laurel.

"Shel," Laurel called, a warning in her tone.

Shelby didn't look back or respond, just stayed by the edge of the quarry. Then Laurel saw the little wires going into her ears. Shelby had her iPod headphones in. That was what Bet had been fiddling with, working the controls to find a song.

Shelby was standing so close to the edge. The water was high, a ten-foot drop into fathomless green.

Laurel was seven feet away. She realized she could hear the tinny echo of some boppy tune pumping into Shelby's ears, an inappropriately cheerful sound track. Bet shifted the brick in her hand as if testing the weight of it.

"You waited this long," Laurel said. "You don't want to."

Bet's original surprise had faded, and her eyes had gone as blank and glassy as the surface of the Frog Hole.

"This is that part now," Shelby said, in the overloud voice of someone with headphones in.

"Please don't," Laurel said.

She had so much more to say. She wanted to tell Bet she saw the difference now, she understood how Daddy had brought Mother down the hill. He'd made a place for her. Laurel had given Bet American Eagle jeans and colored sandals and watched her with a hard, suspicious eye, but she hadn't made a space for Bet. Now here was Bet, leading Shelby to the Frog Hole, trying to make a space for herself.

Bet peeked at Laurel sideways out of one dead eye. There was no time to say these things. Bet's face was expressionless, as if all her focus had turned inward.

She was wavering, and Laurel said, "It can all still be okay."

The words fell flat between them. They weren't true. There was Molly, and that could never be okay.

Bet's body seemed to come to some decision.

Shelby said, "He's saying, 'You better take my heart,' I'm pretty sure. You want to listen?" Her hands were moving up to take out the earphones, and Bet said, "I'm real sorry."

Her hands moved, too. The brick came up.

Laurel was already running toward them, but Bet was too fast, smashing it down into the back of Shelby's bright blond head, at the center part between her braids. Laurel saw the vivid spurt of fresh red blood, and Shelby stumbled forward. Laurel was reaching, her fingers scraping against the bright pink of the T-shirt but finding no purchase. Bet dropped the brick and shoved Shel in the small of her back as she crumpled. Shelby went over the edge.

Laurel went, too, jumping in right after, feeling the sick and dizzy rush of falling, a weightless moment that paused her by the sheer walls of limestone. In that dazzling halt, she heard the splash of Shelby entering the water. Then she was in as well, velocity shoving her under so that her head was in tepid warmth that cooled down the length of her body so quickly that it felt as if she'd stuck her feet in liquid ice.

She could see Shelby's golden hair, one braid reaching up as Shelby's body sank. Laurel grabbed it, hauled up, got her hands around Shelby's narrow chest, and began kicking for the surface. Shelby spasmed in Laurel's arms, coughing, choking on the water with her head lolling. Shelby's eyes were open, showing all white as air came out of her in short bursts.

Laurel was so strong. She'd never been so strong in her whole life. Her legs propelled them up, and she would not have been surprised if the force of her kicks had thrust them up and out to hover three feet above the surface and cough and drip.

They burst into the air, and she got Shelby's face out, trying to rest her daughter's head back on her shoulder as Shelby coughed and sputtered, her body jerking. Shelby's blood pumped out, as warm as the surface water, smearing across Laurel's cheek.

Then Shel got her breath back, and her body stopped spasming, but she wasn't swimming. Her eyes were still rolled back in her head, and her limbs felt loose and easy. She was breathing, though, and Laurel felt the hard, steady beating of her heart. Laurel rolled onto her back, cradling Shelby to her chest, and started towing her to where the access road had been cut, forming a slope out, a man-made beachhead the width of two big trucks.

The quarry was a solid quarter mile away, but Laurel was swimming toward it, strong and certain, when a wave of water rose up in front of them, splashing into Laurel's face. She aspirated droplets and choked, struggling to keep Shelby up.

Then another wave came at them from the side, and she realized that Bet was up there, following their progress and hurling chunks of granite and shale down at them.

"Bet!" she screamed, and then one got her. It was a bull's-eye, a flat chunk of rock that slammed so hard into the top of her head that it pushed her down and she saw stars.

She felt a vague, dazed wonder. She'd always thought it was only an expression, but she saw them, yellow stars like pinpoints of light shining down at her. She realized she was looking up through water at the late-afternoon sunshine sparking off the surface. She was under, the chunk of rock sinking past her and disappearing into the green-black dark.

Shelby sank with her, a quiet string of warm and living flesh in her arms, drifting down into the coolness. The drift seemed slow to Laurel. Everything seemed slow. She was sinking on the inside, too, darkness closing in and the sparkles fading. She took everything that was left in her and she pushed Shelby, thrust her slight weight up toward the light and the air, and then it was very quiet where she was.

It was dark, too, a cold, airless silence where drifting down didn't seem to matter very much. It seemed right to sink, a fair price to pay for the force that had sent Shelby up. Above her, she saw Shelby's legs twitch and then scissor. Shelby's slim arms came to life, and she was swimming for the surface. That was good. It was enough. Laurel's eyes closed and the stars were gone and everything else was following them.

Then she felt strong fingers twining deep into her hair, nails raking her sore crown where the shale had hit her. The hand in her hair yanked hard, and she cried out in a silent string of white bubbles. She was going back up, following the bubbles. She felt her face come into the air, and she heard Thalia say, "Oh no, you damn will not," and Laurel closed her eyes against the bright sun and didn't hear anything for a little.

"Mommy," Shelby was saying. The fear in her voice called Laurel back. "Mommy?"

Laurel opened her eyes. She was lying in the rocky mud of the access road, her feet still down in the water. She had lost her shoes. Shelby was beside her, her pink shirt bloodstained, her mouth turned down, but alive and whole.

"Baby," Laurel said, and then she rolled onto her side and coughed, and water came out, and she coughed more and more until it felt like throwing up. Even after she stopped, she still heard it happening. And then she lifted her head and saw Thalia a few feet away, her shirt gone, on her hands and knees, vomiting up everything she'd ever eaten.

"Are you okay?" Shelby asked, one warm, small paw on Laurel's shoulder.

"I'm good," Laurel said. She crawled toward her sister, Shelby following on her knees. When she got close, she sat up and the world spun and she knew she was lying. "Mostly," she amended, looking at her daughter.

Shelby was pressing Thalia's crumpled shirt to the back of her head. Her eyes were red and puffed almost shut. "I'm so sorry. I'm so sorry," she said.

"It's okay, baby," Laurel said.

"I couldn't stand it," Shelby said. "Gramma brought me home, and I saw Molly's mom on our sofa, and I knew I couldn't stand it if she looked at me. It was my fault, Mommy. I couldn't stand for Molly's mom to look at me and know."

Laurel grabbed Shelby's shoulders and said, "It was not your fault."

"It was. If I had met her—"

"Baby," Laurel said, "I know. And it's not your fault. You can't control the whole world, honey. It was an accident." She gathered Shelby up and held her, rocked her, and Shelby melted into her and let her and wept until her whole slim body was shaking with it.

Thalia finally stopped vomiting. She sat up, tugging on her bra straps. Her red eyes met Laurel's.

Over Shelby's head, Laurel mouthed, "Where is Bet?"

Thalia tilted her head slightly, toward the water.

Laurel looked out at the still expanse of the Frog Hole. The green water was like a sheet of uncracked glass. There weren't even ripples. "We have to—"

But Thalia was shaking her head. She tapped her wrist where a watch would go if she wore one and said, "No point."

Then Thalia started gagging again, tears spurting from her eyes, and she went back onto her hands and knees until she could gulp in enough fresh air to stop.

She crawled to them and sat by Laurel, close on her other side. Shelby rested on Laurel's chest, exhausted, and Laurel put her hand over Shelby's on Thalia's wadded-up T-shirt, applying pressure.

"I have to stop doing this," Thalia said. She looked, in that moment, as young and lost as Shelby. Laurel put her arm around her sister. She understood exactly what Thalia meant.

"What did he say when the deer ran?" she asked Thalia. "I heard Daddy say, 'Get him,' and the deer going. Then Marty said something. What was it?"

Thalia said, "He said, 'Next time, I'd pick her,' and he kinda jerked his thumb at you. He meant because I'd missed such an easy shot. But that's what he said. That he'd pick you next time. He stepped in front of me, going after that deer, and I didn't even think about it. It was something my hands did."

"What are you talking about?" said Shelby.

"Shhhh," said Laurel. "Never you mind." She looked at her sister, wiped down to toddler level again, big circles under both her eyes, her mouth still trembling. The unbreakable Thalia, broken. "I'm not like you," Laurel said. "I wouldn't have said 'I've seen better' or told."

"I know," Thalia said, and then she buried her face in her hands. "I knew she couldn't swim."

"What happened?" Shelby said, struggling back out of Laurel's arms. She was still holding the T-shirt to her head, and now her other hand reached around to feel it. "Wasn't Bet here? Where is she? Did rocks fall on us? I remember rocks falling."

"We couldn't get her out," Laurel said, and Shelby scrambled to her feet, swaying. Laurel tried to get up after, but her body failed her. She fell back as Shelby ran the few feet to the water's edge.

Thalia said, "Put one toe in that water, Shelby Ann, and I will drag you back and spank you till we both die."

Shelby stopped, staring out the smooth expanse of green. "Bet?" she called. "Bet?"

It echoed off the sheer rock walls, and there was no answer.

"I could have punched her in the face," Thalia said in a low voice for Laurel alone. "I could have hit her with a stick, knocked her out. But I thought, 'What if she doesn't go down? What if I'm in the water, trying to drag both of you, and she's still up there beaning us?' Then I didn't think at all. I did things. I knew she couldn't swim."

"Baby," Laurel said in the same voice she'd used with Shelby. She was thinking of Thalia at about Shel's age, taking her thumb out of her mouth to say, *My stupid sister had her eyes shut. She's afraid of guns. She's probably afraid of deer.*

"Baby," Laurel said again. "You didn't know. How could you know that? You didn't think about that. You saw her throwing the rocks at us, so you pushed her out of the way and she fell in. Then you came and got us."

Thalia laced both of her hands over her mouth and looked at Laurel, for once following her sister's lead. She nodded slowly. Shelby, at the water's edge, sank down to her knees.

"Help me up," Laurel said.

Thalia stood, shaky as a newborn foal, and gave her a hand. Together they made their slow way to the slope to where Shelby knelt.

Laurel eased herself down beside her daughter and wrapped an arm around her, and Thalia sat down on her sister's other side. Laurel could hear people moving up the trail, fast. David was coming. He was bringing the sheriff's men in light blue suits, pushing through the woods to find them. Someone with a dry cell phone or a radio would call in ambulances and rescue workers with scuba gear.

Laurel pulled Shelby closer and hooked her other arm around Thalia, bringing her sister in closer, too. They sat in a row, Thalia and Laurel and Shelby, the Gray girls all watching the unbroken surface in the final quiet before the lights and noise and Sissi's monstrous grief and the endless questions came. They waited for whatever would rise out of the water to rise.

EPILOGUE

Laurel is on her knees, digging in the sandy soil of her backyard garden. She's working on the double beds that flank the gate. The last few bulbs are next to her in a basket, firm and still faintly cool from the crisper. By the time the house in Victorianna sold and they had found this place, four miles away, fall had given way to winter, and it was too late to plant. She's putting them in now, at the tail end of February. The blooms will be small, but she wants the hopeful cheer of tulips and daffodils come spring.

Their new house stands on a hill, like the old one, because that's the only way to get a basement in Pensacola. The neighborhood is not gated, but their street is long, and from the hilltop, Laurel can see a long way in both directions. She likes it here, likes the big backyard with its koi pond and patchwork flower beds, likes her country-French house with its sleepy stone lions flanking the walkway. They don't look much like guardians; these are library lions, lollers and slackers. Shelby has named them Lawrence and Miss Iris.

Behind her, Laurel can hear the murmur of Shelby and Yvonne Feng and Carly Berman, sitting close on the stone bench in the very back of the yard, yammering. Laurel shifts her weight. The small of her back aches; she can't kneel this way for long, not since her center of gravity shifted. She gives up and sits flat on her bottom, covering the last of the bulbs with Florida's loose, sandy soil.

When she's finished, she stands up, slow and careful, dusting herself off. She's not far into her third trimester, but this is going to be a big baby. Already he is cramped inside of her. She can feel the press of his feet, a knob poking out of her left side as he stretches. She puts her palm over the knob and feels his legs retract.

"Carly?" she calls across the yard. "What time is your mother coming?"

The girls are sitting in a row, blond, brunette, and redheaded, and they look up in tandem. Shelby has her hair back in a band, and the slight jut of her ears puts a crack in Laurel's heart. She's starting to grow into them, and her baby mouth is firming, becoming her own.

"Before dinner," Carly calls back.

"Okay," Laurel replies. "And then you get right on that homework, Shel, you hear me? I want to get an early start in the morning."

"'Kay, Mom," Shelby yells, and the three glossy heads bend back together to whisper and giggle, silly girl noises from the beautiful tail end of childhood.

Out of the corner of her eye, Laurel catches a flash of color. Bet Clemmens lurks near them, behind the climbing roses on their trellis, her small feet planted in the earth. Laurel doesn't look at her directly. If she does, she'll see it's only a redbird, stirring the leaves of the azalea bush that stands up against the fence behind the roses. Bet doesn't like to be caught watching. She's there, though, at ease in the weak late-winter sunshine. She's Laurel's only ghost now that Molly is at peace and Marty has gone on to get whatever rest he earned.

Laurel doesn't mind Bet Clemmens. Bet seems happy here among Laurel's stone angels and garden frogs and the tacky plastic pink flamingo Shelby gave her for Christmas. Moreover, she is Laurel's best reminder.

Laurel's second-best reminder is peering over the backyard gate, scowling.

"I've been ringing that front bell for all eternity," Thalia says. The gate is white and wooden, only four feet high. Thalia rattles it.

"Well, you're early," Laurel replies. She leaves her basket and spade and opens the latch to let Thalia through. "I was just heading in."

Tomorrow they will get up before six and drive over to DeLop, Laurel and Shelby and Thalia. They go once a month now, on the last weekend of the month, when Thalia's theater is dark between productions. They'll stop by Sissi Clemmens's place first. Sissi will watch them from her vinyl sofa as Thalia restocks her pantry and Shel and Laurel clean a little. She doesn't seem to mind them coming. She seems past minding anything. They don't stay long. They have only the weekend and a lot to do.

Laurel is stealing the babies.

Already Della's three-year-old, Janina, hollers, "Miss Lall, Miss Lall!" and holds her arms up when they come through the door.

It isn't only because of the candy and the board books and the fat wax crayons Laurel brings. It's because Laurel looks at her and sees her, seeking out the little girl under the dirty T-shirt and the jam-ringed mouth. Laurel is learning this child and Della's sister's boys the same way she'll learn the baby Raydee has made with fifteen-year-old Polly Deeks. If they want out, they'll damn sure know they have a way. It's a small hope that even one of them will take it, but if they do, Laurel will be there to walk them down.

"Missionary to the mud people," Thalia calls her these days, but she hasn't missed a trip since Laurel started.

David comes, too, when work allows. With all of them together in one car, the air takes on an electric tang, the taste of their uneasy, silent truce.

"Do you want me to have her stay home?" Laurel asked him after dinner one night, leaning on his shoulder on the sofa. "On the weekends you can come, I mean."

After a thinking pause, David said, "No. Bring her. You have some spooky relatives, and with Thalia along, at least I know we've got someone to gut-shoot anyone who tries to hurt you or Shel."

Laurel whacked him in the leg with the flat of her hand.

"What?" he said, and she realized he hadn't been making a macabre joke. David was just being David, calling it as bluntly as he saw it. "I still don't like her, though," he added.

"Well, she's crazy about you," Laurel said, and then she got the giggles.

It feels right to have her sister orbiting her life again, even if Planet Thalia is prone to loop-de-loops and calls itself the sun. Laurel needs her now more than ever; she's called peace with Mother and Daddy, mostly for Shelby's sake, but it's not the same. Laurel gives her mother party manners and kindness, and Mother, in return, chooses to have no memory of smashed dishes and profanity, all the things she can't forgive. Laurel has forgiven, but she won't forget.

Now Thalia looks her up and down and says, "Hey there, big fat fatty." She leans over and cuts her huge voice loose, calling, "You in there, Mr. Puppethead? Wake up! It's Auntie Thalia," to Laurel's round midsection. The baby thumps at Laurel's bladder like it's his own personal drum.

"Oof," says Laurel.

Shelby has heard Thalia. She's running across the lawn toward her, her girlfriends in her wake. Thalia strides away to meet them and catch Shelby in a hug. Laurel stands back, watching, both hands braced around her belly.

After the second line turned pink, David predicted another little girl. Shelby Junior. But Laurel imagined a loud little boy with a voice like a trumpet and blond hair that stuck straight up.

"He'll want a dog," she whispered to David in the quiet dark of their big bed.

"A dog'll dig up all those flowers," David said.

"I don't much care. A boy needs a good dog, and I'm telling you, we've made a boy here."

The ultrasound backed Laurel up. That very night, she felt his first small flutter. Tucked beneath the velvet of her skin, his movement was too muffled to be felt from the outside. Secret moth wings.

He has quickened and grown since then. He's alive and strong inside her, a hidden thing. Come spring, when the last of her daffodils are tall and blooming, she's going to do the bravest thing that she knows how to do. She's going to open, and she's going to let him out into the world.

ACKNOWLEDGMENTS

Novelists always say, "This book could not have been written without list-of-people," but no, really, this book would not ever have been finished if it weren't for the devious machinations of Caryn Karmatz Rudy and Lydia Netzer. These two women have never met, and yet they acted as a tag team, alternating sugar with judicious pinching to keep me writing (always my best medicine) through a difficult year. I keep trying to amalgamate them into Helen Hunt so I can make Jack Nicholson eyebrows at them and say, "You make me want to be a better man," but they both just tell me to shut up and start work on the next novel.

In order to write about Laurel's career, I spent hours staring, awed and dumbstruck, at Canadian folk artist Pamela Allen's work and the tarot quilts of Deb Richardson. I knew nothing about sewing, so a foaming-crazy batch of wild fabric artists called the Quilt Mavericks took me in, fed me strange berries, and taught me how to say "Bernina." I will never be the same.

Georgia homicide detective Ted Bailey and Pensacola, Florida, assistant chief Chip Simmons explained police procedure during an investigation. Several times. Slowly. These are good, smart, savvy cops, while I am at best a shoddy criminal, so anything I got right is due to their efforts.

Yolanda Reed, Patricia Simmons, Waylon Wood, Hunt Scarritt, and the ensemble troupe at the Loblolly Theatre in Pensacola taught me about black box and its surrounding culture. I am pleased to report that the Loblolly folks don't need nearly as much therapy as my theater people.

Grand Central Publishing remains my home thanks to the unwavering support of folks like Jamie Raab, Martha "angels want to borrow her white shoes" Otis, Karen Torres, the inimitable Evan Boorstyn, and so many more. I was honored to have Harvey-Jane Kowal working her magic in tandem with Beth Thomas, whose rampant purple pencil marshaled the forces of goodness and order to triumph over my wayward gerunds and sloppy typing. Stet! I must also thank my agent and dear friend, Jacques de Spoelberch. You don't forget the guy who pulled you from the slush pile.

Love and thanks to crit partners Karen Abbott (forever my Potsi!), Anna Schachner, Lily James, and fifth monkey Jill James. RN Julie Oestreich has, for three novels now, told me how to properly kill, injure, drug, and maim people. Thanks, Jules!

I pause here and wave to the FTK regs, tireless guerrilla marketeers who remain my Best Beloveds. For them, a little insider information: DeLop is a made-up place, but it's based on a real mining town in northern Alabama. I call it a mining town, but at this point, there's nothing left to dig up. Some of the people stayed, and if you are born there, chances are, you'll die there. The Christmas letters from the DeLop kids are based on real letters. These letters are currently answered by a Birmingham church, since the real kids don't have Laurel and Thalia. Of course, knowing Thalia, perhaps this is better.

My wonderful family—Scott, Sam, Maisy Jane, Bob, Betty, Bobby, Julie, Daniel, Erin-Fishelby-Virginia, Jane, and Allison—are my heart. I am eternally grateful for the way they work together to knit time out of nothing and give it to me so I can write.

Most of all, I thank you for reading.

GODS IN ALABAMA

Joshilyn Jackson

'There are gods in Alabama. I know because I killed one.'

When Lena Fleet went to college, she promised God she would stop fornicating with every boy she met; never tell another lie and never, ever go back to her hometown of Possett, Alabama. All she wants from God in return is that He makes sure the body is never found . . .

Ten years later, Lena's demons are catching up with her. Her high school arch-enemy appears on her doorstep, looking for the golden haired god who disappeared during their senior year. To make matters worse, her African American boyfriend has issued her with an ultimatum – introduce him to her lily-white family or he's gone.

While she would rather burn in a fire than let him meet steel magnolia Aunt Florence and the rest of her eccentric and racist family, Lena realises it is time to go home to Alabama and confront the past once and for all . . .

HODDER